Praise for the novels of
STEPHEN WHITE

PRIVILEGED INFORMATION

"Suspenseful . . . ambushes with moments of real terror!"
—*Publishers Weekly*

"Fascinating and entertaining . . . you'll want to race through
Privileged Information in as few sittings as possible!"
—*The Minuteman Chronicle*

"Stephen White makes a dazzling debut with this thriller!"
—*San Diego Union-Tribune*

PRIVATE PRACTICES

"Detective writing at its best."
—*West Coast Review of Books*

"White weaves a near-flawless web of evil."
—*Publishers Weekly*

HARM'S WAY

"Superb . . . one of the best thrillers of the year."
—*Cleveland Plain Dealer*

"Gripping."
—*New York Times Book Review*

"Taut, tightly spooled storytelling . . . difficult to put down."
—*Rocky Mountain News*

PRIVILEGED INFORMATION

STEPHEN WHITE

Pinnacle Books
Kensington Publishing Corp.

http://www.pinnaclebooks.com

To Rose and Alexander
and for my mother

PINNACLE BOOKS are published by

Kensington Publishing Corp.
850 Third Avenue
New York, NY 10022

Pinnacle and the P logo Reg. U.S. Pat. & TM Off.

First Zebra Printing: 1991
First Pinnacle Printing: March, 1999

20 19 18 17 16 15 14

Printed in the United States of America

Prologue

It starts like this.

I say, men are shits. He waits for me to say more. I'm quiet. Maybe I shift in my chair. Maybe I tug on my skirt or run my fingers through my hair. Okay, I'll own it, I say, I don't feel safe with men.

You chose a male therapist, he says. This is an old conversation. It varies little with us. I think he's waiting for me to vary it. I'd like to, but I don't know how yet.

I don't feel comfortable with women, either, I say. Women? I don't know anything about women. Men, I know. They're the enemy.

I know he's thinking, well, I'm a man, what about me? Why the hell doesn't he just ask? He doesn't. Fine, I say to myself then aloud, I feel safe with you. There. Okay?

I think he knows what I'm thinking. That's how well he knows me. He knows I feel safe with him. I haven't let a man touch me for two years, but I feel safe enough for him to touch me. If he touched me, I could be alive again. He can make it safe for me to feel again. I need to melt. He can be the heat.

He's so formal, coat and tie, polished loafers. But I like loosening ties.

When is he going to say something?

He'd like to touch me. I know when men want me. Sometimes I know it even before they do. He wants me. I want him.

He wants me.

And I want him to want me. It makes it safer, somehow.

We've been here before.

I tell him I have fantasies of seeing him outside the office. He

5

says, you have a pattern of enticing men to respond to you sexually. I translate: you're saying I try to get men to come on to me? He nods, stays formal. It's not necessary to repeat that pattern with me, he assures me, this relationship is different. Given your past, he says, it shouldn't surprise either of us that you are trying to generate sexual intimacy between us. But in this relationship, it's something we can work to understand, not a destructive pattern to act out again.

You use sex as a currency, he tells me, as he has many times. Treasure your femininity, he says, don't barter it.

He says again that he won't gratify my old needs.

But he wants to. They always want to. Anyway, this relationship is different. He said so himself. We both know it.

His office is warm. The afternoons are short. The light in the office is muted by night.

It's only five feet between our chairs. May as well be a mile. But my desire, I think, can reach across it.

He watches me, waiting. I watch, too. His chest, I think, rises a millimeter higher with each breath. That's how I know I'm his.

I get up slowly, all hesitation I don't feel. My eyes are glued to his. His are always glued to mine. They never wander. But I do.

Now, I do.

His eyes stay locked on where mine are supposed to be. For a moment, as I rise, they stray to my breasts, and then, as I stand, he stares at my crotch.

His eyes are surprised. I say, you're too far away. I step once and lower myself to the edge of the table that's off to the side, between our chairs. I don't bother to tug down my skirt. Our knees are less than a foot apart. That's better, I say.

Time passes. But not much. He asks me, a barely detectable crack in his voice, to get back in my chair. Before he's done with his request my hand is on his knee. I say, you're the only one who cares about me, really cares about me. He closes his eyes for an instant longer than a blink. My fingers are moving.

He takes my hand and removes it. He is trying so hard to do what he keeps telling himself is right. He asks again for me to go back and sit down. He says, go back. He says, please. We need to talk about this, he says. Instead I move from the table and sit on the

6

arm of his chair. I embrace him. One of my breasts is pressing against his shoulder.

This is right. I'm his.

He says my name. There's a melody in it I've never heard before. Something is dissolving. There's a plea in his voice. A plea for what? He doesn't know yet. I know.

The power has shifted.

I didn't plan this for tonight. This won't stop with an embrace. It never does. My underwear isn't what I would have chosen. Oh well. He won't see it long.

His pleas continue. He tells me to get back in my chair. He says, don't, as I unbutton my blouse and shed it. This is destructive, he says, as I tug on his tie.

I hear him, but I don't hear him. Why?

Because I need him. Because he wants me. I have to respond to that. I must. He's nurtured me, encouraged me, helped me discover me. He wants me is why. And I don't want him to take me. Part of me says he's earned this. I don't want him to leave me.

And I'll never tell. I've never told.

His protests dissolve as I reach behind my back and arch my chest toward him. He watches, grateful, as I roll my shoulders forward, first one, then the other. Then I extend my arms, to him, and shrug out of my bra.

Part One

The Domain
of the Heart

One

Cicero reacted to the rap on the door with her "attention" bark — an extended "Wooof" without much volume — and raced me to the front of the house.

It was midafternoon on a late autumn Sunday. The dry air held only a rumor of chill, and the light was snug and bright. I had skied in the morning and then driven down the Front Range to my house, planning to crown the day with a couple of sets of tennis. And maybe a bicycle ride.

I chased Cicero to the front of the house, thinking it odd that Peter, who had never before been deterred by my closed front door, would knock rather than saunter in and tell me he was ready for tennis. The big dog skidded on the slick wood floors as she failed to manage the turn from the living room to the entryway. She slid in the same spot every time she attempted that curve at high speed.

My new skis leaned by the door, a long linear gouge on the base of one silently scolding me for not having taken a pair of rock skis so early in the season.

The knock became more urgent.

"Hold on, Peter, just a second," I yelled through the closed door to a man whose prior most grievous sin of impatience in our eight years as neighbors was drinking a glass of wine before it was quite done breathing. I resettled the skis to rest precariously against the painted trim of the hall closet so I could squeeze open the door without releasing Cicero.

The unfamiliar man at the door and I paused at each other's outfits.

I wore pale green flip-flops and yellow nylon bib warm-ups over a maroon T-shirt. The guy at the door wore a sport coat and a tie.

There was no doubt that mine was the less peculiar costume. In Boulder, on Sunday, finding a tie attached to a person in the late afternoon is like getting a phone call in the middle of the night. You've got to be suspicious.

Cicero was. She switched to alert status and cracked her "anomaly" bark — two loud claps with concentrated tenor nuances at a volume illegal in the city limits. The man at the door was unruffled by the eighty pounds of black bear I restrained by choke chain. He offered a wallet with a badge, which he exposed to me for a leisurely examination.

"Detective Purdy, Boulder Police," he said. I lived outside the city limits and found myself wondering why the police and not the county sheriff before I was wondering why any law enforcement officer at all. "May I come in?"

"Sure, just a second," I said to the detective, and then to Cicero, "It's okay. Good girl. Back up." Which she did, right into the skis, which clattered to the floor. I brushed them to the side of the narrow hall with my left foot and welcomed the policeman into my house.

He waited for me to escort him from the little entryway and followed me into the living room. After looking around at the big room that stretched the length of the back of the house and at the great view of the Front Range, he settled uninvited onto the chair that I think of as "mine." It's a very old high-backed reclining chair of unlikely blue-green leather.

Cicero pulled at her chain. "It's okay. Lie down," I said. She sat instead, always heeding my every command, and keenly examined our guest.

"It's 'Doctor,' isn't it? You're a psychiatrist, right?"

"I'm a clinical psychologist."

"Whatever. A therapist, a psych-o-therapist." His treatment of the job description seemed to relegate me to the same New Age stew that gurgled with Boulder's channel-

12

ers, metamorphic reflexologists, jin shin energy balancers, and color therapists, the ones who examine the palette of colors in the food you eat with the same diligence that the IRS examines your money. He took a small spiral notebook from the patch pocket on the right hip of his coat and glanced at it.

"You have a patient named . . . Karen Eileen Hart?"

I paused before answering. The pause was a developed reflex to any situation where I was being encouraged to divulge information about somebody I was treating in psychotherapy, including just the fact that I was treating them. I pursed my lips and stared at the detective, who looked as if he had been wearing his clothes for most of a week. His eyes were tired and red, and his demeanor oozed impatience. He had at least one roll of gut for every decade he'd been a cop. I guessed at two decades, making him early forties. His forehead was the size and shape of Nebraska, like a great expanse of plains ascending to curly, faintly red hair. He held his arms out from his chest the way strong men hold their bodies.

"And if I do?"

He exhaled, puffing out his cheeks like an adder. "If you do, you have a dead patient. If you don't, I'm wasting my time. So which is it?"

I had been sitting slightly forward on the sofa. I fell back and said, "God." Karen Hart, dead? The detective gave me a minute.

He closed his eyes momentarily and recovered some sense of equanimity. "Look, I didn't want to tell you like that. I'm sorry." He had a vague, compassionate smile, silently entreating me not to be an asshole about this.

"She's my patient," I said.

"We found her body this morning after an anonymous tip. Guy said there was a dead girl in an apartment at such-and-such Maxwell Street. We go over," he continued, turning "go" into a two-syllable word. "There was. It looks like an overdose. I'm just tyin' up some loose ends, being thorough."

13

Maxwell Street? Yeah, she lives there. Karen Hart? No, it must be a mistake. "Karen Hart?" I asked, my head thrust forward.

"Caucasian. Aged twenty-four. Dark hair. Blue eyes. Cute kid." The boilerplate language was spoken as a father would speak it. The detective's voice was shadowed by a Minnesota cadence. I guessed the Iron Range, Bob Dylan country.

Two of my other patients came immediately to mind — patients who were depressed enough and suicidal enough to kill themselves. Karen Hart is fine, I thought. He's wrong. "Go on, please," I managed.

When talking to the police, I have a tendency to act like an idiot. I was acutely aware of my inclination then and was striving to keep the imbecile hidden inside.

"So what can you tell me, Doctor? Did she kill herself?"

"No," I said. "Shit. I don't know, Detective. You tell me. Should we be having this conversation about Karen Hart killing herself? No. No. We shouldn't. She shouldn't have killed herself." I was convinced.

"Autopsy's going on now, but the evidence looks like suicide. No note, but an empty bottle of" — he looked back at his little notebook — "imipramine." His unpracticed tongue put the emphasis on the wrong syllable. "Mixed it with alcohol. Pretty lethal, I'm told, low LD-50."

Part of me heard his analysis of the amount of antidepressant Karen would have needed to ingest to have had a 50 percent chance of having consumed a lethal dose, the LD-50. Mostly I was transfixed by the image of Karen's beautiful body slit from chin to pudenda on a stainless-steel autopsy table somewhere across town.

He saw the pain in my face. "Didn't expect this, did you?" he asked, acknowledging the obvious.

"No. No I didn't. She was fine on Thursday. I saw her on Thursday. She's been improving."

He started writing. "History of depression?" My resolve to protect Karen Hart's secrets had cracked, and he leaped to exploit the fracture.

"Yeah. At least two years."

"Tried this before?" he asked. I waited, confused at the question. "Suicide? She try it before?" he pressed.

"No. No. She's thought about it. A year ago she thought about it all the time. Suicide was a companion for her then, always on her mind. Recently, no. No recent plans. No recent ideation."

"Any recent crises?"

"Nothing."

Purdy shifted on his seat. His sport coat had been well made, but either for someone else or a much earlier incarnation of him. Watching the herringbone surrender its geometry as it stretched across his shoulders caused me to squirm. He was thinking, turning pages in his little book.

"You prescribe the drugs?"

"Psychologists can't prescribe drugs. The antidepressants are old. Somebody had misdiagnosed her when she was a student. She got them then. Before I started seeing her."

"Misdiagnosed her? You said she was depressed. The drugs were antidepressants. What's the problem?"

I was in no mood for a tutorial but bulled forward. "There are lots of kinds of depression, many etiologies — causes. Some are responsive to antidepressants; some aren't. Karen's wasn't."

"So she wasn't taking them now."

"No. To my knowledge, no."

"Know where I can find her father?"

I shook my head. "No. Look, I don't have her chart here. Maybe it's in there, but I doubt it. She has a good friend in Denver, Valerie somebody."

"Yeah. Talked to her already. Anybody else might know how we can find her family?"

"She works for . . ." I paused, tasting the *s* that I had allowed to hang on the end of "work." I couldn't have managed any other tense. "She works for Adams and Blount, a big law firm in Denver. They might know," I offered.

He knew that already, too.

15

"Who was she seeing?" he asked.

"You mean dating?" I responded as though he had asked me about Mother Theresa. The village idiot routine was starting.

Purdy smirked, finally generating some interest in what for him must have been a mundane interview. "Yeah, dating."

"Nobody," I said.

"Nobody," he echoed. He stared at me for a short while, maybe considering how much he wanted to tell me. "Well," he said, returning his gaze to his notebook, "we found evidence of a little get-together at her place. Two wineglasses. Two coffee cups. And"—he raised his eyebrows and looked up at me without lifting his boxy head—"the coroner has already said he thinks there's evidence of sexual intercourse not too long before her death."

By demeanor and training I am skilled at shielding my emotional reactions, especially in conversations. Not this time. I gasped quietly, stunned. I said nothing for a minute. Purdy let the silence hang as well. Gathering my wits, I said pathetically, "No. I mean, I didn't know. That she was, uh, seeing anybody."

"We wondered"—Purdy raised his heavy head and fixed his eyes on me—"if maybe, you know, she was distraught about a relationship."

"Detective," I said, "I can't help you with that. I just don't know."

"You don't know the guy, then?"

"No," I repeated.

"Where were you yesterday and today?"

"Why?"

"Where were you?"

"I skied at Copper yesterday and this morning. Stayed overnight at a friend's condo."

"By yourself?"

"Yes. By myself."

"Those the lift tickets?" He pointed at the two colored squares hanging on triangular wires from the clasp of my

16

bibs. I nodded.

"Mind if I take them?"

I was more shocked by Karen's death than I was offended by his implied suspicion of me. "No, not at all." I ripped the tickets, pulled the wires through the clasp, and handed the detective the shreds.

"Did she try to reach you while you were gone, Doctor?"

"She might have. I cleared my calls when I got back from the mountains. The answering service said someone phoned but wouldn't leave a name when they found out I wasn't taking my own calls. I guess it might have been her. Karen."

The detective had probably been doing his job too long. Tragedy didn't affect him anymore, but he was aware that others weren't immune. He folded the little notebook and tucked it into an inside pocket of his jacket. As he capped his pen slowly, he adjusted his face into an expression that resembled compassion the way acrylic resembles wool. I was oddly grateful.

"Thank you, Doctor," Purdy said, standing, and turned toward the door.

"Wait. Please," I said. "Is that all? Is there anything else—"

He held out his hand as if he were directing traffic. "It looks like suicide. This one'll be closed when the toxicology comes back." He watched his words register on my face. "Thanks for your time."

"Detective. She . . . Karen should not have killed herself. I know that."

"Doctor . . ." He was trying hard not to be patronizing, and not quite succeeding. "When you mental health types want to be let off the hook, you plead to guys like me that you can't predict violent behavior. When you want to be taken seriously, you tell me you know the future like you know your hourly rate. Come on, which is it?" He didn't wait for an answer, which was just as well. I didn't have one.

At the step up from the living room to the front of the

17

house, he gestured toward Cicero and said, "What is she, a giant schnauzer?"

"No, she's a Bouvier, a Belgian sheepdog," I managed.

"Real pretty," he said, and showed himself out.

I followed him through the house and watched him get into his car. He sat for a minute, writing something, then drove down the lane.

The house was quiet when Cicero and I walked back in. I phoned Peter to cancel our tennis match, suggesting I was too sore from my first skiing of the season. I had the impression he had discovered something else he'd rather do anyway.

After changing from ski clothes to cycling clothes I exhausted myself with a hard ride in eastern Boulder County. I was trying not to think about Karen Hart.

By the time I pushed my bicycle back into the house, the sky to the west was flaring like an aura over the ragged Front Range. Cicero followed me into the living room and watched me sit down. She sat, too, in front of the couch, her head in my lap, as I watched the dirty pink halo fade and the darkening sky begin to pitch stars at the blank screen above the mountains.

The house was cold. I switched on the furnace and bent to light a fire in the kiva-style fireplace that Merideth had insisted on installing a few winters before. Images of my wife and our life together regularly crisscrossed my mind like threads in a web.

Our separation wasn't yet three months old.

Our little house was a multigenerational hybrid of fake adobe and authentic cinder block on a western-facing slope in the morning shadows of the scenic overlook on Highway 36 coming into the Boulder valley. Deep-set windows and a carved door with a rounded top provided all the charm. The exposed foundation of the downhill level was unpainted gray masonry with aluminum window frames. An addition to the north had all the aesthetic appeal of a barracks at Camp Pendleton.

18

The house had been mine rent free through graduate school in exchange for taking care of the proprietor's three acres of native grasses. My landlady then, Lois, lived on the eastern edge of the property, higher up the hill in a commanding home she and her husband had built to accommodate the one-hundred-mile expanse of the Rocky Mountains that dominated the panorama from the eastern edge of Boulder. Her husband had died years before I met her in 1973. She had placed an ad looking for help with her "ranch" and explained, as I sat with a cup of tea in her living room, that the cast on her arm was preventing her from doing a few things. Lois, then sixty-one, had climbed an ancient elm tree that was blocking her view of the Fourth of July fireworks celebration in town, fallen, and broken her arm.

Seven years later she moved to her husband's native Norway and sold the ranch to a young urologist and her husband, a woodworker. Adrienne and Peter, now my friends and neighbors, offered to buy the whole ranch, but Lois split off the bottom acre and sold it to me with its mosaic dwelling for half its value.

After we married, Merideth and I invested a lot of energy into making the interior appealing and found reasons every spring to postpone a major rebuilding of the structure. The house was ugly, but it worked for us. It was full of dark, primitive, heavy-cushioned wood furniture, some of it antique, or at least old, and some of it built by Peter to the instructions of an imaginative deity who resided in his head. Merideth knew Oriental rugs and beautiful wool softened the scarred oak and scratched ceramic tile floors. Everything flowed to the west in the house, and a series of large windows permitted the Continental Divide to act as the true perimeter of our home.

That night, as I sat on my favorite chair, numbed by the news of Karen Hart's death, I couldn't discern the profile of the divide in the black western sky. Cicero's hulking frame was a dusky shadow as she paced back and forth in her "it's late for dinner" dance. I measured out a cup of chunks from the big green bag in the pantry and checked her water. I poured myself a glass of wine.

Cicero inhaled her food in seconds and amused herself watching me pace. I dumped a piece of hickory in the developing fire and turned down the thermostat.

I needed to call someone. Merideth popped to mind, but my memory of our last conversation was too much of an impediment. We had reached that awkward threshold in our separation where we had committed to staying friends, no matter what.

The bed in the office-guest bedroom where I was sleeping was unmade, and I diverted my energies into grabbing sheets and stuffing the recalcitrant comforter into the duvet. Merideth would never have let us leave the house for a weekend with the bed unmade. Actually, Merideth wouldn't have left the bedroom with the bed unmade. I yearned for her compulsiveness now. I yearned for other things, too.

The telephone was cradled over my shoulder as I walked around the kitchen table trying to decide whom to call. Indecisive, I poured another glass of wine. My reverie was soon interrupted by the acid beeping of the receiver as it reminded me that I wasn't doing anything productive with it.

I called my partner, Diane Estevez, and listened to a Bach fugue accompany her husband Raoul's instructions to leave a message after the tone.

I hung up and returned to my leather chair, deciding that the most soothing thing I could do as I sat in the dark and listened to the fire was to find a way to convince myself that Karen Hart could not have killed herself.

Three days before, she had been in my office for her regular Thursday five-fifteen appointment. It was still fresh in my mind, but no more remarkable than any session with a motivated patient.

She had arrived right on time, gauging with precision the long drive in from the Denver law office where she was a paralegal. She dressed like a lawyer, was required to, I imagined, but her suits had telltale evidence of her low salary, and the polish on the heel of her right shoe was always worn away by the rigors of her commute. She was a tall woman; we stood eye to eye when she wore heels. Karen was lean and very fit. She lifted weights most evenings to keep away monsters she uncovered soon after I met her. Her long dark hair, always a little unkempt by the end of the work day, fenced a pale, wary face and framed vigilant eyes. I had thought her attractive.

Karen Hart had been self-conscious on the Thursday before her death. Her habit of shielding her mouth with her left hand as she smiled was pronounced. She had visited an orthodontist that morning to begin the ordeal of having braces installed to correct the one feature of her face that had been vulnerable to criticism. She talked flippantly about her vanity and then insightfully of the ambivalence she felt about the power her beauty gave her with men. Granting herself permission to feel better about how she looked had been a months-long process. One of the demons in her had professed that the only reason she might correct her uneven teeth would be to augment her attractiveness to men. The metal in her mouth still reflected the light of those doubts.

She dodged a query about how she supposed her appearance, her beauty, might influence me. I pointed out the diversion. She told me she wasn't ready to talk about her feelings about me yet. "Maybe soon," she said with an embarrassed smile. I watched as an unbidden association emerged in her consciousness, an awareness no more volitional than the shadow that dogs a pedestrian in the morning sun. Then tears moistened the corners of her eyes, and she leaned toward the nearby box of tissues.

"I want to kill him sometimes," she said. "If he came to my door, I think I'd drive a knife into his heart." She'd said it before.

Karen had first come to see me almost two years earlier,

feeling quite depressed after graduating from the University of Colorado. Neither her complaints nor her presentation were atypical. She described a succession of failed relationships, a disapproving family, success in school without any satisfaction. High school and her first years at C.U. were marked by indiscriminate sexual behavior; by graduation she was abstinent.

Before six months had passed she was late for sessions and was describing her reluctance to come in at all. She was accusatory of me, charging me with being manipulative and controlling and of trying to undermine her independence. I felt, as she did, that something important was surfacing. Unconsciously we both knew what it was. I waited. She defended, trying to escape the awareness, scurrying away from it as a fly searches the panes of a closed window.

The memory of incest by her stepbrother was a land mine she tripped over while hopscotching through associations related to a few months her family had spent in London when she was a girl. They had lived abroad for a while to accommodate her father's business. The recollections of what happened to her there devastated her.

Karen was in paralegal training while she and I slowly uncaged the memories, and she described many days where her hours at school were her only hours out of her apartment and out of her bed. She stopped dating and stopped working out. She was again the terrified nine-year-old she had forgotten and suspended in time. And she hated me for a while. As a man. And as the guide who seemed unshaken by the territory she was begrudgingly crossing. "If you weren't here," she once said, "I wouldn't have to talk about this."

That chapter in her life was titled "No Relationship Is Safe," and she wrote a thousand versions over the next year.

She was just starting to recover when she killed herself.

Two

The weight in my head shifted with every breath. A shot put was loose in my cranium. I slashed at the clock radio and stunned it into silence. "Shit," I mumbled into the pillow.

Predawn noise filtered in through the darkness. Birds. Breeze. Commuter traffic on Highway 36.

Dread.

Feeling apprehensive in the morning wasn't new. Since Merideth moved out in August, three months before, I awoke each day with a certain foreboding, knowing her side of the bed was cold and empty.

But something was different about this morning's funk.

The cop. Karen Hart. The wine I'd kept drinking. "Oh, God," I mumbled. "Oh, shit." Three Tylenols, a hot shower, and a big mug of coffee took the edge off my misery.

My Subaru was the only car heading west on South Boulder Road as sunlight edged into the valley. The light reflecting off the Flatirons was a beacon, drawing me up Baseline, then across Ninth to Walnut. I parked the wagon behind the converted Victorian that housed my office in downtown Boulder and sat for a few minutes with the window open, listening to *Morning Edition* on the radio.

I walked down to Treats, bought the *Daily* from a machine, and paced outside until the bakery opened. I ordered coffee and sour cream coffee cake, not the ode-to-cholesterol bran muffin that I routinely used as a rationalization for my too frequent trips to the bakery.

Juggling the newspaper, the white waxed bag with the pastry, and the cardboard container of coffee as I walked across Ninth to Walnut, I used the private entrance into my office from the garden and closed the French doors behind me. Until Merideth left I had relished these early times in the office before my first patient. My partner, Diane, rarely arrived before eight-thirty, and the architect upstairs, Dana Beal, sauntered in whenever she chose. I saw her rarely and tracked her tenancy only by attending to small clues, like the absence of her accumulated mail or the presence of a scripted note wondering whether Diane or I had any light bulbs, or stamps, or whatever. I suspected that she had a source of income that rendered her architectural practice superfluous. Diane, I was sure, knew her whole life story. Someday I'd ask. My routine was mindless as I turned on the lights, set the thermostat, and started a pot of coffee in our small kitchen. There was no need to unlock the front door; Diane would do that when she arrived. My first appointment was not until midmorning.

My progressing stupor was interrupted a few minutes later as the electronic chirp of the phone filled the office and jolted me from my mindless review of the day's news.

"Alan Gregory," I answered.

Diane Estevez, Ph.D., was on her car phone, her favorite new toy, careening down North Broadway, her enthusiastic voice as constant as ever. She must not have heard about Karen's suicide.

"Good, you're in," she said. "Surprise, surprise. I'm coming in at the crack of dawn and I'm running late and this patient always arrives early to read the cartoons in *The New Yorker* to get in the mood for me. Will you unlock the front door so she can get in? Does this sound familiar or what?"

"Your coming in before eight o'clock in the morning isn't very familiar. Your running late, well, we all have our faults. Don't worry, I'll get the front door," I said, quickly deciding to postpone telling her about Karen's death until she arrived.

"Fucker!" she said loudly, her voice trailing off.

I maintained my poise. "Excuse me, sweetheart, you've misunderstood, I said I *would* open the door."

"Sorry, some asshole is about four inches from my tail. I've gotta take care of this. Thanks, bye." Diane took driving seriously, and she guarded the well-being of her new 9000 Turbo religiously. A pardon for the offending motorist was unlikely.

"Diane," I said to the dead line, "be nice."

I walked out through the locked door that separated our offices from the waiting area and crossed the rich blue-and-red carpet that dominated the room. I switched on the overhead track-guided minispots and turned the deadbolt in the old oak door. As I pivoted to return to my office, my shoe slid from polished oak to paper.

A pale blue envelope with my first name on it in delicate script rested half-hidden below the edge of the Oriental carpet. I didn't recognize the handwriting. But I knew it would be from Karen.

It was.

Dear Alan,
    I decided to try and break free. I finally had a date.
    But he came back, to my door, just like in my dreams. I didn't even scream.
    I let it happen.
    I'll be dead when you read this. I have to be dead before it happens again. I'm sorry.
    I let you down.
    And you let me down. You weren't in the big house.

25

It's funny, everything's felt safe but telling you that I love you. So there, forever, I love you.

K

I had never noticed that the pattern on the cove molding in Diane's office was different from mine. Then again, I couldn't recall ever lying on her sofa before.

Diane had walked in to say good morning. She found me at my desk, crying quietly and raving in whispers, first at Merideth and then at Karen's ghost. Diane had quickly decided that, regardless of what I thought, I had no business doing therapy so soon after discovering a patient suicide. She called the answering service, giving them the phone numbers of my patients that day and instructing that they be called and their appointments canceled. That was her second good idea. The first was getting me out of my office and into hers.

"Maybe we should talk," she said.

"Yeah. Maybe." I rolled over on my side a little bit so I could see her on the chair across from me. "As you've no doubt gathered, I've got this dead patient I'm a little upset about. A young woman I've been seeing for a couple of years killed herself over the weekend. I think I might've really fucked this one up." A good Catholic in another life, I always framed disasters with mea culpas. "I didn't see the suicide coming at all. No increase in depression, no ideation, no plan, nothing."

"Tell me," she said.

"I'm annoyed at myself about something else, too. After they somehow linked me to this woman's body, I told a cop who came to my house some confidential things about her treatment, despite the fact that I didn't have anybody's permission."

"That's not like you."

"Yeah, well, now I know I'm not at my best with cops in my living room and dead patients across town."

"I think you can be forgiven your lapse in judgment. No harm, no foul."

26

"About telling things to the cop, maybe, about whatever I failed to see coming with this patient, I just don't know." I was mindful at some level of bruised awareness that I didn't have anyone's permission to talk about Karen with Diane, either, but I convinced myself that it was a consultation. I hadn't disclosed Karen's name, anyway.

"People don't get braces who are planning to kill themselves, do they?" I asked. The question wasn't purely rhetorical; my state of mind was as shaky as an adolescent drunk.

She hesitated a moment before responding. The delay was tactical. "Well, there are those of us with sufficient vanity to want to look our best for future archaeological expeditions. It's residue from years of maternal admonitions about clean underwear and emergency rooms." She primped her hair with both hands and saw the desired smile developing on my face. "No, honey, they don't," Diane continued, "braces and liposuctions are very rare in suicidal patients. A comprehensive search of the literature will prove me correct."

I tried to ignore her attempts at humor. "Then, you tell me why, damn it." The fight was out of my voice. The words were still angry, but I was wearing them like a tuxedo after the prom.

"Why do you think?"

My answer was ready. "She was an incest victim. I think somebody raped her. Maybe the guy the police think she went out on a date with. Date rape, maybe. But rape. I think it flooded her with memories. She was overwhelmed. That's what I think." I was close to convincing myself.

"Sounds plausible," Diane said.

"But mostly what I think is that it doesn't fit. She was all done being a victim. She was taking control of her life. You know that stage of therapy where the work is done and all that remains is consolidation? Well, she was almost there. She shouldn't be dead. She shouldn't have killed herself. I've never lost a patient before. Have you?"

27

I already knew the answer to my question; she shook her head anyway. Surprisingly few therapists had experienced patient suicides. "Part of me expects to hear that the police are wrong. That she isn't dead. Or at least that she didn't suicide, that it was an accident or something. I don't know, I feel like I must've screwed this one up somehow. Maybe if I'd been in town to take her call?"

"It may have made a difference, Alan. There's no way to know. You can't watch over your patients all the time."

"But you know I haven't been here, all here, since Merideth left. Maybe I missed something."

"Yeah. Maybe you did. You're not perfect at this, Alan, you're merely damn good at it." She knew her words were not getting through to me. "She killed herself. You didn't kill her. Hey! Alan!" My attention was focused on the gaps in the window mortises.

"Yeah. I know, Diane." I started to get up. "I also know that knowing isn't going to help for a while. Your eight-thirty is waiting." I gestured at the minuscule red light beaming above her desk.

Diane zipped open her appointment calendar and checked her schedule before glancing at the clock.

"How about dinner tonight?" she asked.

"Thanks. Let me think about it. I'll let you know." I walked over and hugged her, and she held me for a while and then strode toward the waiting room to retrieve her next patient.

I left the office and walked two blocks east to the Downtown Boulder Mall. Economic redevelopment motivated the permanent closing of four blocks of Boulder's "Main Street" in the mid-1970s. Coffee shops, pharmacies, hardware stores, and a Woolworth's surrendered their storefronts to upscale shops, and the two-lane blacktop of Pearl Street was transformed into a pedestrian sanctuary of paving bricks, statuary, fountains, playgrounds, and a designer jungle of trees, shrubs, and flowers. Hair nets,

28

hammers, and twenty-five-cent cups of coffee were no longer to be found in a retail district whose shopkeepers sold virtually nothing one couldn't live without. Unless one placed southwestern knickknacks, gourmet kitchen supplies, and outrageously priced clothing on one's list of essentials. Renovated turn-of-the-century buildings loaned charm to the mall, the jutting Rocky Mountain foothills twelve blocks away added a sense of space, and Boulder's peculiar locals had a place to gather.

I sat alone and had coffee at the Bohemia Cafe after exchanging pleasantries with the Czechoslovakian owners and their kids. When I was done I called the answering service from the restaurant phone. I left a message telling Diane no but thanks about dinner.

Cicero was waiting on the front porch of the house when I pulled myself from the Subaru. The rear end of her body wagged as if to parody the absence of sway from her nub of a tail. She jumped in place, all four legs straight up, and her joy was almost infectious as we walked our rural neighborhood. I was surprised to see my neighbor Adrienne's Land Cruiser on a Monday morning and followed Cicero as she chased it down the road toward the house. Adrienne, the urologist, explained something about a scheduled hypospadias repair that had been canceled because her patient had developed pneumonia — so I invited her to have lunch with me.

"Can't, sorry, boychik, I haven't made rounds yet. I left some charts here that my office manager is convulsing about, but I've gotta get back. How about dinner tonight? Peter's making something that's been buried in sodium in the refrigerator since about Passover, and to be totally frank, I'd rather not be solely responsible for convincing him how good it is."

It didn't feel fair to accept the invitation without letting her know that I wasn't in the mood for a celebration. She saw my hesitation. "I have patients who consent to have bicycle pumps installed in their perennially flaccid penises faster than you accept dinner invitations. Think about it, honey, and let me know. Bye."

I was about to tell her of my patient's suicide, but she kissed Cicero and climbed into the big car before I could untangle my tongue.

I'd been advised by Adrienne, among others, that in times of need I was not particularly adept at turning to my friends for support. The criticism had been justified, but the recent series of events that was turning my life to shit was also helping me get better at seeking solace. If it's indeed true that practice makes perfect, at least I was getting a lot more reps.

The house was thick with parched air when Cicero and I walked in. I hadn't turned down the thermostat — another, it seemed, in a series of sins of omission.

Cicero knew nothing but that Merideth was gone. She didn't know about Karen Hart, and I didn't trouble her with it. Instead we commiserated for the thousandth time about Merideth's departure. The big dog missed Merideth as much as I did and would sit in front of the carved door at the end of the day listening for the peculiar hum of her car. Sometimes I sat with her. Sometimes I pointed out that the wait was futile; other times I didn't.

My dog and I were back inside early that evening when Peter's robust yell down the hill beckoned us to dinner. He stood on the gravel drive, his straight blond hair hanging limp to his shoulders. Ambivalently, I headed out the door and started up the hill, Cicero prancing beside me.

I carried a bottle of red and a bottle of white, unsure which went better with brine.

Three

The daily ration of tragedy and despair that I observed in my work had always humbled me and left me feeling beholden to fate. Experience had convinced me that any spirit would crack if exposed to enough pressure, to a sharp enough blow. For almost ten years I had toiled to strengthen and shore up those whose egos were already weakened, perforated, or absent by the time they entered kindergarten, to heal those whose intact psyches had fractured under pressure that I liked to think my own could endure, and to palliate those whose strong psychological constitutions succumbed to stresses so unfair and so monumental that skeletal strength was rendered inconsequential.

In the face of these immense tragedies empathy was inadequate, condolences vacant, pity unhelpful. Often all I offered was tenderness and a willingness to echo essential, familiar voices to my patients until their resistance waned and their defenses permitted the sounds to be heard. And perhaps to heal. I aspired always to offer safety, an environment free of random infection. First, Hippocrates mandated, do no harm.

I felt deep sorrow for the arbitrary cruelties of life that befell these people I treated, always aware of and grateful for my constitutional fortitude and apparent immunity.

When my immunity showed some cracks, I consoled myself by thinking that things couldn't get much worse than having my wife leave me and having a patient kill herself.

I was wrong.

Diane heard the rumors first. But Diane, who nurtured more sources than the Mossad, always heard rumors first.

Initially my colleagues were compassionate to me about Karen Hart killing herself. In the end, though, I think many of them needed to see her death as my failing; if a patient killing herself wasn't a therapeutically avoidable circumstance, then my colleagues could be vulnerable to it happening in their practices, too, and none of us in the mental health business are eager for reminders of that vulnerability. In retrospect, their pointed fingers were understandable. But I felt as though I had been temporarily suspended from the fraternity of competent and caring healers.

Boulder is, in practice, a small town. My peers were going to talk about Karen Hart's death. And those therapists eager for closure were going to come to the conclusion that I had failed to anticipate her high risk of suicide. The unpleasant reality was that there was not much arguing with that assessment. Some would surmise, of course, that Karen's elevated risk of suicide was there to be anticipated. I was quite willing to argue that point, but confidentiality restrictions kept me from the debate circuit.

In the meantime life went on as before. My practice thrived. I bicycled whenever autumn was pretending to be summer, skied when it was unmistakably winter. Most days I no longer thought about Karen Hart. My first Christmas without Merideth was lonely. But I survived.

I first heard the bad news on an early January Sunday morning, the cusp of the same holiday season that had been baptized by Karen Hart's suicide the weekend before Thanksgiving. Chinook gales were blowing through the seams of my house and fracturing my sleep. In the tropics people are evacuated when the winds hit seventy miles an hour; in Boulder, when the chinooks gust past ninety, people compensate by talking a wee bit louder, re-scheduling tennis matches and bicycle rides, and leaning a little bit when they walk.

My house sounded like a soprano sax with a split reed on windy days, and on that Sunday morning I crawled out of bed early for the relative quiet of my southeast-facing kitchen. I made coffee. Grimly soiled slush, residue from a Boxing Day snowstorm, pooled and congealed on the driveway and fouled the otherwise pristine hillside. Up the hill I saw Adrienne silhouetted by the light of her kitchen and imagined a big stack of charts and her porta-ble dictating machine in front of her. Peter, who could sleep through anything, wouldn't be up for hours.

I stepped out into the downslope gale with an anticipa-tory lean that proved unnecessary in the shelter of the house and retrieved the fat newspaper wrapped in orange plastic from my side of the driveway.

Rumor was transformed into ink. Under the fold, but still front page — Sunday front page.

STATE BOARD TO REVIEW ALLEGATIONS
AGAINST PSYCHOLOGIST
Possible Misconduct Prior to Patient Suicide

The local paper, the *Daily*, had obtained a copy of a for-mal complaint prepared for submission to the Mental Health Occupations Grievance Board alleging that Boul-der psychologist Dr. Alan Gregory had engaged in an on-going sexual relationship with his patient Karen E. Hart in the months preceding her death by suicide the previous November.

A particularly vituperative Denver psychiatrist was quoted in the article about the universally tragic conse-quences of professionals betraying the trust of women cli-ents. The implication of her remarks was that if the allegations about sexual impropriety were true, then my behavior was causally related to Karen's suicide. I realized that if I was reading about almost any psychologist other than myself, I would have been nodding my head in agreement. I carried my coffee mug into the living room and wondered how many of my friends, colleagues, and patients were reading my professional obituary.

The big western windows vibrated and hummed in their ancient frames from the force of the pulsating chinooks. The horizon was scrubbed and clean, sunlight brightening the cape of snow on the Indian Peaks.

I screamed at Cicero to get off a small Tabriz on which I had permitted her to rest daily since Merideth left and yelled at the fucking winds to stop. Cicero cowered at my ridiculous outburst; the chinooks ignored me. The phone rang. I yelled at it and caught myself. I wasn't handling this well. With exaggerated calm, I stepped over and turned off the ringer.

Cicero stood and woofed, a lot of bass but more woodwind than percussion, and tore off toward the front door. I didn't hear a knock until after she crashed into the wall by the entryway, missing the curve again.

Standing there, on the cracked concrete slab outside the door, my friend looked like a waif. Adrienne wore a mint green silk nightgown largely covered by an oversize turtleneck sweater knitted from yarn of three or four of the many colors that do not complement mint green. On her feet were red wool and brown leather Acorns. Furry muffs covered her ears.

Every one of her features was finely drawn, save her hips, designed, she maintained, "to give at least one set of triplets the experience of being born simultaneously." Her hair was the color of good topsoil and was cut close to her head. She had spreckled dark irises that looked like a luminescent version of the underside of a Nestle's Crunch bar and pupils that refused to constrict in bright light, which made her eyes appear even darker. Her nose was a pleasant pudge and her rarely closed mouth a deceptive horizontal slash that could spread open as if it were gusseted into a grin that had the power of an infant's smile. Her voice sang accents of Manhattan by way of Brooklyn, and she relished the impact of her unadulterated urbanity on Boulder's version of western life.

"Life's a bitch, huh."

I couldn't help but smile. "Yeah, Ren, it is."

"So. Maybe you could invite me in out of the approaching hurricane?" Years in Colorado and she refused to get her storms straight.

I opened the door enough to allow her in. Cicero greeted her adopted mother with glee. "Want some coffee?" I asked.

"Love some, black."

When I walked back in with the coffee I found that she had invited Cicero up on the sofa in the living room. Adrienne and Cicero both knew that the dog wasn't allowed on the couch. Cicero generally lacked discipline about such things; she was, nonetheless, much better behaved than Adrienne. Cicero looked at me expecting to be kicked off the sofa, but I felt guilty about yelling at her earlier, so she got to wriggle around and twist about an eighth of her body onto Adrienne's lap.

Adrienne took a sip of coffee and nodded her approval before she spoke. "You do it?" she asked, gesturing at the newspaper on the table.

I laughed. "Jesus, Adrienne, you're a little blunt sometimes. You know that, don't you?"

"I'm somebody who tells people to take off their pants for a living. You expect decorum?"

I was silent, wishing I had Cicero to distract me.

She persisted. "It was a serious question."

"I know it was." I sipped from my mug deliberately, as though auditioning for a commercial with Juan Valdez. "The answer is no, I didn't do it." There it was. Out of my mouth.

"Something in your hesitation tells me it crossed your mind." Adrienne made this statement as devoid of accusation as it could be made.

35

"Now you're asking was I tempted?"

She shrugged.

"She was very beautiful, Adrienne." I noted the past tense. "Did I realize she was attractive? Sure. Did I have an impulse to sleep with her? No, I didn't. She was a patient."

"Don't get professionally pious with me, Dr. Gregory." She was giving me her "I can't believe you can be so naive" look. "Find me a male OB-GYN who doesn't occasionally enjoy a breast exam. Go ahead, try. Okay, leave out Aronson — do you know he's gay?" I noted some hesitation, not a trait I often associated with Adrienne. "Even I, yours truly, have performed vasectomies on organs that are attached to men who are *my* patients, and, with a carefully chosen subset of those men, I have had impulses to perform other, more intimate, procedures on those organs. And I'm happily married to a man with a libido the size of Oklahoma, where I've never been, praise God. But you, who to the best of my knowledge haven't even been stung by a female insect in five months, mean to tell me that you weren't the slightest bit tempted by this young lady you call 'beautiful'? You tell Peter I said any of this, by the way, and I'll swear you're psychotic and that I've been giving you scrips for Haldol.

"Anyway, my friend, sometimes we professionals are faced with gorgeous patients being quite seductive with us."

"But you don't fuck 'em, do you, Ren?" I stressed the *f* in "fuck."

She manage to ignore the edge in my voice. "No. But I notice."

I started to pace. "There's a certain trust that gets bestowed on us by our patients. The trust is that no matter what *they* do, *we* don't cross the line. Even if this patient" — I flitted my hand at the newspaper — "or any patient walked into my office and started to take off her clothes and begged to sleep with me, my job would be to tell her to get dressed and to leave the office while she did. The se-

36

duction is just part of the patient's pathology."

Adrienne stared into her cup and mesmerized Cicero by scratching her below the chin. "No argument. But it's not your job not to be interested, even captivated, by the offer that was made."

"Your point is?"

"My point is: Don't delude yourself into thinking you need to be pure in order to be innocent. Not having slept with your patient is innocent enough."

"No. It's not enough. I need to be certain that any feelings I might have had about her didn't contaminate the treatment in a way that was harmful to her."

"Did they?"

"I've gone over this a thousand times since she died. I don't think I mishandled the treatment. Quite the opposite; I'm proud of the treatment. It's more than slightly irrelevant now, but she shouldn't have killed herself. I know I wouldn't have missed the signs. I've even had fantasies about trying to track down the guy she went out with that night to find out what really happened."

"It seems unlikely that he poured the antidepressants down her throat."

"Maybe he forced himself on her. She was still too fragile for sex."

"Maybe yes. Maybe no. Maybe she just killed herself. Even some of your patients get cancer, Doctor."

"Valid point, Ren, but she had survived surgery, radiation, and chemotherapy and then died unexpectedly during her remission. It leaves questions unanswered."

"You can't have it both ways, my friend. Either she was suicidal and you missed it, or she wasn't suicidal and something happened to provoke it. You can't switch back and forth deciding which leaves you feeling more responsible. Well, actually you can, but I'll give you a lot of shit about it."

She noted the absence of mirth in my reaction and reached over and pried my hand from the mug. "Are you all right?"

I shook my head a little. "It may sound terribly self-serving, but I don't need this now."

She stared at me for a moment, then smiled.

"This ain't the half of it, buster. You know you're gonna get sued, too," she warned me with an impish smile. Another hesitation, a big kiss for Cicero, and then she took her leave with, "Call me when you want to talk."

I reread the article. And I got pissed.

No previous allegations accusing Dr. Gregory of sexual misconduct had been filed with the Grievance Committee of the State Board of Psychologist Examiners. A complaint investigated five years before regarding billing questions had been dismissed as without substance. Current state law, the article pronounced, made sexual contact between a psychologist and a patient a felony, but the district attorney reported no charges had been filed against Dr. Gregory.

Dr. Gregory had refused an opportunity to be interviewed about the case. Ms. Hart's father had also refused comment and declined to state his intentions regarding legal action.

The declaration that I had refused to speak with the *Daily* was in the vicinity of accurate. On the day after Karen's November death a reporter, Joseph Abiado, had called to get a quote for a story. I had declined to be interviewed, claiming that confidentiality guidelines prohibited me from discussing any case, whether the patient was dead or not. He pressed me a little to check on my resolve and then relented. He had called twice more on New Year's Eve day and left messages with my answering service to call him about an important follow-up story on Karen. I assumed it had something to do with a review of the year's stories that the *Daily* prepared each New Year's. I wasn't especially eager to listen once again to his arguments about why I should talk to him about Karen. In not returning the calls I thought I was defending Karen's confidences; I didn't realize Mr. Abiado was probing mine.

The guidelines about confidential communication prohibited me from discussing cases with anyone without the permission of the patient. The fact that my patient was dead and that somebody was slinging mud my way didn't free me from the boundaries of confidence.

An argument could have been made that little was to be lost by disregarding the tenets of privileged communication and simply defending myself against the accusations that I had sexually exploited a vulnerable woman. Karen Hart was certainly in no position to sue me for violating her confidences.

But that wasn't the point. The point was that all of my other patients needed to believe that *their* secrets were safe with me, that I wouldn't discard my vow of confidence to them at my convenience. Colorado law acknowledged that psychotherapeutic relationships were special and provided legal sanctuary for therapists to maintain confidentiality for their patients. The law mandated or permitted some exceptions: therapists were obligated to report child abuse and had a limited mandate to abrogate privilege if their patient or any other identifiable person was in imminent danger of physical harm. This exception was known as the "duty to warn." Despite frequent attempts at liberalization by legislators, the exceptions remained tightly drawn, because without the assurance that communications between therapist and patient would be held sacrosanct, psychotherapy could not survive. Confidentiality was to psychotherapy what antiseptic conditions were to surgery. Without confidentiality the risk of proceeding in therapy would be too great. You trusted your surgeon to keep his or her operating room clean. You trusted your psychotherapist to keep his or her mouth shut. In my mind, then, it was that simple.

So my hands were tied. Through my silence I provided my remaining patients and my future patients the assurance that I would not violate their confidences. And through the same silence I left them to wonder whether I might venture to violate their bodies. Ultimately, I stood in solitude to absorb the consequences of unrebutted charges of sexual exploitation of a patient. A patient who had killed herself, no less.

The consequences were prompt. A handful of patients canceled their weekly appointments before the morning was out. I was on call that weekend, and the answering service put the messages through on my digital pager, which was beeping away like a robin in mating season.

By Monday morning the number of cancellations was ten. I was beginning to assume that the rest of my patients didn't read newspapers.

The maelstrom persisted that day at work. I had three no-shows on Monday and two more cancellations instructing me not to call back. Diane visited me hourly, a nurse checking vitals.

I spent some of my suddenly abundant free time going over the financial status of my professional corporation. The corporation had plenty of assets, some cash, some investments, some accounts receivable. If I got half of the A/R receipts, I would be solvent for quite a while. Personal finances were strong. I had learned a lot from Diane and Raoul and had a decent income from downtown Boulder office investments and had a stock portfolio of Raoul's ex-employers. I could liquidate if necessary. I decided not to worry about money. The relief was minor; it was the least of my problems.

I called my lawyer, Jonathan Younger, and got a lesson about libel. He'd read the article and found it carefully worded. He said he would represent me before the grievance committee and to call him when the complaint was filed. I relayed Adrienne's warning about being sued. He laughed and told me that the only people who knew more than lawyers about lawsuits were doctors. "Count on being sued," he said, "and hope you get lucky." He also suggested that I consider explaining the confidentiality issue to the *Daily,* for the record.

I didn't have to wait long for an opportunity. Mr.

Abiado called that afternoon seeking comment about a follow-up article that would inform the *Daily*'s readership that Dr. Gregory had been separated from his wife, Merideth, since the previous summer. I said, "No comment," to that. Then he started into questions about Karen Hart. I gave my speech about confidentiality, for the record. He seemed to listen carefully. His article the next day got most of it right. But not all of it.

Abiado unknowingly presented an opportunity for a little passive aggression, and I jumped at it. Merideth spelled her first name incorrectly (she would say unconventionally). The conventional spelling is *M-e-r-e-d-i-t-h*. Merideth's parents had spelled it wrong on her birth certificate. Since early adolescence my wife had assertively defended her right to spell it the way she chose; she corrected transgressors relentlessly. I was sure Abiado would get it wrong. I liked that Abiado would get it wrong.

He got it wrong. It was a small victory. Like a long foul ball before getting struck out looking.

Merideth's old station in Denver, Channel 9, ran a brief story on the ten o'clock news using file footage of me without the sound. Channel 9 had interviewed me the previous winter for a fluff piece they were doing on divorce. I was interviewed at my desk; behind me a blanket of snow covered the yard outside my office. I was surprised as I watched the silent tape at how much younger I looked then. I wore a mustache but no beard, and my sandy hair was shorter then, but too full around the temples. On camera my eyes were a steely sapphire, what Merideth, in one of her more acquisitive assessments, had called "BMW blue." My nose was long, and the tiny valleys of my dimples distracted from the absence of a smile on my face. Merideth had complained about the gray-and-black geometric sweater that I wore that day, suggesting a suit or a blue blazer and tie. A year later I could begrudgingly admit that the sweater wasn't at its best on video.

As the image reverted back to the pregnant young

morning anchor, I wondered about my next contact with the electronic media. Television images of reporters sticking weaponlike microphones in reluctant faces were all too familiar.

Merideth sent an overnight letter after I neglected to return her calls for a couple of days. She had heard about the allegations from a mutual friend. I reached her at work and used all my guile to convince her I was fine. She knew me well enough to recognize the ruse but permitted me the camouflage. She offered to come out for the weekend. The temptation was strong, but I resisted. A pity visit wasn't the way to work things out with her.

By the end of the week I had seen eighteen patients out of thirty-eight scheduled.

The patients who did keep their appointments were a fascinating mix of the blind and deaf, who apparently neither saw nor heard anything of my crucifixion; the hysterical, who heard and acted as though nothing had happened; and the faithful, who rejected the allegations out of hand. Two severely characterologically disturbed patients, compelled by an intermittent need to see me as evil, stayed as spectators to my demise.

I was most intrigued by the group bound to me by faith. The group was small and consisted of patients who had traveled through personal visions of hell while in my care. Gretchen Kravner, a woman in her late thirties who had suffered as a battered wife for ten years and had recently managed to separate from her tormentor. Elliot Perkins, a small, brilliant scientist who had been paralyzed by panic attacks since his late teens. I had referred him to a psychiatrist for medication and then treated him for the sequelae of his disease. A month ago his work on superconductivity for the National Institute of Standards and Technology had been recognized in *Time* magazine and on the "Today" show. And Paula Smith, a victim of depression and cervical cancer, who was winning the battle against both. She had a good oncologist and, I had to admit, a good psychologist.

The patients who departed were mostly new patients, people I had seen for a couple of months or less, or people whose resistance to the process of change left them in chronic search of a reason not to be in psychotherapy, or adolescents whose parents made decisions, some gleefully, some sadly, that they could not risk leaving their children in my care.

The excuses of the well-meaning were intended to insulate me from the reality of the migration. Some patients reported financial problems, or spontaneous recoveries, or miraculously healed marriages to soften the blow. Hostile, usually depressed patients, eager to feel betrayed by me, left in a spray of accusations or just didn't arrive for appointments anymore.

A Valentine's Day accounting showed seventeen patients left in my practice. During the months between the prior August, when Merideth left, and January, when the exodus began from my practice, I had struggled to keep my nights and weekends full. Now even my days felt empty.

Adrienne was the only friend who asked me whether I had abused Karen Hart. A handful, like Diane Estevez, stood by me. Most just kept their distance. A few confused allegations with proof and joined the chorus singing the refrain of my supposed sins.

Four

My mother instilled in me the surety that tragedies come in threes. She learned the lesson from the skycaps at Midway Airport in Chicago in the early 1940s. The crashes will come in threes, they told her.

Number three had me worried. If Merideth leaving me was number one and the Karen Hart affair was number two, then number three was on the horizon.

It arrived during the springtime: Memorial Day weekend.

Diane Estevez and her husband had invited me to dinner on the Saturday night before the holiday. I hadn't been feeling particularly sociable and had hesitated to accept, but Diane threatened to drive down from their mountain perch and retrieve me from the Ponderosa if I didn't agree to join them for Raoul's paella. I'd finally said I'd come if Raoul promised to make a big plate of cazuela potatoes with lots of black pepper. He argued that the potatoes were redundant given the saffron rice in the paella. Diane argued that it was a waste of food since I seemed to be on a prolonged fast anyway.

Raoul made the potatoes. His family owned a renowned restaurant on the coast near Barcelona; he knew what he was doing. Dinner was superb.

I drove away from their house around nine, using extra

44

care on the oily slush developing on Lee Hill Drive. A storm had blown in with a promise to drop three to four inches of liquefied cement along the foothills by early morning. A few hundred yards from North Broadway I pulled the Subaru off the road to join three other parked cars and four or five shadowy figures moving haphazardly around a vehicle resting in the creek.

By the time I got out of the Subaru, they had already removed the body from the car.

At first I edged just close enough to see her hair shimmering in the glare of the headlights, the dark strands matted into ropes by blood and melting snow. Two more steps and I recognized her.

Anne Hubbard's head rested on a small pink towel, upright, as if searching the sky for stars, but her body splayed awkwardly on the muddy ground, her right arm out and bent at the elbow, her hips twisted. Eyes I remembered as Riesling bottle green shone black and stared away from the accelerating commotion, disinterested. Her parted lips were freshly painted cranberry red, her gaping mouth trapped heavy snowflakes the size of daisy petals.

A tall thin man in an orange all-weather running suit bent next to her on one knee. He touched her wrist and neck with three rigid fingers and held a vanity mirror over her mouth and nose, and then gently, as though not to disturb her, he raised a khaki blanket over her head. The inelegant shroud failed to shelter one burgundy boot, its leather wet almost to black by the snow. The toe was pointing north toward Cheyenne.

A man gripping a cellular phone leaned against an old Mercedes, his spare hand cupped against his ear to retard the whine of tires cutting rivulets in the slush on Lee Hill Drive. After a moment his lips stopped moving. He leaned into the car, came back without the phone, looked at me, and said, "The police are on their way." I nodded.

The stray boot was alluring and immodest, like an inadvertently bared border of lingerie. I knelt and gently

45

nudged the boot from the lip of asphalt where it rested and covered it with a corner of the blanket. Altar boy memories transformed the act into a genuflection.

Her car was perched at an angle on the bank of a small creek not far from the road. Crushed parallel bands of saturated brown weeds and new green grass designated the route from Lee Hill Road to the creek. A large rock shaped like a derby braced the left front fender. The windshield was cracked on the driver's side. The driver's door was open, the interior lights on, the right headlight sending a beam to record the falling flakes. The windshield wipers were set for intermittent use, their swishing and clicking keeping time with the melodious requiem of spring snow, helpless and curious people, and careless death.

I drifted next to the car and spotted her purse on the floor below the passenger seat. A red band of the skin of some exotic animal or reptile encircled the top of the huge black leather bag. This was the farthest I had ever seen Anne from it.

I shuffled back and stood just beyond the circle illuminated by the headlights of the cars. The shrill sirens of rescue vehicles pulsated in the distance.

Soon, rotating blue-and-white lights highlighted the falling snow. The sheriff's deputy jumped from his car and herded everyone but the man with the cellular phone back to stand where I was. I considered stepping forward to identify the dead woman as a Boulder city councilwoman, ultimately deciding that everyone would know soon enough.

I focused on remembered images of Anne's hands and her chin. She had wonderful hands; her long fingers sifted the air like the teeth of a bone comb and always settled in some juxtaposition of perfect choreography, never symmetrical, never without elegance or strength. Her chin was dotted with tiny black hairs. She'd crinkle her chin to help her fight back tears, and the little hairs would capture and play with the room light.

Anne had come to see me for psychotherapy almost two years before. For almost two months she came regularly before she abruptly pronounced herself free from problems and terminated her treatment. She returned again at Christmastime, last year, intent on confronting the intimacy fears that had spurred her previous retreat from therapy. When the allegations about my abusing Karen Hart became public, she again declared herself cured and left. I hadn't seen her since.

"You know what's weird," said an unshaven man with yellow teeth who ended up next to me, "is that after I found her — I was here first, you know — I had to run over to the Bustop, you know, the topless place, for a phone. I mean, shit, I'm dialin' 911 'bout a woman I think is dead, and I'm starin' at these amazin' tits all over the place." He spoke slowly, his battery running out. "Fuck-ing weird. You know, they tried to get me to pay the goddamn cover charge?"

To pretend his soliloquy wasn't directed at me, I treaded toward my car, conscious of my soaking shoes and dripping hair. I sat in the Subaru, lights off and engine running, grateful for its whining heater. From the driver's seat I surveyed the starkly lit stage as the paramedics felt her body and searched for vital signs, danced a vain and brutal dance to inspire their return, and then again covered Anne Hubbard's body with the dirty khaki blanket, professionally this time, not neglecting the burgundy boot.

I steered the Subaru home slowly, in four-wheel drive, mourning a little, shivering a lot.

I decided then that my troika was complete. Merideth was gone. Karen Hart was dead. Now Anne Hubbard was dead. Anne was a nice lady and a promising politician, but if her death was number three, I had dodged a bullet. She had been my patient briefly, that's all. A glancing blow to me at best.

I would tell my mother the next day on the phone. She would be certain my luck was about to change.

47

* * *

"I've always liked you better without the beard," Diane said. We were sitting outside at Nancy's. She was eating lunch. I was drinking coffee. We met for lunch every Wednesday; this one was the day after Anne Hubbard's funeral, two days after Memorial Day. We hadn't talked since dinner at her house.

"Yeah. I know," I said. The stubble, I thought, had barely matured into something bordering on respectability. "Merideth never liked it, either," I continued.

"Oh, that explains it." Diane was talking to her herb cheese omelet.

"Explains what?" I said with prophylactic defensiveness.

"This, this tonsorial experiment, is just like your not eating food anymore"— she gestured at my coffee cup — "or your new touring bicycle"— she said "touring" with a sneer that underscored her lack of comprehension of the value and grace of my brand new Bianchi racing bike with Campi components — "or your wondering whether to keep the Subaru or get something that goes too fast and doesn't have enough seats, or . . . Should I continue?"

I wanted to encourage her to stop. The day was too pleasant to beg immolation.

"This is separation shit." She said "shit" the way Raoul did, with a *c* on the front. When it wasn't directed at me I always thought the pronunciation made the word more elegant. "You have insisted since Merideth got on that plane that you wouldn't do what everyone else does. No Flatirons Fitness Club for you. No, that's where all new divorcees go in Boulder. Instead you ride that ridiculous bicycle and wear those silly spandex shorts all over the damn county to further tune your sparse body with absolutely no, no inclination toward attracting some similarly well tuned young female. Right? Quit kidding yourself. You're on the hunt."

Diane said this without varying her voice even a fraction of an octave. It provided an image of the power she

48

could bring into her psychotherapy. It was inspiring. Diane was just forty, but her face suffered from her inability to stay out of the sun. Laugh lines and wrinkles had definition that they shouldn't. She was medium everything: height, weight, and complexion; her hair was nondescript brown like her eyes. Her face was full, bordering on round, her chin oval and pronounced. Diane was pretty. Not head-turning pretty, but the kind of pretty that keeps drawing your attention from across a room.

Diane Estevez and I had become friends almost eight years before in the insanity that was the psychiatric inpatient unit of Denver County Hospital. We were fresh from our clinical psychology internships — she returning to Colorado from a year in Chicago, I moving across town from the medical school campus. Nothing had prepared us for the quality and intransigence of the lunacy that we confronted at County. Within hours of our arrivals we were preparing discharge plans to eject patients from our care who, only weeks before, in the relative insulation and luxury of our internships, we would have been feverishly admitting.

Our half-time positions were designed, we were certain, to keep us broke and dependent. Private practice was the answer. Together we rented one office in a renovated retail storefront east of the Pearl Street Mall in Boulder and rotated hours there during our time off.

A year and a half later, three months apart, we each resigned from County and went into full-time practice. Diane was older than me, wiser than me, and braver than me. She left first. We found larger space in an old house on Walnut Street west of downtown. Our neighbors were a sheet metal shop, an auto body shop, and a strange company that collected metal and put it in piles of various sizes to rust to ever darker shades of brown. Our landlord considered himself a developer and historic preservationist. He was actually a lazy economics professor at the

University of Colorado who realized late that he was only a coat of paint and some minor carpentry away from rescuing his little rental house from the mercy of unreliable residential tenants by converting it to commercial use.

We skirmished with him for two years over everything from soundproofing to window screens and finally reached a truce by buying the building from him. Diane thought of it, and we financed the purchase with her husband's money. Raoul Estevez had specialized in electrical engineering for a series of high-tech cradle companies that emerged during Boulder's rise to entrepreneurial prominence in the late 1970s. Each move left him with a chunk of stock and a lot of freedom. His current passion involved the genesis of a company that was going to do something with satellites. Raoul spoke of his plans with great fervor as his Spanish accent devoured the niceties of the English words, and I nodded my head a lot.

Our practices flourished. Diane said it was because we were very good. I figured we must be.

My position sitting across from Diane that day in the spring sunshine was precarious. I assumed she would blast me if I said anything to defend my dignity. Her voice told me that she felt I needed to hear what she had to say.

"It's been what—nine months? Meri is not coming back, Alan, and whether or not you want to let it sink into your pathetically bearded head, you are finally starting to act like the newly unmarried."

My silence had already conceded the point. "You're right, Diane," I said. "But that doesn't mean I wanna analyze it."

"Great," she said, leaning back in her chair. "Is this why you started umpiring, too?"

"Denial seems futile. You're on a roll."

"Is that a yes?"

"Having my evenings so free—so empty is more accurate—isn't pleasant. Umpiring gets me out of the house.

No Merideth. No patients. Gotta do something. I might even take up umpiring as a career if my practice continues its current trend."

Diane tilted her head slightly, pointing her chin at her collarbone. "And why the women's leagues?"

"For obvious reasons." I smiled. "I'm beginning to look around some. But first I need to feel a little better about myself."

She found this especially funny. "If that beard helps you feel better about yourself, it's time to get yourself back into therapy."

"You know what I mean."

"Yeah, I know what you mean," she said. "Are you seeing anybody?"

"Gone out a couple of times. I'm outta practice, and to be honest, I hate dating. Anyway, nobody very interesting and, I hope, nobody you know."

Diane laughed again. "I'll find out. You know I will. I look forward to it. I actually have warm memories of the parade of young women with insufficient gray matter and overabundant mammaries who filled your social calendar before Merideth." She was getting into this. "Remember the one who actually had you listening to country music for a couple of weeks? You know, what was her name, the one with the pointy boots and—"

"I remember, I remember," I said to stop her. I still had an album by Loretta Lynn to remind me. "I'm umping your game tomorrow night. I can and will get even with you."

"Not even a malevolent umpire can slow the force of Montezuma's Revenge," she said, quite matter-of-fact. Montezuma's Revenge was Diane's softball team and her sole delusion.

"Perhaps not. But at the game, when I argue with you, I get to decide when we're done arguing, and I get to decide who wins. That's the real reason I became an umpire. Just for the opportunity to tell you what to do occasionally."

51

Diane returned to her omelet.

"I got a referral this morning," I said.

"Really. Maybe your professional life isn't dead."

"That makes two referrals in four months, Diane. Not exactly sustenance."

"Is this one going to stick?" she asked. The previous referral had been from her; the entire therapy lasted forty-five minutes. Actually the appointment lasted forty-five minutes; therapy never started.

"I don't know. The guy didn't say much on the phone. Funny, though, he got my name from Anne Hubbard, our dead councilwoman."

Diane opened her eyes wide and smiled. "Connections with the netherworld, huh?"

"I am assuming," I said, "that the referral came while she was still alive."

"You never know. The business consultants are telling all of us psychologists to adapt to the managed health care environment by cultivating every referral base that we can. Think of the possibilities. If you could somehow manage to tap the afterlife market, you could get dead people to refer all their grieving relatives. What a resource."

"Pre-seance, Diane. I'm sure," I said, shaking my head and wondering what I did to manage to surround myself with so many enigmatic women. I put ten dollars on the table for Diane's ample lunch and my coffee, and said, "Let's go."

As we neared our office I turned to her and said, "Did I tell you I saw the accident where Anne Hubbard was killed when I was on the way down from your house last Saturday night?"

I was pretty sure that Diane didn't know I'd been a witness to Anne Hubbard's death. She despised not knowing things. Sometimes I saved news as long as I could to emphasize that I knew some things before she did. Reluctantly she admitted, "No, I didn't know you were at the accident. Did you stop?"

"Yeah, just walked around for a while. There was nothing I could do." I remembered Anne's crushed car and Anne's inert body and took a moment to reassure myself that my statement was true. "I didn't see you at her funeral, were you there?"

"I was there. I saw you at the cemetery. In back. How come?" She knew the answer. She was asking only to create an opportunity to offer a parable.

"There were a lot of people there I didn't want to have to be pleasant to. So I kept my distance."

Peer support was a tough area for Diane and me. Since the charges against me had begun to accumulate, she had defended me assiduously. She had also refused to join me in criticizing colleagues who I felt had isolated me. Diane never joined posses.

"Our compadres," she said, "are doing the best they can with this. Some are vultures, granted. But I don't think you would handle their position any better than most of them." She continued down the hall to her office. As far as lessons from Diane go, this one was noteworthy for its brevity. In a minute I heard her voice behind me. An addendum, perhaps.

"Raoul wants to see you again. God knows why. He's coming to the game tomorrow, and we're goin' for pizza. Wanna come?" she asked.

"Depends," I said. "What kind of pizza?"

"Asshole."

Five

I was the sole base umpire for the game. The plate umpire was a serious man who seemed Greek. He had a mustache that covered half his face. I tried to joke with him before the game. He chose to study his rule book instead.

Montezuma's Revenge was not a bad fielding team. Their failure to find a pitcher who could put a softball across the plate without denting low-flying planes usually meant that they got to exhibit their fielding for too many minutes each game. They couldn't hit to save their lives.

Umpiring behind second base is much more fun in 16-2 games than it is in pitching duels. Traffic on the bases was like the Valley Highway at rush hour. Players from both teams disputed close calls. I argued back, acted authoritative, and reserved the right to turn and walk away when I'd had enough — umpiring was a perfect antidote for doing psychotherapy.

In the bottom half of each inning I retreated into shallow center field so that I could look at the second baseman on Diane's team. Her teammates called her Lauren. Between innings the Greek suggested I might be standing too deep behind the bag. I told him with a straight face that I liked what I could see from there. I didn't tell him that from where I stood it looked like he had a dead animal in his face mask.

Lauren badgered the other team with inane repetitive

jingles. Her dark hair hung loose to her shoulders, the strands indistinguishable from one another. They formed a smooth, dense armor with the sheen of lacquer. Even when she moved quickly the hairs returned rapidly to their ordained places. Her eyes were gray under the shadow of the bill of her cap, which she wore pointing to the sky, reminiscent of the dorks of my youth who couldn't get their hats on right. Her upper lip was fine, thin, and pink and in its rare still moments had the perfect outline of the top of a drawn heart. Her bottom lip was full and pouty, a soft red cushion. She spent her time on the field with her hands on her knees and her balance on her toes; I got to know well the taut tendons on the backs of her knees and the muscular curves of her calves.

Her move to first was good, and she didn't throw like a girl.

Since I was thirteen I have been able to rely on my absolute inability to be at all charming to any strange female for whom I feel even a modicum of interest. With characteristic aplomb my interactions with Lauren consisted of catchy phrases like "Nice stop," or "Good glove." She seemed amused by me or at least thought that my calls were funny. She contested one failed forceout at second base. I had been tempted to call the runner out just because I thought the second baseman was beautiful. The Greek would understand.

After the game Diane bought a deep-dish from Old Chicago, Raoul a paper-thin from Abo's. Diane and Raoul could never agree on pizza. We ate within spitting distance of a pack of transients playing Hacky Sack on the western edge of the lawn in front of the courthouse on the mall. Diane chose the unlikely picnic spot in order to make a political statement by reclaiming space she felt had been usurped from "the people" through the harassment and bad hygiene of the anachronistic street dwellers of the thirteen hundred block of the Downtown Boulder Mall.

I wanted a beer.

I also wanted to sit a little closer to Lauren, who had joined the party along with the catcher and her significant other and two outfielders who were each other's significant others. I stole glances at Lauren whenever I thought I could get away with it and made eye contact for an instant but generally felt ignored. The cloud of my joint statuses as maritally separated and professionally repudiated served to inhibit my joviality. I was an umpire among ball players. Raoul and I talked about satellites and their impact on rural life.

As the party broke up I moved over to Lauren and asked whether I could buy her an ice cream. I hoped Diane hadn't overheard.

Lauren looked at me and smiled, her eyes now more blue than gray, smoke replaced by sky. She looked away and then back at me.

"Alan Gregory," I said, holding out my hand. "You're Lauren?"

She nodded, her hair moving like the mane of an Afghan hound. Her fingers were long and cool. "I really can't," she said. "Sorry. I need to do some work." She crinkled her nose in punctuation. "But thanks." She grinned and looked at me a little longer than was necessary. I felt a reprieve.

"Maybe another time? Maybe you prefer frozen yogurt?"

Her smile finally broke through pursed lips, and I saw brilliant white teeth. "Yeah, maybe another time," she said, nodding. She turned away, called good-bye to the group, and walked up the mall toward Broadway.

Cicero was waiting at the end of the driveway when I got home. She needs, I thought, to be put on a diet. I made a mental note to talk to Peter, who fed anything and anybody who would visit him in his studio/shop during the day.

The blinking light on my answering machine revealed

a call from Merideth. She was calling more frequently since my life had turned sour. Her concern felt very kind. I feared that it gave us an excuse not to let go of each other. On this night, though, I didn't want to talk to her because it would contaminate my thinking about the second baseman, basewoman, of my dreams. I thought about calling Lauren and realized quickly my only source of her phone number would be Diane. She would probably give it to me, but it would come replete with advice, admonishment, and sarcasm.

It wasn't worth it.

I walked into the living room and had the beer I'd been wanting with dinner. The night was dark, and the lights from Boulder twinkled at my feet. Tomorrow, Friday, my morning was free. I needed a hard workout, maybe a bike ride to Loveland. In the afternoon, hallelujah, I had a new patient — my referral from Anne Hubbard.

Recovery on the horizon? Maybe I'm not going to die of this disease after all.

Six

The tiny circle of light on the wall above my desk shone red. The clock on the small table by my chair said 2:45 exactly.

The office suite was designed so that Diane and I could function without the expense of a receptionist. We told patients to flip a switch with our names on it when they arrived in the waiting room, illuminating a red light on the wall in the corresponding office.

My first glimpse of Michael McClelland was of the top of his blond curly head. His face was down and buried in *People* magazine, his back curved from the waist, his posture defeating the lines of the waiting room chair.

"Mr. McClelland?" He looked up. "I'm Alan Gregory." As I greeted him I flicked off the switch that had illuminated the red light in my office and stepped back to encourage him to enter the hallway before I closed the door. I watched for him to make an invitation to shake hands. He didn't. I led him into the office and at his hesitation suggested he have a seat.

"How can I be of help?" It was always my first line.

I recognized him from Anne Hubbard's funeral. This man and I had stood only a few feet apart at the cemetery. Since Anne had apparently given Michael McClelland my name, I wasn't too surprised that he'd been there.

He settled slowly onto the chair opposite me. He straightened the creases on his trousers and tugged on his

58

suit jacket cuffs before beginning to talk. "I'm not . . ." he finally started, then stopped. It seemed a deliberate gesture, the stopping.

"Her death, I'm afraid I'm not dealing with it well," he said after about a minute.

Anne Hubbard's death? I wondered. "Never assume," was a favorite refrain of one of my ex-supervisors.

I had watched him during his minute of silence. The watching was one of the liberties I cherished about my work. I knew of no other interpersonal situation where it was socially acceptable just to watch somebody.

He sat straight, filling the antique leather chair opposite me, his sculpted hands with their manicured nails resting on the carved wood of the armrests. He looked at me occasionally, more, it seemed, to check on my attention than to connect with me. Eyebrows dominated his face and framed well-rested eyes. The thick blond shrubs perched over irises blue like coral, bright but without much depth. His chin was deeply furrowed, his mouth small and flat. His face was almost without lines, though I imagined that he was about my age, maybe a few years younger, thirty or thirty-one.

I had seen a lot of grief in my seven years in that office. I wasn't seeing any then. I did not reply to him, waiting to see where he would go next.

"Anne spoke very highly of you. I thought you could help me. Get through this."

Nobody is speaking highly of me these days, I reflected. And Anne Hubbard was not a person to disclose casually that she'd seen a psychologist. I guessed that he was beseeching me to say something and take some pressure off him. I just continued my neutral stare. To say something now would be to presuppose.

"I'm not really sure . . . what to say. Do you have any questions?"

"I don't know what might be important."

He sighed and looked out the window at the garden. The irises were unmoving in the afternoon heat.

"I was having an affair with her." He lifted his hands to his face and brought his fingers together across the bridge of his nose. Michael McClelland was very comfortable with the past tense.

"She was on her way down from my house on Lee Hill when she crashed." He glanced at me for a reaction. I sat, entreating him with my silence. His opaque eyes moved to the collection of crystal animals on the table between us.

"I work for her husband."

I still didn't know what was important, but at least his story was getting interesting.

"I'm a scientist at NOAA," he explained a little later in the session, speaking the acronym as a word, like the name of the captain of the Ark, not pausing to see if I recognized the initials of the National Oceanic and Atmospheric Administration. "And my boss, Anne's husband, ex-husband, widower, whatever — Phil Hubbard, has made my job quite a bitch. He travels a lot. I'm new — I haven't even been there a year — and getting established with him has been a pain in the ass. I'm afraid he's going to find out about Anne and me, and, shit, what a mess that will be."

The voice in this youthful body was proper and polite. He spoke carefully, forming his words as if for an audition as a news anchor. But every word approached pianissimo, almost a whisper, quiet and modulated.

Boulder is home to scientific institutions as wide-ranging as the University of Colorado, IBM, Ball Aerospace, the National Center for Atmospheric Research, and the National Institute of Standards and Technology of the Commerce Department; many scientists and academics came to see me for treatment. I was familiar with their eccentric, out-of-date clothes or their department-store suits. Michael McClelland's gray suit was either tailored or off-the-rack Armani or Cerruti.

"This isn't all new with her dying. She was going to break it off. The affair. I didn't know if she was planning to tell him or not. Didn't seem politically wise, though. But I worried. The guy is a cold enough bastard that I could have taken some pleasure in his knowing that his wife was stepping out on him. But I sure didn't need him to know I was the guy screwing her. I guess I don't have to worry about that anymore, do I?" He looked at me with relief in his face. "He's a very influential man in my career." A curious mixture of admiration and contempt lurked in his final appraisal of his boss.

"I gather you're still feeling somewhat vulnerable." I took a shot at being reflective.

"No, not really." Strike one. "I just need to find some way to get something going with him. I don't have full scientist rank. That's where the power is, and that's what I want. He's in the way, know what I mean?" Was Michael McClelland, I wondered, looking for a co-conspirator or a therapist?

"He asked me why I was at the funeral. Can you believe it? I said to show my respect to him. He just nodded. No 'Thank you.' Not a word of gratitude.

"I get real ticked off at him. I do good work, imaginative research, really, but he doesn't notice." There was something very primitive and sad in his affect as he said all this. "He's always gone to some meeting or some conference. He has favorites in the lab — prima donnas, to be honest — and goes over their stuff a lot, provides them with discretionary grant support and encourages other funding for them. He hunts with these jokers, for chrissake. I get even, though. I nicked some of his data once, just hid it in the computer. Moved it back after a while. He never caught on."

"Nicked?" Some new computer slang, maybe? When in doubt, clarify.

"Ripped off. Borrowed." I nodded, making a mental note of the childlike quality of this man's retribution.

"I just needed to find some way to get his attention,"

Michael McClelland explained.

Sleeping with his wife is one way to get a man's attention, I thought.

A few minutes remained. I asked him if he'd like to make another appointment.

He responded by asking, "So how does this work? How many times do I come in?"

I gave a version of my start-of-therapy speech.

"I am not interested in getting dependent on this. Please realize that," said Michael McClelland.

I considered myself warned about his propensity. I wondered when whatever was going on between him and his boss would develop between him and me.

"That's a topic that requires a lot more attention than our remaining few seconds allow." My voice was soft as I said this. Compassionate, at least to my ears.

"I've done this before." Been in therapy? I wondered. It doesn't show. "Had affairs with women I shouldn't get caught sleeping with," he clarified. "Women find me attractive," he said, smiling, "even irresistible."

His appraisal of his presentation was certainly narcissistic, but not necessarily arguable; he had a well-built body and a slightly puffy but attractive face. He was apparently successful. I found his manner mildly grating but could certainly see how other people might be less critical. Anyway, Merideth had admonished me for years that I didn't have a clue about what women found attractive in men. I told him, "We can talk about that next time as well, Mr. McClelland."

"Michael," he directed.

I nodded and opened the door, angling him to the exiting hallway, ninety degrees from where he had entered. He turned back and shook my hand. "So, do you think you can help?" he asked.

"Next time, Mr. McClelland. Michael."

I walked out of the office and looked for Dr. Diane Estevez. Her office door was open. I stuck my head in and said, "Got a minute?"

"I have a three forty-five," she said, waving me in. "Was that your new patient who just left?"

"It was."

"He's kinda cute. Nice body if you like 'em big."

Diane liked 'em big. "You shopping around?"

"No, but I'm never gonna stop browsing," she said.

"When's your next game?" I asked about her softball team. "You playing next Wednesday night?"

"Yeah. Why, you the umpire?"

"Do I detect some continuing dismay at my new activity? As a matter of fact, I'm doing a six o'clock game behind the north rec center."

"Well, we're spared your rotten eyesight. We play at eight."

"Maybe I'll come and watch."

"Watch what? The game? Or Lauren?"

"Lauren?" I blushed, trying not to.

"I know you, Alan. I do. You're scoping out Lauren Crowder. Second base."

I was sitting on the corner of her sofa that afforded the best view of the garden. I was checking out the last of the tulips on the west fence. "Good glove. No hit," I said.

"So you're just scouting her for the big leagues? Please. Admit it. You lust."

"She's cute."

"Deputy district attorneys are generally not referred to as 'cute.' It's considered bad form."

Deputy DA? "Okay, then, I lust."

"Try not to be too obvious."

"Is she single?"

Diane flashed a great big, knowing smile. "Divorced."

"Seeing anybody?"

"Maybe I can find out."

"Maybe?"

"Yeah. Maybe."

"Thanks for her last name, I didn't have that much." I

continued before she could counter with a sarcastic retort, "You're always so kind, so generous. Have you considered a career in the helping professions?"

The light behind her desk blinked on, beckoning her to her next appointment. She gestured to it with the middle finger of her left hand.

"See you later," I said.

"Lauren could do worse than you, I suppose," she said, laughing.

"Thanks, sweetheart."

Back at my desk, I jotted down notes about the first session with Michael McClelland. I was curious about his need to introduce himself through some grief that was absent or at least contained. The collegiality of the process was noteworthy as well. After the first few minutes he was attempting to engage me as much as a friend as a psychologist. I replayed the session, carefully observing my work for unconscious adjustments I was concerned I was making since Karen Hart's death and the recent publicity about my alleged improprieties with her.

Finished with the notes, I sat back and recalled the cemetery, where Michael McClelland and I had been acting like minor league outlaws.

We had been to the rear of the crowd at the interment, back where individuals stood alone, shifting weight from one foot to another, maintaining separation from seemingly more legitimate mourners. He had leaned against a small ash. I had stood in the bright sun on green grass, Anne Hubbard's bronze casket the only reminder of the Memorial Day weekend snowstorm just two days before.

At the time I had envied Michael McClelland his shade.

Seven

I should have tried to see Lauren over the weekend. I kept tripping over images of her. If I carried a notebook, I would have been carving her initials into the cover. Adolescence is a disease from which total recovery is rare.

I umpired a six o'clock game the next Wednesday evening. Afterward I reclined in the grass behind the first-base line of the adjacent diamond where Lauren's team, actually Diane's team, was warming up for their eight o'clock start. I sipped from a longneck bottle of beer, a welcome gratuity from the victorious team of the game I had just finished.

One of Boulder's ubiquitous summer evening thunderstorms also seemed to be warming up for an eight o'clock start. The billowing gray mass shadowed the peaks of the Front Range and obscured the afterglow of the late-setting sun. The laden air preceding it supplanted the day's aridity. Nobody seemed to pay much attention.

I took a seat down the first-base line and watched the women play. Their baggy red game shirts read MONTE-ZUMA'S REVENGE across the back and inelegantly, and inaccurately, stated, WE GET THE RUNS across the front. An explosive thunderclap brought everyone's eyes westward, toward me, and Lauren's spontaneous smile mitigated my doubts about waiting uninvited in the middle of a field in an approaching thunderstorm.

The storm drifted to the south, and she drifted to be with her teammates between innings. Diane visited me between the fourth and the fifth.

"Their pitcher is tough," she said.

I looked at her with a bewildered smile. "I don't even know the score."

"The score is," she said with mock seriousness, "that I think she likes you, too."

I had ceased trying to shield myself from Diane's capacity to read my thoughts. She proved the exception to the rule that psychologists can't read minds.

"You're on deck, smart-ass," I said, gesturing with my head toward the plate.

"So are you, Alan."

"Is she seeing anybody?" I said this as loud as I dared to Diane's retreating back.

Field lights reflected in her eyes as she looked over her left shoulder and shook her head.

Merciful forces delivered the last out. I approached Lauren and asked her to join me for a glass of wine.

She sighed. "Not tonight, sorry." I decided that Diane was setting me up.

"But," she added after a pause that was a measure too long for my comfort, "I will take a ride home. My car's in the shop."

"I'd love to," I said as though she had asked me to dinner at my favorite restaurant. She finished packing her things into a Lancôme bag, stood, and gazed at me. I wondered if I was supposed to take her bag. I compromised with myself and picked up her bat.

"Your car?" she asked. "Which one is it?"

The scent of her, perfumed and sweaty, permeated the stale warm air of the Subaru on the short ride over to her house, which butted against the foothills west of Fourth above the university.

"Can I call you?" I asked as I pulled in front of the

66

house she had indicated.

"Sure. I'd like that."

"Good." We smiled at each other. I was convincing myself that we were flirting.

"Then I'll need your phone number."

She widened her smile, gave it to me, hesitated, then got out of the car and said, "Good night, thanks for the ride."

She was halfway to her front door when I called to her. She stopped and turned.

After having failed to entice her once for ice cream and once for a glass of wine, I decided to determine whether the quality of my inducements was an impediment to getting a date with her. What the hell. "Will you come with me to Sante Fe this weekend?" I called out the window of the car.

She shook her head slowly and laughed. Then she said, "No," drawing it into something more than a simple denial. She was quiet for a moment, composing a comeback.

She said, "But how about Aspen?"

I smiled in a way that made me realize that my facial muscles had been feeling like Plexiglas for the past two hours.

"Aspen"—I paused—"sounds wonderful."

She was still twenty feet from the car. "Can you get Friday off?" she called to me. I nodded eagerly, reflecting on my withered appointment schedule. "Great," she said, closing the gap to ten feet. "I'll take care of a place to stay. And I want to take my car. Pick you up Friday morning at seven o'clock." She waved and went into the house.

I waited outside her house for a few minutes, congratulating myself on having a date. I was reliant on small successes those days.

My answering service paged me the next morning.

The pager read Lauren's name and asked that I call for a long message. I felt certain that she was canceling. The message was simple—she was asking for my address and directions to my house, and was telling me she would bring breakfast in the car.

I called her house and left directions on her answering machine.

Michael McClelland came to see me for the second time that afternoon. He was on time, cordial, and eager. The Wednesday slot at four would work best for him on a regular basis, he told me. We agreed on it as a standing weekly appointment time.

"I know what's been going on with you," he said. "Anne had talked about it and said it couldn't be true. She said that you were able to get her to talk about things she didn't know were on her mind. Her problems, not yours, caused her to stop seeing you. She made that clear. I need to talk about things, too, things I may be unaware of. So you needn't worry about my judging you."

Until that moment it hadn't been a concern.

The tenuousness from our first meeting was gone. He didn't even pause for a reply.

"When I was growing up, my mother was in hospital a lot. She had a series of illnesses that they couldn't diagnose. My father couldn't take it and left us. Her and me. I was seven then. I thought I could understand his leaving; sometimes wished he had taken me with him. She got better; the pains—she called them 'the pains'—went away. She married again when I was ten. I adored him, her new husband. He was so alive, so funny, and he was generous, you know, in the way that ten-year-olds like grown-ups to be generous.

"She started drinking soon after he came. I hated her for it. She drank constantly at first. She was sloppy and ugly. Then she drank only at night. I remember the drinking at night most clearly. I put her to bed more than once. Cleaned her vomit. Hid her bottles."

"Your stepfather?" I said.

"By then, gone. Business. I don't know what came first, her drinking or his traveling. But he was gone all the time. I think she drove him away, and then he wasn't there.

"I hated her. She drove them both away."

"Now?"

"She's dead. Aspirated some puke and died." He might have been talking about a road kill.

He paused here, and I waited. Then I asked, "And your stepfather?"

He exhaled slowly through his nose before he answered. "I idolized him. And I despised him. He cut me off when he cut her off. He would come home, not like my father, who left and that was that. He came home and was charming and loving, and then he'd leave again."

"I doubt if this will come as a surprise to you"—I spoke slowly and quietly during sessions—"but you speak about your mother's second husband and your boss in much the same way. They are powerful and"—I paused for effect—"neglectful." The words spread like powder over him, and I waited for them to settle.

He seemed genuinely moved. "I wasn't aware of that. I hadn't seen that before."

I sat back and watched the vestal insight pulse into him. This, I thought rather smugly, is the stuff of which the therapeutic alliance is made.

He said, "Asses," under his breath. He waited a moment and clarified, his head shaking almost imperceptibly, "You fucking assholes." Each syllable had the definition of the first notes of Beethoven's Ninth.

Not, I noted, a typical reaction to the magic of psychotherapeutic interpretation.

Eight

Independence Pass into Aspen almost behind us, I asked Lauren, "So where are we staying?"

"I have sort of a time-share thing up here."

"Downtown?"

"Actually, no, a little north of Main Street."

Since I had no idea what direction Main Street ran and since we were minutes from town, I didn't pursue it. She drove her Peugeot into a neighborhood near the music festival tent. We crossed a bridge over the Roaring Fork River, and I marveled at the beauty of the setting and the opulence of the housing while she kept her eyes on the road.

She slowed the car as we dropped down to the "time-share thing." It was a wonderful, contemporary, stone, glass, and painted cedar three-story that spilled down a steep bluff toward the Roaring Fork. She looked at it, then at me and my raised eyebrows, and said, "This is it."

We spent the rest of the morning hiking, actually walking, the paved portion of the Rio Grande trail along the river into town. Pine and aspen trees sheltered the path from the bright sun, and the roar of rushing water impeded conversation. Columbines, wild chives, and lupines bordered the trail. In town we lunched outdoors; she insisted on a shaded table. From time to time we touched fingers across it.

She told me about the apple orchard she grew up on in Washington. She described her parent's anguish when she transferred to Stanford from Washington State. She stayed in California and went to Boalt, in Berkeley, to study law, met Jacob, the brilliant child of a Denver railroad family, and married him right after school. They never practiced law, instead moved to Denver and directed real estate acquisitions for an investment firm. Later they "did deals" with money coming to him from a trust. "God, we made a lot of money," she said.

The marriage broke up slowly. He had affairs; she made certain she was never home to miss him. After a couple of years she quit the investment firm and took a job as a deputy DA in Boulder. She commuted from Denver for a while, and when she finally moved out they started a settlement battle that lasted for eighteen months.

After coffee she and I strolled back to the house. Lauren explained that she and her husband had finally reached a settlement two years before. "It — the house — is Jake's, Jacob's, my ex-husband's" — she almost yelled to be heard as we crossed a picturesque bridge over the river — "but I get to use it. Actually the title's in his name, but as part of our dissolution agreement I have unrestricted access three months a year." She sounded like a lawyer. I didn't say anything for a while.

As we were walking back into the house she touched my arm and said, "I'm going to rest for a couple of hours. Please make yourself comfortable."

She disappeared down broad stairs into the lowest level of the house. In the middle of three Sub-Zero refrigerators I found a bottle of vintage Lanson along with a welcome note from Jake, Lauren's ex. I chose a Diet Coke instead of the champagne and found a place on the deck from which I convinced myself I was looking at the Maroon Bells.

This was the first mountain accommodation I had ever stayed in that had sharp knives, which undermined my long-held assumption about the existence of a secret state ordinance intended to protect tourists from altitude-precipitated kitchen mishaps. I chopped serranos chiles, onions, cilantro, and tomatoes into pico de gallo while Lauren Crowder rested. As I began mashing an avocado for guacamole she walked into the kitchen wearing pale yellow sweats. She awoke looking in the afternoon the way I looked in the morning. Her eyes were burdened with sleep. Her soft face was creased from the bed clothes. Her hair verged on not being perfect.

"Are you all right? You look very tired." I hesitated as I said this; I didn't have a good reading on her and didn't know whether she would find my concern critical.

"I am. Tired, that is. I wake slowly from naps. I'll be fine." Her voice was soft and heavy with sleep, like a lilac weighted with spring snow. She eyed the food and took a chip, ignoring my salsa.

"How about a bike ride? Maybe that'll help wake you up." A bike ride was my prescription for most ills.

"I'd like that, but maybe a little later, after it cools off a bit." She sighed.

I said, "Great. No problem." I wondered if something was wrong and whether this was going to be a very long weekend.

"Hey," she said, mobilizing, "you haven't unpacked. Follow me." I grabbed my bag and trailed after her as she escorted me down the white oak stairs. Lauren held the handrail deliberately as she descended to a bedroom with its own bath and a deck overlooking the river. None of her things were there, and the bed had not been slept in.

"This is great." I didn't sound convincing even to myself.

72

She ignored my disappointment. "I'm glad you like it," she said evenly. "Come back upstairs when you're unpacked."

I unpacked by throwing my overnight bag on the floor next to an antique dresser, climbed back upstairs, and found Lauren in the living room. She was facing Aspen Mountain, her back to me. She said, "I'm very attracted to you. I wouldn't have invited you here if I wasn't. But I'm not ready to sleep with you."

She turned, looking over her shoulder, to gauge my reaction. I didn't reply right away. It wasn't a communication ploy; I was taken aback.

"Actually," she said, finally facing me, "I brought you here to see if I wanted to sleep with you."

When in doubt, get paternal. "That . . . is a dangerous move, isn't it?"

"I can take care of myself." There was defiance in her voice. "Anyway, Diane says you're a pussycat."

"That's not what the *Daily* says about me."

"That . . . is another conversation."

My eyes darted around the room, seeking a prop, a dog to pet, a wall to lean against. But I was standing in a room the size of my high school gym facing twenty-foot-tall windows and a herd of cows' worth of pale yellow leather furniture. My thoughts were filled with the absurd notion that ski runs in the summer look like a vertical golf course with very long fairways.

"What makes you think I want to sleep with you?" I asked. Her face sharpened. I wondered if this was how she looked when she received an unexpected answer from the witness stand. But then I couldn't imagine her getting an unexpected answer from the witness stand. Finally she saw my weak grin.

"I'd take you right here on the rug if you'd have me," I offered lamely.

"Not yet." She was shaking her head gently and smiling with pursed lips. "Not quite yet."

I held my ground. She walked over, took both my

73

hands, and kissed me lightly and then not lightly on the mouth.

She had acceded to my desire to take care of meals for the weekend. I made shredded chicken with green chiles, and we ate on one of the decks. The chill of the evening was invigorating, and Jake's champagne surprised us both as an accompaniment to the spicy food.

"You're divorced?"

"Separated." She must have known that already.

"How long?"

"It'll be a year in August." I wanted it to sound like more than eleven months.

"Is there a reason the divorce isn't final?" She looked at me briefly as she asked, then at her champagne as she awaited my answer.

Only the divorced knew to ask that question.

"Neither Merideth nor I have pushed for a settlement. She's in broadcasting. TV. In San Francisco. She took a network job out there with NBC; that's kind of why she left. No, that's not right. That gave her a good excuse to leave." I intended my wan smile to signal a desire to glide on to a different subject.

"How did you meet her?"

"Merideth used to be a real estate broker. She handled the sale of the office building that Diane and I are in. She represented the slimeball we bought it from, and we flirted at the closing." The reality was that Merideth picked me up at the closing, but Lauren didn't need to know how bashful I was, yet. "She moved in with me about four months later. Within a year we were married."

"Why did you separate?"

I was beginning to feel like I was in a deposition. "We, well, we disagreed on a number of things of major importance. But mostly she was—is—no longer sure that she wants to have kids. And I'm ready. She also

74

wanted me to close my practice and start again in San Francisco. I wasn't willing to do that."

"Your career is more important than hers?"

"Actually, no." I felt as if I was tap-dancing on a causeway without handrails. "After we were married, she quit real estate and went back to finish her master's in communication at C.U. Her first job was as a producer in public radio at the NPR station in Denver. She was good. About three years ago she was offered a job at Channel 9 in Denver, as a producer. They loved her. She worked hard, did some great pieces, won some awards, made everybody feel good about themselves . . . and the networks noticed. She got an offer from ABC in Chicago and one from NBC in San Francisco. The Chicago offer was to do what she was doing in Denver in a top-five market. The San Francisco offer was a production job in the national West Coast bureau. She chose California."

I stopped to see whether she was still with me. Her look was that of a trapper watching her prey head for the snare. Eager for the impending trap, sad that the game was so easily lured.

"So she wanted me to go. I said no. I—"

"Your practice came first."

"Please let me finish." At that moment I realized I was telling the story in such a way that I might trap her.

"The network told her the San Francisco position was temporary. Maybe six months. Maybe three years. But temporary. I can't set up a practice that fast. It takes time, a long time, to get established. I suggested that we commute until she knew the time frame. She said maybe she should just go. I told her I'd join her as soon as she was settled. That's when she told me she'd changed her mind about having kids."

"You sound bitter."

"I guess I still am. I loved her. She screwed up a good thing."

"By being successful?"

"No. By changing the rules. Our rules. It was her right . . . but I felt betrayed." I captured her staring eyes in mine, once again hoping to find a way to punctuate the end of her interrogatory.

"This sounds a little self-serving." Not quite the amount of empathy I was hoping for.

"It is," I said quickly. "You haven't heard Merideth's speeches about my 'sedentary proclivities,' about her concern that this child I want would plant roots so far down that she would never again budge me toward adventure. All her fears were valid. I'm not sure they would've come to pass, but she knows me well, the tendencies weren't artificially created. I make it all sound surgical on her part. It's easier that way. The reality is that it's a brave thing she did. Leaving. Stupid and wrong. Like a fireman dashing into a building that's collapsing to save a cat. But brave."

"Do you still love her?"

"Yes. I do."

"That's why the divorce isn't final."

"Probably."

We had begun the "are you emotionally available?" inquiry. I had heard separated patients describe similar vignettes countless times and had sharpened my vigilance to them in my recent dating. I did not want this woman, the first in almost a year whom I found compelling, to decide I wasn't ready for a relationship.

"It's over," I said.

"I know." She paused. "I know the words to that song."

It was she who found the punctuation to end the conversation.

But I found that attractive, too. Learning from mistakes I made with women had never been one of my maladies.

The next morning I rose to a quiet house filled with honey-filtered light flushed from the shadowed perimeter of the little valley. Her door was closed. The night had provided no avenue for reconsideration of her decision not to sleep with me, and there were no nocturnal strolls through darkened halls by either of us.

I squeezed fresh grapefruit juice, made coffee, and sat watching the morning light progress and envelop the face of Aspen Mountain. The river roared and masked the sound of her stockinged feet on the deck. My first awareness of her was when her arms slid around my neck and her hair brushed against my ear. Then I smelled her.

"Good morning," she said. The sound was soft and dense.

I didn't turn. I was bathing in this scene that felt like a greeting of new lovers, not of relative strangers.

"How about that bike ride?"

"I'd love to," I answered, my hope for another invitation evaporating with the morning dew.

After changing clothes, I followed her to the three-car garage and to a choice of mountain bikes or racing bikes. She pulled out a Bridgestone mountain bike, and I did the same. I viewed mountain bikes with the same disdain that I had viewed boogie boards as a teenage bodysurfer. The purist in me knew that racing bikes were the true path to cycling heaven.

The trail down the valley turned from asphalt to dirt a quarter of a mile from the house, and the bike's agility in negotiating the ruts, rocks, and streams astounded me. We rode for over an hour before heading back to the house.

We flirted the rest of the weekend. Lauren retreated and slept in the afternoon, and we parted at night before eleven on the carpeted landing of the white oak stairs.

Saturday night I told her about the allegations against me. She said she knew about them. I told her that I was being investigated by the state board that licensed psychologists. "What can they do?" she asked.

"Revoke my license." I paused and looked sideways at her. "Maybe ask the local district attorney to pursue criminal charges against me."

"That's great," she said sardonically. "Maybe I'll get to prosecute you. I imagine you're safe for a while, though; state boards aren't renowned for their investigatory speed."

"I think you're right about that; they're real backed up. My hope is that they don't get around to my case until the end of the year." I paused. "I'm surprised you know about all this. I figured if a woman knew what I've been accused of, she'd disappear like I had herpes."

"I'll make my own judgments about you. Obviously, right now, I'm assuming Diane's right and that you're innocent of all this . . . stuff." She looked away quickly and then right back at me, a trace of a smile on her lips.

"*Do* you have herpes?"

We packed Sunday night and were back in the Peugeot before dawn on Monday. The ride down was quiet. I rested my hand on her thigh and rubbed her neck to feel her skin and her hair.

In the Eisenhower Tunnel I asked, "Do you want to have kids?" The brashness of my words startled me, as if they were ice water I had dribbled onto my shirt.

"Plural? Kids?" was her initial reply.

The orange light of the sunrise was fractured by a thousand peaks before she continued. "Yes," she said quietly. Though to my ears it sounded qualified.

Nine

Lauren dropped me off at my little hacienda before nine-thirty. Heat already radiated off the dusty earth. The house was stuffy.

Cicero had camped out with Peter and Adrienne up the hill while I was away. I was surprised and disappointed that she failed to bound down to greet me when she heard Lauren's car drive up. I counted on her companionship more than I was comfortable acknowledging.

Peter's call of "Alan, you here?" caught me downstairs with one leg in a pair of summer-weight worsted-wool trousers. I ran halfway up the stairs bare-chested and told him to come down.

In the time it took Peter to meander to the lower level of the house, I had belted my pants, buttoned my shirt, and looped a tie around my neck. For Peter, such a rapid descent was hurrying. He stood at the entrance to the bedroom, deciding, I suspected, whether to editorialize about Western versus Eastern standards of formal dress. I hoped he would refrain.

I always thought of Peter as being taller than he was. In his shop clothes—old dewaled corduroys, regardless of the climate, long-sleeve T-shirt with faded references to some 10K he had run during his "competitive" period, and gray Nikes without socks—his body had little form. He could have been a model for Giacometti.

But like the Italian's sculptures, Peter's lithe formlessness, his fine, light, shoulder-length hair, narrow face, and long thin nose all combined to give the illusion of height. He stood only about five feet eight inches tall.

"Is Cicero with you?" he asked after a moment, fascinated, like a little boy watching Daddy, by the intricacies of the half Windsor.

"No, she's not, Peter. I assumed she was munching on a veal shank behind your planer."

"She didn't come back last night after we let her outside. She did her usual after-dinner prowl around seven-thirty. Then we couldn't find her. I hoped she was here with you. How was Aspen?"

"Aspen was real nice. This lady's different." I sighed, "Look, Cicero's done this before. I'll call the Humane Society before I go to the office. Don't worry about it, okay? She had her tags on, didn't she?"

"Sure," Peter replied, distracted by some creative urge that was rendering our conversation immaterial. When you suggested to Peter that he not worry about something, you could count on strict obedience. "I could do a great wall unit to frame those windows," he said.

"Peter."

"Right. I know. You'll let me know when I can redesign your house. Just a thought."

Peter shuffled back up the stairs and then up the hill toward his shop. Corduroys and long sleeves, and he never sweats.

"Damn you, Cicero," I said absently, and dug out a phone book to find the number of the pound.

Cicero had lived all her life on the Ponderosa and had ventured away on her own only on rare occasions. When we decided to get a dog, Merideth and I had originally intended to choose a hybrid from the Dumb Friends League but ended up searching kennels from Cheyenne to Colorado Springs to find a Bouvier de Flandres after Ron and Nancy kicked theirs out of the

White House. Neither of us could imagine a better recommendation for a breed.

Since two of three people would ask if she was a giant schnauzer, I had to admit that she looked like one, although I'd never seen a schnauzer bigger than the compact model. To me, Cicero looked like a svelte, lumbering bear with a beard. She had legs that propelled her over anything in her path and a vocabulary of barks that ranged from feminine to ferocious. She was going to be the only object of our property settlement that was certain to cause disputes between Merideth and me.

Unless Merideth went after my chair.

I sometimes wondered if the anticipated fight over Cicero prevented either Merideth or me from filing dissolution papers.

The young woman at the pound said no, they didn't have any black Bouviers. When I pressed she said, "Sir. They're not our usual guests. I assure you I would've noticed." I told her what the tags on her choke chain said and gave her my answering service number. She promised to call.

After straightening up the house a little bit, I took the Subaru for a tour of the hills and pastures of southeast Boulder looking for my dog. A couple of other errant pooches checked out the slow-moving wagon, but I didn't see Cicero.

"I don't know very much about your work," I said to Lauren. We were sitting in John's for dinner the night we returned from Aspen.

Cicero was still AWOL. I was the ambivalent parent. My initial righteousness that a day in doggy jail would teach her a lesson had faded into a gnawing fear that she wouldn't turn up.

She looked up from her pale green soup. The words that came from her mouth were, "What would you like to know?" The tone, however, was suspicious and defensive, as if I had made a query about the terms of her will.

I was growing more infatuated with Lauren's beauty. Her eyes, large white orbits and ever-changing irises, were green-blue in the dim light of the restaurant. Her hair was down and had a surface so unbroken, I fought constant impulses to find a way through it with my fingers.

"What it's like. What kind of cases you do. Like that."

"Is this just conversation?" she asked sharply.

"What do you mean? I'm just curious about you. That's all."

"Jake hated, I mean hated, my being a prosecutor."

"So you think I will, too?"

"It's not that. At least not all that. I take this really seriously. I've turned you down twice already when you've asked me out. The reason is that I have cases to prepare. My house is full of case files, police reports, investigative reports, evidence. My work is consuming for me, and to be real honest with you, I've liked it that way. Until," she said, "the last couple of weeks."

"I'd like to hear about it, Lauren, trust me."

She sighed a suspicious sigh. "I do mostly serious felony cases now. Rapes, assaults. I've done two murders. At the beginning, I was in county court, where I did traffic and misdemeanors, then I moved to doing prelims — preliminary hearings — then district court, where I am now. I've also done a rotation in the charging division, where DAs work with the police to determine charges for suspects. Deputy DAs move through a hierarchy, you start with the little stuff and work up to more important cases. I've moved up fast. Just four years with the office and I'm doing some big cases. They get my blood rushing. When I'm doing a big case, I get so focused, so well aimed, I guess, at getting my proof out. I love it, it's why the law is there." Her eyes searched mine as if to find an errant lash.

Whatever stop sign she was searching for in my gaze was apparently absent. "I hated the investment work that Jake and I did. And I was pretty good at it. Not as good as he was, which I think he liked. He was great. Right out of law school, and he could finesse an elephant through a keyhole without any grease."

The waiter interrupted to ask Lauren if she had future plans for her soup. She made some hand gesture that I thought was impossible to interpret. He took the bowl away. "I had always seen myself as a prosecutor. When things went bad in our marriage, I felt free to pursue it. The lack of status pissed him off, the pay pissed him off, the hours pissed him off. I'm not someone who anticipates a lot of support from men for the work I do."

She was decrusting a hard roll as though it were a boiled egg. "I have an offer on the table right now from Horwath and James. They're the biggest criminal defense law firm in Boulder. They want me to come on as an associate. Peterson, my boss, the DA, has told me that I had better get out now or decide to stay for the duration. He says that after four or five years as a deputy DA, the private sector begins to write you off. Others say the same thing. I believe it."

"What are you going to do?"

She wiped an imaginary spill from her lips. "I don't know," she said.

The service at John's was attentive and occasionally cloying. The entrées arrived promptly. We decided later, over coffee, that I, not she, had been the object of our waiter's more overt pleasantries. It was always a toss-up at John's.

"His reaction to you is understandable," she said, deadpan. "You have bedroom eyes and, from what I've seen, a nice body, maybe a little skinny."

I was blushing. "Go on," I said.

"Okay, Alan. You're a handsome man, beard notwithstanding. I'm kidding, I even like your beard. I like

83

your little nose, and the dimples that peek out under your beard." She stopped smiling and looked away from me. "I like that you're not sure of everything. I love that you make me laugh, and I love the fact that you haven't tried to pressure me into bed."

"Besides needing to protect your work, why the caution with me, then?"

Lauren stared right at me, the green gone from her eyes, "A couple of reasons," she said.

"Yes," I said.

"You're not as divorced as I am. That worries me. Anyway, I'm not cautious with you, I'm just not sleeping with you. I find you very attractive, very interesting. If I didn't, going to bed with you would be of little consequence."

"What do you mean? About my not being as divorced as you are." I asked the question I least wanted an answer to.

"There is," she said, leaning forward and smiling self-consciously, "no true separation without murder in the air. And," she continued, her voice conspiratorial, "between you and Merideth Gregory, there is no murder in the air. What is in the air, Alan, is something else. Some passion. Some despair. Some bilateral longing. No felonies there."

This part of our conversation would have gone better with the appetizers: grilled shrimp with warm bitter greens. This was not a conversation for poached peaches in fresh raspberry sauce.

"I'm too much of a risk for you."

"Now, yeah, you are. We'll see what happens. I enjoy being with you. For now, that's enough."

"Since Merideth left, I haven't been tempted, seriously tempted, by another woman. Until you. I find you tantalizing." I was leaning forward across the table. "I want to know where your legs go when they disappear into your skirt. I don't want you to hide from me."

Lauren took her turn blushing. "If the waiter heard

that speech," she said, "he'd take his attention elsewhere."

"And you," I said, "where will you take yours?"

She poured the rest of the wine into my glass, flustered, careless about the grainy sediment in the bottle.

"We will see. I don't know."

She insisted on paying the bill. I didn't argue with her. As she was signing for dinner, I said, "Before, you said there were a couple of reasons for your caution. You mentioned one. What's the other?"

She pulled her napkin from her lap and set it beside her coffee, stood up, and turned to the exit. "I said that?" she said, moving toward the door.

I drove Lauren home and asked to come in. She kissed me as if she meant it, grabbed a cheek of my ass in each hand, and then said no.

A three-quarter moon hung like a pendant over the horizon of the eastern sky and illuminated Cicero's undulating form on the tiny concrete slab that I called a front porch. The return of the prodigal pooch.

She didn't run up and play chicken with the Subaru, which was not so much odd as unprecedented. In the beam from the headlights, it looked as if she had a bandanna or handkerchief or something around her neck. Shouldn't take presents from strangers, Cicero.

A thin piece of twine tied her to a scraggly aspen, one of a trio of eight-foot-tall twigs next to the porch. Maybe somebody had returned her and tied her to keep her from running again.

She bowed down as I approached. Penitent, I mused. The warm tongue darted at my face as I untied the string and asked her where she had been.

"What the fuck," I almost spit the words as I removed the blue cotton handkerchief and saw a neatly shaved one-inch band completely circling Cicero's neck. The pink-and-gray mottled skin made her look like she had been kidnapped by a renegade punk dog groomer.

"Roll over, girl," I said in my "I mean it this time" voice. She gave me a look that said, "Now? Seriously?" I repeated the command, and she obeyed and plopped over in the dust. I stopped her midroll and checked for other mutilations.

Nothing but the bizarre haircut.

"Shit," I said, perplexed. "Where you been, poochie?" I threw a stick, and Cicero ran and pounced, proudly returning it to my feet.

"Good girl." I ran my fingers over her coat, feeling for anomalies. "You all right? Okay?"

She preceded me inside and promptly lost her footing in the entry, crashing to the floor before recovering and finding her way to her water dish, which she drained. I gave her a late dinner of kibble, and she ate voraciously.

The day's mail from my office was crammed in my briefcase. I discarded a few pleas from underutilized psychiatric hospitals desperate for patients, set aside a couple of checks and a couple of bills, and started ripping open the only envelope that wasn't from a familiar sender. The phone rang.

I reached for the receiver and said, "Hello." And then, "Ouch," a paper cut oozing blood from the side of my index finger.

The noise on the line was vacuous for a moment. I sucked blood from my finger, heard a click, and then a dial tone. I said, "Good-bye," to the humming phone and hung it up.

The envelope held a single sheet of paper. After reading it quickly, I sighed, mumbled an obscenity, threw it back in the briefcase, and went looking for Cicero.

Cicero was back on the Tabriz beneath the living room windows. I again examined her bizarre necklace and shook my head. Why the hell would somebody do that to a dog? What really bothered me was that whoever did it must have known where she lived. But that information was on her dog tags. Maybe somebody gave her the haircut and let her go, and a neighbor or somebody else brought her home. None of it made sense. Some anticanine nut could have done it. Maybe Cicero crapped in their flower bed or something, and they were trying to give me a message about keeping her tied up. I could call the cops, but shit, they'd let me know I was wasting their time. And then probably cite me for not having her on a leash.

I thought for a full five seconds about the sheet of paper I'd just stuffed back in my briefcase and decided I had enough problems without inviting the county sheriff to give me more.

Ten

I delivered the piece of paper to my lawyer the next day.

"Alan, good to see you."

My hand was lost in his grasp as Jonathan Younger greeted me. The hair above his ears had grayed since I had last seen him. His tie was loose at the neck, and he wore, as he always did, trousers that hung on his massive frame as if he were wearing his father's clothes. His father would need to be the size of Paul Bunyan. Never had I seen the suit jackets that matched the expansive trousers.

We sat on small, upholstered chairs away from his granite-top desk, the chairs much too small in scale for his office or his body. I actually fit onto these juvenile chairs; he certainly didn't.

"Good to see you, too, Jon. It's been a long time."

"What do you hear from Merideth?"

"We talk frequently. She loves San Francisco, and is doing fine, real well, in her job."

"Please give her my best."

Jonathan was a contact I had gained through Merideth, who had sold his home for him, when I needed some advice in handling a nuisance grievance early in my career. I admired and respected him. He doted on his twin six-year-old boys and felt free to call me for reassurance about their development from time to time. I felt fine about reassuring him.

As he crossed his long legs, they filled the space between our chairs. The Bally brand on the sole of his elegant shoes was barely scuffed. I wondered if they charged more for shoes that size.

"What can I do for you? Wait — coffee?"

"Please. With cream." He called out the door to somebody in a voice that boomed but wasn't harsh. Two coffees arrived in moments in imported ceramic mugs. The coffee was darkly roasted and distracting.

"You know about my problems?"

"Sure. I read about you in the paper even before I read about the Cubbies." His face revealed nothing; in his own way he was as good a blank screen as I was.

"Well, I received this in the mail yesterday." I handed him the single sheet from my briefcase. "I want to think it's benign, but my luck hasn't been running that way."

His green eyes moved deliberately as he read the request for release of confidential information signed by Sheldon Hart for all my clinical records regarding the care of his daughter, Karen Eileen Hart.

"Postmarked where?"

"Don't remember precisely. Boulder. Maybe Denver. Here, in Colorado."

"Does he live here?"

"Didn't used to."

"Did you recognize the return address?" he asked.

"No. It's not Karen's."

"Is he a lawyer?"

"No, international finance or something."

"He had some help with this," Jon surmised, again perusing the language in the document.

"That was my guess, too."

The silence seemed prolonged.

"Tell me about your troubles," he said.

"First, a question about confidentiality," I said. "Does the fact that the state board — you know, the one that licenses psychologists — does the fact that they've opened an investigation of me free me to discuss this case with you?"

"The investigation, does it involve just this case?"

"To the best of my knowledge it does."

"Yeah, you can talk to me. Even if you couldn't, you could, because this confidential relationship"—his long arm swung back and forth between us—"keeps me from divulging the fact that you have told me anything at all."

So I told Jonathan Younger, my legal bodyguard, about Karen Hart, her therapy, the incest, the braces, the suicide, and the note she had left for me. I told him about the stories in the *Daily*, and I told him what it had done to my life. I didn't tell him I didn't sleep with her. He didn't ask.

"So the police don't know about the note?" said Jonathan.

"No. What difference does that make?"

"It means that her father doesn't know about it. From what you say it seems unlikely that he knows about the incest, either."

"She was terrified of telling her father, afraid he'd be furious at her or not believe her. She also wasn't ready to be angry at him, her father, I mean."

"Why would she be angry at him?"

" 'Cause he never noticed. Or noticed and did nothing. Or because he left her alone with him and his drunken mother so often. All of the above. I don't know. We won't know the answer to that one now. Her guilt, though, is a big part of it."

"What was she guilty about? She was just a kid."

"Her arousal. Despite her terror, despite her protests, despite her will, occasionally she was aroused by the sexual contact. Getting pleasure from the forbidden is a pretty good recipe for guilt."

Jonathan was turning over a leaf of his legal pad. I grabbed the opportunity to ask a question. "Where do you think the *Daily* is getting their information?"

"I don't know," Jonathan said. "They don't seem to have much. The articles contain few specifics. The editors must have some corroboration, some documents, enough, anyway, to convince themselves that they don't have to worry about libel. I wish I knew what they had. She have any confidantes?"

"Her best friend, Valerie Goodwin. Karen may have shared this with her. I don't know. As I said, she felt a lot of shame. It's not the sort of thing people feel eager to talk about."

I pursed my lips and raised my left hand to scratch at my temple. Jon waited. "I feel," I said, "like a fighter with his hands tied behind his back. First there was her suicide, then the story in the paper, now this request for her records. I'm being beat up, and I can't fight back. I need to break loose, Jon. I've even been tempted to just call the *Daily* and go on record and defend myself. Is there anything I can do other than just wait?"

He puffed out his lower lip and exhaled toward the ceiling. "Yeah. There's things we can do. They all have their liabilities, though."

"I'm listening."

"First, until somebody sues you for impropriety of some kind, you can't use litigation as an excuse to breach confidence. Once you're sued, the plaintiff automatically waives confidentiality. Absent that, if you breach confidence without permission, your reputation suffers immeasurably and you probably get censured by the state. Maybe lose your license. I can hire a private investigator to find Sheldon Hart and see if he is feeding this stuff to the papers. Down side is that if we get caught, it's not going to look good for you. Not going to look good at all. Even if we find out he is feeding this stuff to the press — so what? We may uncover something we can use to make him stop, we may just find out that he's the one doing it. My advice is that it's a big risk for a potentially low payoff."

"So. I stand pat and bleed."

He wrinkled his forehead and opened his eyes wide. The big shoulders shrugged. "Until you get sued. Then you can fight back."

Jon was trying to wipe an oily brown stain from his hand, some residue, apparently, from the mug he was holding. "I don't think you'll be in this dilemma long because it's obvious that he's planning to sue you, or at least he's thinking about it seriously." He said this as a surgeon tells a patient about a required operation — legal sparring that was routine to him was grave to me.

He got up and said, "Follow me." I watched as his back disappeared into an unmarked door, then followed.

The bathroom sported twin porcelain vanities, marble counters, and brass faucets without knobs. I peed while Jon stepped up to the sink and watched water appear by some divine plan as he placed his hands beneath the faucet.

He registered my querying stare. "Italian. Infrared. Microwave. Ultrasonic. I don't know."

I marched up to the counter, put my hands together, and placed them below the brass spout. Nothing. Shifting my weight didn't help, neither did jerking my hands away and replacing them slowly. Jon reached across the counter and placed his left hand beneath the faucet in front of me, and water gushed immediately. I tried again. Nothing.

Jon stepped back, and I tried his sink. Still nothing. He was laughing. He moved forward, reached in front of me, and held his hand in front of the faucet so the water would run. I rinsed and dried my hands.

"I'm beginning to understand your troubles a little better," he said, and began to explain my dilemma to me.

"Besides being of insufficient molecular weight to assert influence with these wonderful faucets," he said, "you have an irate, grieving father possibly, hell, probably contemplating suit over your treatment, mistreatment in his eyes, of his daughter."

As we walked back into the office, I said, "And?"

"And he wants your help. He wants to finesse you into releasing records he probably doesn't have any right to."

This was good news. "Why not?"

"This"—he picked up the piece of paper again—"Eileen, no, Karen Eileen Hart, was not a minor. He, as her father, does not automatically inherit control of her records. And, I would guess"—he smiled—"I would guess he already knows he doesn't have control of the records."

"Why would you guess that?"

"You and I agree that the language in this release is, well, studied?" I nodded my assent. "Well, if he had control of her estate, the lawyer who provided the studied language would have simply told him to insist on the release based on his rights as either the representative named in the will or the legal representative because his daughter died intestate."

I must have looked as though he was trying to explain Kierkegaard.

" 'Intestate' means without a valid will. Certain laws apply to the estates of persons who die without a will recognized by the court. Remember Howard Hughes? He died intestate. When people like Howard Hughes die without wills it causes big messes; when people like your patient die without wills it causes little messes. But messes nonetheless. I'd bet that Karen Eileen Hart left a will, and didn't name her father as her personal representative. In Colorado the personal representative, the executor, assumes guardianship—control, if you will—over medical and psychological records. Only that person, or the court, can order you to release them.

"Of course I could be wrong about all this. But I don't think I am," he added. "What company underwrites your malpractice coverage?"

I told him.

"And your limits?"

"A million per occurrence. Three occurrences. Jon, if he sues me, I want you to take the case."

He didn't react to the numbers. "Alan, if this joker does sue you, it's up to your malpractice carrier to decide who represents them. You don't get to choose," he said.

"Do you think they'll accept a request by me that you be appointed?"

"You don't get it. They're not too concerned 'bout what you want. As far as the insurance company is concerned, you're just the guy that's got them into this mess. Anyway, they know me; I've represented your company once before. But I don't know whether they'd want me. Depends what they thought of the settlement I negotiated last time. Sometimes insurance companies see an eighty-thousand-dollar settlement as getting off easy, other times they see it as getting screwed."

"I'll call them this afternoon and alert them to the possibility of the suit," I offered.

"Follow it with a letter. Copy me," said Jonathan. "And make a copy of the chart and send it to me."

"Why do you want the chart? If Sheldon Hart doesn't have access to the records, I'm safe, aren't I?"

"No. The bad news is he can sue you for malpractice first and try to get civil court to force the personal representative, whoever that is, to yield access to the records. Or he can petition probate court to replace a resistant personal representative." Jon's voice took on a paternal, slightly authoritarian air. "You need to keep in mind, Alan, that the records belong to Karen Hart's estate. All you own is the paper. The words are hers."

I sighed.

"Should I respond to this request?" I held up the form I received from Sheldon Hart.

"Sit on it awhile. Then write a note saying you lack the authority to release the records. That's all."

"And send you a copy?"

Jon's thin lips traced a line from one cheek to another as he smiled. "That's right. Send me a copy."

Eleven

Wednesday morning, no patients scheduled, I sat in the back of Division Six and watched Lauren Crowder, deputy district attorney, prosecute an underachieving sociopath as a habitual criminal. I don't know if she saw me. I observed a demeanor in Lauren in court that I had only seen glimpses of in our time together. She was calculating and pleasant. Modulated but unmoved. I wondered when I would get a larger dose of it.

The beeper on my hip vibrated twice while I was observing Lauren in court. The digital messages were succinct but unnerving. Philip Hubbard phoned regarding an appointment. And Valerie Goodwin called asking that I call back. No message.

On the brief walk across Canyon Boulevard to my office, I wondered what Phil Hubbard wanted. I was in no position to see him for psychotherapy. But talking with him inspired less guilt than talking with Karen Hart's friend, Valerie Goodwin, so I dialed his phone number at NOAA first.

"This is Alan Gregory returning your call."

"Hello, Dr. Gregory. Just a moment please." Muffling noises and a closing door preceded his return.

"Thanks for returning my call. I'd like to set up an appointment to see you."

"May I ask what this concerns, Mr. Hubbard?"

"Actually, sure, I want to discuss your treatment of my

wife. Her psychoanalysis with you."

"That information, the record of your wife's psychotherapy, is confidential." I detested sharing clinical records only slightly less than I hated people using "psychotherapy" and "psychoanalysis" as though they were synonyms.

"My brother's a lawyer" — he paused and let the words linger on the wire — "and I asked him whether I could see them. He told me that I could."

"On what authority?"

"I think because I'm the one who runs her estate. I'm pretty sure I have the right to those records. Doctor." The tone of these words was more academic than confrontational.

"I wasn't aware of your role as personal representative, Mr. Hubbard. I'll need to have you, as guardian of the records, sign a release of the confidentiality. But I'm happy to meet with you." Just thrilled.

Sufficient posturing accomplished, we set an appointment for the following Monday.

The resolve needed to dial the Denver phone number of Valerie Goodwin was more difficult to muster. Her name yanked me back to a phone call I had made to her a couple of days after Karen Hart's suicide. She had been the "Person to contact in case of emergency" in Karen's chart. Valerie Goodwin had been quietly accusatory and frigidly proper during that brief conversation. As I dialed the phone to return the call I had just received, old feelings about Karen washed over me, like a wave that no longer crashed.

"Dr. Gregory. I'd like to start by apologizing for being so abrupt with you when we talked last fall. I was reeling from Karen's death."

"As was I. No apology is necessary, Ms. Goodwin." Anticipatory dread about the confrontational intent of her agenda began to subside.

"I'm calling about another matter related to Karen. Actually Karen's estate. I'm her personal representative."

96

Jonathan Younger was right. Hallelujah. "And I've received a request from an attorney representing Karen's father, Mr. Sheldon Hart, to permit him access to the records of Karen's treatment with you. For a number of reasons, I'm not inclined to comply. But as an alternative I'd like to see those records myself. Is that agreeable, Dr. Gregory?"

"Certainly. What's a convenient time for you?"

"Actually, Doctor, I live and work in Denver and was hoping you could come by my office, perhaps this Friday."

I had no appointments Friday and hadn't been to Denver for a while, so I agreed. Being cooperative with anybody who was inclined to interfere with Sheldon Hart's march to my door seemed like a good instinct, anyway. We found a satisfactory time. The red light above my desk was lit after I replaced the receiver on the phone.

Michael McClelland had arrived for his regular four o'clock Wednesday appointment. I had the tautness in my bowels that preceded sessions with patients whose hostility could erupt at any time. Until then I hadn't been aware of viewing Michael with trepidation. Maybe the twin phone calls were responsible for the dread.

His whisper was precise. "Where were you over the weekend? Why didn't you tell me you were going to be gone?" No evidence of hostility graced his face. He leaned forward on his chair, intruding on the neutral ground between us.

I sat silently and tried to decide if, and how, to respond. Had he had an emergency? Diane, who was covering for me, hadn't said anything. Why the intensity?

"What if I needed you? What if her death sent me over the edge? Jesus," he said.

"You tried to reach me over the weekend?" I asked.

"Brilliant," he said in his hoarse whisper. "Yeah, I called to try to change this appointment. And you just disappear. No warning. Nothing. Shit.

"I'm supposed to trust you," Michael McClelland continued, "when you just split whenever you please."

"I wonder, Michael, if the feelings you are having now might not be reminiscent of other circumstances."

"What? Don't muddy the water. This has to do with last weekend. With your leaving. Period."

"There may be other situations, similar, that could be aggravating your reaction to what happened," I offered. Come on, wake up, Michael.

His hand slapped the Formica table next to him with an intensity that caused me to jump. He grew three inches and gained fifty pounds.

"Cut the shit"—the whisper was accelerating—"just admit that you blew it."

"I admit that I didn't tell you that I wasn't going to be available over the weekend. I also feel certain that's not all that's going on here."

"You feel certain. Great. You know it all."

"It's apparent that you are very angry with me. It's also clear, to me, that my efforts to explore the intensity of your reaction are not welcome right now."

The silence in the room hung for five minutes like crystal balanced on the edge of a table. My heart attacked my chest wall with echoed drumbeats.

He terminated the silence by changing to a discussion about the research project he was charting, appropriately enough, on the genesis of severe storms.

I was quiet, avoiding traps invisible to my eyes and ears.

Michael McClelland stood fifteen seconds before time was up and walked out of my office, telling me he would see me next week.

I couldn't wait. I checked the drawer in my desk for antacid.

Two days later I took I-25 into Denver for my meeting with Karen Hart's friend, Valerie Goodwin. Temperate morning air belied the searing heat that engulfed the eastern plains by the time I arrived for my early after-

98

noon appointment. I turned onto Lawrence into downtown and then right on Seventeenth to find the building that matched the address in my hand. Fifteen futile minutes passed looking for on-street parking before I relented and parked the Subaru in a lot that charged some multiple of a dollar for some fraction of an hour.

The parts of Denver's lower downtown that had been spared the vision of modern developers were charming and full of character. But Seventeenth Street was almost fully the vision of contemporary developers and was lined with parallel twelve-block-long curtains of glass-and-aluminum-clad towers. I felt I could have been walking in any of fifty different cities. The mountains were as obscured as if I had lifted my hand in front of my eyes.

Valerie Goodwin was a paralegal for a law firm that occupied two floors of Denver's tallest building, the Republic Plaza. I judged myself underdressed without a suit in few places in Colorado. This law firm was one of them. Ms. Goodwin's office, I guessed, was one of the chin-high cubicles partitioned from fabric-and-aluminum panels that filled an acre or two of the thirty-second floor. She escorted me, instead, to a conference room furnished in French Provincial. The view was east and brown and flat and boring. I felt certain the fabric on the chairs cost more per yard than I made in an hour.

Following her down the hall to the conference room, I noticed that the most striking feature of Valerie Goodwin's body was a carved definition that her pleated white skirt and navy blazer could not disguise. Calf muscles jutted beneath her pale hose, and full hips and shoulders accentuated a narrow waist. Her buttoned blazer could not hide the fullness of her bosom as she turned in profile to allow me into the room.

When Valerie Goodwin smiled, I could have discovered if her wisdom teeth had been removed. A wide mouth and open grin quaked across her face. Her chin was as broad as her wide-set eyes. She was not a pretty woman, but she could certainly, in opportune shadows, be arresting. She wore makeup not to enhance, but to conceal; I was as aware of the heavy powder and dark eyeliner after five minutes as I had been after five seconds. She sat at my right side, keeping her face in profile as much as possible.

"Thanks for coming, Doctor."

"Certainly. Before we begin, I need to have you sign this release so I can disclose the information in Karen's chart."

Valerie Goodwin reached into a thin leather portfolio and extracted a sheet of white paper. "I've already prepared a release for you," she said. "I think you'll find it adequate."

I looked at it quickly. The language authorized Valerie Goodwin to have access to the records of Karen's treatment. It was signed by Ms. Goodwin, Karen's personal representative. It was notarized. When I had finished reading, she handed me another sheet of paper. It was a photocopy of a page from Karen's will, a paragraph highlighted in yellow designating Valerie Goodwin her personal representative. "In case there were any questions," added Valerie.

"How can I be of help?" I said, mindful that it was the first line I had spoken to Karen Hart.

"This is awkward, Dr. Gregory. But for me to reach a decision regarding whether or not to grant Sheldon Hart the right to Karen's treatment records, I need to do something which I have no desire to do, and that is to know more about her treatment with you. I say 'more' because Karen told me a lot over the time she was seeing you. She and I met at paralegal school and became good friends, initially, I think, because we were both body builders." Her chest seemed to puff out and her shoulders retreat as she spoke about her obvious avocation. I stifled an impulse to disagree; although it was apparent that Valerie Goodwin was, indeed, a body builder, Karen Hart had been only a weight lifter.

"She thought an awful lot of you, you know?" said

Valerie Goodwin.

"Yes, I know," I said. I was acutely aware of how foreign it felt to be discussing a case of mine openly with a nontherapist.

"Why does he want the records?" I asked.

"I imagine he wants to use them to build a case in order to sue you."

I did my best to look nonplussed. "And you'd like to do your best to judge whether that's a reasonable endeavor?"

"Partially. Mostly I want to try to understand why she died. She wasn't depressed. Not like she used to be. During school. I want to know why this father who didn't talk to her for years at a time and who berated her for becoming a paralegal rather than a lawyer, why he is suddenly so interested in her. He's very wealthy. He doesn't need the money. And" — she began nodding her head gently — "I want to convince myself that Karen was right about you. That you didn't abuse her." She sat even straighter on her chair. "If I think you did, I'll sue you myself."

"And if this" — I held up the manila file — "helps you line all those ducks up in a nice straight row, you will decide not to give Mr. Hart the information he's looking for."

"What it means, actually, is that I will resist him. Whether or not he gets the records is ultimately probably up to probate court, if he decides to pursue it that far. My goal today is to decide whether I will sue you or not. If I decide not to sue you on behalf of Karen's estate, then I won't turn over the records to her father. If I decide there are grounds to sue you, I'll do it myself. The partners in the firm" — she opened her hands to call my attention to the legal lords who ruled this domain — "have given me assurances of their assistance."

I played my cards. Jon Younger would have preferred, given Valerie Goodwin's overt threat, that I walk out the door at that moment. But I hadn't even told him about the meeting. I double-checked my hand and had kings over jacks, so I called her.

101

I told Valerie Goodwin about my time with her friend, Karen Hart. I told her things that made her laugh, and I told her things that made her cry. I reminded her of things she knew about Karen, and I exposed things that shocked her about Karen. She asked how much I knew about her, Valerie. I replied that Karen had talked about her frequently. She didn't pursue it.

I mentioned nothing about the blue note. I had temporarily placed it in my "Correspondence: In" file, not in Karen's chart.

Valerie turned the yellow pages of the clinical record slowly, teasing me about my handwriting and asking intelligent questions about my abbreviations and the meanings of clinical terms. The last few sessions received special attention. Her bold script filled pages of legal pads with notes.

After two hours she led me from the conference room, almost as an afterthought informing me that she had already given permission for the state board that licensed and disciplined psychologists to peruse Karen's records. I reacted to the nauseating pronouncement with my best therapist mask.

While she shook my hand good-bye, she said, "The newspapers say that you're separated." It was almost a question.

"Yes, that's right." Survival instincts told me to flirt my way onto safer ground with this woman. A drink, perhaps? The words that came out of my mouth were, "There's something you may be able to help me with."

She waited. "Did you know Karen had started dating?" I asked.

Valerie nodded. "Yes. She told me she had a date. She was pretty nervous about it. Some guy she met at the club where she worked out in Boulder. I don't know anything about him. Not even his name." She eyed me critically. "Is it important?"

"I don't know. I was surprised to learn she had seen somebody. That's all."

She looked at me quizzically. "You don't even know she'd started going to the bars again, do you?"

I shook my head. My ignorance was no longer a shock to me.

"She'd said she was getting better. Wanted to get out of her shell."

An awkward moment ensued that required a transition I couldn't manufacture. I said, "Good-bye, Ms. Goodwin," shook her hand a second time, smiled pleasantly, and headed down to ransom my car.

Twelve

The following Monday I kept the second of my appointments with the representatives of the dead.

Red skin stretched above the thatch of Philip Hubbard's left eyebrow, looking like an uneven blister that had flattened but never healed. The index finger and thumb of his left hand were of the same rose tint, mottled here, taut there. At first glance it seemed that the left eye was pinker than the right. Actually it just lacked eyelashes.

He was oblivious of my entering the waiting room. His once burned right hand held a pen that scratched away at folded computer printouts. The papers covered a closed brown briefcase whose gussets had long ago yielded to gravity and abuse.

Anne had only alluded to the accident that had spilled molten metal onto her husband's left hand. And to the reflex that splashed it into his face.

Phil Hubbard responded to my clearing my throat and followed me into my office, his papers and briefcase folded together under his arm. I fought an impulse to focus my vision on the disfigured side of his face. He signed the release I handed him without so much as a glance at the typed words. Those words granted me the right to discuss Anne Hubbard's treatment with Phil Hubbard, something I couldn't do without the permission of either the patient herself or, postmortem, her legal representative. Phil Hubbard was the designated representative.

Before putting his pen away, he picked a printout from the pile beside him on the couch and scribbled a note.

"I was in love with her," Phil Hubbard finally said. The words were straightforward and unselfconscious.

"She loved me once, too. My last years in graduate school. God, how much fun it was then. But that died. My work" — his scarred hand swooped over the papers next to him — "has a tendency to consume me. I neglected her. I'm awake most nights now. Since the accident. I rewind and replay scenarios that don't have her in the car in that creek. That bring her back. I'm not sure I was ever that great a husband to her. I'm sterile. You probably know that. My sperm lacks motility. But she was a good wife to me, and I, I didn't take care of her. Of what I had." Phil Hubbard was looking right at me, his pink hand and his good hand intertwined on his knees like twisted taffy.

"She wasn't a saint. She wasn't that great a wife. Not at the end, anyway. It's because I'm not sleeping that I'm here. Or rather because of why I'm not sleeping. I don't believe in what you do. I handle my own problems. Sometimes I mishandle them. But I don't believe in psychiatrists and psychologists. I don't want counseling. I want to know where Anne was before she died. Maybe then I can sleep."

In Boulder, "where Anne was," was more likely to refer to a psychological space than to a physical one. Concretely, where Anne was before she died, according to Michael McClelland, was in his bed. What Phil Hubbard wanted to know wasn't at all clear.

"She probably talked to you more than she did to me during the past couple of years," he concluded.

"What would you like to know?" I began.

Phil Hubbard wasn't certain. He displayed a disarming openness and naïveté. "I guess I really want to hear you tell me that she still loved me. But she didn't." He paused and laughed a laugh of self-deprecation. "I don't attract many women," he said, touching his scarred fingers to his scarred face. "Just the pieces, I guess. I don't know what the puzzle is. I just want the pieces."

Anne Hubbard hadn't had any affairs that she ever told me about. She was a frightened woman who found the public spotlight more comforting than an embrace. She stayed with the man sitting across from me, not for love, nor for comfort, nor for the financial security he provided. She stayed with him because he didn't ever get too close. She called him the "NOAAwhere man." She left therapy because she was frightened of the intimacy involved in having someone there just for her. Even for only forty-five minutes a week. Her problems with intimacy told me a lot about her. They told me a lot about the man she had chosen to marry, Phil Hubbard. And they told me a lot about the man she had chosen to sleep with, Michael McClelland.

I spared Phil Hubbard the nickname. I told him about his wife's problems with intimacy. He seemed relieved. He came into my office believing, from the bed of nails that guilt had built, that he was Anne's only problem.

I told Phil Hubbard some of the stories Anne had told me about her childhood.

I told him about her fears that someone would discover she was a charlatan in her political life.

I told him she was very ambivalent about his infertility.

I didn't tell him I had seen her dying, or just dead. I didn't tell him that I saw her big black purse twenty feet from her. I didn't tell him I had touched her wet boot.

And I didn't tell him that one of his employees had been fucking her.

That information was privileged. And it seemed unlikely that Phil Hubbard would ever get permission from Michael McClelland to hear it.

Before he left, Phil Hubbard said, "Thank you," and stuffed his papers unevenly into the satchel. "We probably would have divorced," he said, mostly to himself. His head was nodding up and down, like a car with bad shocks, as he walked out the door.

I told myself that he had to know. His own employee? He had to know about the affair.

And then the doubt crept in.

Maybe, the doubt said, Anne Hubbard never had an affair with Michael McClelland.

Thirteen

The hypnotic whir of the spoked wheels mesmerized me as my legs pumped and extended on the pedals. I shifted gears without thinking and traversed twenty miles of winding, hilly back roads through dried wheat fields before circling back to Longmont.

The Diagonal Highway slashed straight back to Boulder, and I hammered hard past Niwot, a town whose slumber had been interrupted by town houses and condominiums forced north by Boulder's growth control. IBM's mile of low-rise industrial castles was flanked by berms that obscured from my view the cars of thousands of employees.

Rather than squander my energy against the traffic generated by the strip commercial districts of Twenty-eighth or Thirtieth streets in east Boulder, I cut across Fifty-fifth and took as many winding lanes as I could back to my house to shower and to change clothes.

My only afternoon appointments were with a married couple who were on the verge of separation, and with Gretchen Kravner. My usual eleven o'clock, Elliot Perkins, was out of town, so my morning had been free.

Too many couples had exhibited the death throes of

their vows in my presence, and I recoiled at the prospect of my appointment with the Parkers. They had managed to manufacture a week of artificial bliss from the decay of their marriage, and their simmering separation slipped farther away. Neither of them wanted to see the road that they were traveling. Despite my best efforts they left full of denial and full of vacant hope.

The red light on my wall announced Gretchen's arrival.

Most patients are creatures of habit. They sit on the same chair in the waiting room, reading new issues of the same magazine, finding the same spot opposite me in the office. Once I know their habits, I demonstrate mine and automatically seek them out in their preferred lairs.

When I walked into the waiting room, Gretchen wasn't sitting on her chair below the Ed Singer print.

Michael McClelland was.

Across the room, Gretchen smiled from behind *National Geographic,* and Michael gave me a look that said I'd screwed up. I reviewed my appointments in my head. Today was Tuesday. It was four. That was Gretchen's time. Michael's appointment was Wednesday at four. He was a day early.

"Michael, please come in. Gretchen, I'll be with you in a moment."

I led him down the hall to my office.

"I'm afraid we have a mix-up, Michael."

"Yes, we do," he said, a glimmer of glee evident in his appraisal of the dilemma.

"Your appointment is tomorrow at four. I'll see you then."

"I don't think so. You're mistaken." I was listening for menace in the grainy whisper. The glee was gone.

"I don't have any time to discuss this with you right now. We can talk about it more at four tomorrow."

Michael examined his perfect fingernails. "So be it," he said. "Tomorrow." He walked slowly down the hall to the exit door.

I took a deep breath and returned to the waiting room for Gretchen, who was amused by the theater.

"I've been seeing you for almost two years, and that's never happened before. The switch was already on when I got here. I figured something was wrong."

"What did you guess was going on?"

"I assumed you blew it. Scheduled somebody for my time. Is that what happened?"

"This is your time, Gretchen."

"Not gonna tell me, huh? That's fine. I didn't mind. He's not bad looking."

I expended some effort into exploring what meaning the mixup might have for her. She resisted and finally said, "You've been under a hell of a lot of stress, Alan. If this is as bad as it gets, it's not a problem."

Great, I told myself, I'm getting sympathy credits from my patients.

Before I could decide how to respond, Gretchen was off recounting tales of separation and divorce woes from her restaurateur husband. "The Jerk," as she referred to him, was obeying the restraining order but wasn't budging at all on the divorce settlement. She said she was making threatening noises about disclosing the source of the tips he used to make almost a million dollars in the stock market over the past few years. The tips were generated by a friend in the legal department of the Pacific Coast Stock Exchange in San Francisco. The information was all inside, and all illegal. The friend was now a minority partner in the Boulder restaurants. Gretchen was sure her husband didn't want a scandal and would agree to her terms after he screamed and pouted for a while.

"It amazes me," she said, "but he doesn't frighten me anymore. Two years ago I couldn't even visit my sister in Grand Junction without his permission. God, it was awful. I've come a long way." Her eyes were moist with tears as she gazed at me. "I don't know what I would have done if I hadn't come to see you. When I think about what

110

would have been, everything just goes black. It's too terrible to imagine. Now I just want what's mine. And I think I'll get it.

"You know, I'm not an unattractive woman." Her skirt extended below her knees, which were together directly in front of her. She wore a high-collared white blouse and a bright porcelain-and-gold necklace. "Men hit on me all the time. You haven't. I don't believe you slept with that other patient." The spaces between her sentences were solid gaps, not vacuous. "There were times when I fantasized about sleeping with you." Gretchen was staring at the garden, swallowing frequently. "This is hard to talk about. I wished you would ask. I wanted you to hold me. I wanted you to give me more than you were giving. It's only been the last few months that I realized that I was trying to get you to take advantage of me like Doug did. Like so many have. You knew, didn't you, that I wanted you?"

I said nothing. Her knees had not always been covered, her breasts not always so far from view. We both knew it. Gretchen was a paradox. Brash in some ways, passive and naïve in others. Elegant and demure at times, abrasive and confrontational at others.

"I'm gonna get through this. You've spoiled me as far as men go. I want somebody like you, and then I don't. There are parts of you I love," she said, "but I hate that you don't need anything from me. At first I thought you were perfect. You're not. But you're decent." I watched her hazel eyes glisten as she remembered. "And I needed decent."

At four P.M. the next day Michael McClelland missed his appointment.

My initial response was relief. I searched for some meaning in his confusing the days for his appointment. I hypothesized about the consciousness of his acting out by missing this appointment. I wondered if he was being straight with me. Then I thought about Lauren.

A full week had passed since I had spent time with her. We had talked almost daily on the phone. I had watched her play a softball game on Monday night. Tonight we had a date.

She met me at my office at around six. She wore a flowered silk shell that left little doubt that her breasts were untethered. A deep burgundy cotton skirt stopped inches above her knees. Her long legs were bare, and she wore simple black flats. "You're something," I said, shaking my head in appreciation. Before approaching her, I hesitated, digesting some of her reticence, then bounced across the room and kissed her newly painted lips.

"So are you," she mumbled, our lips still touching, my tongue tracing the hilly outline of her upper lip, tasting Crest and lipstick.

In the summertime, the Downtown Boulder Mall was an ecumenical version of Main Street in Disneyland. From the west end, where a lone Laundromat is the last evidence of the real world, there mingled a solid mass of browsing couples, wandering tourists, teenagers on the make, adults on the make, and members of sundry societal fringes.

Taken at its full length, it was a sociological microcosm of counterculture America since the beat generation. Aging Kerouac-inspired men somehow found sustenance sipping coffee at the Trident or the Bohemia. From their outdoor seats they were inured to the punks, stoners, and heavy metalists who sprawled across tiny lawns or surrounded planter boxes and benches. Teenagers spilled from subterranean video dens, sub shops, pizza by-the-slice parlors, or an absurdly broad selection of ice-cream and frozen yogurt vendors. The most outrageous of the teens always seemed to stand sentinel at the ends of blocks, their bizarreness creating reasonable bookends for what lay in between.

New Age devotees carried take-out salads of unlikely vegetables to the small lawns in the eleven hundred block, or lined up for falafel or designer cookies farther down the street. Time-capsule hippies and hypomanic street people shared centurion duty on the lawn in front of the thirties deco courthouse. Constituents of the indigenous culture were present in small congregations, too. Adrienne called the natives "Bouldoids" but could never quite describe their mores, instead insisting that, like obscene materials, "I just know 'em when I see 'em."

The affluent were conspicuous mostly by their purposefulness, the fact that they had destinations distinguishing them from the majority merely in search of a place to be. The dollars the middle and upper classes dropped in galleries, boutiques, and restaurants kept the four-block playground in the black.

In a town where ice-cream trucks are illegal for making too much noise, where airplanes pulling banners violate the city sign code, and where municipal employees are prohibited from smoking even when alone in city vehicles, the mall was a bit of an oasis of noninterference. As long as you didn't want to skateboard, ride a bike, panhandle, or run your dog, it was Boulder's most tolerant four blocks.

Lauren and I held hands and wandered through the throngs beneath the Victorian storefronts and anachronistic architectural oddities that contained the press of people. A good magician drew a crowd in front of Potter's, and an energetic piano player, who had pushed an aging baby grand on wheels to the brick walk in front of the New York Deli, played ragtime mostly to himself. He had more enthusiasm than talent.

We landed awhile beneath an umbrella on the roof of the West End Tavern and watched the western light fade over Mexican beer. Our aimlessness ended at Juanita's, where we flirted over Mexican food and too loud roadhouse music.

"So you've just been creating a mood?" Lauren asked

in response to my shouted question. Juice from salsa and orange-marinated pork was leaking out the back of a flour tortilla and down the spine of her hand.

"You've got a problem," I said, gesturing at the developing mess.

"You?" she said, tortilla back on the plate.

"You haven't answered my question. Will you come with me to Baja?"

One side of her mouth turned up, her eyes in counterpoint in the opposite direction. "You certainly do travel a lot."

"Nothing else to do." I grinned, feeling my second beer of the night. "I'm virtually unemployed, you know. Merideth used to say it was my most visible neurosis. Something gets me anxious and I need to take two flights and sleep in a strange bed before I can feel better. I guess I could fly round trip to Colorado Springs and back and sleep in your bed, but—"

"Where in Baja?" she interrupted before my developing entreaty settled anywhere in her proximity.

"Cabo San Lucas. Been there? It's great. A little finger of rock and sand. Sea of Cortés on one side. Pacific Ocean on the other. Only a few hours away. You'll love it."

"Why do you persist with me, Alan?"

"Because," I said before a reply was formulated in my head. I sighed and took her hand. If I'd had something romantic and convincing to say, taking her hand would have been the perfect move. "Because you're the only good thing in my life right now. I'm a mess and you're clarity. You're fun. And, well, you're gorgeous." She was looking at me skeptically. I plowed on. "You seem to like me at a time when I don't feel particularly likable. You've been straight with me at a time when I can't handle too much confusion."

She made a face that expressed continued doubt. The correct answer to her question, if there was one, apparently hadn't made my list. "I have this concern," she said, tracing a fingernail over the pale lines on the palm of my hand, "that my not being totally available to you is part of the attraction. That if I were sleeping with you, I'd be a threat to whatever is holding you and Merideth together."

"Shit," I said quietly. "Like I said, you're straight with me. Merideth and I are done with our marriage. We're not, I admit, done with whatever it takes to say good-bye to it." I broke off a tortilla chip in some concretizing refried beans. "I saw a couple this afternoon. Their marriage is a shipwreck. Hopeless. They move close to acknowledging it, and then they dream lovers' dreams for a while. They did that today. It's touching — and it's frustrating. But they'll end it at their own pace. My role, with them, is to try and mitigate the destruction as they salvage things, emotional things, to take with them as they get on with their lives." The waitress cleared our plates. We ordered coffee. "My marriage is over. You're part of my trying to get on with my life. That's why I persist."

"I've said it before, 'There's no true separation without murder in the air.' "

"I can't make you believe me."

"I actually want to believe you," said Lauren. "I really do. The problem right now is that I think you believe you. And that's dangerous for me."

I punted on third down. "So how about Cabo San Lucas?"

"I'll pick a place to stay," she said, exasperated. "You take care of the plane."

"Have you noticed that you tend to end every discussion with some sort of directive that leaves you captain of the ship?"

"No. I haven't noticed that." She smiled and raised her left hand. "Check, please," she called to the harried waitress.

The masses seemed to have condensed when we returned to the mall.

"What are you anxious about?" Lauren asked as we walked.

"I'm not sure what you mean."

"Before. You said that your wife associated your travel with anxiety"

"You do pay attention, don't you? You, for one. You make me nervous. It's like you've got one foot in the door, and I don't know which way you're leaning. But I'm also a little weird about this guy I saw today. I can't get a handle on him yet."

"Want to talk about it?"

"No. I want ice cream."

Fourteen

Tuesday morning at ten-thirty I followed the electronic trail of the illuminated red light to the waiting room to get Elliot Perkins for his appointment.

The tiny scientist, no bigger than five feet three, was perched on his usual chair, his feet bent forward so the toes of his shoes could graze the floor and provide the illusion of not just hanging in the air. Gray curls covered his head and dangled onto the forehead of the carved features of his bronze face. He looked like an aging, miniature, colorized version of Michelangelo's *David*.

A college-age man in running shoes, athletic shorts, and a tank top sat on another chair. I guessed he was waiting for Diane.

I guessed wrong. He stood up and said, "Are you Alan Gregory?"

My impulse to flee could not have been stronger if a skunk had been wandering around the room. If Elliot had not been there to catch me in a lie, I would have said, "No." Or simply run back through the connecting door and locked it behind me.

Instead I exhaled through my nose, looked straight at the young man, and shook my head slowly, side to side.

He mistook my exasperation for denial. "You're not him?"

I thrust my right hand out in front of me, palm up, and said, "I'm him—he. I'm Dr. Gregory."

He handed me the trifolded papers, their backs protected by a sheet of slick, sky blue bond.

"Thanks," he said.

I replied, "You're welcome," intent on not blaming the messenger.

When the front door closed behind the process server, I turned to Elliot and said, "Come on"

He never asked what the drama was all about.

The papers formed an eight-and-a-half-inch-long hollow triangular loaf on my desk. I knew what was in them.

Early in my career I had done a lot of forensic work. Psychological evaluations of criminals, assessments of accused abusive parents or battering husbands, custody evaluations. I spent more time in court than most lawyers. During those years I received more subpoenas than Christmas cards.

These papers, I knew, were different. And I didn't want them.

I was being sued by the father of Karen Eileen Hart for malpractice in the care of and treatment of his daughter. I was specifically accused of not foreseeing her suicidal intent when a reasonable practitioner would have done so. An additional specification stated that I had acted in a way that caused, aggravated, or precipitated the depression that led to her suicide.

I picked up the phone and punched buttons. A receptionist asked my name and made the connection.

"I pay you to be right. This is one instance where I hate it that you're right."

"He's filed a suit, then." The calm words from Jon Younger's mouth did not form a question.

"Yes. It's in my hand as we speak."

"Can you come by at five, Alan?"

"See you then, Jon."

At four forty-five, after Gretchen Kravner left the office, I walked into the bathroom, threw cold water on my face, dried it with one of the soft fresh towels Diane kept in the bathroom, and loosened my tie. I walked down Walnut to Jon's office on Broadway near Spruce. The still heat of August was unmitigated by clouds, and I wished I had driven.

Jon always came out to the reception area to greet me. I wondered if he did it as a courtesy to me or whether he did it with all clients. Maybe all lawyers did it. I doubted it.

In his office he sat almost sideways on the armchair to keep his extended legs from using up all the space between our seats. The two sheets required just a couple of moments to read.

He ran his hand through his hair. I found myself surprised at how far his hairline had receded.

"Kind of what I expected. Good law firm, Spencer and Kates. They must feel that they have something. I'm surprised by one thing, though." He flipped the second page back and quickly reread the first. "Wrong, I'm surprised by two things.

"First, I'm surprised that they filed this in Boulder. Spencer and Kates is a Denver firm. Near Cherry Creek. Second, I'm surprised that the allegations that have been made in the *Daily* are only alluded to here. No specific allegation of sexual misconduct is made."

"I think I can explain that one," I said. I, too, had been bothered by the fact that there was no mention of sexual impropriety. The answer had come to me an hour before while Gretchen Kravner was reciting the Jerk's latest escapades of predivorce madness.

"When did you last do a psychologist's malpractice case?"

"I do mostly psychiatric cases. My last case with a psychologist was three, maybe four years ago."

"Things have changed, Jon." I reached into my briefcase and extracted my malpractice insurance policy. I handed it to him. "If you take a look at paragraph four, under 'Special Provisions,' you'll see that the insurance company limits coverage to twenty-five thousand dollars where damages are awarded for acts related to 'erotic contact.' Hart's attorneys can go for the full million if they ignore that allegation."

"Interesting restriction. But it makes sense out of this." He shook the papers in his hand. "And it's the sort of thing that Spencer and Kates would know."

I climbed up on a soapbox. I had an audience who was being paid $160 an hour. He was no fool. He listened. "Actually, Jon, although I understand that the restrictions might be necessary from a risk management perspective, I think they're insidious for consumers. If someone is seriously injured by the sexual misconduct of a malignant therapist, they're basically shit out of luck. They get screwed twice."

Jon said, "So to speak." I waited a moment for more of a response. One was not forthcoming. I doubt that Jon disagreed with me, but he was smart enough not to encourage me, either.

"There's some other things I should fill you in on, Jon. Sheldon Hart has been trying to get permission to get the treatment records from Karen's friend, Valerie Goodwin, who is the personal representative. As you guessed, Karen appointed her friend, not her father, as her personal representative. As far as I know, Ms. Goodwin hasn't agreed to release the records to him. She did review them at length, in my presence, however, and seems to see Sheldon Hart's motives as being more suspect than my actions."

"You should have called me before you met with her."

"Probably," I said, granting the point and then being silent.

"Go over your whole meeting with her. Everything you can remember. Write it down. Drop it by here tomorrow."

I nodded a nod of acquiescence engendered by twenty-two years of homework assignments.

Jon bulled on. "The fact that Sheldon Hart isn't the personal representative is good news and bad news, Alan."

Jon was extinguishing the only ray of hope in this mess. "What's the bad news?"

"The bad news is that since we are going to argue that

Karen's father doesn't have legal standing to sue you, since he's not her personal representative, you're also going to be unable to defend yourself publicly against the charges we're assuming he's making through the press. We can't argue on one hand that the litigation is without legal justification and therefore Sheldon Hart can't have Karen's records, and then, on the other hand, argue that his suit is the legal justification that permits you to waive Karen's privilege and provide the same records to the media."

What bothered me most was that I understood him.

"What did you hear back from your malpractice insurer?"

"Not much, just a form letter acknowledging my correspondence. Please stay in touch, that sort of thing. But no reply to the question of you participating in my defense."

"Where are they? New Jersey? Connecticut?" He looked at his watch, mentally adding two hours for the time zone change. "Too late to call today. Call them tomorrow and tell them you're being sued. Ask for a reply to your question. They'll be more responsive now that you have this," he said, pointing to the lawsuit documents.

"Where do we go from here?" I asked.

"First we find out if I'm on the case, and then . . ."

"Jon, if they don't retain you, I will. You're on the case."

He opened his mouth as if to tell me it wasn't that simple and then thought better. "This needs to have a reply drafted. That's the next step. Before I get started on it, though, I want your notes on your meeting with the personal representative, and I want to hear what your insurance carrier has to say. Okay?"

He stood up without waiting for my reply and walked me out to his wood-paneled reception area. The receptionist was gone for the day.

"No more meetings without informing me."

The words that formed in my head were, "Yes, Dad," but they stayed there, and I nodded and said I would make the call the next day.

That night, sitting at the word processor, I drafted a

summary of my meeting with Valerie Goodwin. I sipped bad red wine and ate take-out pizza while I wrote.

I called Lauren to get some sympathy but got her machine instead. My mind drifted quickly from self-pity to jealousy, and I wondered whether she was out with somebody. As in "somebody else."

Part of my defensive structure was an ability to manufacture a worry that could temporarily overshadow a real anxiety. I was usually conscious of the tendency. It was something I had learned at my mother's knee. She had polished and refined the techniques of diversionary worrying during my prepubescent apprenticeship. Despite my awareness, the habit occasionally snuck up on me, and hours or days would pass before I recognized what I was doing.

So I wandered around the dark house reviewing whether Lauren and I had ever discussed seeing other people. Of course we hadn't. Shit, Merideth and I hadn't even discussed seeing other people.

Lauren was distant with me. Or at least reserved. Surely she got other offers. Of course she did. She went out with me. She went to Aspen with me. So she must go out with other men. Of course she's out with somebody else tonight. The logic was impeccable.

For almost an hour this insidious dialogue deflected Sheldon Hart from my awareness, and I was tossing and turning in bed before I remembered that Diane had told me that Montezuma's Revenge had a nine-fifteen game that night and realized that Lauren was standing at second base throughout my temporary insanity.

The new problem solved, I fell asleep.

Fifteen

Lauren's kitchen looked out over a wooded lot and a neglected lawn. A green hose snaked across the yard and fused with a sprinkler shaped like a piece of earth-moving equipment disguised as a helicopter. During its last journey, which had apparently been in the distant past, it had run into the trunk of an ash.

White cabinets with glass fronts and brass knobs dominated the kitchen, which managed to feel cool after a succession of warm August days. An old gas range with porcelain so brilliant it looked as if it could have been delivered yesterday sat comfortably along the north wall at a right angle to a black glass-fronted dishwasher with digital controls. The pine floor was sanded and clean. No dirt hid beneath the molding.

The experience of being in her house for the first time was distracting.

She was toasting bagels in the broiler of the old range, a toaster oven sitting unused on an opposing counter beside a wooden knife rack holding a selection of fine knives with European lineage. She sliced the bread with something from the cutlery section of the grocery store.

"In my family, growing up, barbecue potato chips and Mister Salty pretzels were considered fancy appetizers when company came over. I'm more than a little uncomfortable cooking for you, you know." I didn't say anything. She asked, "One or two bagels?"

I sipped at the orange juice in my hand and said, "One."

The cheap knife sliced tomatoes and scallions that she blended into a mound of puffy cream cheese. An exotic-looking coffee maker sat unused beside the toaster oven, as coffee finished dripping into a Chemex carafe whose wooden saddle had cracked from the effects of age and water.

"It's nice seeing you and not feeling like one of us needs to rush somewhere." I said "one of us," but we both knew I meant her.

She looked over her shoulder and smiled a patronizing smile in return.

"You know, this is the first time you've let me in your house."

"There hasn't been opportunity or motive before this, Doctor."

"I've had motive," I corrected, "and intent, Counselor."

"You can see it after brunch. Okay? Eat."

She laid a platter splashed with red lox, rainbow cream cheese, and a full spectrum of sliced melons between us on the small table. The bagels were in a basket wrapped in a napkin that failed to contain the aroma of toasted onion.

"Do they do autopsies after traffic accidents?" I asked.

Lauren paused and gazed at the raw salmon she held suspended by a fork over her plate. She gave me a look that questioned my timing. I took a bite.

"When I was a rookie," she responded, ignoring my query, "I got assigned a suspicious unattended death of a fifty-six-year-old guy. The neighbors complained about the smell coming from the house. That's how they found him. Because of the smell." She finished assembling the bagel and then raised it to her mouth and took a bite that left no cream cheese on her lips. I was impressed.

"The cops on the scene treated me like a high school girl who was there for career day. They told me where I could stand. They told me what not to touch. One detective gave me something to put over my mouth and nose and . . . suggested I could go back to the office. It was, he implied, no place for a girl.

"So when the post was scheduled for late that afternoon and the same detective said to his partner, right in front of me, that he was gonna go, I said, so was I.

"This guy, the dead guy, smelled like—he smelled like death times twenty. I walked into the room a couple of minutes after they started the post and watched the pathologist slice his chest and gut from here to here. The stink didn't seem quite as bad as it had been in the closed house. Big exhaust fans sucked up the fumes. These two macho detectives just watched me, waiting. After a while they took their little masks off. So did I. What a mistake. I rocked back on my heels and felt behind me for that cold tile wall. The detectives had their hips leaning against a high lab counter on the other side of the autopsy table. One cleaned his fingernails, the other was doing some sort of solo chiropractic abuse to his neck.

"I tasted vomit and death for the next hour. I watched bloated organs thrown onto a scale, like a butcher weighing sweetbreads. I became so clammy at times, the damn tile felt like it was sweating.

"When it was over, I crooked my finger at Purdy, one of the detectives, asking him to join me. He sauntered over like he was sure I was going to ask for help leaving the room. If I had any energy left, I would have hit him.

"I checked to make sure no vomit was waiting to escape my mouth, unplastered my tongue from my teeth, and said, 'Detective, I think we should discuss this further. How about some dinner? Italian okay?' I brushed past him, held the door, and said, 'Coming?'

"We had lasagna and red wine. For the first twenty minutes he just sat there waiting for me to puke. I think I became a bit of a legend. And Sam Purdy became an ally. I dry-cleaned the suit I was wearing and gave it to the Salvation Army."

Lauren took another bite of bagel and said, "So I can

talk about autopsies during meals. Can you?"

My bagel had only one serrated half-moon-shaped indentation in it. "No," I said, "I don't think so."

It didn't slow her down. "The answer to your question is 'Yes.' They sometimes do perform autopsies, postmortem examinations, after traffic accidents. They do them whenever there's a question about the cause of death. Does this fall into the category of information you've always been dying to know, or is there a mission behind your curiosity?"

I took a bite of bagel. "I know Sam Purdy. He interviewed me — interrogated me? — after a patient of mine killed herself."

"He's a good cop," said Lauren. "Do you know he has a master's?"

"Everyone in Boulder has a master's," I replied, instantly wondering about the derivation of my hostility toward Detective Purdy. Since I didn't want Lauren to wonder, too, I changed the subject. "Maybe it's not right to ask you to do this. But, is there a way you can get me permission to see an autopsy report? One of my patients, a woman — she died in a car wreck — I want to find out if she had sex before she died."

"You mean was she a virgin? I thought that's one of the first things shrinks learn about their patients."

"Don't be a smart-ass. No. Did she have sex just before she died? The last few hours."

"Why do you want to know?"

"Her husband came to see me recently. I'm just curious about the facts surrounding her death." I had no permission to tell Lauren the real reason.

"You don't need my help. You can read it yourself. Under Colorado statutes autopsy reports are public records. It's not part of an active investigation, is it?"

"No, I don't think so. Where do I go?"

"County Coroner's Office. Sixth and Canyon. They'll even make you a copy for a fee. Maybe you could get a whole stack of them and take them on vacation with you."

She stood and began clearing the table.

Lauren's living room contained a pool table. Big, carved wood, deep green felt. Leather pockets. No other furniture.

"No comment?" she said.

I shook my head from side to side. "You're full of surprises."

A quick survey revealed no rack of cues. A short, hard case rested on the deep sill of the window on the western side of the room. "Where are the cues?" I asked.

"I wouldn't bother to play with anybody who didn't bring their own."

"Oh," I said.

"Sounds arrogant, doesn't it? But think, Alan. Have you asked me to ride bikes with you? I mean one of your rides, to the mountains, or to Nebraska, any of the places where normal people take cars or airplanes. No. I can't keep up. I don't belong."

"And I don't belong here?" I pointed at the table.

"I don't know. Do you?"

"How good are you?" I asked.

Lauren said, "Very good. Tournament good."

"Then I probably don't belong here."

"Don't be offended, Alan, we all don't belong someplace."

"Do I belong here?" We stood in the doorway to her bedroom. A contemporary brass bed was an island in the middle of the room. It was covered with enough pillows to sleep a family of twelve.

Lauren nudged me in the ribs with her elbow.

I turned her toward me and kissed her. I felt her respond, her thin body slackening for most of an exhale. Then she pulled away, reached across the hall, and opened the door to her office.

An ancient oak teacher's desk floated in a sea of books, files, boxes, papers, and plastic bags. An antique lounge chair of shiny mahogany and cracked brown leather sat beneath an Italian halogen floor lamp. The seat was swamped with files.

I was enchanted with the chair. "Don't you use it? It's beautiful."

She said, "I did. But the light bulb burned out in the lamp." As though that were sufficient explanation.

"Why didn't you change the bulb?"

"It's one of those weird halogen bulbs. I don't have much patience with mechanical things," she replied, looking over a pile on her desk.

"What's wrong with the toaster oven and the coffee maker? I'm guessing your good knives are just dull." We were walking along the greenbelt above Chatauqua a few blocks from her house.

"Smoke comes out of the toaster oven. The coffee maker gurgles and burps and drips too slow. You're right about the knives, they're dull. You're thinking I need a man in my life. Aren't you? Christ."

"Actually, Lauren, I'm just amused at the occasional lacunae in your otherwise complete mastery of the world."

"Speaking of lacunae," she said, "what're you doing with all your time?"

Subject changed.

"Long bike rides. I do them in repertory. Mountain rides, up Flagstaff, or Sunshine, or Left Hand Canyon. Foothills and plains rides, to Loveland, Erie. Circuit rides, the Morgul Bismarck. I'm in the best shape of my life."

The conversation was choppy, like the ocean in the afternoon.

"Have you picked a date for Los Cabos?" I asked. Her court schedule was going to be the main determinant of the dates for our vacation.

"As a matter of fact, yes. How about the weekend after Labor Day? Leave Thursday, come back Monday. I get the beeper at five on Monday afternoon. I need to be back for that."

"I'll call my travel agent."

"Great."

Lauren stumbled twice as we walked back to her house. I was tempted to ask her what was wrong, but the issue of frailty and vulnerability had developed into something competitive and I said nothing. She entwined her left arm with mine and rested her head on my shoulder as we walked.

She played pool with determination and concentration. Observing her, I was reminded of the hours I had spent in Peter's shop watching him shape and smooth wood. And she was good. Crack, thud. Shot after unlikely shot left balls in leather pockets.

"I drove my brothers crazy. I could beat all of them by the time I was eleven." She spoke of her superiority with competitive glee. "I played some tournaments until I transferred to California for school. I was the sixteen-year-old female champion in Washington."

"I believe it," I said. "You're very good."

"And not just at this." I interpreted an invitation in her eyes.

I stood and walked over to her, the bright light from the lamp over the table highlighting half her face. She relinquished the cue, and I laid it on the table. She kept her eyes fixed on mine. She responded slowly when I kissed her, her mouth opening, then closing, and then widening again, my tongue sliding over the smooth surface of her upper teeth.

I tugged her pink camp shirt from the waistband of her shorts and moved my mouth down to kiss her neck, smelling flowers in her hair. I could hear her breathe. She shivered as my hands moved over the skin at the small of her back and then up her sides, where I could sense the slight swell of her breasts.

Her hands hadn't moved from her sides.

I turned her so her butt pressed against the polished hardwood rail of the table. She reached back with both hands and supported herself on the green felt. I leaned in to feel the contours of her arched breasts against my chest. My right knee found soft warm skin on the inner thigh of her left leg.

And her beeper went off.

She flew out of my arms with the determination of a volunteer firefighter answering a call. After disappearing for five minutes into her study and returning retucked and with steady breath, she said from across the room, "That was nice." As in, "That is over."

My erection persisted until I left a few minutes later. She hugged me at the door in such a way as to not aggravate my arousal and not remind herself about the versatility of pool tables.

"Did I tell you about the journals?"

The husky voice of Valerie Goodwin filled my left ear.

"What journals? No." I was returning a call to her home the day after brunch at Lauren's.

"I can't believe I forgot. Karen's father has a journal of hers. You know, like a diary. I found it under her bed when I cleaned out her apartment. I put it in a box of personal things — effects? — I turned over to him."

"What's it about? What's in it?"

"That's what's odd. I knew she kept journals. I'd seen them around, she'd showed me passages. But there were lots of them. 'My volumes,' she used to call them. You know, typical journals. Certainly stuff I wouldn't want my dad to read. But typical. And then there was one about you and her. She called it *Domain of the Heart*. It was where she wrote down her thoughts and feelings about therapy, I guess, about you, about you and her. I didn't read very much of it. It was embarrassing. Very personal."

"You said her father has 'a journal.' Which one?"

"That one. The one about therapy."

"Is the incest in it?"

"Not in the part I read. I don't know."

"When did he get it? Mr. Hart?"

"A couple of weeks after she died. A long time ago."

"Where are the others? Do you know?"

"No. That's what's so weird. When I cleaned out her apartment they weren't there."

"Thanks for letting me know, Ms. Goodwin."

"Please call me Valerie."

"Sure. Valerie. Thanks."

I could now make a guess where the *Daily* had been getting its information. But I had no idea what was in that journal.

That journal. *Domain of the Heart.*

The title was borrowed from a monotype by David Barbero that hung in an unfinished oak frame above and behind the chair where I sat during sessions. She had loved it from our first meeting, rising from her chair after the session to examine it closely and to read the artist's name.

Domain of the Heart.

Primary colors and primitive childlike strokes of rounded mountains and green-and-purple glens. Two box houses, lollipop trees, fences drawn without regard for perspective.

"I live there," she told me once in relating one of her fantasies, "in the little house on the hill. You live in the big house. No matter what I see coming, they have to get by you first. You protect me. You're the guardian of the *Domain of the Heart.*"

Sixteen

Tuesday, 4:00 P.M.

"I feel funny about this, I mean about how I know about this. But I heard that you're going on vacation. With somebody. Mexico, right? A friend of mine works at Front Range Travel. She told me." Gretchen Kravner shifted on the chair, tugging her skirt down below her knee. "These last few times I've been here, I keep feeling embarrassed. Wonder why that is? Maybe because I'm breaking the rules by doing things like this?" She nodded to herself, answering her own question.

My home phone was unlisted, always had been. Answering machines and answering services provided a buffer between my private life and my professional one. I bristled when that zone was crossed. Considering the details of my life that were now public knowledge, though, it was a bit like a prostitute defending her chastity.

I bristled anyway. "What reaction do you have to knowing about my trip?" I asked, my voice as bland as I could make it.

"That's what's nice, Alan. I mean, sure, I wonder who you're going with. Are you taking a lady? Are you back with your wife? I know you won't tell me, but I'm curious. But I'm not crazed about it. Before, I would've been jealous. Angry. Would've convinced myself that if I wasn't your patient, I could be going with you. Should have been going with you.

"What's great is that I'm just curious. Like if you were a friend or something. I hope you have a great time. It still infuriates me that I can't know. That there is this line drawn down the middle of this room." She arched an arm into the space between us. "But I can live with it."

She swung her head from side to side while gazing upward with both eyes. Gretchen used affectation as punctuation; this gesture indicated a change to a new paragraph.

"I think the Jerk is going to settle." The change in direction was abrupt. But then, so was Gretchen. "The flames are dying down. I think he knows he's lost. The fight. And me."

I told her that I thought part of her would miss the fight. She concurred. We talked about that for the rest of the hour.

My mind wandered. I thought about errands I needed to run before the flight to Mexico.

I decided to change travel agents. The brown leaves of the irises needed to be removed and cleared. I needed to make sure that Peter and Adrienne could watch Cicero while I was gone.

Wednesday, 4:00 P.M.

"It's like a hall of mirrors," said Michael McClelland, "the reflections are infinite, and I lose perspective." A cologne I didn't recognize filled the room. "Sometimes I just respond to him, without thinking. Other times I feel like he's intentionally pricking the balloon, trying to get me to burst. Mostly, though, he's just not there. He's kind of a monster." He was talking about his frustration with his boss, his dead mistress's husband, Phil Hubbard. "Has these huge scars on his face and hands from some kind of burn. I think I need a plan."

"Does he remind you of anyone?"

The whisper changed tone. "My dissertation chairman was the same way. I never knew where I stood with

133

him. I slept with his daughter. Did I tell you that?"

Minute droplets of water emerged on his temples. He took a handkerchief from his pocket and dabbed them away. I didn't respond to his question.

He chuckled, remembering. "She was something. Nineteen when we started. Big tits. So firm it was like they were sculpted on." For a moment he detoured into the apparent luxury of the memory. "Anyway, she was a freshman and she loved sneaking around behind her daddy's back. It was more her idea than mine. I saw her for over a year. After a while I got tired of her. Gorgeous, but not very bright. You know the type. Anyway, she threatened to tell her dad. I just dropped her. Called her bluff. Don't think she ever told him. They never do.

"I told you a long time ago that I've been involved with women I shouldn't have been screwing. You've never asked." Michael McClelland had assumed his challenging posture. Elbows on knees, hands together. Head down. Then he raised his head and looked straight at me.

"Don't you pay attention? Or don't you care?" His tone was as conversational as an almost whisper could be. The menace was engraved in his words.

"That sounds like your complaint about your boss. Or your dissertation chairman." This ball belonged in his court.

More dew on his forehead. "It's my complaint about you."

My mind raced, reviewing the last couple of sessions to check my bearings. They had been bland, wandering, not provocative. I had confronted the meandering as a way of not dealing with something important. We kept coming back to this primitive transference theme. Men not caring. Not paying attention. He acted out his anger through women, never directing rage at the man.

Because of Michael's resistance to accepting the genetic link between his current feelings and his past, I decided to continue with my plan of interpreting that

134

resistance to him.

"I'm not saying that you don't have a complaint with me. I'm saying that some of the intensity of your reaction may be determined from someplace else."

"There's always a reason. Always an explanation. Always something more important." His head was down. "Well, I know what's more important, too."

"It's not clear what you mean, Michael."

It was his turn not to respond.

The door closed with a thud and a *whoosh* of air. The tight fit and rubber gaskets that improved soundproofing also diminished the impact of slamming the door.

At least I had waited until he was gone before I flung it closed. It was a symbolic act, I told myself, signifying the end of work, the beginning of a break.

Most of my notes on Michael McClelland were still in the form of questions. I was a clinician who believed I was doing my best work when my questions outnumbered my answers. Trying to identify another case where the ratio exceeded ten to one proved an elusive exercise, however.

I reread his chart. I needed to put Michael McClelland to rest before I boarded the plane the next day.

My treatment plan was simple. Confront his resistance. Reflect inconsistencies. Stabilize the therapeutic alliance.

Little headway had been made with his resistance to looking at antecedents to his current predicaments. He would recall personal history reluctantly and with the detachment of a surgeon. As if the precise cuts were in somebody else's body.

Pointing out inconsistencies in his presentation resulted in impulsive counterattacks and finger pointing. Or with denial of the contradictions.

And the alliance. The adhesion, the bond, in the therapeutic relationship. The elastic that stretched during the intimate anguish of psychotherapy and always returned to a form that permitted the patient to come back into the private room for more private pain. Usually the alliance was built on trust. Usually visceral trust. Initially unearned, transferential. Trust in someone from the past temporarily bestowed on me. But not with Michael. With Michael, the honeymoon of positive transference was terribly brief, supplanted quickly by the pall of inherited mistrust.

Maybe, my thinking continued, I am overestimating the alliance. Maybe he'd drop out of therapy. Maybe he needed to see me as incompetent and uncaring so he could reject me. My relief at the prospect was troubling.

It was evidence of countertransference. Previous relationships in my life could be contaminating my view of Michael McClelland. Countertransference was, after all, what everyone was assuming was responsible for my alleged improprieties with Karen Hart.

Transference, yes. I was thinking of Michael McClelland's transference. I was being treated like someone from his past. But so was everyone else. His boss, his dissertation adviser. Both men. In some authority. Paternal transference. Sure. So what? An insight of little utility if I am the only one who is curious. What interferes with your search, Michael?

There are the affairs, sure. Acting out his conflict should have reduced the associated anxiety. Maybe he was right today. Maybe I need to focus more on his illicit relationships. Interpret the acting out.

Okay, I'll focus some attention on the acting out. Good. An addition to the treatment plan. A decision formulated. I sandwiched the yellow sheets between the manila halves of the chart and began to shove it somewhere in the *M*s in the filing cabinet.

What the hell is Karen Hart's chart doing in the *M*s?

After shoving Karen's chart back into the *H*s and chiding myself that I should start a "dead" file, I told myself how badly I needed these five days in Mexico, and locked the drawer.

The remainder of my meager caseload tumbled through my head as I reviewed the list for other cases with unresolved questions that might cause them to visit me unexpectedly during my time with Lauren in Mexico. Nothing.

I called Jon Younger's office to check on the status of the lawsuit. His paralegal told me that they had received interrogatories for me to respond to, but Jon had decided to spare me until after my vacation. I dialed the answering service, cleared my calls, and turned my practice over to Diane for the long weekend.

By the time I crawled into bed that night, my mind no longer festered. My blue-and-yellow Churchill fins and my mask and snorkel rested in the suitcase. The airplane tickets were tucked in my carry-on bag. I had already risen from bed once after remembering to call Peter about taking care of Cicero. Plants were watered. Alarm set.

A recent habit had developed where I looked around the bedroom before lying down. I'd decided weeks before that I was looking for someone to say good night to. Cicero, without fail, opened an eye or rustled an ear during my surveying. That night the shrill siren of the telephone interrupted the ritual.

"A promise. Please." It was Lauren. She had an annoying habit of skipping salutations when she generated a phone call.

"And what might that be? Something asexual, I imagine."

"Feeling a little deprived? I'm serious. I just wanted to see whether you had any luck getting the autopsy you were looking for. I don't want to be bothered by any mention of work until we get back to Boulder. I want a promise."

I hesitated. Lauren Crowder took promises seriously.

"Since I'm tired and it's late, I plead lack of capacity. But," I told her, "to the best of my ability to think this through — yes, I promise."

"Jesus, you have more disclaimers than an auto ad on TV. Okay. Did you get the autopsy? Did your patient fornicate before she died?"

I sighed. I had gone to the County Coroner's Office earlier in the week. "Yes, she did. She still had her diaphragm in." I didn't bother to mention the fact that the presence of the diaphragm caused the coroner to conclude that Anne died not knowing she was pregnant.

"Disappointed?" Lauren said, misinterpreting my tone.

"About her? No. Considering the cost, I hope she really enjoyed it. No, the sigh was about something else. I think I'm getting jaded. Enough. No more work talk. Thanks for your suggestion about the coroner. I'll see your pretty face at seven-fifteen tomorrow morning."

"You're welcome. Good night, Alan. Dream about me."

I hoped I would.

I didn't.

I dreamed about Michael McClelland. And then I lay awake.

Wondering if I should transfer him to someone else. Wondering if I was still in any mental condition to do this work.

Tomorrow morning, 9:10 A.M. Mexicana Airlines. Cabo San Lucas.

Thank God.

138

Seventeen

The Volkswagen minibus from the airport at San José del Cabo dropped Lauren and me and our spartan luggage at the stone portico of the Hotel Cabo San Lucas, which was perched on the rock and sand above Chileno Bay.

Viewed from the cliffs above, the sandy beach of Chileno Bay formed the profile of a proud eagle with spread wings. The crystalline waters of the Sea of Cortés sparkled in brash tropical light and were brushed by breezes that varied endlessly, washing gently from the narrow peninsular sea or blowing boldly over the hills that fenced the Pacific.

Our one-bedroom villa topped a bluff just off the southern tip of the cove. A terrace adjacent to the cottage was shaded in northwest light, its southern wall a ten-foot expanse of porous ivory-and-pink-tinted rock flanked by sickly palms and scraggly bougainvillea in terra-cotta pots. The patio bordered a small kidney-shaped pool, apparently just for our use. The view was south and east over the spare landscape; the volcanic terrain — rocky promontories, sand, and barely vegetated desert — appeared to have been just snatched from the sea.

Our early afternoon arrival had almost interfered with Lauren's siesta. While she slept, I sat alone on the stone deck overlooking the bay, a Bohemia from the minibar sweating away its chill in my hand. My previous visits to

Los Cabos had taken me to the Solmar, a miniature canyon and a world away from the sleepy town of Cabo San Lucas and its adjacent port. The Solmar had never cost me more than sixty dollars a night. I was wrestling with discomfort at my suspicion that Lauren's nap alone would use up our first sixty dollars at this elegantly aging beauty of a hotel. I reminded myself that we were on vacation, that Lauren was probably going to insist on paying for the room, finished the beer, and began to seep into the serenity and safety of foreign soil, no beepers, and plentiful *cerveza*.

Later, Lauren was collapsed on a leather chair on the terrace when I returned from a swim in the bay. "It's hot," she said. "Whatever happened to ocean breezes?"

I kissed the top of her head, slid open the heavy glass doors behind us, and pushed open all the windows and slatted shutters on the west side of the cottage. A gecko, no bigger than my finger, clung to the shady side of the sill. Momentarily, a strong, tepid breeze washed away the stale air.

"It's a Pacific wind, now. In the morning it'll come off the bay," I offered, trying to sound reassuring, not really knowing what I was talking about.

The breeze seemed to brighten her spirits. She rolled a cold bottle of Penafiel orange soda across her forehead and cheeks. I grabbed another beer from the minibar.

"Well, Doctor, what does today hold?"

"Do you fish? Supposed to be great marlin fishing."

Lauren raised her eyebrows higher than nature intended and shook her head.

"No whales to watch this time of year," I said. She mimed a frown.

"Actually, my sweet, I come to Cabo because there's nothing to do. No shopping worth mentioning. No Mayan or Incan sights to explore. There's nothing to do but sleep, and read, and swim, and eat, and drink. There is tennis. But we brought no rackets. And some provocative desert. But we rented no car." I paused to consider whether she was enjoying my speech and sipped from my beer. "There is sex as well. But wait" — I pulled out the waistband of my shorts and peered in — "he did bring his genitals."

She laughed. "That's sick. Awful."

"Thank you." I bowed from the waist, pouring beer on my foot.

We had late afternoon *antojitos* in the hotel bar, swam in our private pool in the late day sun, and ate a light dinner facing equatorial waters from the hotel's outdoor restaurant. Later, back on our terrace, we sipped bitter Mexican brandy on ice and luxuriated in the sweet mix of ocean and desert air.

Sometime before ten she yawned, left the cradle of my arm, kissed me full on the mouth, and said, "I'm tired, good night." She closed the door of the only bedroom behind her.

I waited an hour for the door to reopen. No invitation was forthcoming.

The next morning I woke early and tugged the cushioned sofa that had been my bed onto the patio.

She said, "Alan." I turned to find her standing naked in the billowing curtains behind me.

Sex with Merideth had always been good. Certainly, neither of us would have listed it as a precipitating factor in our separation. We survived times when each of us yearned silently for the other to make an initiating caress, and we weathered storms when each of us feared our presumptive touches would be rebuffed. But mostly we relished leisurely, quiet episodes of fingers and

141

tongues and thrusts and counterthrusts and gasps and shudders. Sometimes our coupling was fast and furious and fingernailed, but those times were cleansing rains in generally sunny skies.

I'd been abstinent, though, a long time.

A step, and Lauren was beside me. Her long thin fingers raised me to my feet as though I were weightless. She slipped off my shorts and helped me raise my shirt above my head.

The hard tips of her breasts were what I felt first. Then her lips were soft on my neck. She entwined my fingers in hers and extended my arms down my sides. She moved closer, the firmness of the front of her legs, then the liquid fullness of her breasts, then a raised leg, the coarse heel scraping against the back of my knee, then hair against my thigh. I felt her wet. Her perfume drifted in with the breeze from the sea.

When she released my hands I traced the firm muscles of her back and then lightly scratched the swell of her breasts that escaped the compression of our chests. Her tongue was on my mouth, her lips and teeth first capturing, then releasing me.

I said something about a condom; she responded with a tongue in my ear and whispered something about a diaphragm.

The Chevy II we took into Cabo San Lucas for dinner was a mobile shrine. Plastic statues of saints, postcards of cathedrals, and crucifixes of Jesús Christo adorned the dashboard and visors of the dilapidated taxi. The driver dropped us at the restaurant on the bay in Cabo San Lucas without a word more than the negotiations over fare required.

Lauren and I ordered margaritas and asked for a plate

of limes to sour them further. She had a small, whole red snapper, floating in olive oil, wine, and a bushel of garlic. I had grilled shrimp. The thatched dining room was open to the bay, thirty yards away, and the beauty of the setting offset the chef's propensity to overcook.

When the plates were cleared we ordered coffee, hoping to find something other than Mexico's ubiquitous powdered Nescafé.

"I have MS," Lauren said.

"Excuse me," I replied, her words not registering.

She touched a clear-lacquered fingernail to the cleft between her nose and upper lip and gazed left toward land's end. She raised her eyes to search the moonless sky.

"I have multiple sclerosis." The words were softer. She had used much of her resolve, it seemed, to say it the first time.

"Oh, God," I said in a quiet voice. "I'm sorry, Lauren."

"Don't be. I've known for a couple of years. I didn't just find out."

"I don't know what to say."

"Please don't feel like you need to say anything. I just wanted you to know."

The waiter brought coffee. His *guayabera* was stained and wrinkled, sweat beaded on his forehead and drenched the white cotton under his arms. The coffee was Nescafé. The cream was milk. The milk was suspect.

My eyes were wide open. I exhaled through my mouth. "Tell me about it, the MS."

"You know what it is?" She seemed to want a reply. I shrugged and nodded simultaneously. She continued, "It's a demyelinating disease of the white matter of the central nervous system." The lawyer had become a doctor.

I nodded. "I knew that much, I guess. I also think I know that there's no cure. And that it's progressive."

It was Lauren's turn to nod. Sadly.

"For me," she began, "the disease started about five or

143

six years ago. I think. I had a brief episode of blindness. Ten minutes. No more than that. In my left eye. It got better. I told my gynecologist about it, and he told me not to worry — I had probably popped a blood vessel or something. Then, about a year and a half later I had some paresthesias, tingling and numbness, on my right side. They were annoying, lasted almost a month. I didn't see anybody for that. Finally they went away.

"And then . . ." Lauren looked at me only intermittently, very intent on her story and her words. "And then, two years ago May, I got dizzy. Hold-on-to-the-walls dizzy. The-room-is-tipping-and-the-bed-is-moving dizzy. I ended up seeing an internist who sent me to a neurologist who took a long history, discovered some problems in my reflexes, some difference in color saturation between my eyes, and told me he thought I had MS. A spinal tap and an MRI, a magnetic scan, confirmed it.

"I seem to have the exacerbating-remitting form of the disease. That means I have exacerbations every once in a while, then full or near full recovery, and then more good health. The episodes of symptoms can last days or weeks or months. Some symptoms never go away. My vertigo has never totally gone away."

"Why didn't you tell me before tonight?"

"I don't advertise it."

"That's not fair, Lauren. I don't think I'm just anybody to you."

Her voice changed in intensity. The courtroom remembered. "Okay, you tell me what's fair. This isn't AIDS, Alan, you can't catch it from me. I have no moral duty to inform — you or anyone else. Telling you weeks ago would've been for your benefit, not mine. So you could've decided whether to hang around with a sick woman. And you wouldn't have seen me. You would've seen somebody like me with a disease that's misunderstood and distasteful. Now you have to deal with me. I think I'm somebody to you. And that somebody has multiple sclerosis." As she leaned forward to make her point, her hair formed a grotto around the forgotten coffee mug.

"You don't place much faith in me."

"Faith." She shook her head, slowly, back and forth. "Last year I saw a guy I really fell for. In love, from moment one. A personal injury attorney." She filled her lungs with air and exhaled loudly through her mouth. "Someday I'll tell you about litigators. . . . Anyway, after we had spent every waking and sleeping moment together for two weeks, I told him about my MS. He left my bed the next morning, didn't return my call that afternoon, and left a cardboard box on my doorstep that evening with a few things I'd left at his house. No goodbye." Tears welled in the corners of her eyes. "Not a damn word. Yes, you tell me about faith. My neurologist told me at the beginning, very matter-of-fact, that men leave women with MS. I believe him.

"You want faith," she challenged, "earn it."

The cab ride back to the hotel was silent. The miles passed slowly. I pondered what had happened and was irritated at being set up. Not by her guilt-by-association attack at dinner, but by the timing of her announcement. On this trip. Right after we'd made love the first time.

Back in the villa, I told her I was angry.

"You probably have every right to be," she said, "but I didn't plan anything. After making love this morning, I knew the time had come to give you the chance to decide whether or not you could stay with me. And yes, now I do get to watch you react for a few days. That's probably to my advantage."

"It feels manipulative."

"My response, Alan, is 'Too bad.' You may want to homogenize your response to all this for my benefit. I'd rather see how you really feel about it." With those words she walked resolutely to the bedroom, leaving the door ajar.

I left the couch where it was and slept outside on the terrace, where her scent clung to the pillow. I wasn't sure whether the cracked door had been an invitation made or a trap set. My best guess was that she wasn't sure, either.

The next morning, Saturday, I suggested, paradoxically, a visit to Lover's Beach, a stone's throw from the land's end. We hired a boat at the Hotel Hacienda in Cabo San Lucas and visited the famous arched entrance to Baja before landing on the Sea of Cortés shore of the beach. The narrow strand had both bay and ocean exposures and a sandy knoll between them where both were visible. The Pacific was raucous, waves reaching high and crashing in shallow water, the wind-borne spray a relief in the developing heat.

We sat back to back on the knoll, Lauren facing the Pacific, me the bay. The temperature was becoming oppressive. I recalled Lauren's telling me the night before that heat was one of the aggravations to the fatigue that was a constant feature of her illness.

My concern for her evaporated as I watched a couple approach from the shallow tidepools lining the entrance to the Sea of Cortés. A shiver tempered the heat radiating off my skin.

The young woman in the red-and-yellow maillot was unfamiliar. The man, however, I knew. It was Michael McClelland.

He approached as though we were running into each other on the sidewalk outside my office. "Hello," he said. Lauren made a half turn, the sun in her eyes.

"Hello." I returned the salutation.

"On holiday? Out of town again?" Michael's throaty almost whisper was the same timbre as the hissing ocean spray. He and the striking blonde continued their pace to the Pacific shore. She left us with a whimsical smile and a shy wave, he with a smirk.

I said, "Good-bye," to their retreating backs.

"Who's that?" Lauren asked.

"Just somebody I know."

"Right. Let me guess. If it was her you seemed to know, I'd guess she was an old girlfriend. Since it's him, I'll guess he's a patient."

"Very good, Sherlock." I sighed.

"Your muscles got very tense," she offered.

"You ready to go back?" I asked in diversion.

She hesitated, looked again at the ocean, and said, sounding unsure, "Sure." She took my hand as we moved down to the sparkling bay.

She tugged on my arm to assure my attention and asked, "Do your patients always follow you on vacation?"

The tension between us continued to ease as the day progressed. I forced thoughts of Lauren's illness to chase away the intrusive image of Michael McClelland's arrival in Baja California.

"How does it affect your work? The MS?"

"I'm blessed there, actually. Roy Peterson, the DA, his wife has MS. He's been great. He covers for me whenever he can, gave me an office big enough for a couch so I can sleep when I need to."

"I thought you said that men leave women who have multiple sclerosis."

"Most men do, yes."

"But there are exceptions?"

"Yes, dear man, there are exceptions."

"So most people at work don't know?"

"Just Ray and my secretary. Maybe Ray's first assistant. I've never told him, but he acts like he might know."

She thought for a minute before going on. "The worst part is the dizziness, the vertigo. So far I've blundered my way through the times when it was almost unbearable. A couple of times I've asked for a recess in court because I just couldn't go on. I'm sure the judges thought it had something to do with blood dripping down my thighs or particularly bad cramps or something. But I've gotten away with it."

We were back on our stone patio, both wet from a swim in the villa's private pool. I kissed the back of her neck and folded my arms around her from behind.

"This is difficult for me, Lauren. I'm not done processing it. So far I feel very sad for you, for what it must be like. I am also scared for me. I don't know what all this means for us. That's the part that I'm tripping over."

The fingers of her left hand caressed my face, and I heard her say, "Yes."

I slept with her for the first time that night, both of us naked in the desert heat. We touched and kissed, eyes open, genitals off limits, for a long time before we felt assured that a bridge had been built to span the chasm that had quaked between us. In the end, sex was sweaty and loud.

Afterward she slept. I marveled at her beauty. Her chest rose with each breath. But a bee buzzed around my head, distracting me from joining her in sleep.

The bee was Michael McClelland.

What the fuck was he doing in Baja?

The flight back to Denver was buffeted by thunderstorm-spawned turbulence as we approached Stapleton. I wondered if this particular atmospheric disturbance met Michael McClelland's criteria for a severe storm.

We had left the Subaru in the airport long-term lot, and Lauren waited in the terminal while I rode the shuttle to the lot to retrieve the car. I found her sitting on the luggage outside baggage claim exactly where she'd said she'd wait. I drove back to Boulder. Lauren's fatigue was palpable as I dropped her off at her house and headed back to Spanish Hills.

Cicero came bounding up when I dragged myself from the car. I grabbed my bags and walked in to the insistence of a ringing phone. I toyed with ignoring it but answered it instead.

"Do you have a patient named Gretchen Kravner?" The voice was a measured version of the one that had whispered into my ear the night before. The question was like a punch in the kidney.

"What is it?" I managed.

"She's dead, Alan. Murdered."

I felt pressure in my throat and wondered whether the taste would be bile or vomit. Tears and rage conspired to force blood to my eyes.

"Tell me, Lauren, please."

"Last night, apparently, someone broke into her house, maybe a burglary, and killed her after a struggle. They found her body less than an hour ago, and I caught the call a minute after I put on the beeper. Sam Purdy's at the scene, remembered you, told me one of your bills was sitting open on her dresser." She was breathless and silent for a moment, then said, "We'll get whoever did it." The concept of justice hadn't edged its way past more primitive stirrings in my mind. My knuckles were mottled pink on the receiver that I choked in the fist in front of my face. "I need to go to the scene, sweet man. Okay? I'll call you later. . . . Alan? Honey, you all right?"

"Sure. Please. Call me later."

"You're not all right, are you? Listen, I promise I'll call."

And she hung up.

In case I had any doubt, the vacation was officially over.

Part Two

The Baccarat Turtle

Eighteen

A morning chill presaged autumn. The air felt light, crisp. The warm blanket of Mexican heat that had comforted me for five days was only a memory; endless brash Baja light was supplanted by the dwindling rays of the abbreviated high country summer.

I ground some frozen coffee beans and started brewing a half pot. A bosc pear that shouldn't have been soft yet, wasn't. I tried for a moment to remember how to ripen pears in brown paper bags, but igniting my resistant neural synapses proved too troublesome. The hard, grainy mouthful of pear was particularly distasteful; I spat it into the sink.

The tiny blond hairs on top of my little finger caught in the rubber band of the *Daily* as I unwrapped it. Gretchen Kravner's murder was the story at the side of the front page.

The local paper would soon assign a reporter to me full-time; I was developing into my own beat.

The article ran a full column. A few facts were sprinkled about, but the clipped paragraphs were mostly stuffed with filler about what wasn't yet known. Fortunately, for me, included in what wasn't yet known was the fact that the murdered woman was my patient. I reserved little hope that my tangential tie to Gretchen would remain unknown.

Strangled. Evidence of a struggle. Interrupted burglary or a rape. Autopsy results not available. The reporter raised questions about connections to a series of nighttime burglaries that had plagued the Wonderland Hill and Sunshine Canyon neighborhoods over recent months. The police would not comment on possible similarities.

With the remote control, I flicked on Channel 9 news in Denver. I watched as a medical reporter tried to provide, without offending anybody over their morning coffee, an informational update on the use of cryogenics for hemorrhoid treatment. She was so oblique that the ignorant could have been left with the impression that hemorrhoids were a disease of the foot. At the bottom of the hour the morning anchor switched to a minicam the station had live outside the crime scene. The reporter's copy sounded like a digest of what I had just read in the paper. It probably was.

But Merideth would have been proud of her old crew. The camera angle was carefully chosen, the handsome young reporter seemingly suspended like Peter Pan against the backdrop of Gretchen's expensive home, with the dramatic profile of the Flatirons knifing to the sky a couple of miles to the south.

Gretchen's house was a cedar contemporary ranch at the southern edge of Knollwood, an enclave of lavish homes of varying architectural distinction that bordered Boulder's western greenbelt. At that early hour her home was shaded by the looming rock formation that was Knollwood's centerpiece. Yellow tape ribboned off the screen in all directions. A uniformed cop stood by the driveway guarding the crime scene. I punched the remote and switched off the set.

Lauren hadn't called back the night before. Diane had phoned; somehow she had found out about the murder. She had asked how I was and joked that she was beginning to wonder about her own safety. I told her I was numb, that it seemed reasonable that she be worried.

The cold air of the bathroom assaulted me as I stepped out of the shower. I couldn't remember whether I had shampooed my hair. It was wet. Was it clean? I said, "Fuck it," to myself and slid on some warm-ups and old running shoes. I drank more coffee and read about the cuts the Broncos made to get down to the final roster limits. I had a growing empathy for those who had failed to make the cut.

The phone rang.

"Hi, honey." And after a pause, "It's Merideth."

I said, "I know. I know. How are you?" But I hadn't known.

"I'm fine," she said, poignant concern in her voice. "I just read about a Boulder murder on the AP wire. I had this weird premonition that—"

"Not weird. Accurate," I said. "She was one of my patients."

Merideth whispered, "My God," and fell silent for a moment. "What's going on, Alan?"

"I wish I knew, sweetie. I wish I knew. Just be glad you were only married to me. It could be worse. If you'd been seeing me in treatment, your life would be in danger."

She corrected me. *"Are* married to you. Not were. Anyway, that's not funny. This is just a string of bad luck, babe. It doesn't have anything to do with you." I could picture her as she spoke. Her left earring was on the table in front of her. She twirled the phone cord with her right hand. I recalled her gestures and her smells as though she had left me yesterday. "What can I do for you? Would you like to come out here for a while? Just get away? I can't travel now, but you're welcome to come here."

"That's a tempting offer. I may take you up on it. But I think I'll let the dust settle a bit first."

We chatted, like the intimates that we once were, for a few more minutes. She asked about our dog. I hadn't told her Cicero had been kidnapped and defaced. I had pledged to take good care of her and wasn't ready to admit frailty in that area, too.

Almost every time I talked to her I felt so good that I wondered why we were getting divorced.

Merideth said to call if I needed anything. I promised vacantly that I would. I hung up and called Lauren and heard her sweet voice on her recorder. I decided not to call her office. She'd said she'd call.

I changed from warm-ups into cycling clothes and hammered the pedals hard from the moment I left the house. When I turned onto Arapahoe I passed one of Gretchen's husband's restaurants. It was supposed to look like a country inn from somewhere in generic Scandinavia. The simple Victorian lines of pioneer Boulder architecture were apparently not very marketable. Curiosity and hunger almost succeeded in conspiring to compel me to stop for breakfast. Objectivity prevailed. The guy owned four or five restaurants and bars in Boulder—did I really expect him to be standing behind the counter at this one at eight o'clock on a weekday morning?

Since the night before I'd been wondering if Douglas Kravner, the Jerk, had killed his wife. Based on what Gretchen had told me, he certainly had motive. She was blackmailing him. But the police would find that out. He couldn't be so naïve as to think that motive would stay undiscovered. Maybe he killed her out of rage, not self-protection. Maybe he had gone over to her house to talk about the divorce settlement, got enraged at her stubbornness, and killed her. That made more sense.

Or maybe it had been a random murder. An interrupted burglary. Or rape. Boulder averaged only one or two murders a year; in a bad year there might be five or six. Few were of the stranger killing stranger variety, though. Statistically the most likely person to murder a wife was a husband.

The aah-ooo-gah of a tractor trailer jolted me from

my musing. I was in the middle of the northbound lane on Seventy-fifth going a good fifteen miles an hour. When I turned to apologize to the driver of the rig, I was greeted with him flipping me off and blasting his howitzer of a horn again. I shifted the Bianchi, feeling the smooth glide of the Italian derailleur as it responded to my fingers, hammered hard, ass in the air, and left the fucker in the dust. I turned left on the next side road. While I relished my acceleration advantage, I wasn't quite fool enough to think I could maintain it for long.

An hour later, back home, the digital readout of my pager showed no calls during my absence. Lauren's failure to phone was annoying. Before long, however, I knew she had been thinking of me.

I answered the phone, heard the detached voice ask if I was available, and suspected that Lauren had given Detective Purdy my home phone number. I also suspected that propriety would prevent her from calling me before the police had completed any part of the investigation that included me.

"I am calling in regard to —" Papers rustled. The victims' names all ran together after a while.

I decided to assist. "Gretchen Kravner."

"You heard? Good. Can I come by to talk with you about her? I understand she was your patient."

Yeah, I thought, I specialize in the barely predeceased. "When, Detective?"

"Now. I hoped, now."

"That's fine. I live at — you know where I live."

"Yeah, I know," he said, and hung up the phone.

The white sedan kicked up a lot of dust as Purdy steered it onto the shoulder of the lane above my house. In profile, I could see his head was down, probably checking something in his little notebook. After an absentminded pass beyond the driveway, he doubled back and drove down to the house.

I waited for him outside.

"Hello, Detective."

"Hello, Doctor." Purdy propped his left hand on the open door to lift his large frame off the seat. His sport coat rode up his back, sharp creases evidence of a hundred wearings between dry cleanings.

"Been a while," he said. I just nodded.

"Nice view up here. See the mountains real good," Purdy tried again.

"Thank you," I said, taking proprietary kudos for the central Rocky Mountains.

"May I come in?"

"Please." I stepped back and let him into the house. Cicero was being nice to him. No barks. I didn't interfere when she stuck her big snout into his balls.

In the living room, I grabbed my chair before he could usurp it. The chair that I offered him faced the mountains. I hoped it would distract him.

"This one isn't suicide, Doctor."

I didn't reply. I was in no mood for this interview, for this intrusion, or for the judgmental glare of some cop who wondered why my patients kept dying.

It crossed my mind, during the ensuing quiet, that with the right cop and the right psychologist, an entire interview could be conducted, or not conducted, in silence.

"Got any coffee?"

I marveled at his chutzpah. "Cream or sugar?"

"Two sugars," said Detective Purdy.

"I've thought it over, Detective, and I don't think I can talk to you about Gretchen." I raised a steaming mug to my lips and watched him gulp from the one in his left hand as if it were a cold beer on a July afternoon.

"She's dead, Doctor."

"But her confidentiality isn't. It becomes part of her estate." I was tempted to explain to him that I had been

158

getting a lot of unofficial continuing legal education on the topic lately.

The large man sighed. Exasperation with the technicalities of the judicial process was an unwelcome, but familiar, companion.

"I just want the same kind of information you gave me about that other patient, the one who killed herself." Cordial had decomposed into hardly pleasant.

"That was my mistake. I shouldn't have told you what I did. I won't repeat the error."

"Jesus. I don't want to know about her conflicts with her mother. I don't care when she lost her virginity. I don't even fucking care about her goddamn dreams. I want to catch the guy who murdered her. That's all. Gimme a break." I recognized the now familiar don't-be-an-asshole tone.

"Detective. Let me call somebody and get some advice on this, and I'll get back to you later in the day. I won't say anything about Gretchen until then."

He didn't thank me for the coffee before he left.

Within a half hour the phone rang again. I hoped it was Jon Younger returning the call I'd made the moment the detective was out the door.

"God, you can be a pain in the ass."

"Hi, Lauren." There was no continuing evidence of concern for my well-being in her tone.

"I just talked to Gretchen Kravner's mother. In Cleveland. She's the sole heir and executor. She says to talk to us. I've got her number if you want to hear it for yourself. Here's Purdy. Jesus, Alan, is this really necessary?" She dictated the long-distance number and handed the phone to Purdy.

I heard the detective's voice again before I could formulate a rhetorical reply to her rhetorical inquiry.

"Hello again, Doctor. Twenty minutes, okay?"

"Fine." My front teeth scraped the skin below my bottom lip as I said it and hung up.

I filled his coffee mug when I heard the car outside.

I was tempted by an impulse to insist that I have the authorization to release information in writing. I would be within my rights. Lauren would be incensed if I did. What was confusing was whether that was an argument for or against being a stickler for legalities. My ultimate decision to go ahead and cooperate with the deputy district attorney was a surprisingly conflicted one.

Purdy took the mug from my hand as he walked in the door and proceeded to the chair I was in before. His presence had become mundane to Cicero, who acknowledged his reentry with one raised ear.

"So." He put down the mug, scratched the side of his thick neck with the index finger of his left hand, and reached into his coat for a notebook. "What can you tell me?"

"What would be helpful, Detective?" My words were much more conciliatory than my voice.

"Know anybody who would want to kill her?"

"I thought it looked like a burglary?"

"That's the problem. It looks like a burglary. Some stuff was moved around, trashed. Her wallet thrown open, money gone, credit cards gone. If it was a burglar, it was an amateur. We're not sure it was. So we're being thorough, and considering the possibility that we're dealing with somebody who thinks cops are stupid. Which unfortunately doesn't narrow the field too much."

"Have you talked to her attorney, Elizabeth Warren?"

"Outta town. We're trying to track her down."

"Her husband. You need to talk to her husband."

Purdy just waited for me to continue. I appreciated his interviewing skills.

"She was blackmailing him in her divorce proceedings. Blackmailing is probably too strong a word. He did some illegal stock things some years back, and she was using that as leverage to get a better settlement. I'm sure that Elizabeth Warren knows more about it than I do."

"Doesn't sound like blackmail is too strong a word."

"That's your arena, Detective. Not mine."

"How was she doing with you? You know, in . . . whatever you call what you do."

I swallowed in an attempt to ignore the dig. "Very successfully."

"Seeing anybody? Dating?"

When he asked, I wondered if he remembered our last interview and my embarrassing ignorance about Karen Hart's dating habits. He probably did.

"Yes, she was. A marketing somebody from Ball Aerospace. Frank. I don't know his last name. And a guy named Robin. I think he's a commuter airline pilot. I don't know what airline. She wasn't serious about either of them. They were just guys she met at the Broker."

"Were they serious about her?"

Good question, Detective. "If I had to guess, I would guess no."

"Anybody else she was having troubles with?"

"No. Just her husband. She isn't the — she wasn't the type of woman to have a lot of enemies. She gave in to people, had a hard time standing up for herself. She got used by many people in little ways. By her husband in big ones."

"A victim," said Purdy.

"A Victim. Capital V."

"Her husband beat her?" Another good question.

"Yes and no. There were some times when he beat her up pretty good early in their marriage. Not the last few years, though. But don't get me wrong — she was a battered wife. She finally left him after he pulled her hair one too many times. But most of his abuse was domination and criticism and interrogation. He needed to know everything she was doing. He was intimidating. Just a bully. In its own way, every bit as devastating for her as if he beat her every day."

"How'd she manage to get so feisty with him in this divorce?"

"With my help." As I said it, I wondered whether the statement was self-congratulatory or self-accusatory. Purdy just nodded.

"Her last session with you was when?"

"Last Tuesday. Four o'clock, her regular appointment. Nothing unusual about it. She talked a lot about how she felt that the end of the fight with her husband was close at hand. She felt they were on the verge of a settlement. Nothing remarkable that I can remember. My notes are in the office."

"We'll need her file. The whole thing. A subpoena is in the works. If you think of anything else, give me a call. And by the way, the prosecutor sends her regards." A faint outline of a smile graced his sour face.

As he walked to the door, he stopped and turned and said, "She was ready to get a grand jury together to get your records. By the end of the week you would have had to choose between silence and jail, Doctor."

I parried. "I assume, Detective, that along with your subpoena you'll provide me with a written copy of the release you received over the phone from Ms. Kravner's mother."

He glared and smiled simultaneously. He was a bully by training, not demeanor, and had grudging respect for someone who would stand up to him.

"Sure, we can do that. I'll even forward the request to the deputy DA personally. She, I'm certain, will be tickled by it. And enamored of its source."

Cicero pranced beside me as I followed Purdy out to his car and watched him drive away.

Nineteen

Instinctively, late that afternoon, I looked at my watch: Tuesday, 4:45.

On any normal Tuesday, Gretchen's time would be up.

My eyes teared. I stood, walked into the kitchen, rummaged around the back of the refrigerator for a half bottle of champagne once set aside for a long forgotten celebration, popped the cork, and poured a glass. Flute in hand, I returned to the living room, to the company of my once radically coiffured dog, and toasted the sunset and Gretchen Kravner.

In the dark, that night, I sat listening to old songs. Joni Mitchell. I played "I Don't Know Where I Stand" a half dozen times despite an annoying click in the second verse. *Music from Big Pink* by The Band.

I sipped more wine.

Not much left to feel. I found Janis Joplin's version of "Nothing Left to Lose" and recalled the simplicity of my adolescence when four-measure poets sang about my life on AM radio.

I walked out into the night to steal a tomato from Adrienne's garden. Peter was picking beans and peas for stir-fry.

He had been giving it a lot of thought and had decided that the collar shaving of my dog might be the result of unexplained forces, like the almost-surgical mutilation of cattle genitals that sporadically puzzled eastern Colorado ranchers.

When Peter was in one of his "bizarre universe" moods, I never disagreed with him. Out loud, anyway. I usually counted on Adrienne to be close enough to fulfill her marital compact and steer him to less controversial ground. She was nowhere to be found, however, so Peter and I spent ten chilly minutes discussing the wisdom and efficacy of higher beings communicating with us through mammal butchery. I got a few tomatoes and an eggplant that I didn't want along with a recipe for turning them all into a miraculous soup.

My dog and I walked home. I made two grilled cheese sandwiches with Adrienne's tomatoes and coarse mustard and gave one to Cicero. She had previously refused to respond to my queries about her experiences during the dognapping and maintained her silence while listening politely to my growing suspicions that maybe all these things happening in my life were not merely coincidence. Evidence to link the disparate disasters eluded me, but Cicero was not a stickler for objectivity.

Polite canine attention became intense interest as she realized I hadn't finished my sandwich. Without a half bottle of champagne bubbles causing my otherwise acute perceptive skills to misfire, I probably would have realized that she was looking upon me with the same self-serving attention that I had awarded Peter in the garden as I coveted his wife's tomatoes.

No matter. Cicero listened as I talked about Lauren. Clinical acumen is rarely heightened by alcohol. But then neither is judgment, so I barely downshifted as I moved to an assessment of whether Lauren's ambivalent treatment of me had to do with her own problems with commitment and intimacy. Fearful of sounding like a guest on the afternoon TV talk show circuit, I couched this in terms of ego boundaries and ego defenses and dropped in some Kohutian reflections. The dog's interest waned as my sandwich continued to disappear.

She was curled on what I now considered her Tabriz by the time I turned the discussion to multiple sclerosis, fears of rejection, ego ideal, body integrity, and the like. I expounded on my tentative conclusion that Lauren had chosen the personal injury lawyer because she knew he couldn't deal with her illness and that she was terrified of me because maybe I could. Cicero seemed to concur.

Maybe I could. But did I want to?

My discomfort with the question pushed through the alcohol with the fluidity of an airliner finding clear skies about the clouds.

Sleep eluded me as I made the transition from dark living room to dark bedroom, from chair to bed, from old albums to old movies. Cicero slept fine.

I finally slept. But not well.

Michael McClelland could keep me awake. Lauren Crowder could keep me awake. Merideth, after all these months, could still keep me awake. Gretchen Kravner, no doubt, would start to keep me awake. But Karen Hart could merely interfere, turning rest into restless. And that despite the fact that she was the nuclear threat, the only one of the lot that could blow the earth out from beneath me.

That night was Karen Hart's night.

Mostly, I didn't believe it was going to come down. I wondered why I was not more debilitated, and it was because I didn't yet believe it could happen to me.

Worst case. Worst case was the Karen Hart thing going to trial, me losing, being smacked with a settlement that wiped out my insurance coverage and all my financial reserves. Worst case was the burned black brand in my professional flesh, the mark as an abuser of patients. Worst case was Diane, and Merideth, and Adrienne, and Peter, and Jon, and yes, Lauren, acting like it was true and the subsequent isolation of having no one believe me. Worst case was going to jail for the felony of sexually abusing a patient.

Invisibility was the worst case.

Invisibility meant becoming transparent, not from lack of substance, but because others chose to see through me. Like the homeless on the Downtown Boulder Mall. Some of them hadn't volunteered to be homeless, but most days I walked by all of them, not seeing, unable and perhaps, yes, unwilling to distinguish the painfully destitute from the professional panhandlers and volitional street people. I, too, was beginning to taste what incipient invisibility was like; apparently I was already altering my molecular structure. Faces that once smiled in greeting and mouths that once formed "Hello" stayed immobile or managed only cursory nods as I passed. I checked at times to see whether leaves crackled beneath my feet and wondered if breezes bothered to part over me.

Other times my presence could catalyze events. I could enter a room and mute conversations. I could stifle laughs. I could precipitate departures and cause the remembering of forgotten engagements elsewhere.

Worst case was unimaginable.

I couldn't believe it would happen or I couldn't go on. So I lived in the relative luxury of disbelief. I told myself that something was going to break.

Most nights I didn't sleep well. Sometimes I barely slept at all. My weight had dropped ten pounds. Food was something I always thought I wanted, but getting it in my mouth was a chore.

Nights I did sleep, I dreamed of treading water in an immense sea, swells passing beneath me. Against a dark sky, a big set of waves mounted against the horizon—the Karen Hart mess, Gretchen's murder, my divorce, Lauren's ambivalence, my dying practice. In the foggy myth of dreams I just watched the waves mount, as though they would never arrive. If they did, I guess I was convinced I could dive under the first ten-footer and get outside the line of breakers. Certain they wouldn't get me.

Awake, I believed it all the time, and I didn't believe it for a minute.

Twenty

An artist I was pushing too fast in treatment once admonished me that I "rush to get paint on canvas. Sometimes," he said, "you need to spend time with the preparation. You can't paint before the gesso is right."

It was a lesson I was trying to apply to my therapy with Michael McClelland as I waited for him to arrive for his four o'clock appointment the next day. My stomach was a miniature geothermal resource as I anticipated the venom that would be associated with the discussion of our brief encounter in Mexico.

The *Daily* had not yet linked Gretchen Kravner to me. But her picture had been in that morning's edition, and I had steeled myself for the likelihood that Michael McClelland, who didn't seem to miss much, had made the connection with the woman he'd seen in the waiting room almost a month before.

The impulse to defend myself with him was unfamiliar; I was rarely defensive with patients. I vowed to fight it. Let him be angry with me. Let it be safe here. Focus on the acting-out.

I picked up one of the crystal turtles from the coffee table. Its heft and clarity were reassuring. Like psychotherapy, the pace of the tortoise was slow and steady. Question: How long does psychotherapy take? Answer: As long as it takes to read a book. It depends on the length of the book and how fast you read.

The vibration of my pager on my left hip preceded the illumination of the light that would signal Michael McClelland's arrival. I pulled the small black pager from its plastic saddle and pushed the buttons necessary to retrieve the message from memory. The call was from Michael McClelland—a cancellation. The liquid crystals instructed me to call the answering service for more details.

After using the same answering service for almost five years, one would expect that I might occasionally recognize a voice on the other end. No such luck. This voice was more efficient and businesslike than most and read from a computer screen as I heard the muted clicks of her ministrations to the keyboard. "He says that he needs to cancel. He's on his way to Florida to fly into Hurricane Frances, then is giving a paper in San Francisco, so he can't reschedule. He'll see you at his regular time next week."

I told her thanks and felt my abdominal muscles relax. Michael McClelland really did study severe storms.

Morning Edition had done a report on Hurricane Frances that morning. She was an especially rapidly developing storm that had matured from tropical depression to Category Three hurricane in only twenty-four hours. She was still strengthening and threatening to veer north toward the Atlantic coast of Florida and the Carolinas.

My own storm had a much longer life span. It seemed to be bouncing around the coastline of my life like a silver orb in a pinball machine, inflicting moderate damage, returning to water for renewed vigor, and picking another exposed spot. What was bothering me was my lingering suspicion that this was indeed one ferocious storm and not a series of haphazard meteorological events.

Merideth, Karen, Anne, and Gretchen. Maybe Merideth could be eliminated from the list. What connected the others? Me. I was the only common denominator. I saw them all for psychotherapy. One death was a suicide, one a traffic accident, and now, apparently, one a homicide. So far only one lawsuit had been filed. Only one allegation of sexual impropriety had been made.

The three patients had no threads tying them together. They lived in the same medium-size town, but their lives had nothing in common. I should know. All my musings swirled down the funnel to me and my office. I was the only commonality. And I didn't know where I fit at all.

I walked down the hall to Diane's open door. We had missed our lunch that afternoon so she could cover an emergency.

"You done for the day?"

Diane responded, "Yeah, I am. My last appointment just canceled."

"Are you up for a drink, or dinner?"

She hesitated, her round eyes and full mouth co-operating in an exaggerated squint. "I'm not sure it's that safe to be a female in your company."

"I know what you mean. I don't find the thought amusing, though. It's part of what I want to talk to you about. Are you willing to risk it? I promise that we'll only go to brightly lit places full of witnesses."

"Are you buying?" she asked.

"For this consultation, the corporation is buying."

170

"Then the answer is yes. I want grilled fish at Winston's."

"You don't ask for very much."

"I know. Everybody says I need to work on my assertiveness."

We walked over to Pearl and through the west end to the mall. Summer lingered, and the late summer crowds, minus the tourists, kept the area busy. The outdoor cafes and bars were crowded with Boulder's young professionals relaxing after work. Diane said hello to at least three people I didn't know as we moved slowly across Broadway before turning north on Thirteenth to the Boulderado Hotel.

The carefully restored late-nineteenth-century lobby of the Boulderado was cool and quiet. A few people lingered on velvet settees, reading papers or just browsing under the stained-glass canopy of the beautiful room. We moved across the room to the restaurant, asked the blond receptionist for a non-smoking booth, and followed her to the table.

"Is the corporation buying a bottle of wine tonight?" I held up the wine list.

"Just a glass. Maybe two."

"If you think it'll be two, the president of the corporation will spring for a bottle."

"Let me see." Diane pulled the booklet from my hand and gazed at it briefly. "Is the Sonoma-Cutrer Chardonnay too much? If sooo"—she flipped a page in the book—"then the Phelps Sauvignon Blanc."

The waiter waited. I told Diane she could have the chardonnay. She ordered it and he left.

I said, "You know that you have no concept of money?"

"Of course I don't. Raoul does. He has no sense of direction. I could find my way out of a forest with a blindfold on. We're perfect for each other." She looked at me with a mildly scolding glare. "Anyway, I just asked you to bring me here for dinner. . . ." She paused to taste the wine the waiter had dribbled into her glass. "Fine," she said, looking up and nodding for him to pour, "but you're the one—the virtually unemployed one, I might add—who agreed to pay for this feast. So who at this table has no concept of money?"

"Why do I still do this to myself? After eight years with you I continue to invite your color commentary on my life without ever, I mean ever, recognizing how I do it."

"You need me, sweetie. I keep you honest." Her grin was huge. "Nice wine. Maybe a little too much acid."

The bespectacled waiter returned after a while to take our food order. Diane ordered grilled roughy, I ordered calamari. She ordered ceviche to start. I passed on the appetizer. Rarely in my life have I had great squid, but on menus I was drawn to it inexorably and was almost universally disappointed in the texture, flavor, or abundance of grease. My learning curve was not always what it should have been.

For a few minutes we sipped wine in silence. Then Diane asked, "So is it different having a patient murdered than it is having one commit suicide?"

"That's a rude question, Diane."

"Somebody has to interfere with your galloping moroseness. If it takes bad taste, so be it." She sat back to make room for the small plate of ceviche.

"Yeah. It's different. My anger is more externalized this time. When Karen killed herself, I was more angry at myself. Wondering if I'd screwed up. I feel awful for Gretchen. Her death is like being hit by a car after finally being let out of jail for a crime she didn't commit." I raised my glass to my lips. "You have good taste in wine."

"I have good taste in everything. Partners included. Want some?" She held out a forkful of a stringy, unrecognizable creature of the deep.

"No thanks." Her vote of confidence had splashed away without note. "Remember when Cicero was barbered over the summer?" She nodded. "Peter thinks it was aliens. Like the mutilations where cattle genitals are removed."

"Peter would probably know. They probably came down and removed something from him, too." Peter and Raoul got along. Peter and I got along. Diane couldn't understand it.

"If all this isn't being perpetrated by a demented version of ET, do you think there's something other than coincidence involved in what's going on with my patients?"

"I must admit to wondering about that myself. Do you see any connections?"

"Just me. That I saw them all in treatment."

"Well, to the best of my knowledge, that excludes Merideth and Cicero from the pattern. You don't do wife and pet work on the side, do you? This is Boulder, after all."

We talked about a trip she and Raoul were planning to the Galápagos. The waiter cleared Diane's appetizer and brought the entrées. Diane took the bottle from the bucket before the waiter had a chance and refilled our glasses.

With surprising trepidation, I decided to ask the question doing calisthenics on my tongue. "So you

173

think this stuff going on, all the deaths, you think it's all unrelated? Seriously."

"Seriously? Probably unrelated. But I'm one of those believers in the interconnectedness of the universe. A butterfly flapping its wings in the Amazon eventually affecting our lives here in Tomorrowland. But I draw the line at aliens and heifer vulva. So until you come up with some evidence, I'll say probably unrelated." Diane dug into her fish. "You have any women left in your practice?"

"Five. But who's counting?"

"If any more die, then probably unrelated will become definitely related."

"That sounds like putting up a stop sign after the fourth pedestrian is killed in a crosswalk."

She shrugged her shoulders, looking at my plate. "You not gonna eat that?"

I picked up my fork, speared a ring of squid, and shoved it into my mouth. It was reminiscent of sautéed balloon lips. l should have had the ahi.

Twenty-one

"I think we're very different." My ears registered conclusion in Lauren's words, not merely observation.

"I disagree." I omitted "vehemently" from my meager protest.

"Look at where we live, Alan." From my living room, where we were sitting drinking coffee, it wasn't a difficult directive. Her little house was nestled in the border of green pine where Boulder nudged the Rockies a few miles from my home. "You're as far away from the mountains as you can be," she said. "You're a watcher. You always want perspective, a peripheral view, an expanse. My backyard is the mountains. I get close enough to things so that sometimes they block my view. I see a single tree from my living room. You see a hundred miles of mountains. My job consumes me when it's going well, yours when it's going badly. You maintain 'therapeutic distance' in your work; I don't, I go toe to toe with people.

"I feel those things," Lauren said, examining me carefully as she wet her lips with her tongue and then rested her teeth on the smooth painted skin of her lower lip, "that frightened Merideth. You're too settled, too sure of what you want. That's good and it's not good. There're other things besides home and kids. When I need to soar, Alan, I'm afraid you'll be ballast."

My experience told me that serious relationship conversations routinely have one or two rehearsed lines. The "soar/ballast" bit had my vote.

I broke the lock of her gaze and watched downy clumps of clouds spill over the honed edges of the hogbacks north of town. A cloudy day, no upslope winds to disturb the progress of autumn.

"I think you're frightened," I said.

"Bullshit. Of what?"

"Of me. I'm a man who isn't going to run because of your illness. I'm a man who can tolerate and even be amused by your overdetermined need to take care of yourself. I'm a man who is only mildly threatened by your appetite for control. I think you're frightened because we, you and me, are possible. The differences you're talking about are just the spice that makes things interesting."

Lauren's silence fueled my momentum. "This case—Gretchen's murder. It's just a vehicle you can use to ride away from me. So we have conflicting professional responsibilities. It doesn't need to be divisive. You do your job. I'll do mine."

"I've already apologized for not calling."

"Fine. Apology already accepted. But it's not the point."

"The point is that you don't want to hear what I'm saying. I'm saying that—"

"I hear you, Lauren. I'm trying to get you to look at what you're doing."

"If this is what it's like to argue with a shrink, then I'm glad I'm backing out."

"Backing out. Good description."

The knit dress she was wearing hugged her figure as she stood, her back to me. "I'm not saying we're

176

over, Alan." She tilted her head forward and brought her hands together behind her neck. "I'm saying I'm not sure. I want to slow down. Maybe see some other men. I'd still like to spend some time with you." Turning, she lowered her hands, trying to slide them into pockets that her dress lacked. The linen blazer with the truant pockets lay folded carefully over the arm of the sofa. "I don't think I can sleep with you again. For now, anyway."

"This is crap," I said to myself as if she had already left the room.

"Pardon me?"

"Nothing."

"I need to go. I have a meeting. Let's have dinner tomorrow night and talk some more. Okay?" The black blazer now covered the suggestive lines of the clinging knit.

"Sure. I'll fix something here."

"I don't think so," she said, not even hesitating. "How about the Fourteenth Street Grill? Eight o'clock."

This was her bus. If I wanted to go along, I could. But she made it clear that she was driving. I nodded and stood. She kissed me on the cheek at the door and half walked, half ran to the Peugeot.

I toasted a bagel and covered it with too much chive cream cheese.

Lauren had come over a little after seven in the morning to apologize for not calling and for being overly aggressive in her quest for Gretchen's records.

And, by the way, to sort of break up with me.

The case was stuck. No witnesses. The physical evidence was confusing. The police remained unsure

177

as to whether the crime was a bungled burglary or a straight homicide. Douglas Kravner's alibi was lame, but Gretchen's attorney maintained that she knew nothing about any blackmail involved in the divorce negotiations. My statement to Purdy was the only link to that particular motive. Gretchen's divorce lawyer was not celebrated for her ethics; I was sure that she knew and saw no advantage in disclosure. In other words, she was generally better at covering her ass than I was at covering mine. I wondered what role she had played.

Purdy seemed convinced, according to Lauren, that the killer knew Gretchen. That he had been in her house earlier in the day or evening and had left a window unlatched for easy reentry. There was no sign of forced entry, but there were some footprints outside a spare bedroom window and some fibers caught on a rough section of the wooden frame. The Jerk had told the police that Gretchen was a fanatic about keeping the house locked.

And, Lauren had said, Gretchen had intercourse, maybe with her killer, sometime that evening before she went to bed.

The bagel was forgotten on the tiled counter. I showered and went to the office to see three patients. At midday I returned a call to Jon Younger's office.

"Your insurance company has retained me. Begrudgingly, I think. They insisted that a woman from Peterson, Graves, and Meikeljohn, in Denver, be co-counsel, which is fine. So we're on.

"First, I will begin drafting a response to the allegations in the suit. Mostly a formality—"

"Jon, I think I know where they're getting their information."

"Go on."

"Sheldon Hart has one of his daughter's journals. Her friend, the paralegal, turned it over to him. It's apparently about her therapy with me."

"Do you know what it says?"

"No. The friend, Valerie Goodwin, only read a little of it. She says it's quite personal. Can we get it through discovery?"

"I'm not sure. Since we're going to argue that Mr. Hart has no right to the records, they can probably delay us getting hold of their information." Jon paused for a moment. "Let me think on it."

"You hear about the murder in Knollwood?"

"Yes. I saw it in the *Daily*."

"The dead woman was another one of my patients. That makes three."

"Three?"

I told Jon about Anne Hubbard.

"Do you see any connection?"

"I can't find a connection, Jon, but I feel a connection. I don't know. There's too much unexplained in all this."

"Well, if you come up with anything, let me know."

"Will do. What about the interrogatories?"

"We'll ignore them for now."

On the way home from the office I stopped at Alfalfa's and bought some groceries. Most of what I was buying lately ended up rotting in the trash. When I passed by the travel agency on Arapahoe, I was tempted to pick up a ticket to San Francisco for the weekend and go see Merideth. The red light changed to green before I gave in to the regressive pull.

The afternoon was unmistakably autumn. Isolated trees were changing from green to gold, and the air lost its warmth early. I changed into my riding clothes at home, mounted my bicycle, and did two circuits of the Morgul Bismarck to exhaust myself. There were a few other riders on the route, and three of us did the last go-round together. My endurance held, and I outsprinted them to the finish.

When I got back home, Cicero was up the hill with Peter where I had left her. She came running down when I called. I checked her carefully for sequelae to prior abominations and found none. That morning, seeing Cicero, Lauren had been certain that somebody was sending me a message with their clippers. I agreed. Although a note tied to Cicero's collar would have been sufficient.

The phone was ringing as I walked in the door. Hollow silence preceded a click after I answered it.

I showered, put on some jeans and a sweatshirt, and paced the living room as a pale skin of clouds absorbed the last pastels of sunset. My beeper sang in its charger, and I paced over to read the tiny screen. "Michael McLend, wants to reschedule, please call," it read, giving his phone number. The operators at the answering service delighted in the development of imaginative spellings for callers' names.

After hesitating, I dialed the proffered number, and it was picked up immediately.

"Hello." The whisper.

"Hello. Michael?"

"Yes." There was a lot of background noise. Voices. Music.

"Alan Gregory returning your call."

"Good. Can I see you tomorrow? I'm back in town."

"What happened to San Francisco?" I asked vacantly as I opened the appointment book in my hand, knowing the question to consider was whether

180

I wanted to see him, not whether I had time.

"I gave my paper. Tried to look somebody up. It didn't work out, so I decided to come home."

It's not my style to chat with patients about inconsequentials. I returned to the business at hand. "How about eleven-thirty?"

"Fine. See you then. Thanks."

Just like a conversation with a normal person.

The normalcy carried through his appointment. Michael McClelland was cordial, nonconfrontive, and wound up like a little kid about his experience inside Hurricane Frances. Phil Hubbard had let him go to Florida because one of Phil's pals was "in hospital for surgery." Michael gave me a long introduction to pressure differentials and the variable velocity of winds at different distances from the eye. I permitted him to fill the time with a science lesson because it was easier than pointing out the diversion. Finally I asked him about his feelings on seeing me in Mexico.

"Just one of those things, wasn't it?" he said. "Nothing really. You like that girl I was with? Something, huh? Am I supposed to have some feelings about seeing you?"

I reminded him that he had experienced some anger the last time he'd discovered me to be out of town without warning.

"That was then. Nothing now."

I suggested that there might be some feelings that he was resisting dealing with, and he told me to blame it on Hurricane Frances. I pressed him a little on the meaning of his decision to cut short his trip to California. He was evasive.

We agreed to meet at the regular time the following Wednesday.

I sorted the mail and paid some bills during the afternoon. Michael's use of the phrase *in hospital,* minus the article, bounced around my head like a rattle in a dashboard.

Diane and I locked up the office and walked together toward our cars. She chatted about her plans to spend the weekend in Aspen with Raoul, a yearly ritual for them during the turning of the mountain foliage. When we reached the backs of the cars, parked side by side at the end of the drive, she walked left to her Saab, I moved right.

"What the hell?" Diane said, her voice quivering. I ran around the front of my car and saw her smashed windshield. A hole the size of a fist on the driver's side. "What the hell?" she repeated, her left hand covering her mouth. "Well, I guess all the bad luck isn't yours," she finally managed. "Who the hell would throw a rock through my windshield?"

"Give me your keys," I said, distracted, and opened the driver's door. Beads of glass littered the dashboard and upholstery.

"It wasn't a rock," I said. "And the bad luck isn't all yours."

She moved away from the hole in the windshield, which had her mesmerized, and stood next to me at the open door. A crystal turtle was beached on the fabric of the driver's seat.

"I'll bet that's mine."

"I will, too," Diane concurred.

I told her not to touch it and walked the slow walk of a man who will find what he doesn't wish to find. I went no farther than the French doors from the garden. The turtle wasn't on the table in my consulting area. It was in Diane's Saab.

I put my hands in my pockets as I sauntered over to stand next to my partner. "So," I tried. My lips obeyed the command to construct a smile. "Wanna borrow the Subaru for the weekend?"

Diane's insurance agent said she could get a mobile van out to the car for a windshield replacement by five forty-five. I told Diane I would wait; she could take the Subaru for errands she needed to run before she left for Aspen. Diane elected not to call the police right then, preferring, she said, to make a report on Monday when she got back. The gesture felt like a gift to me.

I picked up the turtle with a towel from the bathroom, slid it into a big envelope, and left it in my file cabinet. The windshield guy was annoyed by the late Friday afternoon call and was disinterested in the etiology of the hemorrhage in the Saab. Since I preferred he remain disinterested, I walked down the street while he worked on the car and bought a six-pack of Budweiser. I sipped one while he finished and gave him the rest. His mood improved.

Diane drove up in the Subaru a little before seven. She swung her legs out of the car and stood quickly. "Probably unrelated has become possibly unrelated. The forecast is for possibly related. We'll discuss it next week. Okay?"

I nodded. I wanted to discuss the roster of the few people who could have taken the turtle. Diane wanted to pick up Raoul and see a few million golden aspen trees. "Have a good trip. Drive carefully."

"It was pitted anyway," she said.

"Right. You're gonna need to stop somewhere and vacuum up the rest of the glass."

"Yeah. And you're gonna need to buy a gun." Diane looked at me funny, seemed to think about whether to add some additional commentary, and, of course, did. "A patient did this, you know."

"Yours or mine?" I conjectured lamely.

She laughed at my primitive defenses. "Mine are well behaved. I don't tolerate acting out," she declared, smiling.

"And mine?"

"Yours seem to be doing all sorts of crazy shit."

As she pulled out of the driveway I thought how much I liked the hum of a well-tuned Saab. And I realized that if she was right about a patient of mine being responsible for the vandalism, there was no point in reporting the destruction to the police. I couldn't tell them whom I suspected or why.

Privilege belongs to the patient.

So, apparently, does advantage.

I wondered what was involved in buying a gun.

Twenty-two

The champagne was Lauren's idea. She poured me a glass while I slipped out of my jacket as I joined her for dinner after rushing across town to feed Cicero. I was ten minutes late.

She may have said, "Hello, darling," as I sat down. If she did, I missed it.

The first line I heard was, "The fingerprints on one of the dirty glasses in the dishwasher aren't identifiable. They're good prints, but we don't know whose. The Crime Scene Investigators think somebody wiped a few things clean in the house and just didn't think of looking in the dishwasher for a glass they used. And"—Lauren paused to take a sip of champagne—"one of the deceased's girlfriends says that she'd been dating somebody new. So we think maybe somebody she'd invited over that night came back, killed her, wiped up his prints, and messed up the house to make it look like a burglary. Or maybe somebody else just broke in and killed her and wiped up after themselves. But that somebody screwed up by not looking in the dishwasher." She looked at me as if I should raise my glass and say, "Congratulations." I was still pondering the Baccarat turtle.

"So it means we're off dead center," she concluded.

"You don't think that her husband did it?" I offered that question to Lauren and struggled with one myself. Why didn't Gretchen tell me she was dating somebody new?

"I didn't say that. He may be the guy she had over. Even if he was, we need evidence."

"The fingerprints on the glass aren't his?"

"Nope. And they're good clear prints."

"So you can match them with somebody?"

"Maybe. From the placement on the glass, they think they might be left-hand prints. If the guy has a prior record, we can get a match from his jacket or from the FBI. If he's clean, no priors, then there's some problems, since we can't use AFIS. If he's served in the military—maybe. I don't know what we'll be able to find out. At this point, I'll try and track down this new boyfriend and see if he's a match. How hungry are you? Want to split some things?"

"Sure. I want some French fries. You can pick the rest. What's AFIS?"

"Automatic Fingerprint Identification System," she said as she signaled the waiter. He seemed to take an inordinate amount of time to walk ten feet to our table and, silently, by tilting his head and opening his eyes wide, let us know it was A-OK to grace him with our order. Lauren ordered a grilled halibut salad and two plates, an herb pizza and two plates, and an order of French fries. Our waiter, the mime, and I both looked at her funny. "It's what you asked for," she said in my general direction.

I looked up at him and said, "She's right." He picked the bottle of champagne from the bucket and refilled our glasses.

For a few minutes we talked about the weather and popular predictions for the timing of the season's first freeze and for the first dusting of snow.

The waiter dropped off the salad, which had been divided onto two plates in the kitchen. After my first bite I said to Lauren, "Do you know who the new boyfriend is?"

Lauren chewed and swallowed. "No. The friend says that she only heard his name once. Says that the deceased was uncharacteristically secretive about him. Playfully. Said she couldn't tell. The friend figured the guy was married. Thinks his name might have been Nick or Mick. We'll find him."

"Could you please call her Gretchen? Or Ms. Kravner?"

Lauren slowed. Her salad lost its intrigue, and she quietly set her fork back on the plate. As she leaned forward her hair caught the dim lights. She looked up and away and then back to me.

"I continually need to apologize to you. I'm sorry. I'm treating you like a colleague. And you're one of the victims. I'm sorry, Alan. Forgive me."

"Apology accepted."

"How are you? With all this, I mean."

"All this"—I raised my hands, a glop of champagne sloshing to the tiled floor—"keeps getting bigger. I don't know the parameters, though. I have these crystal animals on a table in my office. Two turtles, a snail. The first one was a gift from Peter and Adrienne when I moved to my current office. A turtle, just this big." I held my thumb and index finger three inches apart. "A symbol. A joke. About how long therapy takes. Moves slow like a turtle. Anyway, after work tonight, Diane and I found that turtle had been thrown through the windshield of her Saab."

"It was your turtle?"

"Mm-hmmm."

"When did you see it last?"

"I've been trying to remember. Yesterday or the

day before. I didn't notice it missing."

"Do you look at it often? Would you notice it missing?"

"I like it a lot. I think I look at it a lot. But I'm not sure I'd notice it missing right away."

"Any idea who did it?"

"Doesn't fit any of my patients. But some of them get pretty angry. I'm not sure. I'm not too popular these days, you know. Could be a lot of different people. I'm popularly accused of sexual impropriety and accessory to suicide, after all. I have to wonder if it's a way of telling Diane to cut her ties with me. She denies it, but she must be under a lot of pressure from people to cut me loose."

"Makes sense. But an anonymous note would do the same thing."

"You know Diane. If she received a note, she'd ignore it."

"Ask her, then."

"She and Raoul went to Aspen for the weekend."

"Oh, that's right. I forgot." Lauren paused, remembering. "They're staying at my place. Jake's place."

Quietly we both raised our glasses and sipped the bubbly wine, set the glasses down, and returned to the salads. Memories of our weekend in Aspen and the agenda for tonight's date joined us at the table.

When the crescendo of chewing and swallowing mimicked the roar of the Yampa River during spring runoff, I was forced to attend to the discomfiting absence of conversation.

"So how's Cicero?" asked Lauren.

Thank you. "She seems okay. She looked so odd for so long. I just came across the bandanna again. It gives me the creeps."

"Bandanna?" She barked the word, and her features stilled in freeze frame.

"Yeah, when I found her tied outside the house, she had this blue-and-white bandanna around her neck, over the place where she was clipped."

"Boy, that's eerie," Lauren said, pressing back on the wooden chair, her long fingers stretched on the white table cloth. "The deceased—I'm sorry, Gretchen Kravner, had a bandanna around her neck when she was found. It was used to strangle her. It's one of the facts we haven't disclosed publicly."

My eyes closed involuntarily. I released my hold on the silverware, which clanked to the plate. My hands dropped to my lap.

Lauren reached across the small table and touched my cheek with the fingertips of her right hand. "Alan," she whispered, and a shiver washed over my body.

The waiter, insensitive to the poignancy of the moment, asked if there was a problem with the barely disturbed salads. I said no. Suddenly loquacious, he then wondered if we would like the French fries as a separate course or with the pizza. I said it didn't matter. He gave me a look like it didn't matter to him, either. I said, "Anything else?" And he left.

"This is spooky, Lauren."

"Yes. It may just be coincidence, though." And Vietnam was just a police action.

"You don't believe that. Do you?"

She shook her head and said, "I don't know what I think. Can I have the bandanna?" This was no more a request than a police officer asking, "May I see your driver's license?"

"Sure. Do you want to test it for something?"

"See if it matches ours. Give it to the CSIs—the Crime Scene Investigators. I don't know." The French fries arrived. She grabbed one and held it between her thumb and index finger. "Remind me. When did all this happen? With the shaving?"

"Cicero didn't come home from her evening run the last night we were in Aspen. I found her tied in front of the house the next night. Why?"

"I don't know why. Just trying to understand what happened."

The waiter returned with the pizza, which wouldn't fit on the crowded table.

"Please wrap everything to go," I said.

He smiled a smile usually reserved for the mentally incompetent and retorted, "But of course."

"And bring us coffee, please. Decaf. And the check."

I turned back to Lauren. "Can I come over to your house?"

Lauren's eyes were gray and moist. She shook her head as if its movement were restricted by a brace. "No, Alan. That's not a good idea. We still need to talk about us. And I don't think I'm up to that tonight." A tear carried mascara downstream toward the corner of her mouth.

"Then, umm. I'll get the bandanna to you tomorrow. Leave it at your office?"

"No. I'll send an investigator to pick it up. I'll call you to let you know when. And, you and I still need to talk."

"Yes."

"I'll call you," she repeated.

"Fine."

I paid the bill. Neither of us touched the coffee.

At her car she insisted I take the large bag of food from the restaurant. I kissed her on the cheek to preclude her taking the initiative and doing the same to me first.

When I opened the door and sat in the Subaru, it was cold. I recalled the night sitting in the car near Anne Hubbard's body and couldn't recall the car being so cold in the intervening months.

I drove home and lit a fire. Cicero shied far away until the hickory stopped crackling and then settled close to the warmth. The phone rang as I munched wilted salad and cold pizza. Click. Dial tone. I fought an impulse to throw the can of beer in my hand through the window in the living room.

The phone rang again. I lifted the receiver to my ear.

"Can I ask you a question?"

"Hi, Lauren."

"The new guy Gretchen was seeing. You know anything about him?"

"No. I didn't know she was seeing anybody other than the guys I told Purdy about."

"I'm reading her chart. Didn't see any mention of it and thought I'd ask. Thanks."

"Sure. It was good seeing you tonight."

"You too, Alan. I'll call to set something up. Good night."

"Good night."

I reached down and scratched the new growth of hair around Cicero's neck. I gave her a hunk of pizza crust, which she swallowed without chewing.

"Who did it, poochie? Who's your barber?"

Twenty-three

The thoughts that precluded easy sleep Friday night joined me for coffee Saturday morning.

In the time since I remembered seeing the crystal turtle in my hand, which was Wednesday afternoon during Michael McClelland's canceled appointment, and when I picked it up off the maroon fabric of the driver's seat of Diane's Saab, which was Friday afternoon, a lot of people had been in my office. I had seen three patients on Thursday and Michael McClelland on Friday. The janitors had cleaned twice. I was pretty sure that there were two of them. I could call the janitorial service and find out. Diane had easy access to my office, but I had a difficult time developing a motive for her to hurl my crystal turtle through the windshield of her most coveted possession.

Leaving my office door unlocked while I walked around downtown during breaks in my day was a habit I had developed because of a tendency to forget to carry my keys. I had probably left the office unlocked at least a couple of times since Wednesday.

So. Four patients. One partner. One to four janitors. And possibly one uninvited intruder.

I sipped coffee in the living room and distracted myself marveling at how the golden patches of autumn seemed to double each night in the trees that hugged the meager streams running west to east across the valley.

I decided on two theories.

First, somebody was giving Diane a message about affiliating with me. Maybe one of her patients. When I included Diane's thriving practice, it greatly increased the list of people with possible access to the office. Or maybe a colleague with an ax to grind against me or Diane. Or maybe a self-righteous, unaffiliated, equal opportunity vigilante.

Second, somebody was giving me a message. Which meant that Cicero's barber and the turtle hurler might be the same person. Or they might not. When I pondered who might be giving me a message, I needed an expansive frame of mind. At the top of the list would be Sheldon Hart. Mr. Hart, however, didn't strike me as the breaking-and-entering, mischievous, vandalizing type. But then, I reminded myself wistfully, his daughter hadn't struck me as the suicidal type, either.

Motive? To scare me or to get me to stop practicing or to punish me for the sins of which I was popularly accused. But why Diane's Saab? The easiest answer was that the hurler thought it was mine.

Okay. Then what did a turtle in a Saab and a shaved dog's neck have in common? Sounded like a question for some esoteric IQ test.

I slapped cold bacon into a cold pan as I tried to remember for the zillionth time whether you should never put bacon into a cold pan or always put bacon into a cold pan. I chopped a cold, wrinkled baked potato and diced some onions and peppers and drowned them in melted butter in another pan. I gently scrambled together two eggs in a small bowl. Merideth would have derived significant joy from criticizing away the pleasure I felt at filling a heavily buttered English muffin with egg and bacon and rejoicing in the melody of fat and cholesterol in my mouth. I didn't eat like that very often. When I did I certainly wanted to relish it.

I cleared my plate to Cicero's chagrin and poured more coffee. The solution to all my cogitating wasn't so much eluding me as I was avoiding it.

The truth was that I was sure that Michael Mc-Clelland did the turtle in the Saab. Which meant that he also may have done the bandanna around the dog's neck.

And then I recognized the logical equation that I was avoiding. If the turtle in the Saab was linked to the bandanna on the pooch—and the bandanna on the pooch was linked to the bandanna on Gretchen—then the turtle in the Saab was linked to the bandanna on Gretchen. So if I was sure that Michael McClelland had done the turtle hurling, then I was indirectly accusing him of murdering Gretchen, which made no sense at all.

Did it?

I revisited all the theories as I showered and, on a whim, shaved off my beard. Halfway through the shave I interpreted my behavior as an attempt to keep the bad guys from recognizing me. By the conclusion of the shave I let Michael McClelland off the hook about the turtle and decided that my suspicion was just countertransference talking. Michael was a frustrating patient, so I was accusing him of all manner of mayhem.

The manila envelope I pulled from Merideth's desk made a more than adequate package for the bandanna. I fought an impulse to put it in a plastic Ziploc bag like the ones I had seen in Lauren's study. I'd already decided that I had better things to do with my Saturday than wait for Lauren to call with her investigator's itinerary.

Outside, I started the Subaru and then ran back inside for a sweater while it warmed. I cut off South Boulder Road at the Foothills Parkway and then went west on Arapahoe to Thirty-third. After parking the car, I grabbed the manila envelope and walked into the new headquarters of the Boulder Police Department. At the desk, a woman in street clothes, about my age, looked at me with a pleasant smile and asked if she could help me. She had sparse blond hair, fluffed to take up more space than it should, and skin so white that it looked bleached.

I smiled back.

"I'd like to leave this for Detective Purdy." I held up the manila envelope.

"And it is . . . ?" She managed to be courteous and suspicious simultaneously. Something they teach at the Police Academy. I wondered if she was plainclothes.

"Evidence. I guess." I was having another one of my village idiot attacks.

"Evidence. In what case?" She continued smiling, remained quite pleasant. The last time I had seen that face, however, it had been on a state patrolman querying me about my cruising speed.

"Gretchen Kravner's murder."

"Oh." My mention of Boulder's only active murder investigation apparently propelled me from the category of crank to that of novelty. "Please have a seat. And your name?" I told her. "Someone will be with you in a moment." She crinkled up her pink-and-white nose and gestured toward some chrome-and-leather seating that was inappropriately fashionable for a police department lobby.

She waited until I was on my chair before she picked up the phone, punched a couple of numbers, and spoke too quietly for me to eavesdrop.

A minute later I heard, "You shaved your beard."

Purdy looked almost fresh that morning. His shirt and tie were clean, the herringbone was absent. I would have guessed that he had slept better than I had the night before. I also would have guessed, eyeing his girth, that we had eaten similar breakfasts.

"Detective," I said. It was hard to fit a foot in my mouth if I opened it just wide enough to say "Detective."

"You have something for me, Doctor?"

I held up the envelope and didn't say a word.

"Come on in. Show me what you got."

Purdy's office was a partitioned cubicle with a window. The furniture was more like that of a mortgage company than what I expected from a detective's office. Black metal desk with a laminated fake oak top. His chair matched the desk, the one he pointed me to came from my preconceptions about police departments. Gray metal frame, torn Naugahyde cushions, armrests carved by amateurs with penknives and ballpoints. A hinged metal frame rested on the corner of the desk, only one photograph visible from my chair, a carefully composed snapshot of a two- or three-year-old boy giggling down a slide. A thin black vase held three tropical flowers.

"My wife's a florist," he said, as though he had felt compelled to explain the flowers before.

I just nodded, feeling like the little boy playing a game to see who could go the longest without saying anything.

He started playing, too, holding out his hand for the envelope in my lap.

I handed it across the desk.

His stubby fingers pried apart the thin metal clasp. He peered in and then slid the bandanna out onto the desk pad in front of him, never touching it.

There was a glimmer of recognition in his eyes when he identified what it was. But he was good at this game and said nothing. His hands hovered over the front of the desk, supported by wrists balanced on the edge. In unison he raised his orange-tinted eyebrows and lifted the index fingers of both hands.

To keep the game alive, I was tempted to shrug my shoulders and make a perplexing face. My sense of self-preservation told me that this was a game I could lose by winning.

"Lauren Crowder thought that might be important," I said, motioning at the neatly folded dusty fabric dotted with black dog hair.

He sat silently for about fifteen seconds, perhaps not realizing that he had just won. Then he said, "And."

"And. I don't know."

"Where didya get it?"

"From around my dog's neck. You remember Cicero?" As I silently reprimanded myself for asking a homicide detective whether he remembered my dog, I apparently missed his next question.

"Well. Is it?"

"Is it what, Detective?"

"Is it yours, Doctor?"

"The handkerchief? No. It's not."

"So why's it sitting here on my desk?"

After a harmony of sighs of exasperation, Purdy on bass, me on tenor, I told Purdy about Cicero's shave, about my comment to Lauren about the bandanna, about Lauren's concern that it might not be coincidental that they were being so carelessly left around Boulder, and about her desire to give it to somebody for analysis. I didn't tell him that I assumed she had already called to tell him about the new lead and that I would thus be spared the humiliation I was going through. And I didn't tell him about the crystal turtle.

"You've touched it?"

Back to nodding for me.

"Anybody else?"

"My neighbors, maybe. They might have touched it. Cicero spends a lot of time with them."

"The twine. You mentioned some twine. Where is it?"

"I don't know. Maybe still around the tree. I can look for it."

"Do that. Check the trash, too. Your neighbors see anybody bring the dog back?"

"No. They were both gone that afternoon."

"Have any pictures of the dog right after the shave?"

"I might. I'll look. There may be some in the camera."

"Check. Hold them for me. I'll come and get them. Negatives, too."

"Sure. I can do that."

Purdy gave me a look that told me the interview was over. I said, "Is it the same? As the one around Gretchen's neck."

"Don't know. Could be. Thanks so much for bringing it around." Any efforts to avoid appearing condescending had evaporated.

"Who do you think did it? Killed Gretchen?"

Purdy shook his massive head slowly. "Don't

198

know." His eyes rested on mine. "Maybe her husband, maybe a burglar, maybe a kerchief fetishist. You should feel fortunate, Doctor, that you've got the alibi of the century."

He attended to the blue-and-white fabric, scooping it deftly back into the envelope. "Keep this information to yourself. Is that clear?" I nodded. "Good. That's all," he said, dismissing me.

"Do I get a receipt?" I asked.

"You're somethin', Doctor Gregory. A few days ago, I'm chomping at the chance to get you before a grand jury to get evidence you're keeping to yourself. Now"—he waved at the envelope—"you're delivering the stuff like Federal Express or something. If I were a suspicious man, I might suspect that the way you're being treated by the local media," he said, making it clear that "media" was a three-syllable word, "might be having an impact on the level of cooperation you are providing to the . . . authorities.

"And if I were a very suspicious man, I might wonder if the, um, affections of a certain deputy district attorney might be influencing your civic-mindedness."

"Anything else, Detective?"

"Not today. Doctor. But, please"—he motioned again at the manila envelope—"do stay in touch. We sincerely value assistance from the civilian population."

I left without my receipt.

The University of Colorado Buffalo football team was scheduled to play an early afternoon match-up against Nebraska, a perennial Big-8 powerhouse that they beat just often enough, like once a millennium, to keep the faithful hoping for an upset. Skinner's laws regarding the power of intermittent reinforcement were operationalized by the masses as they clogged the streets heading west toward the stadium.

A bicycle ride was the only reasonable antidote to the sour interview with Purdy. I drove home, bent and grabbed the *Daily* from below a scraggly piñon, changed into biking clothes and shoes, and checked Cicero's water supply. My last act before pushing my bike out the door was to glance at the local morning paper.

Purdy, apparently, had already checked his copy.

MURDERED WOMAN BLACKMAILING HUSBAND read the headline in section two.

Halfway down the first column, a two-sentence paragraph informed Boulder that Gretchen had been my patient and reminded them that I was under investigation in a prior case by the Grievance Committee of the State Board of Psychologist Examiners.

To me, that wasn't news. The news was in a sidebar entitled "State Reviewing Journals in Misconduct Investigation."

I had little fight left in me. With the paper in my hands, I walked to the sofa in the living room and stared straight ahead at nothing, the paper open on my lap.

Sometime later I read the articles and their continuation on the back page of the second section. The parts that weren't news to me were factual. The reporter, Abiado, had discovered only the broad outlines of the purported blackmail. He knew that Gretchen Kravner, murdered a week before, had been my patient. Friends contacted by the reporter uniformly judged her to be in good spirits

200

despite her pending divorce. "Because of her pending divorce," said one friend. The police continued their investigation of the murder, with a source close to the police department stating that an indictment of her estranged husband seemed likely.

In the accompanying article, Joseph Abiado, in his continuing unauthorized serial biography of my life, reported that the *Daily* had obtained copies of "papers written by Karen Hart" that seemed to detail erotic contact with her psychologist, Dr. Alan Gregory, during her treatment prior to her suicide in November of the previous year. The material in the journals had been made available to the state committee investigating Dr. Gregory's conduct. Dr. Gregory had repeatedly refused comment on the allegations, which Abiado reminded his readers weren't new, only supported by new evidence. The papers in the *Daily*'s possession contained detailed descriptions of erotic and sexual contact, always in the psychologist's office, ranging from the psychologist holding the patient and rocking her, to erotic touching, to sexual intercourse. Abiado wrote that there was no evidence in the materials that Ms. Hart was other than a willing participant in these activities.

Great.

Twenty-four

I was angry enough to ride all the way to Cheyenne and back. Instead I took country roads across east Boulder before heading west at Valmont Road and then north on the continuation of Twenty-eighth Street where it curved up to the foothills.

The ride was easy, but I rode hard, pushing to maintain my spin over one hundred and sweating profusely in the bright sun. When I neared the intersection at North Broadway, I hesitated and turned the bike south one block and stopped it in the field where I had last seen Anne Hubbard months before. The creek was almost dry; snow was accumulating at higher elevations, not melting and running off as it had been the previous May. I wandered around for a few minutes, imagining the placement of the car, and the body, and hearing again the voices and melodies of that night, recalling the dark and wet and cold.

I smiled ironically at my misguided assurance that my triad of tragedies would be over with Anne Hubbard's death.

My original goal had been to ride hard to Lyons, twenty miles north of Boulder, but I scrapped it and started the gradual, then precipitous climb up Lee Hill Drive. Michael McClelland's house was someplace behind that long hogback. I wanted to see it.

Some riders liked to climb. I found it torture. I did it because I was convinced it was good for me.

Half a mile beyond the turnoff to Boulder Heights I passed the long driveway to Raoul and Diane's house and kept climbing, feeling the familiar acid burning in the long muscles in my legs, exhaling loudly through pursed lips. The house number in my head that echoed like a mantra was 2888, and I rode until I came up to a galvanized mailbox with those numbers painted boldly in black.

On the front of the box, in the same black paint, was the name "MORTON." Below it, in Kroy-type letters covered with transparent packing tape, a white band read "McClelland." A loaf-shaped plastic box attached to one side of the mailbox was splashed with the name of the local paper in its familiar stylized black logo.

The macadam drive rose to the west at a right angle from the road and disappeared about twenty yards away as it doglegged south behind a ridge thickly crested with ponderosa pine. I lowered the bike into the dry culvert beside the road and clacked up the driveway in my cleated bicycle shoes, staying in the shadows of the ridge and trees as much as possible. Only when the house was in sight, another twenty yards up the hill, did I let myself wonder what the hell I was doing there.

The house was a simple, suburban-type split level with composition siding. It was painted a green that clashed with the depth of the color in the pines and was trimmed in a brown too chocolaty for the surrounding earth. A concrete walk passed a huge pile of cut wood from the asphalt to the front door. There was no garage, just a prefab storage shed in an incongruous red barn motif.

And there were no cars.

This far from anywhere, with the closest bus two and a half miles away, the absence of cars meant that nobody was home. I walked into the open space in front of the house as if calling on my patients wearing skintight black shorts, a pinhole black-and-yellow jersey, and shoes that looked like lightweight rejects from a bowling alley were an everyday occurrence. I smiled as I told myself that house calls were in the best tradition of the healing profession.

I was on autopilot. Even a moment's reflection would have convinced me of the insanity I was perpetrating sneaking around somebody else's house. Especially a patient's house.

One-inch blinds were turned slightly up in the windows of the lower level of the front of the house, blocking my attempts to peek in. I walked around back, where sliding glass doors were situated to maximize the steep view up the mountainside. The living room and dining room were sparsely furnished.

The furniture was ski condo. Heavy, lightly stained oak with earth-tone cushions. Sled chairs at the dining table. A large cabinet between the rooms held a large TV monitor, VCR, and three or four audio components. There was no art on the walls. Next to me on the deck was a miniature kettle-type barbecue grill.

Another deck provided a platform to view the bedroom that ran along the back of the house on the north corner. A queen-size Danish teak platform bed with attached night tables dominated the room. A bright polyester quilted comforter provided a splash of color. The dresser matched the bed. A small wooden box sat on top of the dresser. The bed was made to withstand morning inspection at Camp Pendleton. Two doors, apparently to a bath and closet, were closed.

It seemed sad that this sterile, unimaginative room was the last place that Anne Hubbard had made love. Or had sex. As the case might be.

I qualified my impression, needing to consider that this might be the bedroom of Michael McClelland's roommate. Whose existence had previously been unknown to me.

I stared in the bedroom for quite a while, looking for clues. It was as fruitful as looking into an unoccupied motel room.

A Princess-style phone sat on one of the nightstands. A Sony clock radio rested on the other next to a remote-control unit, which I assumed operated a television that was blocked from my view by the off-the-shelf draperies that were open only a few feet.

The room at the northeast corner of the house was apparently another bedroom, but it had no deck, and the elevation of the house kept me from looking in the windows.

My domestic spying was interrupted by the whine of a high torquing engine negotiating the steep drive to the house. Given my experience at this kind of clandestine activity, I did what was natural.

I froze.

When my brain clicked back in, I jumped over the rail and off the deck to the north side of the house, where I hoped there wouldn't be too many windows. Crisp clicking of shoes on concrete shared percussion with the thudding of my heart. I heard the front door open, then finally close.

Bicycling shoes are not made for quiet walking on pine needles and twigs. Bicycling shoes are not made for walking, period. The huge, rutted cleats under the balls of my feet were superb at locking my feet to the pedals of the Bianchi; on any other surface they forced me to rock back on my heels with each unbalanced step. I was making a racket as I tried to cover the distance of six or seven yards that would take me to the top of a small ridge and some cover. Between crackles I heard the *swoosh* of a sliding glass door opening. By the time the scratchy squeal of the screen had pierced the air, I had stopped midstride and was imagining Morton or McClelland or both standing at the open door, listening for a refrain of the indelicate sound of retreating feet. I perched on one foot, arms out, my back turned to my pursuers.

Clomp, clomp. Hard shoes striking cedar deck. I waited for more clomps, my balance wavering. No more clomps—it was either Morton or McClelland, not both. I grabbed a tree branch to maintain some semblance of the required catatonia. The brittle wood snapped off in my hand, sounding like a gunshot going off. I waited a picosecond for the thud of the impact of a bullet into my body and then scurried up the hill, trying to outrace any subsequent slugs.

The top of the ridge was more table than precipice, and I flattened myself as best I could. At least fifteen seconds passed before the bulky frame of Michael McClelland turned the corner at the back of the house.

He carried a large rifle.

To keep that assessment in perspective, it must be acknowledged that I am someone terrified of guns. There are no small rifles.

"You kids stay away from here. You understand? Go on. Get outtahere!"

The whisper yells.

He turned and walked back toward the house.

I waited two minutes and scurried over the top of the little mesa to a saddle that led back to the road.

My bicycle was still in the culvert. I jumped on it and rode as though I was wearing the yellow jersey in the Tour de France. The back wheel skidded, and the bike almost went down as I crossed the sandy demarcation from road to Diane and Raoul's driveway.

I knocked for almost five minutes before I remembered they were in Aspen.

The whole time, I shook in my funny little shoes.

Twenty-five

If Peter hadn't invited me to dinner, I would have invited myself. Or I would have begged him and Adrienne to try the new Cambodian restaurant on Arapahoe with me.

The ride home from Lee Hill Road left me feeling like the bow of an icebreaker. The mild morning had become a wintry afternoon, western breezes replaced by southeastern upslopes. Autumn's leaves and summer's dust mingled together in the swirling clouds of debris carried by the chill wind. Soon my skin felt dry and leathery and the inside of my nose as if it had been treated with Scotchgard. Somewhere in my escape from Michael's house my sunglasses had fallen from their perch on top of my head, and I blinked and teared all the way home.

There was a message from Purdy on the front door. He'd come by to get the twine and the photographs. "Fuck him," I mumbled. After greeting Cicero, I plodded straight to the shower. Every few minutes I increased the pressure from the hot water valve, and after three or four increases the chill began to seep from my extremities. I padded gingerly into the steamy room, grateful that the fogged mirrors precluded any vision of my reflection. I feared that it would accurately depict my stupidity.

The phone rang as I dried myself. Dropping the

damp towel at my feet, I stepped into the cold bedroom and picked up the receiver just to hear it click and die.

This, I thought, is getting old.

After dressing in my best Patagonia fleece warmups, I fumbled with the recalcitrant thermostat. From the living room I could see a solid wall of clouds spilling over the Continental Divide. Invisible to the eye, the cold dry northern air began a pitched battle with the moisture-laden upslope winds from the gulf. Boulder was Manassas. The smart money was on the Confederacy.

Cold water from the fridge diluted the dust and dirt from my mouth and throat. I spit out what I could; the rest poured into my digestive tract, which was doing double duty as a waste-water treatment facility. After exchanging the plastic jug for a beer, I sat at the long thin dining table. The views were west and south, toward Pike's Peak.

With a slight shake of my head, I pondered what I had done. What had provoked me to go to Michael McClelland's house? I had, I admonished myself, absolutely no right to be creeping around other people's houses. He had given me no reason. None.

Sure he had. The man was deceptive.

Face it.

The *Daily* chided me from the coffee table where I had left it.

What was in the damn paper wasn't Michael's fault. Impulse was the culprit. No, it wasn't. Having an impulse wasn't the problem. Giving in to it was.

One thing was for sure — and I didn't even argue with myself about this: it was time to terminate the treatment of Michael McClelland. Transfer him to somebody else. Somebody who was capable of viewing him in a neutral fashion. Somebody who didn't consider him a suspect in dog abuse, malicious mischief, and murder.

Somebody shot at me. Okay, don't exaggerate. I could've been shot. Certainly. Michael had a big gun and I was a trespasser and Colorado had this stupid "Make my day" law that let everybody be sheriff of their own OK Corral.

"Mea culpa, mea culpa, mea maxima culpa." The words busted me from my recrimination. No. It was not all my fault. Somebody shaved my dog, somebody threw my turtle, and somebody strangled my patient. Putting it that way was probably unnecessarily proprietary, but it assisted me in putting down the whip I was turning on myself.

And Michael McClelland had been misleading. He'd never told me about his roommate, Morton—I stopped.

And mostly he hadn't been a good patient. He'd been angry, resistant, and threatening. He'd been late to appointments, canceled appointments, and even showed up on the wrong day for appointments.

But I'd had many other patients who had done and been all of those things and more, and I'd never snuck around their homes. Who knew why I was doing what I was doing?

I picked up the phone and called Raymond Farley at his home in Denver.

His preadolescent daughter didn't bother to cover the mouthpiece as she yelled in undisguised disappointment, "Daddy, it's for you."

A moment later Dr. Raymond Farley said, "Hello."

"Ray, Alan Gregory."

"Alan, nice to hear from you." I was getting pretty sensitive to subtle echoes of judgment in people's voices. I didn't hear any reverberation in Ray's solid tenor.

"And nice to hear your voice, too, Ray. It's been too long."

Ray didn't respond. I learned almost everything I know about not responding from Ray Farley. He was my primary supervisor during my internship at the medical school and taught me many of the good things I did in psychotherapy. Mostly he taught me to listen and to stop trying to make things better for everybody. "This patient isn't your mother," he would say patiently, over and over again.

"Ray, I need to discuss a case with you. Urgently."

"Now? That urgently?"

"No. Monday or Tuesday. Just sometime before I see him, the patient, on Wednesday."

"Just a second. Let me get my calendar."

The phone was silent for a few seconds. Then I heard his daughter yell, "Dad, are you off the phone yet?"

Ray boomed, "No," and the silence resumed.

"Got it. How about" — he paused, perusing — "six-fifteen on Monday evening. My office."

"I'll be there. Thank you."

"You're welcome, see you Monday."

Dinner at Peter and Adrienne's house was usually a hands-on affair, and that night was no exception. Adrienne fought a pitched battle with pizza dough that wanted to rise to world record heights. Peter stood over a skillet of tomato sauce, adding dried

211

pepper flakes, stirring, tasting, adding more pepper flakes, stirring and tasting some more. I chopped bell peppers and red onions and grated varied cheeses as I sipped a Spanish red that Diane and Raoul had once left at my house. The wine was my contribution to the celebration.

Neither Peter nor Adrienne commented on my absent whiskers. They were accustomed to the periodic disappearance and reappearance of my facial hair.

That night's celebration commemorated the installation of the last major piece of cabinetry in the rejuvenation of Adrienne and Peter's kitchen. Peter rarely delivered a commissioned piece late to any customer, but the massive island in his own kitchen had been due months before. It was worth waiting for. Not a square line or angle was visible. Its rounded shapes moved from concave to convex, from circular to oval, from aesthetic to prudential. A small sink filled one bay, a cooktop defined another. Granite counters yielded to one lagoon of flush marble.

We toasted Peter, and I insisted that he promise to take a commission for my kitchen when I remodeled.

"That," said Adrienne, "is one commission you can't take to the bank."

As she fussed with the recalcitrant pizza dough, she finished telling us about the day she had completed on Friday. "TURP Day," she called it.

"Transurethral resection of the prostate," she explained to me. Peter was raising his eyebrows and feigning a yawn. Adrienne noticed. "His tolerance for my talking about kidneys and ureters and urine is rather limited. But, as I always say"—at this point Peter joined her in an obviously familiar refrain—" 'it may be piss to you, but it's gold to me.'

"Anyway, I did five of them, TURPs, in the morning." She reacted to her husband's continued disinterest. "You guys—your day will come, you know. Can't count on that old prostate much past fifty. And when it starts to strangle your defenseless little urethras, I'll be there to ream it out through your penises." She smiled. "Only as a last resort, of course. Gently. And I promise, as a special favor, to use anesthesia."

She wasn't finished. "I had a zillion appointments in the afternoon, which I started an hour late despite skipping lunch. People are backed up in the waiting room, my staff is bitching, the patients are steaming, and this couple comes in shopping for a vasectomy. They want to talk. I almost referred them to you, Alan. Jesus.

"What are the emotional consequences of vasectomy? Will the wife really believe that it works? Should they tell their kids? She's so naïve she asks me why on earth a man would change his mind and want a reversal? Because, I say to myself, after he dumps you, honey, he's gonna hook up with somebody whose clock has barely started ticking. I'm looking at my watch, trying to stay calm. Finally the wife says, 'This may sound sort of funny, Doctor, but I mean, where do the sperms'—she called them 'sperms'—'where do the sperms go when the vasectomy is done?'

"I say, 'Philadelphia.' The wife looks at me with this sweet face. And I repeated, 'They go to Philadelphia.' "

"No. Seriously," I said with some disbelief to Adrienne, "you told her the sperm go to Philadelphia?"

"Yeah." Adrienne was washing dough remnants

from her hand. "I'd had it. The husband was amused, more at his wife than me. I don't even think I managed to insult her. Anyway, they finally get up and leave. What a day."

She still wasn't done. "Something else that never ceases to amaze me is how messy you men are when you pee." This was something she had apparently given a lot of thought to. "I mean, sure you *can* stand up to urinate. The real question is *should* you? Just the splashing is bad enough. But you ask a guy to fill a specimen cup or, God forbid, do a split-stream, it's like you asked him to pee standing on his head into a test tube across the room. He almost always gets some into the cup, but the rest is everywhere. On the floor, on the toilet seat that no man ever admits he leaves down — at the end of the day, I swear, the patient's toilet in my office looks likes it's been sprayed with yellow syrup."

Peter looked at me. "She's almost done. Don't defend your gender."

Adrienne screwed up her face into a semblance of irate. "Alan, get involved with somebody. The Ponderosa is short one pair of ovaries."

Peter let the words settle, kissed his wife gently on the lips, and asked how my ride was that day.

"I rode up Lee Hill and prowled around one of my patient's houses and almost got shot."

Peter was parsimonious with everything but wood and chile peppers, both of which he used in abundance. "Say what?" he managed with a tilted head, raised brows, and wide-open eyes.

I vaguely explained about my visit, not mentioning Michael's name, and offered my conclusion that my aberrant behavior was ample evidence that it was time to sell them the bunkhouse and move back to California to seek anonymity.

Adrienne diverted. "You know, they actually give tickets for jaywalking there. I mean, like it's a real crime. I got one on Christmas Eve—the actual eve, mind you, seven o'clock in the evening, Beverly Hills. Prime goyim Santa Claus time. He gave one to my aunt Ida, too. She keeps saying, 'So those little lines, that's not a crosswalk?'

"Certain laws were never meant to be enforced; they're there like little reminders. Noodges. But they don't know that in California. Noooo. There are signs by the freeways in California that say '$1000 FINE FOR LITTERING.' You are actually considering moving to a state that assesses a thousand bucks for an errant Snickers wrapper and thirty-two fifty for successfully crossing a street? And the damn place shakes like some maniac is dropping quarters in its bed."

"Is dinner ready yet?" I asked, knowing Adrienne would corner me later about my escapade in the foothills. And about the new articles in the *Daily*.

Diane called Sunday night and told me she wasn't going to file a police report about the turtle unless I wanted her to.

"I appreciate the gesture, more than you know. But won't your insurance company insist?"

"I told them the damage was done by a rock. They'll right it off as vandalism. If they don't, Alan, I'll send you the bill and discover whether it's worth three hundred and forty-two dollars for you to not have to talk to the police anymore."

"You see yesterday's paper?"

"No. We just now got in. Don't you want to know how Aspen was?"

"Aspen was beautiful, Diane. It always is. Especially in late September. And Lauren's house is magnificent."

"How do you know about Lauren's house? And boy, do you know how to take the fun out of talking about a vacation."

"Sorry. Take a look at the paper. We'll talk tomorrow. Say hello to Raoul."

After I hung up the phone, I called Merideth to get some moral support and to find out if there was still vegetation on my oasis. Her answering machine was low on reassurance.

With some trepidation I tried Lauren, who answered on the fourth ring.

"Alan . . . Hello?" Her voice was distracted. I wondered if someone was with her.

"Is this a bad time for me to call?"

"No. Not really." The tones in her voice sharpened, then quivered. "Alan. I'm blind again. I'm scared."

"Blind? What do you mean? The one eye again?"

"That one totally. The other one partially. God, the house feels so small and dark. I can't read, or watch TV, or shoot pool. I'm scared to go out of the house." The words popped out between reluctant sobs.

"Lauren. Oh, Lauren. I'm sorry." A dozen years of clinical training and experience did nothing to help me choose the right words in the face of tragedy. "What can I do? I'll come over."

"Would you? Just for a little while?"

Twenty-six

After dressing in cords and sweater I hustled Cicero into the back of the Subaru and pushed the speed limits to west Boulder. I detoured downtown, by the mall, picked up some matzoh ball soup at the deli, used Ninth Street over Boulder Creek, then turned up Arapahoe to Sixth toward Lauren's.

By the time I parked on the gravel shoulder in front of the house, I had convinced myself, budding expert that I was, that Lauren's problems were related to too much stress. Everything I read said that stress was a culprit in exacerbations of MS.

Every light in the house was on. The face that answered the door looked worse than I had imagined. Her creamy white skin had paled to ghostlike, and her perfect hair hung limply to her shoulders. She looked toward me, our eyes failing to connect by two or three degrees. Her right hand held firmly to the edge of the open door, her left hand leveraged to the door frame. She wore the pale yellow sweats I had seen first in Aspen.

"Hi," she said.

My impulse was to scold her for opening the door when she couldn't see who was there, but I fought it and stepped in slowly while saying, "It's me, Alan." I put my hands around her and hugged gently, the chicken soup sloshing in Styrofoam behind her. Lauren never let go of her supports. Even when

Cicero stuck her snout into Lauren's crotch, she didn't let go of her supports.

"I'm dizzy, too. Vertigo. Blind and dizzy. Not a nice combination, more like some kind of sick comedy team, don't you think? You brought your dog," she said absently. Her eyes, which had lost all luminance, were moist, dark, accents to her black hair, as useless as costume jewelry.

"Come on, let's sit down," I said, taking her hand from the door, "I brought some soup. Have you eaten?"

She didn't answer my question but suggested we go to the kitchen. "It's brightest in there." She reached up and touched my face. "You shaved your beard."

And it was brightest in the kitchen. I was certain that Adrienne did TURPs in rooms with less light.

"When did it start?" I pulled out a chair and helped her settle at the heavy oak table.

"When did you shave your beard? I was getting dizzy when we had dinner on Friday night."

"I couldn't tell." I felt like apologizing. "I shaved today."

"Nobody can, except Jake, I hide it pretty well. Then I woke up Saturday and my eyes were going, I was going—blind." She exhaled quickly and swallowed to fight back the tears. Her head was bowed. I hoped we could narrow our conversation to one topic at a time.

"What does your neurologist say?"

"I haven't called him. He'd just ask me if I want to take prednisone or maybe start some IV ACTH. I hate how the steroids make me feel. It'll go away, the symptoms always go away." The last words were more plea than declaration.

Lauren looked up and fashioned a smile. She removed one of the hands that were wrapped around the chicken soup container. "You gonna make me find my own spoon?"

I rummaged in drawers and found a spoon and poured the soup into a deep bowl. After she tried and failed to raise a few spoonfuls to her mouth, we simultaneously realized the futility of bringing a bowl of matzo ball soup to the newly blind. Lauren said, "Hey, at least I'm fun to watch."

I carried her bowl back to the counter, removed the three-inch matzoh, and poured the broth into a large mug with elephants on it.

"Better," she said, sipping.

"Maybe you're working too hard."

"Yeah. Maybe."

"This murder, it's a difficult case, and stress can cause your symptoms to get worse."

Lauren raised her vacant eyes and looked toward me. "Been doing some reading, have we?"

"Yeah. I have," I said, unsuccessfully trying to keep the defensiveness out of my voice.

"Listen. Listen good. You're such a goddamn good listener. This disease is my problem. Not yours. I don't need your patronizing suggestions on how to live with it or how to treat it. Life goes on, and this illness will not interfere." The mixture of defiance and determination was difficult to assay. I could have pointed out the irony of someone who was too blind to get a spoon to her mouth claiming noninterference, but I didn't.

"Sometimes it's necessary to accommodate," I said softly.

"Bullshit," she said.

"Your body's talking, Lauren. You're the one who's not listening."

"What the fuck do you know? You read a couple of articles. *Reader's* fucking *Digest*, for all I know. And

219

you're ready to tell me how to live with this? Since I've been sick, I've heard it all. I've heard people tell me that my symptoms were caused by allergies, by the goddamn fillings in my teeth, by my 'attitude.' "

She started to cry, tears running to the corners of her mouth. "I have lesions in my brain. I've seen the pictures. Little dots of electrical disturbance—uninsulated wires. To me it feels like my brain is dying, and, I'm sorry, I'm not gonna slow down and prepare for the funeral."

I walked around the table and raised her to her feet, and she sobbed. Her hair smelled like hair, not perfume. Her body heaved as the sobs deepened. She was small in my arms, and I felt very helpless.

Later, Lauren left her sweats on as she climbed into bed among the dozen-plus pillows.

She told me she didn't want me to stay. "Being sick is something I'm real good at doing by myself," she told me.

"I'm going to leave Cicero with you. Don't worry about feeding her, I'll bring something when I come by to check on you tomorrow morning."

Lauren nodded and curled onto her side. I scrounged around to find a bowl to give Cicero some water, let her out the front door for a few minutes, and idly picked up the papers from Lauren's front walk. Neither Saturday's nor Sunday's *Daily* had been retrieved.

Cicero and I walked back into the bedroom. Lauren's breathing was regular; I had little doubt she was feigning sleep. I kissed the back of her head, patted Cicero, told her to stay, and locked the front door behind me as I left.

Twenty-seven

On the way to the office Monday morning I stopped to check on Lauren and my dog. Cicero was definitely the happier of the two females to see me.

Lauren said she was less dizzy and was seeing better out of her good eye and she was fine. She thanked me for my concern and for Cicero but suggested I take her back home. I asked what was wrong. She said, "Nothing," as though I should believe it. I was angry enough to argue but exited with as much equanimity as I could muster.

The drive to the office was only a couple of minutes. I parked the Subaru in its usual spot and let Cicero into the small yard behind the building. She found some shade and plopped down.

Of three patients scheduled, I saw only one. He asked me if I had grown a mustache. One left a message claiming illness, the other just didn't show. When accusations are magnified enough and repeated enough, even the staunchest of supporters begin to doubt.

Diane was booked solid all day Monday, and we barely said hello passing in the hall between our offices. She said "I'm sorry" with her eyes. She left a note offering to meet for dinner. I scrawled one back telling her I had an appointment in Denver.

Jon Younger called with another tutorial about libel

but no new weapons for our anemic arsenal.

After taking Cicero back to the ranch, I left Boulder around four for the drive to Cherry Creek in Denver. Driving against the grain of rush hour, I planned to make it in forty-five minutes and would have if the construction crew rebuilding the Mousetrap at the interchange of I-70 and I-25 hadn't been late in reopening the last southbound lane for afternoon drive time.

I got to Cherry Creek around five and spent an hour wandering around the expanses of the Tattered Cover bookstore. It was my favorite place in Denver. The Tattered Cover did for books what Saks Fifth Avenue across the street did for clothes. The store invited you with warm green carpets, stained pine bookshelves that extended far beyond your reach, high ceilings, bright, helpful staff, and antique chairs and sofas for leisurely reading and browsing. But mostly the Tattered Cover was books. It filled four huge floors of a once department store with floor to ceiling, every nook and cranny, books. It was Disneyland for the cerebral set.

I read about MS, convinced myself that I was right and that Lauren was full of shit, looked at some new volumes on transference and countertransference, and bought a book with advice on what to do if you're sued for malpractice.

I walked from the bookstore to Ray Farley's office. The door from his waiting room was open when I entered, and he called my name when he heard the door shut behind me. He stood from his leather desk chair when I entered, and I imagined he had grown even thinner. Ray was my height but at least thirty pounds lighter. His white teeth sparkled and stood out against the deep brown of his skin. The tops of his cheeks were slightly pink and full, and he, as always, reminded me of an equal opportunity version of Thumper from *Bambi*.

We sat on the consulting chairs in his office.

"How's Cyn and the kids?" Raymond's wife's name was Cynthia.

"They're well. And Merideth?"

I explained about the separation in a cursory fashion. Ray didn't push it.

"I need some help with a case."

Raymond Farley nodded and waited.

And so I began to present the case of Michael McClelland.

"The patient is a thirty-one-year-old white unmarried male employed for approximately one year as a meteorologist at NOAA in Boulder. He has been in once-a-week outpatient psychotherapy since . . . He was referred by . . . At the time of initial evaluation he complained of . . . And demonstrated or reported symptoms or signs of . . . ,"

Ray held a buff legal pad in front of him and took sparse notes as I spoke and gave the details of my treatment with Michael McClelland, although Ray never heard my patient's name. I spared nothing else with Ray, not even my farfetched suspicions about Michael killing Gretchen. He couldn't provide consultation to me if I wasn't straight with him.

I spoke nonstop for at least ten minutes before I paused.

Ray finally spoke, and his words surprised me.

"As you described this man to me, you stated his presenting problem as a history of illicit relationships with women, but you relate history replete with acting out of conflict with authority males. That's point one. Point two: You've mentioned another patient, one who committed suicide, twice during this discourse."

"Karen Hart," I said to myself.

"Whoever," said Ray.

"I'll have to think on the meaning of that. I don't know why I'm bringing her up when I talk about him. Maybe I'm so preoccupied with that case that it contaminates all my professional work. That's why I'm here, to sort that out."

"What's your question about the weatherman?"

I smiled at his portrait of the meteorologist. "I want to transfer him to somebody else. And I think I should. What I want to try and determine is whether that is an instinct born of a reasoned response to out-of-control countertransference or whether it is just acting out the countertransference?"

"What I hear you asking is whether you're considering transferring him for reasons related to his mental health or reasons related to your mental health. Is he crazy or are you crazy? Regardless of the answer, there are arguments to be made for proceeding with the transfer. Are there any other explanations for your instinct to transfer him?"

Ray was asking for my reflections on previous experience or previous relationships that might have engendered some bias toward Michael. "None I am aware of, Ray."

He tapped the end of his pencil on the top edge of the pad. "What if he's doing what you suspect him of doing? Lying to you, or intentionally misleading you. Abusing your dog. Stealing from your office. What have you got?"

I heard an editorial lurking in his failure to include murder on his list of Michael's supposed transgressions. "I'm not sure what you mean, Ray."

"The problem is not that you don't see, it's that you don't wish to."

I waited, my mind as pure as a February snow.

"You are describing a psychotic transference, Alan. Or a figment of your imagination. I've known you a long time. I know your work well. You don't seem any crazier to me than you used to, so my bias is to disregard the latter explanation."

"I didn't used to have a propensity for breaking and entering. Well, prowling, anyway."

"I'm not arguing about the judiciousness of your response to this guy. You already know that was clinically stupid and generally impulsive and inane. I'm simply presenting a case that states that because you made one crazy move it doesn't automatically follow that you made all the crazy moves that preceded it."

"So I need to consider whether the therapeutic relationship is causing a regression into psychotic transference for my patient?"

"That, yes. And if your judgment says that it is, what should you do about it? Tough call."

"You're not going to tell me what to do, are you, Ray?"

He smiled warmly — all lips, no teeth. "Tell you what to do?" he replied, his tone auguring a change in voice, creating just enough room for irreverent punctuations of vernacular. "In treatment? Noooo. But, but, but. You do seem to think you've got a vandal, a burglar, an animal abuser, and a homicidal maniac across the room from you forty-five minutes a week. What you gonna do about that? Ethicswise, legalwise?"

I waited at the feet of he who taught me about waiting.

Ray smiled again and said, "What you gonna do is nothin'."

My protest was feeble, barely sufficient, I hoped, to keep Ray talking. I wanted to hear his point of view. "You must know how frustrating that is, Ray."

"Ethics aren't there to keep you from being frustrated, my friend. They are there to protect that person across the room from people like you and me gettin' to rewrite the rules whenever we judge it to be convenient. Sometimes ethics may not feel like they serve your interests well; and sometimes they may not serve the public's interests well. But that's not why they're there. They're there to serve the patient's interests well — in this case, the weatherman's interests. And in the weatherman's interest, you keep your mouth shut. You're a clinical psychologist, not a cop.

"If this guy was liftin' strangers' car stereos, you wouldn't call the police, would you?"

I thought for a moment and then shook my head.

"Well, then. Just because you feel like *you* are this guy's victim, it doesn't change the rules. But. When you can come back here and tell me that he's hurtin' people *and* you know who's gonna be the *next* victim — well, *that,* that changes the rules."

His smile straddled from one acre of cheeks to the other.

Twenty-eight

I hoped my upcoming appointment with Michael on Wednesday would end this chapter in my life.

On Tuesday, after two insistent phone messages from Purdy about picking up the evidence of Cicero's haircut, I went looking for the twine. It was still twisted around the base of the pale trunk of the skeletal aspen tree by the front door. I unraveled it, tried for half a minute to uncinch the fused threads, went inside, grabbed a kitchen knife, and sliced it off a foot from the base. Then I cut again inside the loop around the trunk of the tree.

The long piece, maybe five feet, I shoved into a manila envelope and included with it two photographs of Cicero and their negative strips. I addressed the whole thing to Purdy, intentionally didn't add a note, and plastered enough stamps on it to insure that the postal service wouldn't ask him for postage due. I put it in the mailbox at the top of the drive for the carrier to retrieve and left Purdy a phone message that his stuff was on the way.

On Wednesday I saw two patients in the morning and Michael McClelland in the afternoon.

"You can't." His eyes flashed.

I had just told him that I was terminating his treatment.

"I need to, I have the responsibility and the obligation to make the clinical decisions that I feel are in your best interest."

"You can't just stop. You've no reason for this. No evidence to warrant this."

"As I explained, I'll help you find a new therapist, and I'll meet with you again to help you make the transition to someone new. And I'll be happy to consult with whomever you choose as your next therapist."

"No."

I sat silently. Michael McClelland and I were not hearing each other. He was no more culpable than I. I had been hoping that he would be relieved that therapy was ending and guessed that he would probably refuse a referral to a colleague. What was more likely, I knew, given his history, was that he was going to throw a fit.

"I am not the best person to be treating you, Michael." I tried again.

"Are you dumping any other clients?"

"I'm not 'dumping' anyone. And no, the answer is I'm not transferring others." I immediately regretted my candor. He didn't need to know that.

He sat, leaning forward, elbows on knees. His face was perfectly shaved, his suit perfectly pressed. Beads of sweat were appearing on his brow.

"So. It's me. Well, well, well. Here we go again."

"I'm not sure what you mean."

"That's the point, dumbshit. You haven't been paying attention. You'll understand. Before we're through, you will understand."

He stood up and towered over me. "I'll take you up on part of your offer. I'll be here next week at this time. You can count on discussing this further at that time. And," he continued, "you do not, repeat, do not, have my permission to speak to any other therapist about me." Sometimes he spoke in a way that helped me visualize the punctuation at the ends of his sentences.

He left, closing the door gently behind him. There

were still thirty-five minutes left in his session.

I felt as if I had been holding my breath for ten minutes.

The day didn't get any better.

The digital readout on my pager advised me to call Lauren at her office before six.

"I'm surprised you're at work."

"One eye's fine. I'm less dizzy. Listen, I have a question about Gretchen Kravner's chart."

"Okay. Go ahead."

"Who is 'M'?"

"I don't follow."

"In one of your session notes, in mid-August, you say, if I can read your scribbles with any accuracy, 'Appointment confusion with M, who arrived for patient's session. She denies reaction, has sympathy with my px.'

"By the way, what's 'px'? And who is 'M'?"

Here we go again. I exhaled. " 'Px' is shorthand for 'problems.' And I can't tell you who 'M' is. That is why it's only an initial in the chart. It's confidential."

Lauren exhaled. "Do I need to remind you that I have permission to have this chart?"

"But you don't have permission to read M's chart. Lauren, Jesus, what are you making a case about? It's irrelevant."

"How do you know what's relevant, Alan? I'm eating and breathing this case. I decide what leads to pursue."

"And I decide when you have pushed too far into the confidential relationship I have with my patients. I will not release information about other patients in order to help you pursue blind leads."

"It's not your call."

"It is my call. Damn it. You've just indicted her husband, Lauren. It's in this morning's paper. I'm not convinced you're not being intentionally divisive with me." A photograph of Lauren Crowder, deputy district attorney, had accompanied the story of the indictment.

"I won't discuss legal strategy with you. Suffice it to say there's sufficient evidence to indict her husband. That doesn't mean I'm convinced he's guilty. And I have no reason to be provocative with you."

"Lauren, face it, you're looking for a way to push me away. Whether it's because you're afraid of my getting close, or because you don't like fraternizing with a suspected felon, at this point I don't care. Just cut the crap with my practice. Got it?"

"You're getting paranoid, Gregory. And you don't know what you're talking about."

"Bullshit. The more shit hits the fan, the farther you get from the breeze. Don't worry, you won't be soiled by me anymore. And I mean what I said — I'll fight you on access to any tangential records. Call your grand jury. Good-bye."

I must admit, it felt pretty good to hang up the phone before she spoke another word. Acting out isn't always bad for the psyche.

I had been worried that Lauren would write me off when she finally heard about the *Daily*'s story the previous weekend. It was getting to the point where I could barely recognize myself through the mud. I wasn't worried anymore, I was sure she had written me off.

I tried to convince myself that it was all for the best. She was so tormented that life with her had been more crazy making than my loneliness. And I still wasn't sure I was interested in being with somebody with a progressive neurological disorder. Somebody else could play Florence Nightingale. Or more likely nobody else would. Lauren seemed plagued with a need to have men fall for her and then disappoint her because of some serious character flaw.

There was probably something in her relationship with her father. But it was not my job to figure out what.

When knocking on doors didn't garner a response, I had a tendency to pound on them with my head. The time had come to recognize that this door was locked.

"Our first date was a weekend in Aspen. No, she didn't sleep with me."

Diane Estevez smirked. "I didn't ask whether she slept with you."

"You would have."

"A little testy today?"

"She drives me nuts, Diane. I don't imagine we'll be seeing each other anymore."

Diane had worked through lunch hour again. We met for dinner — burgers at Tom's.

"How come when I'm paying, we have grilled fish and chardonnay, and when you're paying we have burgers and beer?"

"Feeling a mite oppressed? I guess you have some justification. The article in Saturday's paper was pretty tough." She spoke through a yawn.

I knew Diane wanted an explanation and that she didn't want to ask. The period of blind allegiance had ended abruptly.

I took the bait. "My patient apparently kept a journal about treatment. Including her fantasies about me. I haven't seen it. My conjecture is that it's largely transferential and is being quoted out of context by its current custodian, her father. I'm guessing its full of sexualized fantasies that he is choosing to read as real life."

"Ouch. How do you fight it?"

I stopped wrestling with a ketchup bottle and smiled. "Fight it? Shit, I'm barely breathing. They can fight publicly. I can't. I can't defend myself without betraying confidence, and I can't even prove that it's Karen's father feeding the shit to the paper."

"Isn't confidence automatically waived when a lawsuit is filed?"

"Generally, yes. For litigation purposes. Not to give interviews to the press. And our current legal strategy is to argue that Karen's father doesn't have standing to file this suit. So I can't argue on one hand that it's okay for me to release information because I'm being sued, and argue on the other that the suit isn't warranted.

"So I sit feeling oppressed." Diane had eaten half her hamburger. I hadn't started, so I took a bite and continued my argument. "Anyway, there wouldn't be much sympathy for my position. My trying to get the public to understand erotic transference would be like getting an accused drug dealer to argue for the medicinal uses of cannabis. I'm tainted."

We ate silently for a few minutes. The burgers were great.

"What about the turtle?" asked Diane.

"Barely scratched. It's fine."

"That's not what I meant, jerk-face. I meant what about your dog's shaved neck, what about the turtle, what about the epidemic of fatalities in your practice?"

"Coincidence? Bad luck? Who knows?"

"What if it's not coincidence? Then what is it?" she asked.

I smelled an ally in my paranoia. I proceeded cautiously.

"One explanation that fits the facts pretty well is that somebody was trying to give you a message about continuing to be affiliated with me. You haven't said anything, but I have to assume that you've been under some pressure to cut me loose."

"I have," she said, "but nothing threatening. Everybody knows I'm a maverick, Alan, that I do what I want. I probably get more slack about this sort of thing than most people would. I haven't gotten anonymous notes or strange phone calls. Your theory makes sense, but I don't buy it. I don't think you do, either."

"Then what," I asked, "are you thinking?"

"If all of this isn't coincidental, then it's related. You

232

have three dead patients. Related means that something ties at least two of them together. Related means that the dog neck and the turtle are related. And what could all this be related to?" She paused dramatically, eyebrows reaching for hairline.

"To me." I knew my lines.

"Wrong. Incomplete answer," she scolded. "That's the problem. If these things are related, then something other than you must tie them together. What could be coincidental is the fact you're involved at all."

"You lost me."

Diane's voice had more patience than her face. "If these things are related, then one somebody is doing them all. That somebody is the important person. Not you. And that somebody has a motive of some kind. And that motive, however crazy it is, requires that somebody be in your role in all this. Because the dog and the turtle are giving you messages. Which says to me that you, and not the women, who are dropping like flies, may be the target. And my guess is that you're a phantom target."

"So I shouldn't take this so personally?"

"I take it that was a joke," she said, barely pausing. "Actually I think you should take it personally. Just not rationally.

"Who else is involved with all your dead patients, Alan?"

I said, "Nobody," but I thought, M. He was having an affair with Anne Hubbard. He had met Gretchen Kravner in my waiting room. "Nobody," I repeated.

"Well, when you think of somebody, and that somebody is on your short list of people with access to your turtle, I think you have a suspect."

"There's something you're thinking and not saying, Diane. You think one of my patients is involved in this, don't you?"

"Yes. I do. I think you have a crazy patient, or ex-patient, involved in all this. And I think the patient's transference to you is psychotic. One of your patients isn't just having feelings about you like you were somebody from their past. One of your patients thinks you are, flesh and blood, somebody important from their past. And not somebody that they're fond of. Somebody they need to torment. And I think you're blind to it because you feel so guilty about your work since Karen Hart killed herself."

"I'm not blind to it. I've wondered about it for quite a while. Even went and saw Ray Farley to check out whether it was countertransference on my part to be suspicious of this one patient. Mostly, though, I think it's been hard for me to believe that anyone else would agree to see this mess as being anything other than my fault. I mean, really, how does it look? I've got one patient who kills herself and leaves a goddamn diary pointing her finger at me. I've got another patient dead in a traffic accident and I'm waiting for the *Daily* to discover I was treating her and tell the world. And now I've got still another patient who gets strangled in her bed, and I'm supposed to think anybody's gonna believe me when I argue that yet another patient is guilty? Shit, I'm reluctant to believe it; I'm sure as hell not gonna convince anybody else that a patient of mine is involved. And certainly not without revealing privileged information."

"So you do have somebody in mind?" she asked.

"Yes, as a matter of fact."

"Patient or ex-patient?"

"Yes. Both."

"Don't spin riddles."

"A guy I've just told I'm gonna transfer."

"How crazy is he?"

"On the surface, not very. He's not hallucinating. If he's delusional, so far he's kept the details of his delusions to himself. But his ego is a colander. The disintegration and regression in the transference is what's so concerning. Successful, bright guy. But odd. He has an affective range that runs the gamut from angry to rage-

234

ful. Other times he looks mostly flat."

"Borderline?"

"Diagnosis is hard, and, you know the way I look at these things, not particularly relevant. Sure there's borderline character organization. For what it's worth, he probably meets criteria. But there's something that feels more sinister than splitting about all this. He's narcissistic as hell. He's got some islands of neurotic development — triadic relationships, obsessive-compulsive defenses. But sitting with him is like sitting in the den of a hibernating bear. I find myself being careful of how I breathe and move so that I don't provoke the release of vast reserves of potential energy. And I have no doubt that the force of that energy will only be destructive. My instinctive response to him is that his underlying rage is a loaded Uzi.

"He acts out a lot of this shit. I may have screwed up by not focusing enough attention on the acting out. That probably interfered with my recognizing how he might be acting out the transference with me. You know, missed and changed appointments, then Cicero, then the turtle in your car. But I'm still at a loss to explain the transference developmentally. He's largely avoided my gentle and persistent invitations to talk about his past. Pieces can be surmised, though. If he's really doing this stuff, he wants me to be suspicious of him, but not be sure it's him. He wants me to feel vulnerable — he wants me to know that he can hurt me close to home. Literally home, office, patients, you. His expressed rage at me is for being insensitive to his feelings, especially his fears of being abandoned. He wants to hurt me when he feels he has been hurt. An instinct says that he wants me to know it's all going on but be unable to prove it. When I told him I wouldn't continue treating him, he didn't say, 'You have no reason to do this,' he said, 'You have no evidence to warrant this,' or something like that.

"There's other strange stuff, too. I found out indirectly that he has a roommate, but he never mentioned one. And I don't think I've told you this, Lauren and I ran into him on a little beach in Cabo San Lucas. That meeting never felt quite right. I was surprised to see him, but he, he seemed to have almost expected to run into me."

"Did he know you were going out of town?"

"Not from me. His appointment time wasn't involved, so I didn't tell him."

She was quiet for a moment, reflecting. "Is this the big one, the one I run into in the hall in the afternoon?"

I nodded. She grinned a little. "What's his reaction to being transferred?"

"So far, he's pissed. I don't expect it to be pleasant." I smiled my most impish smile. "You looking for any new patients?"

"Don't do me any favors, partner."

"The other day," I asked, "were you just joking about a gun?"

Nothing remained on her plate but a greasy piece of green iceberg lettuce.

"No," she said, "I wasn't joking. Wanna get some dessert someplace?"

Twenty-nine

Jon Younger had called to schedule a meeting to talk about the most recent revelations in the *Daily* and to address some clinical issues he didn't understand. On the phone I caught him up on the unpublicized mayhem in my life, telling him about the crystal turtle and about Cicero's haircut. He asked if I had any suspects. I told him that I thought the events were unrelated to the Karen Hart mess and that my best suspect was a patient who was pissed off that I was ending his treatment.

We agreed on Thursday lunch and met in a back booth in a new Thai restaurant on Thirteenth. I was privileged to see Jon in an entire suit, the encroaching autumn propelling even him out of shirtsleeves.

What he wanted to understand a little better, he said, was erotic transference.

I nodded, not so much in agreement, but rather in an acknowledgment of the desirability of understanding eroticized transference a little better myself. Freud had once said that he recognized the existence of erotic transference reluctantly. When one or two patients fell in love with him he could convince himself that they were responding to his innate beauty and kindness; when it kept occurring he realized something else was going on.

Discussing transference and countertransference with nontherapists usually left me feeling like a proponent of the occult. They tended to look at me the way I looked at Peter when he discussed almost anything but furniture.

While I contemplated how to respond to Jon's request, I ordered Pud Thai, Jon ordered something with green beans and chicken and curry, and we both requested a level of spicy heat just below searing.

"You know what transference is?" I began.

"Pretend I know as much about all this as you know about torts."

"How about I copy a few articles for you?" I offered lamely.

"Just talk."

I sighed. "Transference is a component of virtually all human relationships. It's the process of reacting to or responding to someone in a current relationship as if that person had important traits, motivations, behaviors, et cetera, of an important someone from the past. It's often based on purely unconscious motivations, or can be stimulated by traits that the current person may have in common with the important person from the past. The 'as if' part is crucial. Transference is an 'as if' experience; it's not real, but it feels real to the one experiencing it." I thought about Michael McClelland and psychotic transference and droned on. "If the 'as if' experience is absent, if somebody's experience of the person they are having these feelings about begins to ignore the confines of reality, like John Hinckley's experience of Jodie Foster, then the transference is called psychotic. Psychotic in the sense that a disorder of thinking, of reality testing, is present.

"God I hate this," I said.

"Hate what?"

"Trying to explain intrinsic psychological principles to laypeople, like you."

He ignored my protest. "Give me an example of transference."

238

"Okay. My transference to you. You're big, physically, and built a little like my dad. And like my dad, you're somebody I turn to when I'm in a mess of some kind, seeking advice. Have you ever noticed how I'm usually quite deferential to you and am usually very eager to please? That's transference. I treat you, in some ways, in the ways I treat my father. You may just think I'm a nice, obsequious guy. Actually, I treat you differently because of the nature of the transference. With other people I'm not that way.

"Transference can be either positive or negative. Mine to you is largely positive. Most of my feelings about my dad that get transferred to you are positive, or at least neutral.

"Transference in psychotherapy is simply the totality of the feelings, impressions, treatments, and so on that are bestowed on the therapist by the patient. The purer a 'blank screen' the therapist provides, the less contaminated is the transference. It was Freud's recognition of that principle that was a foundation of the psychoanalytic method. If the therapist reveals no details about his or her life, the patient has nothing to react to, so feelings about the therapist are considered to be transferential—generated within the patient, not generated by the therapist."

Our lunch arrived. "Still with me?"

With a full mouth he nodded to me, held up a finger to stall the waiter, and, after swallowing, ordered a beer. When the waiter looked at me, I said, "Sure, me too."

I turned back to Jon. "The more that a patient knows about his or her therapist, the more contaminated the transference will be with reality. If a therapist is late for appointments, is sarcastic with a patient, demeaning to a patient, it's difficult to argue that the patient's resultant anger is transferential. In reality, the patient may be justifiably angry at being mistreated.

"It's imperative, in the forms of psychotherapy that

rely on the analysis of transference, like some of the therapy I do, that therapeutic distance be maintained, so the therapist always has a clear idea which feelings and actions are being dictated from a patient's past."

Being a much better listener than talker, I have found that I finish my food much more quickly than my dining companions. They talk, I eat. As Jon Younger set down his chopsticks, my plate was mostly full. I took a sip of beer.

"Okay. Cut to the chase," Jon directed me. "Add in the sex."

I looked at him and shook my head in mock dismay. Then I continued my lecture. "Erotic transference is simply the transference of sexualized feelings to a therapist in the course of psychotherapy. It's not different from other transference other than the presence of the erotic component."

Jon poured himself a cup of pale tea and said, "So when you tell me you think this diary we think is being quoted in the *Daily* is a product of erotic transference, what you're saying is that Karen Hart was reacting to you in sexualized ways, with fantasy, for instance, because of experiences from her past she was transferring to you?"

"Simplistically, yes."

"Complicate it for me."

I pushed my plate aside before I continued. "Karen, like many sexually abused children, had a narrowly destructive range of experiences with men. Her father was quite close to her when she was young, maybe until the age of five or six, and then he traveled a lot, was very distant and unavailable. She felt deserted by him and convinced herself that she was the reason he was away so much. If she was a better girl, then he wouldn't leave. You need to remember her mother died when she was six, and from six to eight she lived with caretakers and from eight on with her stepmother and stepbrother.

240

"Therefore, one view of men was that they are distant and punitive. They stay away and are ungratifying when she is 'bad.'

"The other experience that had poisoned Karen's relationships with men was, of course, the sexual abuse. It probably started when she was around nine or ten. From the very first time her stepbrother assaulted her, he threatened to disclose to her father what she had done with him. She was terribly torn. Father was protector, probably the only protector she had from him, but she also saw her father as punitive and distant. She feared being deserted by her father if she told him what was going on. She told her stepmother once, and she laughed it off as being nothing serious, refusing to listen.

"So the sexual abuse went on. He'd corner her each time her father left town, always threatening to disclose their last sexual encounter if she refused. Needless to say, her relationship with him became sexualized. In the sense that she related to him through three currencies: violence, intimidation, and sex.

"When she started seeing me she was at a loss as to how to relate to me. I was consistent. I was accepting. I wasn't deserting her. And I asked nothing from her. Specifically, no sex.

"So she went through her limited repertoire based on her experience with men. She was late for appointments, canceled some, was late paying me. Sometimes she just sat, silent and petulant, for much of an hour, trying to piss me off, to see if I would leave her, like her father did.

"When that didn't cause me to back off she became provocative sexually. You need to understand that she didn't want me to respond to her sexually, but she didn't know another way of relating. She did what she knew. She would wear revealing clothes, go into tremendous erotic detail about previous lovers, ask personal questions of me. She made herself available to see if I would

241

take advantage of her, like her stepbrother did.

"But I stayed level. I treated her with an even amount of respect and acceptance. But the eroticized phase of the transference was quite persistent — it lasted for most of a year.

"I imagine that she sublimated much of her erotic fantasy into the diary. The acting out — the provocative behavior — only lasted a couple of months. She said she had dreams about me she wasn't able to remember details of — they were probably erotic. She admitted thinking about me and having feelings about me quite frequently but felt unable to tell me about them. Yet.

"Some of my last notes, if you reread her chart, were about my sense that she was on the brink of dealing openly with some of her feelings about me.

"It sounds very lame, Jon, but she was getting better. It had been a very successful treatment."

I picked at the cooled mass of congealed noodles and broth with a chopstick. Deciding I could eat later, I cracked open one of the fortune cookies that perched on top of the check.

Jon poured us each a small cup of tea and drank his like a shooter of whiskey. "One of the secretaries in our firm is about fifty-five or sixty," Jon said, "and she drives me nuts. She has this 'poor me' look she gets on her face when something is bothering her. Just like my mother. The same damn face. I have, at times, felt like firing her, and then I feel guilty about it and try and make adjustments in how I treat her.

"No matter what I do, I still feel crazy. If I'm understanding you right, that's transference."

I smiled and nodded. "And if you really thought she was your mother, that'd be psychotic transference. All in all, pretty astute for a lawyer."

"What's it say?" he asked, gesturing toward the white strip I was pinching between my thumb and forefinger.

"Serenity and prosperity will continue," I read.

"I think you got mine," he said. I smiled.

He put a credit card on the table. "Okay, I got it. I understand this transference stuff. Lunch is on me."

I looked at my watch. "And the hour and a quarter at a hundred and sixty an hour?"

"On you, Kemosabe."

Thirty

After leaving Jon, I meandered up the mall and back to the office, kicking my way through the scattered leaves of ash trees only recently picked clean by chinook-impersonating winds.

Meeting with Jon tended to move the cursor on my problem checklist next to the necessity of defending myself against the mounting charges associated with my psychotherapy of Karen Hart. Rational arguments, like those related to professional survival, insisted that her case deserved the highest priority, though Michael McClelland easily infiltrated and impeded attending to it.

The bulky charts I pulled from my file cabinet wouldn't fit into my briefcase. I wrapped them in rubber bands to keep the papers from flying all over the Subaru and threw the pile onto the passenger seat.

The conversation with Diane about Michael McClelland was spawning some serious rumination. I was certainly growing less conflicted about being suspicious of him but for the life of me couldn't discern a motive, either criminal or psychological, for shaving Cicero's neck or for throwing the turtle into Diane's car. And Gretchen's murder was out of the question.

But, as a suspect, I liked him. Partially because I had no one else.

Fifteen minutes later, back at home, my stomach churned from the hunger of talking through lunch with Jon. I fixed an early dinner of linguine, olive oil, garlic, and red and black peppers and ate on the sofa while the sun set in front of me. Cicero begged for a few seconds and sacked out on her rug.

After eating, I attacked the stacked charts chronologically. That is, in order of death.

First Karen Hart, then Anne Hubbard, then Gretchen Kravner. Michael McClelland, who was very much alive, was last.

Reading Karen's chart was a mindless exercise. In the months since her death, I had virtually memorized it.

The pale blue note always shocked me back to her death: ". . . he came back, to my door, just like in my dreams. I didn't even scream. . . ." "You weren't in the big house. . . ." "So there, I love you."

Anne's chart told me nothing. A twice aborted treatment. She was sprinting from the intensity of the therapeutic relationship. Nothing new there. If the allegations about me and Karen Hart hadn't become public knowledge, she would probably have stayed in treatment the second time. Her resistance had been diminishing. There was little doubt that she had been acting out a bucketful of anger at her husband by having an affair with one of his employees, but that information wasn't in her chart. It was only in Michael's.

Gretchen's chart caught me by surprise.

Lauren's concern about the waiting room encounter between Gretchen and Michael yanked me to my notes about that meeting. I found nothing revealing in those scratches. But in the subsequent session, Gretchen had revealed that she knew about my vacation in Cabo San Lucas. I hadn't remembered the comment she'd made about, "breaking the rules," either.

"What if, poochie"—Cicero cocked an ear—"after that waiting room introduction, Michael asked Gretchen out? Or vice versa? What if Michael was the new guy that Gretchen's friend told the cops about? What if Gretchen told Michael about my vacation in Los Cabos? What if those were the 'rules' she was breaking?"

Cicero's tolerance for the repetitive drone subsided. The ear went back down.

What if Michael had come to Mexico to follow me? That would explain his lack of surprise at seeing me in Mexico. What if he'd come back to Boulder before Lauren and me? Then he would have been home in time to kill —

The small matter of motive remained unaddressed. I couldn't fathom a reason for Michael to do any of it.

Exercising a need either to impugn Michael further or to exculpate him, I picked up the phone and, after a few futile attempts, finally found someone who could speak English in the billing department of the Hotel Hacienda in Cabo San Lucas. My deduction about Michael's appearance in Mexico was that he had learned about the trip from Gretchen, who'd learned about it from her friend, my ex-travel agent. But the travel agent could not have revealed the hotel at which Lauren and I were staying because Lauren, not I, had booked our room. We had run into Michael after renting a boat at the Hacienda to float out to Lover's Beach. My guess was that Michael saw us at the Hacienda and followed us out to Lover's Beach. My other guess was that he had been staying at the Hacienda.

"This is Mr. McClelland. I was a guest at your hotel in early September, and I would like to correct an error on my bill." That's how I began.

Clipped tones, only faintly accented, asked me to wait *"un momento."*

The polite voice returned and said, "I am very sorry, *señor,* but I haff no record of your visit with us."

"You are certain?" I asked.

"Sí, señor."

It took almost an hour to have similar conversations

at the Finisterra, the Solmar, and the Twin Dolphin. I couldn't find any record of where he stayed or how long he was in Mexico.

Michael, Michael. Were you home in time to leave a bandanna in Gretchen's bedroom?

Thirty-one

Shortly after breakfast Friday morning I called NOAA and asked for Michael McClelland's extension. The patient information form he had filled out had no office phone number, only a penciled notation never to call him at work. I ignored the warning. I wasn't planning on talking with Michael or even on identifying myself. His voice on the phone would tell me all I needed to know before I hung up.

"I'm sorry, I don't show an employee by that name. Do you have a department?"

"Severe Storms. Is that a department?"

"It's a laboratory. Let me check. Just a moment, please." Light tapping of fingers on a keyboard preceded ruffling of pages. "I'm sorry, I can't find a listing under that name. I checked alternate spellings as well."

"Thanks for your help."

"You're welcome."

There was no way for me to know whether the failure to find his extension was evidence of bureaucratic bungling by NOAA or sinister misinformation by Michael. Maybe he was making up a story about being a scientist at NOAA as part of the crazy transference. But he knew a lot about Phil Hubbard and seemed to know a lot about hurricanes.

Unable to get any information legally, I put my bike in the rack on top of the Subaru, dressed in faded black jeans, old Nikes, and a heavy turtleneck, threw a couple of tools into a day pack, and drove up Lee Hill toward Michael McClelland's house to do something stupid. The small piece of twine from the aspen tree was in the back pocket of my jeans.

I stopped at Raoul and Diane's house, parked the car at the bottom of their driveway, took the bike off the roof rack, and headed up the hill toward Michael's.

I lowered the bike into the culvert by the road and walked nonchalantly up the curved drive. When I reached the sharp turn to the left, I crouched and stayed close to the thick wall of pines on the western edge of the pavement. When I raised myself to peek through the trees, I could see the southern end of the house where the macadam ended. No cars.

My breathing at that moment sounded like the puffs of an H.O. version of *The Little Engine That Could*. I reminded myself that nobody was home, that Michael was at work, and so, apparently, was his roommate. It didn't help. As I edged closer to giving up the cover of the thickly vegetated ridge, I examined the house for any signs of life and saw nothing. Then I stood up and sauntered over to the red storage barn.

By breaking into his little barn, I was hoping to find something tying Michael to one of the sundry criminal acts I was suspecting him of committing. If I didn't find anything in the barn, I was prepared to break a window and go into his basement.

The barn was about eight by eight. It had asphalt shingles, double doors with one-by-four white trim, and a medium-weight keyed padlock. I took a final look around, listened for sounds in the atonal hum of breeze through the forest, took a bolt cutter from my pack, and snapped off the lock with only moderate effort. The loud snap caused me to spin around as if I hadn't generated the noise. I was sure that the big gun was pointed at my back.

Before I opened the latch I pulled on some old leather

249

handball gloves. I twisted the broken lock into an unbroken-looking configuration and hung it back on the hasp, opened the left-hand door, stepped in, and quickly closed it behind me.

Inside, it was dark. Only the outline of the door was illuminated. The little room had a ceiling so low, I felt like I should crouch. I expected to trip over a lawn mower or snowblower if I moved, so I didn't.

The little high-intensity flashlight I found in the backpack needed new batteries. Its dim beam illuminated a rack of tools on one wall—snow shovel, rake, broom, gas-powered string trimmer—and a big Toro snowblower on the back wall. The other wall held a narrow workbench, maybe twenty inches deep. The wall above the workbench was lined with pegboard engraved with outlines of a dozen hand tools, all in their prescribed places. Two studded snow tires sat upright beneath the bench next to a stack of fiberboard shelves. A stout round cardboard barrel with a sheet metal rim sat in a corner by the door.

Right in front, second shelf, was a large cone-shaped spool of spun brown twine. I remembered the guy at the Christmas tree lot on Arapahoe had one every year. He cut off lengths to tie the bulky trees on top of cars. I took the twine from my back pocket and held it near the spool. It looked like it matched to me. In the light available from my rapidly fading flashlight, I probably could've convinced myself that fiber-optic cable was a perfect match, too.

I stuffed the sample back into my pocket and found a wire cutter on the wall above the workbench before I heard the whine of overtaxed cylinders echoing in the little barn.

Within seconds I heard harsh braking and the sound of rubber trying to grip asphalt. I guessed the car was parked about five feet from the door of the barn.

"Hello, Michael, mind if I borrow a wire cutter?" Despite the rehearsal of my next line, which I rejected, I maintained enough control of the few synapses necessary to order the extinguishing of the faint torch in my hand. I was left crouching in the darkness, holding a doused flashlight in one hand and a wire cutter in the other.

The car door slammed. Slammed intentionally. One one thousand, two one thousand, three one thousand. Footsteps. Pivot. How long does it take to walk five feet?

The steps faded to the north. God. He's going to get the gun. Another door slammed. Front door?

I waited. It was mid-October when I entered the shed. I waited, I was certain, until about Thanksgiving.

No more slamming doors, no more footsteps. Maybe he hadn't seen the missing lock.

Chirping. Beep, beep, beep, beep. God help me, my beeper was going off. Why didn't I set the damn thing to vibrate instead of chirp? I shoved the flashlight into my mouth, but with the gloves on I couldn't operate the tiny buttons that would silence the damn beeper. Since my mouth was full of flashlight, I couldn't use my teeth to pull off the glove. Exasperated, I methodically placed the tools on the workbench, pulled off a glove, and pressed the little button. Out of habit I lifted the box from its holster while I waited to be discovered. Another little button illuminated the horizontal screen, which read, "Please call Michael McLendan before 1:00 today."

Did I see a phone someplace? Sorry, Michael. I'm not free to return your call. When you come out to kill me you can tell me what you want.

I wondered whether somebody in the house could see the front of the shed. It was parallel with the front of the house, maybe ten feet to the west. I decided it was probably safe to open the door closest to the house, slither out, and stay in the shadows of the shed as I escaped into the pines. I pulled the gloves back on and returned the wire cutter to its peg.

The front door of the house opened just as I cracked

the door to the shed. The light blinded me, and the sounds of footsteps terrified me. I froze again. I was a statue memorializing the unknown idiot.

Mostly, then, I thought about the gun. Would he shoot first? Through the door, no warning? At least, if he did, I'd be dead before I was humiliated. I quickly decided that I preferred that. There was nothing to be gained by being humiliated first.

The steps came closer, right to the door, and stopped. I heard jingling, keys. He wanted to open the shed!

No. He opened the car door. I heard it close. Then nothing. He'd noticed the missing lock. No. The car started. It backed up a little. Then it came forward and faded off to my left and down the drive.

I exhaled. I really needed to pee. Or to throw up. Competing needs.

I counted to one hundred, listening for signs of his return, heard nothing, and cracked open the door. I put the flashlight back in my mouth, retrieved the wire cutter, and cut a couple of feet of twine off the spool and stuck it in my pocket. The wire cutter I replaced on the pegboard. I turned back toward the door, and my eyes fell on the contents of the cardboard barrel. Mixed in with the wood scraps, paper, and wire was a widely scattered arc of black hair. Dog hair, no doubt.

Michael McClelland had done it.

Why?

I retrieved some of the hair from the barrel and threw it into the day pack. I should probably have started carrying evidence envelopes. I'd ask Purdy for some the next time he interrogated me, which would most likely be for breaking and entering.

Shock at not being wrong interfered with my registering the now familiar whine as the car I had never seen assaulted the incline on Lee Hill Road. When the scratching on gravel began and the rumble of downshift exploded, I finally processed the sounds. My hand was on the shed door, which I threw shut. I ran to the ponderosa pines ten feet to the south, and was diving for cover before I saw the car turning through the dogleg. I rolled and landed behind a ridge parallel to the driveway.

After edging to the top, I could see Michael McClelland get out of a red Honda Prelude and walk, fists clenched, to the open door of his little red barn.

"Shit." He offered the profanity evenly. "I'll get you fucking kids. I will." These words were clearly promise, not threat.

He looked inside the shed, inventoried its contents, and then lumbered to the front door. I scurried backward down the ridge and ended up using the neighbor's driveway as a trail back to the road and hopped on the Bianchi.

Halfway to Raoul and Diane's I heard a car approaching the bicycle from the rear. I straightened my arms and lowered my head into the protected space between them, only looking up when the Prelude was a red dot a couple of hundred yards ahead.

Follow that car.

Maybe another time. In a couple of minutes I was at Raoul and Diane's house.

I carefully rested the bike against their mailbox post before the battle of competing needs was won by throwing up.

As I lay on my back in front of their starkly contemporary house on a lumpy bed of pine cones and pine needles, breathing deeply to diminish the urge to vomit up additional bodily fluids best left undisturbed, I thought, People really do this for a living?

Thirty-two

Certain that I had transgressed the boundaries of good taste, fair play, legal conduct, and ethical behavior, I did next what any conscientious psychologist would do — I returned Michael McClelland's phone call as soon as I got back to the office.

The all-too-familiar voice droned from the answering machine tape. Beep.

"This is Alan Gregory returning your call. It's just after two o'clock. I'll try and reach you at this number again later today or this evening."

Next I walked the few blocks to Lauren's office at the Justice Center. The secretary who stood guard over the office stalls that radiated from the central desk asked if I had an appointment. I said I didn't but would wait.

She seemed to fight an impulse to tell me that I hadn't been invited to wait. She picked up her phone, stared straight at me as I held my ground an inch from the front of her desk, hit one button, and said, "A Mr. Gregory is here to see you. Without an appointment." She listened for a moment and shook her head just enough so it was arguable whether it had really moved.

"Ms. Crowder will be with you in a moment."

"Thank you," I said, my demeanor changing from arrogant to gracious.

I waited a long time, given that a few minutes of reading *Modern Maturity* is included in most people's definition of a long time. Finally Lauren stood in her doorway and said, "Come in."

The gatekeeper raised her chin and sniffed a little air through her nostrils as I walked past her to the doorway. Lauren pushed the door shut and, before she gave me an opportunity to apologize for barging in on her, proceeded to blast me with a tone chilling enough to have been carved from ice, "I don't appreciate you dropping in here without calling."

A forest-colored pine needle on the sleeve of my sweater caught my attention. I walked over and let it flutter into the wastebasket by Lauren's desk. "If you want to discuss courtesy—let's discuss the propriety of not returning phone calls. Or not keeping promises to set up a time to get together."

"I've been busy," she said.

"Good reason. Good excuse. I'll make a note of it. Mind if I pull it out someday to blow somebody away with the urgency of my neglect of them?"

"Sarcasm doesn't become you, Alan. Anyway, you hung up on me the last time we talked."

We were both still standing. She had shuffled enough steps to put her desk between us. A wooden-frame Scandinavian-style couch with inadequate brown cushions was across from the desk, behind me.

"As far as I can tell, you find little of what I do 'becoming.' I've tried being caring and concerned and been met with the receptivity that a Klansman gets at an NAACP meeting. You've made it clear, lady, that you don't need me. It's written in neon on your forehead. There's a billboard in my living room that says, 'She doesn't need you, stupid.' So you can stop showing me how well you handle every—and I mean every—aspect of your life, without my assistance or intervention.

"Well, I'm not afraid to admit that I need you. You brought"—I emphasized the past tense as much as I could afford to—"some light into my life, and I liked it. A lot. Maybe too much. It was a break in the sky on a cloudy day.

But I'm fine without you, too. I'll miss you. I already miss you. But at least I don't have to run from the fact" — I saved enough emphasis points to lay a few on "fact" — "that I really care for you. I will not, however, put up with your mistreatment of me so that you can salve your insecurity over being sick, or work through your maladaptive attraction to dominating men."

She sat on her desk chair and twirled it ninety degrees. In profile her perfect hair demarcated a straight line from temple to the nape of her neck. Her nose had a little bump I'd never noticed before. Barely opened lips carved a deep, sensual gash into her mouth. Without turning back toward me, she said, "Are you done?"

I sat down on the hard sofa. I folded my arms on my chest. "I'm not sure. Maybe." I wanted to bite her bottom lip. Just a little harder than a kiss.

The afternoon sun caught a tear swelling in the lashes at the rim of her right eye. It hung there, generating microscopic rainbows. "What do you want from me, Alan?" I waited, suspecting that the question was rhetorical. "I can't give you what you want right now. Yes, your kindness scares me. Yes, I'm safer on my own. Or at least I feel that way. But no. I really don't want you to go away. In Cabo San Lucas, you said that you were struggling with your reaction to my illness. Well, I'm struggling now. With my reaction to you. I fear that when I say I want you, you'll be gone. Running from me. Running to Merideth. Don't get this wrong; this isn't jealousy, it's not that simple. This has to do with trust. In my life men can do decent things. At the end, Jake did. My boss, the DA, he has. But men can't be counted on." She paused as the tear tracked down her cheek, disappearing into the darkness shadowed by her hair. "I can't afford to count on them. On you."

"Lauren, I —" I stood up and moved toward the desk.

"No. Don't, please." She waved an open hand across her chest. Her voice cracked. "Sit down." She tilted her head back so that the fine skin on her neck was stretched tight. She had done that, too, in the shy passion of making love.

The moments had little in common but their intensity.

"Please give me some time, Alan, and I'll try to be more . . . gracious"—these next words tumbled out reluctantly—"and more considerate, in how I respond to you."

"Sounds like an apology to me," I said.

She turned toward me, shoulders and up only, shaking her head. "It's as good as you're going to get. Now, please go. I have work to do."

"I'll call," I said.

"Fine," she assented.

I reached down into my day pack and put the manila envelope from it on her desk. The bundle thudded heavily on the laminate. "You might want to check the prints on this. And compare them with the ones on the glasses at Gretchen's house." I closed the door behind me as I left.

I stopped next to the guardian angel's desk and at the tilt of her head and widening of her eyes said, "Business." I smiled and walked back to my office.

When I got home around five-thirty, I called Michael's number again. The machine was still on duty. I left another message.

The afternoon had warmed, and the warmth lingered in the graduating darkness. I lit charcoal in the kettle on the deck of the house and prepared to grill the swordfish I had picked up at Alfalfa's on the way home.

My appetite felt foreign; I moved quickly to take advantage of it. While the coals were firing I tore lettuce and cut strips of snow peas to make a salad. And I opened a bottle of Oregon Pinot Noir. Wrong wine, even I knew, but it hadn't been a day for adhering to social conventions.

The doorbell rang after dinner, answering my question about how long it took to compare fingerprints in a large suburban police department.

"You're not going to tell me whose they are, are you?" Lauren was wearing the same blue suit with a jacket tailored at the waist that she had been wearing that afternoon.

"Would you like to come in?"

I disappeared into the kitchen and grabbed another wineglass, filled it halfway, and handed it to her.

We each took a sip before I spoke. "I can't, Lauren. I wish I could. I really do."

"What if I threaten you with the fact that yours are there, too?"

"Mine are on the turtle, Lauren, not on the glasses."

"Where'd you get the turtle?"

I knew she would be asking that question and had batted around whether I could answer it without divulging confidential information. I decided I could. "You like it? It was a gift."

"Alan—"

"It's from my office."

"These fingerprints are from one of your patients?" The words formed more statement than question, and I could probably have assented through silence. I couldn't argue that the communication was privileged if I didn't acknowledge that a patient was involved. I gestured for her to sit beside me on the couch.

"There's a good possibility of that. Yes."

She had spoken evenly to this point, like attorneys in the movies who ask benign questions prior to raising their voices and pointing their fingers in accusation at simpleminded witnesses. "One of your patients killed Gretchen Kravner."

"I doubt that I need to point out the frailty of the support for that argument. The person who handled that turtle, perhaps a patient of mine, had a glass of wine with Gretchen Kravner."

"How did you know it was wine? Has he talked about this with you?"

Two could play this game. "How do you know it's a 'he'?"

She sighed. "Alan. A murder has been committed. A man who might be innocent has been indicted and arraigned. And you have evidence that might bust this case. You have to tell me."

"What do you mean, 'a man who might be innocent'?"

"Hair identification is back. The hairs in the victim's bed that aren't hers aren't her husband's, either. Likewise the ones vacuumed from her body. The seminal fluid was fresh and dispersed in her reproductive tract. She probably came during sex; anyway, it doesn't look like rape. The seminal fluids are from a secretor. Her husband isn't a secretor. Somebody else was there. Either in addition to her husband or instead of him. I need to know who was there, Alan. You've got to tell me."

I had expected a better argument from her. "You're not feeling well, are you?" I asked.

She looked down at her wine and shook her head. But, with Lauren, any invitation to compassion was short-lived. "What is *so* precious, *so* inviolable, about confidentiality? We are talking about a brutal murder, Alan. God, there need to be exceptions made sometimes."

"When? Let's imagine — no, no, no — this goes beyond imagination to pure fantasy. Let's fantasize that you, she who relies on no one, are in psychotherapy with somebody here in town." The look on her face told me that my sarcasm was barely being tolerated. "And that you told your therapist about your MS. And you were running for district attorney of Boulder County. And let's say your therapist thought, considering your health, that holding elected office wasn't a good idea but couldn't convince you not to run. So your therapist told the *Daily*. In the uproar you're forced to drop out of the race. Is that a good enough reason to breach confidence?" She started to reply, but I held up my hand; her open mouth closed slowly, like it was hinged by a hydraulic closer. "What is most germane in this argument is that if you, or any patient, thought your therapist had any latitude in choosing what to disclose, you couldn't tell them your secrets, fearing that they might release them to your boss, your spouse, your priest, your mother, whoever. And without knowing your secrets, that therapist couldn't help you. If a patient's secrets were not inviolate, the patient would never walk in the door to therapy the first time. The patient would never seek help. The entire process of psychotherapy rotates on the bearings of privileged information. Confidentiality is so precious, Lauren, because without it there is no psychotherapy.

"Does the existence of privilege create dilemmas? You bet it does. Last year I was seeing a patient who was the adult daughter of a very prominent family practitioner in town. She told me, over time, about a lot of unseemly things her father had done. Alcohol abuse. Battering her mother a bit. And then my patient told me that her father had fondled her on a number of occasions when she was a kid and that she wouldn't leave her daughters alone with him."

I had Lauren's attention. "So what should I do? Report him to the medical examiners? Take out an ad in the paper warning parents that they're taking their children to see a pedophile? Please keep in mind that she didn't accuse him of any abuse of her children. The child abuse reporting law only permits me to break confidentiality when I know of abuse or suspect abuse of a child. It does not permit me to break confidentiality in the absence of that suspicion. I drive by his office now and I pray he's not hurting any children in there.

"Case two. Again, last year, I'm treating a pilot for one of the big airlines that fly out of Stapleton, in Denver. He tells me he's panicking when he's forced to land in the vicinity of thunderstorms. In Denver, on summer afternoons, that's like a ship captain panicking when he's forced to dock on water. He describes his panic to me. He freezes. Can't think. Sometimes closes his eyes. He's terrified he's going to crash. Sometimes he dissociates, finds himself on the runway in the plane and doesn't even remember how he got there.

"Do I report him? To his employers? To the FAA? On what grounds? There aren't any grounds to break confidentiality, despite compelling arguments that it would be for the public's welfare to do so. And if I were permitted to break confidentiality with that one pilot, five hundred other pilots with similar problems, or thousands more with closet alcohol or drug abuse or bad reality testing would never choose to get help. Where does virtue lie? In protecting the public from one sick pilot, or in permitting thousands more to continue flying without any avenue for getting confidential help?

"I encouraged the daughter of the family practice doc to consider some action. She refused. I encouraged the pilot to take a leave of absence while he was treated. After a couple of months he did. None of his planes crashed in the interim. Was I frightened they would? You bet. I have many more examples of times when somebody might benefit by my breaking the privileged communication my patients are entitled to with me, but the legal criteria to do so are very limited. And, unless and until the 'duty to warn' provisions of *Tarasoff* are activated, I don't have one with the case you're working on."

Tarasoff was the landmark decision in California that had begun to spell out the parameters of what became known as the "duty to warn" when a psychotherapist learned of a threat by a patient to another, identifiable, person.

Lauren raised herself from the sofa in a single graceful motion and stepped in stockinged feet to the western windows, becoming part of a collage set against the pastel sky and shy, interlocking mountain peaks. "Why did you give me this much? The turtle? And the lead?"

"I can't answer that without divulging other information." The other information was that I had rationalized giving her the turtle because it had been discovered outside the boundaries, so to speak, of Michael's therapeutic relationship. The other information also included the reality that Lauren had told me that she couldn't identify the prints on the wineglasses. Having two sets shouldn't change that reality much. Anyway, even now all I knew was that there was a match; I still didn't know that the prints were Michael's. But I needed Lauren to believe I knew whom they belonged to. Otherwise my claims of confidential relationship evaporated like virga on a Colorado summer afternoon.

"Is this 'M'?" Lauren asked, as much to herself as to me.

I didn't respond. Instead I got up, went into the kitchen, and put together a plate of fruit and cheese and bread. Lauren had moved back to the sofa when I returned from the kitchen. I set the plate down close to her; she didn't touch it but said, "Thanks." She hesitated, then looked at me, then continued. "The 'M' stands for 'Mickey.' That's what Gretchen's friend finally remembered. She said that the new guy Gretchen was dating was named Mickey." She stared straight at me for the first time, trying to read some reaction in my face. One of her eyes failed to track correctly. And the pupils were different sizes.

"How's the blindness?" I asked, trying to visualize my soon to be ex-patient with a nickname of Mickey.

"Okay. I'm still blind in one eye."

"And still dizzy?" She nodded and sipped her wine.

The phone rang. I picked it up and listened to the line go dead when I said hello. I set the receiver back on the hook and sat down next to Lauren on the couch.

"You're not going to argue with me anymore?" I asked.

She sighed. "Not tonight."

Her arms were crossed over her breasts, each hand grasping the opposite bicep. She lowered her head and rested it against my chest. "It's tempting, you know," she said.

"No. I don't know. What's tempting?"

"Letting you comfort me."

That had been my second guess.

Thirty-three

She stayed in my arms until she excused herself to go to the bathroom.

Upon her return, I was hoping for another button to be loosened on her blouse. Or for her to be wearing my bathrobe.

"Is this the turtle that was thrown through Diane's windshield?" She asked. I didn't answer.

"I don't think the question of whether you can refuse to divulge this information is as clear as you think it is, Alan."

I had forgotten that I had told her about the broken windshield and had not anticipated this line of questioning. "It's the same turtle that went through Diane's windshield. But I'm not free to discuss how the fingerprints may have gotten on it."

"Are you saying the fingerprints aren't those of whoever threw it through the windshield?"

"I'm not saying."

"God, you can be exasperating."

"You're right. I can be. But standing up to you doesn't make me evil. I can be just as firm and principled as you can, and that doesn't mean I'm going to mount a coup and take over your life. I want you to solve Gretchen's murder. I may already have gone too far in helping you do so. But I won't divulge confidential information or information culled from my therapeutic relationships."

Her voice warmed a bit with her next words. "I hope you're not fucking with evidence in a murder investigation. They'll hang you. I'll"—she paused and looked up to the heavens—"hang you."

I felt some salvation in my appraisal that she would, at the very least, build the gallows with a modicum of remorse.

The Peugeot's tires screeched, and it dragged its oil pan as it cleared the top of the driveway. One of the pathetic aspen trees by the front door relinquished its last golden leaf at my feet as I watched her go.

The next morning was Saturday. Around nine-thirty Michael McClelland picked up his phone on the first ring.

"You didn't call me back yesterday."

"I returned your call twice. Each time I left a message on the answering machine."

"Returning my call after I have indicated I'm not gonna be available is not my idea of responsible professional behavior." An agenda was being proposed. I decided not to try to enlist his vacationing observing ego further. Actually, his ability to muster a rational assessment of the world around him seemed to be suffering an abject decline.

So I waited.

"I want to meet with you about your deserting me."

"We're set for our final meeting on Wednesday."

"I want to meet before that. Actually, I want to meet today."

"I don't go in to the office on weekends. Except for emergencies."

"Consider this an emergency."

"Is it an emergency?"

"Yes," he said calmly. "Yes, it is. It's about me hurting somebody."

We agreed to meet at noon.

* * *

Before leaving the house for downtown, I dressed in black corduroys, an old button-down collar white shirt, and a bulky red-and-black sweater. I covered up with a leather jacket.

Michael was as casual as I was. His Italian suit had been replaced by acid-washed brown denim and a turtleneck. He was wearing the sunglasses that had fallen from my head the first time I visited his house.

I waited patiently while he pushed up the sleeves of his sweater to reveal his birch-branch forearms. He rested his elbows on his knee, hung his head for a moment, and began.

"It's called 'abandonment,' " he said.

I was angry enough at Michael McClelland to respond with defensiveness. "I'm not abandoning you; I'm acknowledging that the treatment is no longer helpful, and I'm assisting you in finding another therapist."

"It's called 'abandonment,' " he repeated. "In the professional literature—it's a legal concept—what you're doing is called 'abandonment.' " The almost whisper was reedy and soft, the face that of a poker player laying down a full house in front of a big pot.

"Tell me," I said.

"It's an ethical and legal violation to desert me like you are. Ethically, it's covered under the responsibilities of psychologists to provide 'continuity of care' for their patients. Legally, as I've noted, simply terminating me when you acknowledge that I need continued treatment is probably sufficient to convince a court of your liability. Should I sue."

"What have you been reading?"

"Ethical Standards, some journals."

"I don't understand why you're pushing this. I've told you clearly that I'm not the best person to be treating you."

"I don't agree, obviously. I suspect that there're tangential reasons that you're not divulging. Regardless, it's my intention to continue treatment with you."

"It's not an option, Michael. My ethical responsibility is to provide you with reasonable care. In offering to arrange a transfer I've met that criteria. I'm in no position to compel you to pursue such an arrangement. My legal responsibility is met by the same act. I'm not abandoning you; quite the contrary, I've offered to assist you in finding appropriate continuing care. If you read enough of the literature, you'll discover that it's occasionally therapeutically indicated for a therapist to restrict appointments or to transfer certain patients.

"Regarding your veiled threat to sue, I'll take my chances. Get in line."

Michael McClelland's head was down during my discourse. He raised it to look at me. The timbre of his whisper had lost its cushion. "I've never told you that I can be dangerous. I can hurt people."

The image in my head was of the bazooka at his house. "Are you making a specific threat? Are you currently having an impulse to hurt someone?" Like me?

I assumed that he had read enough of the literature to know what I was asking with my questions. If he made a threat that permitted me to identify a potential victim of violence, I was required under the *Tarasoff* ruling to exercise my "duty to warn" by making some reasonable effort to protect the victim, either by warning them, telling the police, or doing whatever else the court in hindsight might or might not deem to have been reasonable. In addition, if I could determine that Michael was in "imminent danger" of hurting either himself or others, I could admit him to a psychiatric hospital against his will for up to seventy-two hours under Colorado law.

Either act would bring significant joy.

He backed off. "No. Just offering additional evidence of my need for continued treatment. And suggesting the consequences of not providing that treatment."

"Once again. Do you currently have plans or impulses to hurt anyone in particular?"

"I've answered that question."

"Then I'll restate my position. I'm happy, eager, to arrange appointments for you with two psychologists, so that you may choose one to continue your treatment. Should you refuse to accept that offer, I'll interpret your refusal to mean that you've chosen not to continue in psychotherapy and that you've made a judgment that continued psychotherapy is not right for you. My recommendation is that you continue in psychotherapy with a qualified therapist; not doing so will be evidence of your acting against professional advice. In no circumstance, however, will I agree to meet with you again after today."

I picked up a business card on which I had listed the office numbers of two colleagues whose work I respected. In addition I had listed the number of the twenty-four-hour crisis line of the local mental health center. As I held it out to him, he didn't move to accept it. I balanced it, phone numbers up, on the ball his intertwined fingers made in front of him. When I leaned forward I could smell his cologne and feel his breath.

His next movement was abrupt and set the card flying. He retrieved the sunglasses from the table and held them in his right hand. With his left hand he gestured at the table and said, "One of your menagerie is missing."

The hair on my neck bristled. I used every smidgen of my self-control not to throw the Steuben snail into his face.

"Anything else?" I asked.

His thin lips pursed, and he pushed the sunglasses onto the top of his head. "You don't get it. What you're trying to do doesn't work." He stood up and left, carefully stepping around the card on the floor.

When my pulse subsided to a number that was reasonable for an IQ, I began to try to make some sense of whatever craziness was motivating Michael to target me, my patients, my dog, and my partner for his evil retribution.

I had thought about it much of the previous night. The only motive I could develop for Michael McClelland to kill Gretchen Kravner was if she was threatening to divulge their relationship to me. If, indeed, they were having a relationship. The barbering of Cicero was intended to get me to feel paranoid. It worked. Okay? The vandalism of Diane's Saab was to repeat the same message. I'm vulnerable to him. So what?

The arguments were cogent but not particularly compelling. Some important pieces were absent. Transference always implied repetition; I didn't know what Michael was reenacting.

Errands, Frisbee with Cicero, and a solitary late day bicycle ride through eastern Boulder County all intervened before the pieces tumbled a little closer together.

The matrix of little lines on my pager announced that Philip Hubbard had called and wanted to hear from me as soon as possible. So much, I thought, for having weekends off.

He answered my call on the first ring. I identified myself, and he said, "I want to ask you a question."

I waited.

"Was Anne having an affair, Dr. Gregory?" His voice got shallow and soft as the words spilled out.

Quicksand. "She never mentioned an affair to me, Dr. Hubbard." I knew that he had been asking for a statement of truth, not merely one of fact. He didn't have the key to open the door to truth. Apparently unbeknownst to him, his employee held that key.

"I had her car checked out by a mechanic before I turned it over to the insurance company. Looking for mechanical failure, sabotage, whatever. He didn't find anything, said she must have lost control.

"She'd been drinking. I have her autopsy report. But she wasn't legally drunk. Only impaired, .06, but enough, I guess, so she blew that turn on the wet road."

I remembered that turn, the sounds of the tires on the slush, the crumpled fender, the khaki blanket. The burgundy boot.

"And she'd been fucking somebody that night. Said so right in the report. Somebody, I guess, who lives up Lee Hill, or Boulder Heights, or Bow Mountain. Somebody up there, she'd gone to see somebody up there and have sex with him. My wife was killed on the way back from a goddamn tryst.

"And it wasn't the first time. She was pregnant. Five, maybe six weeks."

"I hadn't seen her for over two months when she died, Dr. Hubbard."

"Do you know how stupid I feel? I mean, I should've known. I didn't suspect a thing. And what's gnawing at me now is a perverted twist on the typical husbandly reaction to an unfaithful wife. I can't let go of the possibility that the baby was mine. And that some bastard killed my baby."

I felt despondent, for the second time, at the news of the pregnancy. And deep compassion for the thrice scarred man on the other end of the line. I waited, questioning my role.

"You would tell me, wouldn't you? If you knew?"

I phrased a reply rapidly, fearing the impression of a carefully worded response. "If there was anything in her records, I'd tell you. I assure you of that."

He hung up, still tormented.

My memory served me, usually, with the reliability of a well-trained dog. A dog unlike Cicero. Psychotherapy was made easier for me by my natural capacity to recall sessions with patients—they said, I said—as if I were playing back a videotape. Over the years many patients had questioned me about or accused me of taping sessions. I didn't.

I straddled a dining room chair. My hand still held the phone that had connected me with Phil Hubbard. I remembered a memory fragment from Michael McClelland's first session.

It was too important not to check it.

Cicero failed to respond when I called her. She rocketed to me when I rephrased the question to include going in the car.

The big dog could never decide where to sit in the Subaru. If it was warm, she wanted the universal dog position—shotgun with the window open. On cold days, like this one, she fought canine ambivalence. Sometimes she balled up on the floor in front of the passenger seat until the heater began to curl her hair. Other times she tried to balance on the seat, facing forward, like her master. Curves and deceleration usually rendered this a precarious choice. The best place for her—she knew it and I knew it—was in the broad expanse of the back of the wagon, but it was at least four feet from me, and she rarely gave it a try without some verbal coercion.

On our way downtown she started off in the shotgun-please-open-the-window position. By the time we arrived she was in back where she should have been all along.

At the office, Cicero was checking out new smells and imaginary intruders while I pulled Michael's file. I had copious notes of my early sessions with him. They had thinned just a little as he had become more familiar to me.

The first session was what I wanted. He was talking with disgusting ease, as though he were relating the trade of the Broncos' sixth-round draft pick, about the death of Anne Hubbard and his feelings about his boss,

Anne's husband, Phil.

I read my process notes on his comments on Phil Hubbard. "The man," I had written, paraphrasing Michael, "is a cold enough bastard that I could've enjoyed him knowing his wife was having an affair. But I didn't want him to know I was the one fucking her. I don't have to worry about that anymore, do I?"

My big dog roamed around the empty old house. The outside lights were on, the inside lights were on, and all the locks were locked. I didn't feel safe.

Because I knew what Michael was doing. I knew the repetition. And I knew he was doing it to me.

Michael had been fucking Anne Hubbard. Anne may have been having an affair with Michael, but there was no doubt that what Michael McClelland was doing to Anne Hubbard was fucking her. Actually, by fucking Anne Hubbard he was trying to fuck Phil Hubbard. It was the impoverished revenge of the neglected: If you don't pay attention to me, I will foul something you cherish.

Anne told Michael, in a fit of self-respect or simple remorse, that she was going to break it off and suggested that she might confess to Phil. Maybe she did it to cleanse her soul, more likely to grease her departure from the marriage.

Then Anne died. Did Michael sabotage her car? Phil Hubbard's mechanic said no. My suspicion was that it was a death of convenience for Michael. Anne's death eliminated the risk of her telling Phil about the affair. Her death let him off the hook. It also created a vacuum, a need for someone to succeed Phil Hubbard as the object of Michael's transference.

Michael unconsciously chose me to replace Phil Hubbard as the desired but neglectful male. He barbered my dog when I was out of town and unavailable to him. He started dating Gretchen. Gretchen told him that she was going to tell me they were seeing each other. He couldn't permit me to know that. The solution was, for Michael, familiar. If Gretchen would just die, he would feel better. His secret would be protected.

So he killed her.

He apparently didn't sense enough vulnerability in me after Gretchen's death, so he stole the turtle and dragged Diane and her Saab into things to insure my suspicion of him.

Jesus. If his imagined rejection by me caused two incidents of mayhem and one of murder, what the hell was he going to do now that I had really rejected him?

As I pondered the distasteful possible answers to that question, I reminded myself that what I had ended that afternoon was the psychotherapy of Michael McClelland.

His psychotic transference might not be so easy to terminate.

Thirty-four

One of the more disturbed ambulatory patients I had ever treated had been a private detective. By the time he succumbed to family pressure to get some help, he was no longer in the investigations business. By then he was complaining of severe depression and frequent outbursts of rage and was barely hanging on to a job cooking in the almost superfluous kitchen of one of the singles bars on the mall. One week he would profess allegiance to AA's 90/90 philosophy—ninety meetings in ninety days—and get to a meeting every day. The next week he would be too busy, too angry, or, more usually, too drunk. In my early years in practice, I tended to err in being too lenient with addictive behavior that interfered with treatment, and I allowed him more latitude than was prudent. When I began, belatedly, to set more appropriate limits, his anger surfaced, and some of his primitive rage was directed at me. I could handle the verbal tirades and the transferential references; what I couldn't handle was when he started investigating me.

The dossier he dumped in my lap, literally, was a disturbing mixture of fact and fantasy. He had used old contacts to uncover my driving records and the records of my appearances in court as an expert witness, had visited the county clerk and researched the history of my property transactions in the county. He had somehow found out about Merideth and had taken a tour of the television station in Denver trying to get a look at her. He had examined the information the state board that licensed psychologists made public, had reviewed my listing in the directories of the Colorado Psychological Association, the American Psychological Association, and the National Register of Health Service Providers in Psychology, and had even pulled my dissertation out of the library at the university.

My sense of outrage at being investigated rivaled the pervasive aura of intrusion I experienced after a burglary of my apartment during my internship in Denver. The thief had stolen my privacy and sense of control along with my cameras and stereo. This patient had managed similar larceny during his impromptu investigation.

Convincing myself that my inquiry into Michael McClelland's affairs was any less noxious than my ex-patient's investigation of me was a consuming effort of rationalization. The more my inquiry became a crusade, the more effectively I was required to rationalize.

Mostly I rationalized by declaring myself cornered. When faced with an impossible situation, one had to do something possible. My impossible situation was the stark reality of Karen Hart's death. I knew that even if I could dodge the boulder of culpability for her death that was careening toward me, my impotence in defending myself from the landslide of rubble that accompanied it down the hill seemed almost assured.

But detecting Michael McClelland seemed possible. Probably stupid. But possible. Gretchen Kravner's death was unsolved, and the minor league terrorism of my life showed no signs of abating. Without the confidential information that I possessed, I felt close to certain that the police were going to be unsuccessful in pursuing Michael. And the failure of the police to capture Michael undoubtedly meant that one or more of my few remaining female patients was in danger of physical harm. I'd gone over the list a half dozen times in my head and couldn't discern any reasons for suspecting that one of my women patients was a more likely next victim than another. So I focused my attention on interfering with the lethal crusade of my one and only suspect.

I had ulterior, less compelling motives for my quest as well. Despite my best efforts to avoid her challenges, I was competing with Lauren. And I wanted to win.

The Boulder County Clerk's Office wasn't any help. The matronly woman who guided me through the maze of records was as patient as she could manage to be. She reminded me three times that it was Monday morning.

The property at the address on Lee Hill was owned by a partnership with a Longmont address. Michael and his roommate were renting.

I wasn't expecting much help with his car. The red Prelude still wore Illinois plates. My only contacts at the police department, Purdy and Lauren, were unlikely to search out information for me without taking a peek at it, and that closed the door of access to law enforcement files and, for all practical purposes, I imagined, to the Department of Motor Vehicles as well. I tried anyway.

To my surprise, the clerk at the Department of Motor Vehicles in Denver was willing to copy Michael McClelland's driving record for a small fee. The catch was that he couldn't locate a record for a Michael McClelland in Boulder with the birthdate I had provided him. Did I have a Social Security number? Sorry. Did I have a driver's license number? No. My concern was that Michael didn't even have a Colorado driver's license. I certainly didn't know the number. "Sorry," the clerk said. He seemed to mean it, and I was sure he wasn't long for DMV.

So I started tailing Michael McClelland.

I rented a Camaro from Budget, assuming Michael knew my Subaru. An L.A. Dodgers baseball cap and

275

some absurd mirrored sunglasses completed my disguise. I imagined that I looked like a thousand other almost hip, almost adult males driving around Boulder.

Tuesday morning's dawn wasn't even a promise when the alarm jolted me out of bed. After donning my disguise and bracing for the cold, I raced the Chevy through Boulder's deserted streets and parked it up the hill from Michael's house, around a sharp turn in Lee Hill. Dawn was due in about half an hour. Being inconspicuous at five-forty-five in the morning walking alone on a mountain road wasn't easy. My only advantage was that no one was likely to be around to notice. No one was.

I climbed the driveway until it doglegged and then traversed the ridge that paralleled the north side of the house. The down ski jacket and long underwear retarded the cold for about ten minutes, and then I started to ache from the subfreezing chill. Finally a light shone through the curtains of the bedroom I had examined during my prior prowl. A few seconds later the light moved to another window, this one smaller, of glass bricks.

That light didn't go off for almost twenty minutes, and, shower finished, Michael or his roommate, Morton, moved off to another part of the house. I scurried from the ridge to a thick stand of pines just east of the front entrance and squatted behind a big rock. It took a few moments before I realized what I was seeing. Or wasn't seeing.

There was only one car in front of the house. Just the red Prelude. Where was Morton's car?

Where was Morton? Out of town on business, sleeping at his girlfriend's house, working the graveyard shift. Or . . . what?

My mind was like a diesel engine. It didn't start well in the cold. By then I was very cold. My ass was numb. My fingertips and toes were history. I decided to worry about Michael's roommate after my gray matter

276

thawed.

Michael McClelland came out the front door wearing a knee-length, deep brown overcoat that must have cost a thousand dollars. I wanted desperately to wrap it around my legs and go back to sleep. Instead I managed to fight the malaise precipitated by the cold and made my way on leaden feet back to the Camaro. He apparently warmed the Honda for a few minutes because I had to wait for him to come down the driveway. I gave him a cushion of a couple of hundred yards and then pulled around the curve in the road in pursuit.

I couldn't imagine that he was worried about being followed. I certainly had no way of disguising the fact that we were going in the same direction. If my suspicion was accurate, he would make only two turns before he arrived at work. The first turn was a right on Broadway from Lee Hill.

By the time a break in the traffic permitted him to turn, I had been sitting behind him at the intersection for about fifteen seconds. His face was illuminated by the sun rising in the east, and I could see his eyes and nose reflected in the rearview mirror. There was no glimmer of recognition that I was behind him. What attention he diverted from the traffic was placed on the folded newspaper he held in a nattily gloved right hand.

I cut off an old Ford pickup to enter traffic four or five cars behind Michael. When Broadway went from two lanes to four, I changed lanes and kept the red car in sight without any problem. This is easy, I thought. Near Community Hospital we edged into heavy traffic that thickened as we missed lights on each side of the mall. I watched him make a green at Canyon that I missed and pounded the steering wheel at the frustration of losing him. Near the university, a block ahead of me, I saw the red Prelude trapped by a flood of jaywalking students heading to early classes, and I moved as close to him as I dared, perched only a car length back, one lane over, vowing not to miss another light. Traffic thinned south

277

of Baseline, and the Honda accelerated past the Commerce Department Labs.

The second anticipated turn was a right on Table Mesa Drive up the hill toward I. M. Pei's architectural homage to the Anasazi cliff dwellings. The National Center for Atmospheric Research sat on an island mesa high above the demarcation of Boulder's greenbelt. The voters had approved construction of the labs on cherished public land to lure the prestigious institution to Boulder. Pei had designed twin sandstone high rises that managed against odds to do justice to the spectacular site. The morning sun created a pink tint on the sandstone as Michael and I joined the stream of early arrivals winding up the mesa.

I stopped in a short row of cars on the edge of the lot to watch him park his car, lock it, and walk across the asphalt lot to the northern tower. The research laboratories of the National Oceanic and Atmospheric Administration—NOAA—were somewhere in this complex. Apparently Michael McClelland had some business there. I pondered following him inside to his destination but realized, despite my short-circuiting brain, that the disguise that had made me invisible in Boulder traffic would render me absurd in the halls of NCAR.

Near the entrance he was greeted by a tall woman in a white wool cape who held the heavy door for him. They were speaking as they walked in to work.

The door of the Camaro thudded despite my effort to muffle the sound.

My ex-patient, the private detective, had been a proponent of the acting-like-you-belong-is-the-best-disguise school of skulkery, and I tried to act nonchalant as I plodded over and peered into the Prelude. The backseat was empty, the dash uncluttered. The folded *Wall Street Journal* on the passenger seat was the only evidence that the car hadn't just been driven from a showroom. Dark tint on the windows obscured any easy view. As I cupped my hand to peer inside the driver's side window, my breath froze on the glass and blocked my gaze. The tint was lighter on the windshield, and through it I could read the address label on the paper. It was made out to M. Morton.

Michael's roommate was out of town, and Michael had taken his paper. Easy enough to check out. I sauntered over to the south tower and found a pay phone off the lobby, near the bathrooms. First I dialed Information and got the correct number, then I dialed a second time.

"Severe Storms Laboratory," said the helpful voice.

"Mr. Morton, please," I said.

"May I tell Dr. Morton who's calling?"

"Peter, from the National Hurricane Center," I lied. Click, Musak, click.

"Dr. Morton," Michael McClelland rasped.

I hung up.

Pseudonyms, I conjectured, were usually employed when someone anticipated needing one.

Michael Morton, AKA Michael McClelland, AKA Mickey (?), was using a pseudonym with me. With me alone? Who could tell? I decided to pretend it was just with me because the assumption permitted me to narrow the range of possibilities I was required to consider. Anyway, this play was starring him and me. He was playing at least two roles; I was reluctantly cast in a part that seemed to be leading to my character becoming extraneous early in the third act. Unless I began to make sense of some of the pieces that didn't fit, I would be of little influence in the finale.

So why did Michael need an alias with me? The name Morton meant nothing to me. I certainly hadn't recognized him, and he had made no attempt to disguise his relationship with Anne Hubbard, so protecting that affair could not have been the reason. If the craziness around the dog and the turtle were part of a psychotic transference, it seemed unlikely that it could have started before he came to see me. Yet, obviously, he had started the pseudonymous ruse with the first phone call.

Two possibilities, then. First, the mayhem, Cicero, following me to Mexico, Gretchen's death, the Baccarat turtle, were all a premeditated plot with a motive that eluded me. Or second, the psychotic transference preceded the first phone call. He somehow knew enough about me to cast me in the role of the male who disappoints.

Number one seemed more unwieldy than number two, so I chose two.

Anne Hubbard had referred him to me. Although she may have talked to him briefly about her therapy, her reticence about self-disclosure made it unlikely that she would have proffered any of her feelings about me.

Michael was acquainted with Gretchen, but he'd met her in my waiting room, so he hadn't known her before his therapy commenced. Unlike Anne, Gretchen would have had no reluctance about discussing her relationship with me with a new acquaintance. But they hadn't known each other before the day Michael confused the appointments.

I was forced to assume that the limited information that Michael had heard from Anne had somehow sufficed to cast me in the antagonist's role.

With a self-patronizing smile, I sat back to observe my neurotic style at work. I was absolutely denying that the newspaper articles about me had started months before I met Michael — and I was forgetting that he had acknowledged knowing about "my problems." I had been focusing on Michael knowing me through Anne Hubbard and Gretchen Kravner. He might have "known" me through Karen Hart as well.

By late May, early June, when Michael McClelland Morton called for his first appointment, the papers had suggested that I had coerced Karen Hart into a destructive sexual relationship as part of her treatment. I could assume, I suppose, that Michael knew that much.

But it wasn't sufficient. I kept running into the brick wall of ignorance of Michael's past. He had never given me enough history to make sense of any of this. And I still couldn't explain the pseudonym.

The next step was not a problem.

The road from NCAR blended into South Boulder Road just east of Highway 36. The Camaro was underpowered but hummed nicely well above the speed limit over the few straight miles to the cutoff toward Spanish Heights. I maneuvered the Camaro through the curving lanes to my house just a little faster than I would have run the Subaru. That's what rental cars and disguises were for.

My notes yielded the number, and I punched about a dozen buttons to connect with the Hotel Hacienda in Cabo San Lucas. Fearing I might find the same gentleman I had spoken with earlier, I employed a new ruse.

"Buenos días," I started, trying to sound cosmopolitan, "this is Mr. Morton from Colorado. I'm afraid that during my stay in your hotel in early September I lost an important address book. I've called Housekeeping to ask them to search the room for it, but I couldn't remember the room number. Could you please check your records so I can give the room number to Housekeeping?"

"Sí, señor. Your date of arrival, please?"

"The first Friday or Saturday in September. I don't have a calendar in front of me."

"Sí. Your name *es* Morton."

"Sí."

"Un momento.

"You arrived Friday and left on Sunday, *señor. Es* that correct?"

"Yes, that is correct."

"Your room number was cabaña 126. Shall I transfer you to Housekeeping Services?"

"That would be most kind. Thank you."

As the repetitive clicks signaled failure of circuits to find mates, I placed the receiver gently back into the cradle.

Once, when Lauren was rattling on about one of her cases, she talked about criteria prosecutors used for determining probable cause in a felony investigation. I remembered means, opportunity, and motive easily enough. She also said something about LOVID, but the translation of the components of the acronym were suspended in some foggy microclimate of my brain.

She had said, "LOVID is what saves you." At the time I thought she had said, "Loving is what saves you," and had gotten my hopes up.

L was location. D was date. Could the suspect be placed at the location on the given date and, I assumed, time? Basic stuff.

V? Venue. Was the crime in the prosecutor's jurisdiction? She told me she got burned once when she was still in the charging division for not checking location of a crime carefully enough.

L,V,D. Well, at least I had my consonants.

O? Nothing.

I? As in ID. Identification. Did she mean, can you identify your suspect properly? Sounded good to me.

Back to O. It had something to do with getting the charges right. Offense. That's it — offense. Make the charges fit the crime.

Location.

Offense.

Venue.

Identification.

Date.

Means, opportunity, motive.

LOVID and MOM.

The crime in question was Gretchen's murder. Were my LOVIDs straight?

Location. Not in question. Everybody seemed to agree the crime took place at Gretchen's house.

Offense. Lauren's problem, not mine. Rape-murder. Burglary-murder. Murder-murder. For Gretchen it was splitting hairs at this point.

Venue. Boulder.

Identification. Of the victim, no questions. Of the suspects? The Jerk, easy. Michael? Who the hell knew who he really was?

Date. Not in question.

Now MOM.

Means. The Jerk, Douglas Kravner, and Michael McClelland both were big and strong enough to have overpowered Gretchen. Blue bandannas were not hard to come by. Michael had come by one once before.

Opportunity. Both Douglas and Michael had had access to the house. Gretchen had probably been more receptive to Michael, currently. Douglas was under a temporary restraining order to avoid contact with her, which he had apparently been obeying. But he didn't have an alibi for the night of the murder.

Motive.

For Douglas Kravner: thwarted love, blackmail, money. Good list.

For Michael: he didn't want his therapist to know that he had been dating another of his patients.

Not a good list.

Thirty-five

The day had warmed by the time I was back in the NCAR parking lot just before lunch. I was toying with the idea of going in the building and hanging out near Michael's laboratory to follow him around over lunch.

At precisely eleven-thirty Michael spared me the recklessness of my impulses. He exited the same tower he had entered a few hours before and walked purposefully to the Prelude, started it, and moved quickly down the mountain toward Boulder. The Camaro struggled to keep up with the Honda, and I reconsidered my earlier conclusion about how easy it was to follow someone unobtrusively.

The left-hand-turn arrow cleared both of us onto the wide stretches of Broadway heading back into town. The Prelude was doing forty-five or fifty in the slow lane as we passed the old Bureau of Standards complex. I had fallen a good quarter of a mile behind him and would lose him for certain if he made the light at Baseline.

The Honda slowed without braking and turned without signaling into the L-shaped strip shopping center at Baseline and Broadway. I watched as he found a parking place by the cheese store and hurried down the covered walkway into Le Français.

I found a parking place a little closer to the restaurant and bakery than he did. The restaurant had one cavernous dining room. I left the disguise in the car; if Michael spotted me, I decided, I would pretend our encounter had been by chance.

He was sharing a table by the window with an older man who was speaking quite forcefully. I could hear syllables floating across the room where I was trying to pick a table that gave me a good angle on Michael without giving him a good angle on me.

In the profile view my roost permitted, I was impressed by how familiar Michael's posture and demeanor were to me. He sat erect, disinterested, looking at his hands while nodding. He sipped from his water. The older man spoke on, unconsciously adjusting his position to try to get some eye contact from his recalcitrant companion.

The older man was fifty-five or sixty, professional looking: a colleague of Michael's, I conjectured. Despite his age his hair was dark and full. He sat taller than Michael, gesturing occasionally with large, pale hands. Syllables ricocheted around the dining room from his sonorous voice.

A waitress came, and I ordered coffee and a brioche. When I looked over again, Michael was talking. His thin lips pantomimed a conversation. The older man's voice was thunder, Michael's was a spare breeze. Michael finished saying something, folded his napkin carefully, stood up, said something to his waitress, and walked directly toward me.

Looking away abruptly is much more apologetic than maintaining a discovered gaze. So I maintained my gaze in his direction as Michael walked toward me, then beyond me, praying I hadn't been spotted. His footsteps stopped somewhere behind me.

My best option was to sip coffee and nibble brioche—not to turn around and see where he was. He hadn't headed in the direction of the door.

He said, "Hello, Alan."

I said without turning, "Michael."

"Eat here often?"

"Sometimes," I said.

His voice took on the tone of water escaping a cracked pipe. "Very nice" — he paused — "seeing you."

I turned and nodded.

He continued to the back of the restaurant in search of the bathrooms. I dropped a five-dollar bill on the table, briefly made eye contact with Michael's lunch companion, and hurried out to my Chevy.

The Camaro lurched as my left foot tried to use the brake as though it were a clutch and my right foot floored the accelerator.

Smooth. Very smooth.

After changing into work clothes that I had stored in the trunk of the Chevy, I fumbled my way through my four and four forty-five appointments, then fought traffic on North Broadway and Iris while trying to choose a route across town at rush hour. The Budget office was just closing as I arrived at six, but the clerk agreed to take back the Camaro. I rescued my Subaru from the street in front of the store and took the Foothills Parkway to South Boulder Road toward home.

The autumn light lingered in the western sky, but night was manifest everywhere else. Some of the hackberries and elms still held their brittle leaves, but most of the trees on the narrow lanes were bare. Indian summer was going to end soon.

When I pulled into the driveway, I saw Peter up at the mailbox by the road. I called up to him to get my mail, too, and watched Cicero paralyzed by ambivalence as she tried to determine whether she would romp up the hill to the mailbox or chase the Subaru down the driveway.

She ran down the hill to greet me, jumped up and touched her paws to my chest as I stepped out of the car, and then bounded up the hill to Peter at the mailboxes. I followed her up the drive.

My eyes were just level with the roadway when everything happened at once.

I think, like Cicero, I saw the rabbit first, before I realized that it was frozen in the headlights of an oncoming car. Next I saw Cicero dart across the road in chase. She looked so young and black and shiny in the instant the headlights illuminated her before she sank into the shadows of the bumper that seemed to lower itself to her as the screech of brakes filled the air. A scream got lost in my lungs, and my hands gripped the hair on the sides of my head as I watched Cicero disappear and heard the thud.

The scream escaped—"N*ooooooooo*." The shrillness echoed off the hills.

She wailed once and was quiet and still before I got to her a step before Peter. Peter screamed at the driver of the car, who screamed back, and I held my limp dog and looked for blood.

I said, "Cicero, it's okay, girl. It's okay."

And I rocked her heavy body and I cried and cried.

Thirty-six

Tragedy was stalking me, it seemed, like a hunter. I knew how the doe felt in the forest in autumn.

Peter and Adrienne had taken Cicero's body from me after I sat with her forever on the quiet road. They wrapped her limp body in a blanket and drove it to the vet for cremation. When they returned they knocked quietly on my door. I didn't answer.

The next day, Wednesday, my eyes were swollen and red. Each dark shadow in the house was the outline of Cicero's furry body, and each creak was the sound of her treading across the scratched wood floors. Her water dish begged for clean water, and I fought the impulse to fill it. It didn't occur to me to put it away. Four-thirty came, and I walked to her bag of dog food, forgetting and remembering.

The dementia was familiar; Merideth's exit had been obscured in a mist of denial that ebbed like the fogs of the city that had stolen her away. Photographs of her and me brought sharp stabs until only recently — and now I couldn't look at images or relics of Cicero, either.

The pale tile on the kitchen floor preserved the ubiquitous trail of her wet paws. I had cursed the stains a hundred times while on hands and knees with a rag — and now I couldn't bring myself to wipe them up a last time. When Merideth departed, the sheets

and towels that had safeguarded her smells stayed un-
washed for weeks.

The images of light and dark of the night before replayed themselves over and over again, my silent voice
commenting and critiquing as though the call could be
reversed on review of the instant replay. I saw the rabbit and the dog and the headlights and felt the screams
lock in my throat and then be released too late and
heard her wail and stop and heard my wail and saw
me frantically looking for blood to make it real.

Cars never come down our lane. Cicero never darts
across the road.

She would fail to catch a rabbit no more.

My heart was in pieces.

My friends came over again the night after Cicero
died. Peter hugged me first. Witnesses embracing.
Adrienne hugged me and handed me a fist full of
choke chain and dog tags. I was unable to restrain the
sobs that I had promised myself were over. My neighbors said kind words, and I knew their loss was almost
as great as mine. I fumbled with words that felt inadequate to comfort them. Cicero had been loved all over
the Ponderosa.

We laughed a little that night, remembering Cicero
before the rabbit and the car. The laughter echoed in
the chilly house, as if the space on the Tabriz that she
called her own had once absorbed the reverberations
of our voices and no longer did. Peter and Adrienne
were reluctant to leave and stayed later than they
should have. When they left I cried some more,
watched some television, didn't let Cicero out, took
one of the Halcion tablets Adrienne had left for me,
and slept a dead sleep till morning.

Cicero was still gone when I woke up early on
Thursday.

* * *

Dread flushed me each time I moved to call Merideth to tell her of Cicero's death. I managed to complete the call at eight-thirty Thursday morning. It would be seven-thirty in California. She'd be getting ready for work.

If her offer was still open, I would be on a plane to San Francisco that afternoon.

"Hello," said the strange female voice. I asked for Merideth. The voice said that she wasn't there. I asked when she would be back. The young woman said, "In a few days. I'm housesitting."

"Is there any way I can reach her? It's urgent." My voice was hollow.

"She left a number. Do you want it?"

"Please."

She gave me a number with a familiar area code to which I couldn't assign a locale. California, probably.

I punched the buttons methodically, and the voice on the other end said, "Good morning, Ventana."

I stammered before telling the voice that I had made a mistake, had dialed a wrong number. She said it was no problem.

Merideth wouldn't go to Ventana—an inn on the hills that tumbled down to the ragged coast of Big Sur—alone. And she wouldn't go there with a woman friend. She would take someone there to seduce him, as she had me, a few weeks after we met.

I tried to get back to sleep, couldn't, got up and wrote Merideth a letter about Cicero and how she hadn't suffered and how she had been loved. I didn't write about Ventana or coming to visit.

As I wandered around the quiet house, I attempted to figure whether my tragedies were now coming in multiples of threes, or squares of threes, or logarithms of threes.

It all depended, I finally decided, on how you computed.

Thirty-seven

Until Cicero's death, futility was the fuel that kept me moving. Now, it became clear, anger was the engine.

It required most of my energy just to return my pages by the end of the day. I jumped each time the beeper chirped and made decisions of dubious judiciousness about which calls could wait to be returned. When the gray lines on the screen of the pager read Michael McClelland's name and number, I thought for only a moment before hitting the button that would erase it from memory.

What could he want? Who the fuck cared? I erased his name from the screen.

Twenty times in the last thirty-six hours I'd reminded myself that Michael hadn't really killed my dog.

The bell on the phone at home was turned off. Twice that morning a call came in and the answering machine sputtered to life in response to a silent signal. After Jon Younger had left two messages at work and one on the home machine, I decided it was prudent to return his calls.

He was, of course, not available, and I assumed that we could extend our game of telephone tag ad nauseam, so I told his receptionist that I would be available at my home number until four and would he please call. I turned the bell back on.

Jon would be calling with bad news. That was my conclusion by the time the phone beckoned shortly after three.

"Please don't hang up," said Michael when I answered.

I didn't. "Yes."

"It's Michael . . . I need to talk to you." He didn't use a last name. Maybe he knew I knew.

"Our therapeutic relationship is over. I suggest you call someone else for assistance." I wasn't pleasant.

"I already did," he said. "I went and saw Rebecca Washburn. She said I needed to meet with you again to terminate more effectively. I agree with her. Please. I know it'll be our last meeting. But I think it's important that we talk, come to some conclusion."

Shit. Rebecca had done what I would've done had I heard whatever version of the end of therapy Michael had told her. She sent him back to me to clean up some of the mess. To terminate more cleanly.

"Okay," I said, "one last visit. Tonight at five."

I hung up before he had a chance to reply.

Jon never got back to me, so I left the phone on and the answering machine off until I left for the office. It stayed silent.

I dressed in wool slacks, shirt, and sweater before driving downtown. Diane's office door was cracked open. I knocked a warning and walked in.

Her face said she knew about Cicero. "How are you?" she asked, standing.

"I miss her," I said, and we embraced.

"I've called a few times, you know."

"I know, Diane. I haven't felt like talking."

"Can I do anything?"

"Yeah. You can buy me dinner tonight. I'd really appreciate that."

"You got it. I'll call Raoul and tell him to make other plans."

"Diane, if you've got plans, we can do this—"

"It's done. I'm finished at five forty-five. Okay?"

I nodded and said, "One more thing. That guy I told you I was worried about, you know, the one I was terminating?" She nodded some acknowledgment. "He's gonna be here at five for a final session. If you hear some screaming from my office, call the cops."

"Are you serious?" she asked.

"I'm serious."

"Which one of you will be screaming?" she wondered with a smile.

"Good question. Let me rephrase my request. If you hear me screaming, call the cops. If you hear him screaming, write it off to catharsis."

Diane continued to smile. "Got it," she said.

The red light above my desk flashed on at five exactly. I sighed and reminded myself that however bad it got, it was only going to last for forty-five minutes, and if it got terrible, I could just tell him to leave.

He wore the same double-breasted suit I had seen on him at the cafe. His eyes bore a hint of apology and conciliation.

I didn't even try to be cordial. Too much had happened already. For all my rationalization skills, I couldn't convince myself that the man across the room from me was not a murderer. I even blamed him for Cicero. No rational reason. It just felt like his fault.

I had rehearsed my first line. "About your bill. You owe me three hundred and sixty dollars before today. Including today's session, your balance due is four hundred and fifty. I think it will make the termination more complete if we resolve the financial issues right now."

Michael reached into his coat pocket and handed

me one of the return-mail envelopes I enclosed with my statements. It was unsealed. In it were four one-hundred-dollar bills and one fifty.

I became silent. Merideth would have said I was brooding. She would probably have been right.

Michael leaned forward on his chair and stared at his hands for two long minutes.

"I've had trouble accepting your decision to stop seeing me." He waited for a reply. "And I'm grateful for the chance to clear a few things up." Despite his obvious attempt at deference, I didn't have anything nonsarcastic to say and had barely enough self-control to keep my mouth shut.

"You're not going to make this any easier, are you?" Michael didn't look up when he asked this.

No, asshole, I'm not.

He continued. "Do you know the man you saw me with the other day?" He looked up as he spoke this time.

"Is that important?" I asked, wondering what difference it could make.

"Do you know him?" he pressed.

"You know me well enough to know that I don't answer questions like that in therapy."

"Were you following him?"

This didn't make any sense. I was mildly concerned about being broadsided with accusations about following Michael around, and he wondered if I was following the guy he was having lunch with?

"Michael. How can I help you terminate this relationship so that you can proceed more effectively with Dr. Washburn?"

"I never saw Dr. Washburn, Gregory, I made that up." As I tried to process the deception, he continued, recognizing his advantage. "This is our last therapy session. Wednesday, the last week in October." He stared at me, bemused, as he said it. "Right?"

"You bet, this is our last meeting."

"In therapy?"

What was this all about? "Yes, in therapy." He slid his left hand into his jacket pocket, and I heard a click.

"You figured out that I killed her, didn't you?"

I moved mechanically, sliding my hands into the pockets of my trousers and slowly filling my chest with enough air to guard against forgetting to breathe. Although I knew, I said, "I don't know what you mean."

"Don't play dumb." Conciliation and amusement were replaced by earnest menace.

"Killed who?"

"You can't touch me, you son of a bitch. I've admitted it now during a therapy session. You can't tell fucking anybody."

"Killed who?"

He answered my question with a smirk. "I shaved your bloody dog as well."

"Get out of here!" I shouted, standing, realizing. "Get the hell out of here!"

"And I did the trick with the turtle. Sleight of hand, magic."

"Therapy is over. Now. Get out!" I was still shouting.

"One more thing, Doctor. Don't rest too easy. I know the way to San Jose. And points north."

"You fucker!" I screamed.

He stood slowly, walked over, opened the door, turned, and said, "Thank you," smiled, and left. He paused a moment in the hall to straighten his suit.

Diane was in my office in a flash. "Are you okay?"

"I'll be fine. Go finish your session. I'll be fine."

She moved back down the hall to her office, looking back over her shoulder.

I was shaking, I was so mad. I'd been trumped.

Thirty-eight

Diane Estevez and I walked silently from our little office building to a fish house a couple of blocks from the mall. She requested a booth and pried one from the reluctant maître d'. During their discussion I watched colorful fish swim in the immense saltwater tanks above the bar. Although the fish were enchanting, I couldn't help comparing the experience to displaying choice steers in a corral in the middle of a steak house.

I was last in the procession to the table. "Chardonnay and cioppino okay?" Diane asked. She knew she was better off in charge of minutiae for the time being.

"Fine. Sure."

The waiter took the order from her and left. Diane said nothing in the minutes it took him to return with the bottle of chardonnay from some obscure California winery. Despite the fact that Diane had read the wine list, picked the wine, and ordered it, he somehow managed to assume that I was the only one capable of tasting it. As he leaned toward my wineglass, I caught his eye and shook my head.

"No wine, sir?" he asked.

"The lady ordered this bottle," I said. Diane smiled.

He turned toward her. "Would you like to taste this, ma'am?"

"No, thank you, I'm sure it's fine. Please go ahead

and pour. And, please, serve my guest first."

I removed my hand from above my wineglass. The wine was poured, first for me, then for Diane. The waiter left silently.

"So," Diane said, still grinning, "we're apparently done being pushed around today, aren't we?"

I lifted my eyes from an examination of repairs previously made to the worn pink tablecloth and looked at her. "Yes. But not just today. Period."

"Tell me," she said.

"There's not much I can tell you. For a few reasons. Number one, if I told you some things, you'd be in the same ethical dilemma that I'm in. And I don't wish that on you. Second, if I told you some other things, you'd be ethically compelled to report me to the state grievance board, which, given the facts, you probably wouldn't want to do, and that would leave you in yet another quandary.

"This guy, my five o'clock today, has boxed me into a corner by tricking me into having a last termination session with him and then admitting some criminal acts, so that I can't discuss what I know with anyone. What's even more galling is that I was on the verge of collecting significant evidence against him outside of therapy about these crimes, and now, I'm sure, there's no ethical way I can make that information available to the police. And even if I did, I'm not sure I could get anyone to believe me."

"I am probably not supposed to ask this, but how did you 'collect' this outside information?"

"You don't want to know."

"Shit."

"This would not be so bad if—no, that's not right—this is made worse by the fact that I am already under investigation by just about every judicial and professional board authorized to investigate me. Another set of complaints and I can kiss my malpractice insurance good-bye. I'm already at risk of being booted from the state psychological association and from APA, and my license to practice is attached to me by a very slim thread."

"Something you said is confusing. You said that if I knew some things, I would feel obligated to report you for ethical violations. But if I knew 'the facts,' I probably wouldn't."

"I've done some things that I can't believe I did. Nothing terrible. Well, not capital crimes, anyway. But I did them to try and keep some worse things from occurring. My gut feeling says if you knew the details, you would agree with me. I have morally rationalized my behavior as choosing the lesser of two evils. On a more basic level, my hands were being tied behind my back, and I had to do something."

The cioppino came in immense covered bowls that bellowed aromatic steam as the waiter removed the lids with what he mistook for a flourish. The flourish permitted the beaded water to drip from inside the lids onto the tablecloth and to foul Diane's waterglass. The waiter was oblivious. He asked us how everything was. I told him that we didn't know since we hadn't started eating yet. He departed with offense on his face and a prayer that I wasn't the one who would decide on his tip.

I started with a piece of garlic bread. Diane headed for the shellfish.

"What does this have to do with? The suicide? The murder? What?"

"Do you really want to know?"

"Yes. I do. But maybe I shouldn't." She paused. "What're you gonna do?"

"I don't know. The last card has, I imagine, been played. I've been an unwitting accomplice to the perfect crime. The bad guy goes free. And I'm left wondering about the quality of the clinical judgment that permitted me to fall prey to all of it." I scooped up my spoon and left it hovering inches about the stew. "Would you break a privileged communication to report a serious crime?"

Diane set down her spoon and sipped some wine. She supported the tulip glass with both hands.

"There is," she began, "not much, if anything, to be gained by breaching confidence. Let's say you report him. He gets the evidence thrown out by falling back on the confidence. You get censured and maybe sued for your indiscretion. No, I wouldn't report a crime reported to me in therapy. In little ways, it happens all the time. You know that. Shoplifting. Dealing. Drug use. Theft. Burglary, even. Patients talk about that stuff all the time." She sipped some more wine. "I've just started seeing a guy who has two convictions in another state for child molestation while employed in child care facilities. He knows he needs help. Yet he's just taken a job at a residential treatment facility for kids. He maintains he's not going to do it again but says he isn't qualified to do anything else. He says it's like the alcoholic tending bar in *Cheers*, the TV show. No harm done, right? I would love to report him—my gut tells me he'll molest another child. But I can't. What I can do is treat him. And I will." She went back to her cioppino with gusto.

I had always envied Diane her capacity to resolve internal conflict. She turned things over, looked carefully, decided, and that was that.

Diane said, "What about an anonymous phone call to the police?"

"I've thought of it in my case, Diane. What about your molester?"

"I see what you mean," she echoed into her wineglass. "You gonna eat those crab claws?"

My stew was untouched. "Please help yourself." She did.

"Then I repeat: What're you gonna do?"

"Put my energies into fighting the malpractice suit, I guess. I don't know. My professional survival depends on my winning that battle."

"What does Jon Younger say?"

"He's neutral about my chances at this point. A major issue is whether the malpractice insurer is going to invoke the physical intimacy clause and restrict my defense fund to twenty-five thousand dollars. If they do that, I'm sunk."

"They can do that?"

"Sure, they can argue that this is a sexual misconduct complaint in disguise and, if they're successful, limit my coverage."

We talked about Cicero through dessert, for Diane, and coffee, for both of us.

Afterward we strolled the west end shops on Pearl, had more coffee at the Trident, found our cars where we had left them, and each headed home.

The phone was ringing as I entered the house without Cicero. Maybe it's Jon, I thought.

Only silence. Click. Hummmmmmmm.

"Asshole," I said to Michael.

The phone clicked loudly as I moved the ringer switch back to the "off" position. I turned the answering machine back on.

I redialed the number that Merideth's housesitter had given me earlier. Michael had threatened me that he "knew the way to San Jose and points north." I had to assume that he had already tracked Merideth down. At least to California. "I looked somebody up," is what he had said a while ago about his abbreviated trip to San Francisco. "But it didn't work out." I hoped that meant that he couldn't get my wife to agree that he was irresistible. For now, until I warned her, I

300

couldn't be too certain of her safety in Big Sur. I took some paradoxical solace in my suspicion that she wasn't alone.

There was no answer in her room at the hotel. The desk clerk came back on the line and told me she had a reservation at the inn's restaurant for a "late dinner." I left a message asking Merideth to call me and told the clerk to mark it "urgent."

I poured three-quarters of an inch of Armagnac in a snifter, turned a torchère on low in the back of the living room, put on a record of Moussorgsky's *Pictures at an Exhibition,* and sat to watch the stars and the moon above the mountains, contemplating how long I could hold out before making the inevitable move to compact discs.

When the sound exploded out of the darkness, I reacted by diving to the rug in front of the sofa. I could feel glass shards flying all over and could hear the tinkle of the larger pieces as they tumbled on the wood floor. The tinny treble was syncopated by the thunderous bass of something heavy bouncing across the room behind me. I waited for more bombs, more bullets, more rocks. But the room grew progressively more silent except for the sounds of the night, now invited in along with the cold autumn air.

Using the full sleeves of my sweater to brush glass out of my path, I crept over to the windows and raised my head high enough to see outside. Nothing.

Then, fifty yards to the south a flash of light flickered, the dome light of a car—on, then off. An engine started. The dark shadow moved away, around the bend, without benefit of lights.

The turntable clicked itself off.

Part Three

All Saints'
All Souls'

Thirty-nine

Like a fool, I stood silhouetted in the window hoping for a flash that might illuminate the traveling shadow and reveal it to be a red Honda Prelude.

No more bombs or bullets or rocks were propelled my way. As I pivoted to check on Cicero, my stockinged left foot found a shard of glass, the blood oozing through my sock just as I remembered I had no dog to be concerned about. I was surprisingly calm as I hopped to the kitchen like a seven-year-old in a hopscotch game designed by a sadist.

The wound glistened bright red but looked free of errant bits of glass. I sat on the kitchen counter and ran cold water over the cut for a while, then pressed a blue-and-white-striped bar towel against it until it stopped bleeding. I hopped across the hall to the guest bathroom, retrieved a butterfly bandage, and stretched it over the wound. After pulling off the other sock, I found the green flip-flops that I kept by the front door, put them on, and began pushing a broom in front of me to clear a path through the debris back to the living room.

The amount of mess that one broken window could make was astonishing. The top half of the pane was intact, the shatter spreading down from a roughly semicircular arc a couple of feet from the lower sill. The bottom pieces had tumbled to the floor just below the window and shattered widely. Specks and crystal shards clung to the heavy yarn of my sweater. I didn't disturb the shards, treating them like insects that could be startled into stinging, and elected to take off my sweater outside, padding and clicking my way toward the front door while dodging crystal pungi stakes and smears of red and drying blood.

A bright dot registered in the corner of my eye. As I turned I saw a two-inch purple orb resting on the tight wool of Cicero's Tabriz.

I shuddered.

Solids. Purple. The four ball.

Lauren.

Family-style pool halls were briefly in vogue during my preadolescence. The trend lasted almost as long as slot-car parlors but left me knowing my billiard balls. The purple ball on the floor would reveal two small white circles with the number 4 inscribed in each.

The game with Michael had progressed to the point where he was calling his shots. Four ball, which pocket? The billiard ball meant that Lauren was now part of the equation. Where did she fit into all this? Was she the next victim? If she was next, was it because she was the DA prosecuting Gretchen's murder or because of her relationship with me? Actually the question of motive was probably academic because the billiard ball screamed that, regardless of motive, Lauren Crowder was now on Michael McClelland Morton's new list of called shots. The important question was: How was I going to convince her?

Cutting cardboard and packing tape with shivering hands was not easy, but the late-October night air rushing through the broken window made it imperative to close the wound in my house before I tackled the mess on the floor and furniture. I measured the window frame, cut two pieces of cardboard from the box my television had come in, and taped the make-shift cover over the hole. The cleaning tools developed a rhythm in my hand; I swept and brushed and vacuumed and wiped, finding minute shards and specks scattered over half the living room and dining room.

I worked methodically, searching out every little crystal dot. I found glass floating in balls of dust and Cicero fur that hid beneath furniture. I found pieces in my hair and resting on my skin.

After cleaning the house, I cleaned myself, showering for a long time, letting the water carry away the sharp specks, not wanting to rub them into my skin or step on them before they floated away.

Shower time was thinking time, but cogitation failed to solve the puzzle.

The three ball was missing.

Anne Hubbard was number one. Gretchen Kravner was two. Who the hell was number three? If Lauren was four, there had to be a three. Probably Merideth. Michael's threat to her was so overt, though, I was tempted to minimize it. Or maybe the bastard had just hurt or killed another one of my female patients. Or maybe the three was pending, too. Or it could be that the three was part of my already completed triad. Maybe the three was Cicero.

But most likely the three was Merideth. At least she'd listen to my warning about Michael. Merideth was prudent.

But Lauren? Sure. I could call Lauren and warn her. Warn her about what? That I thought some guy she didn't know was going to do something annoying or deadly to her. How did I know? she'd ask.

Well, I can't tell you.

Has he made a threat to hurt me?

No, not in so many words.

Well, then?

307

I think he hurled a pool ball through my living room window.

And that means he is going to hurt me?

Of course.

Wait. He had to know her pretty well, or how had he known about her billiard skills? How did he know her?

I dialed quickly, hitting the four instead of the three for the third digit, hung up to recover the dial tone, and punched seven more buttons. That it might be late hadn't dawned on me until I heard her sleepy voice.

"Lauren, it's Alan."

Silence for a while, muted voices in Kansas echoing in a corner of our line. "What time is it?"

There were no clocks in the living room where I sat, and my watch was not on my wrist. "Late. I don't know."

"What is it?" Her voice guarded the sleep she had barely left. She spoke as if she could return to her slumber more easily if she didn't enunciate.

"Are you dating anybody, well, anybody else?"

"Please don't tell me you woke me up to ask me that. There are," she prodded, "more opportune times for your jealousy."

"Lauren, please, I'm not prying. I'm not jealous. Well," I corrected, "I am jealous, I guess, but that's not why I'm asking. Please answer me. Are you seeing anybody else?"

"I've told you I was going to see other men."

"I know. I know. But are you?"

She emitted a sigh a sentence long. "Yes."

"Will you tell me who?"

"No! I will not tell you who. It's none of your god-damn business." She was awake now.

"You're right. It's not." I paused, searching for perfect words and not finding them. "I'm worried you're

308

in danger. I, um, think that someone intends to hurt you, and it might be someone you're seeing."

"I can't believe this. Alan. Enough. I won't discuss my personal affairs with you, nor will I encourage your pathetic jealousy. End of discussion."

"Are you missing any balls from your pool table? Someone threw a four ball through my living room window a couple of hours ago."

"And you think it was me?"

"No." This wasn't going well. "I'm wondering whether somebody you're seeing may have stolen it."

"I'm gonna hang up."

"Okay. Okay. I'll stop. Will you go out to dinner with me Saturday?"

"Saturday's Halloween, Alan, I'm going to the Mall Crawl. I have a date. Okay? Anyway, I'm not sure I want to see you right now. This conversation is too strange."

"What are you gonna be? You gonna dress up?"

"Alan. Please pay attention. I—have—a—date. Don't bother me on Saturday."

"Fine. I won't. What are you going to be?"

"Depends how cold it is. Maybe a clown. Maybe an Eskimo. You going?" The tone of her question clearly stated her desire for a negative response.

"No. I did once. That was enough. What about tomorrow night? Will you see me then?"

"I have a bar association meeting, and then I'm meeting with a partner from a law firm that's recruiting me."

"Sunday?"

"No."

"I'm worried about you."

"Don't be. I'm fine."

"How's your eye?"

"Good night, Alan."

"Good night, Lauren."

309

* * *

I called Merideth's housesitter and left a message urging Merideth to call me as soon as possible.

It was ironic. Merideth was having a romantic week in Big Sur with somebody. And I was glad. Glad, mostly, that the somebody wasn't Michael. Which meant that she was safe for now. I must be getting over her, I thought. I'm much more relieved than jealous.

For the first time in over a year, I slept in the bed I had shared with my wife. Considering my state of mind, I slept well, dreaming about Cicero and times I had been inattentive to her.

Ten minutes after I woke up on Friday morning, the phone chirped.

"Alan. Jon Younger."

"Good morning, Jon. I apologize for being so hard to reach."

He ignored my attempt at expiation. "I got a call from Mark Brodsky. He suspects you of harassing his client."

"Who's Brodsky? Who's his client?"

"Brodsky is Sheldon Hart's attorney. Have you been free-lancing again, Alan?" There was an edge to his voice that was unfamiliar.

The pieces suddenly all appeared. I didn't know what sense to make of them. But I wasn't surprised.

"No, Jon, I haven't."

"Not at all?"

"Not at all. I don't know what he's talking about. I assure you."

"Okay. He accused you of trying to overhear a conversation Hart was having. Don't be tempted to screw around with this. Promise me."

"Jon, don't worry. I'm innocent." At least I'm not

guilty. "Any word from the malpractice carriers?"

"Yeah, they're trying to classify this as an erotic contact suit. I've contacted the national psychological associations to get support from their practice directorates. I hope to hear something next week."

"Keep me informed."

"Fine, I'll call when I know something."

Only one appointment was scheduled to interrupt my unemployment that Friday before Halloween. I canceled it.

Peter had planned a field trip to scout weird wood in Denver on Friday, and Adrienne was in surgery all morning. I spent the morning unsuccessfully trying to fathom a definitive answer to the puzzle about the three ball that hadn't been thrown into my living room. In the meantime I dusted and scrubbed and vacuumed the downstairs bedroom and moved my clothes back into the closet next to Merideth's unclaimed garments. Cicero's things—two crusty saliva-dried tennis balls, a largely unused grooming brush, water bowl, food bowl, dog biscuits, and half of a forty-pound bag of dog food—I moved into the storage room.

Merideth called midmorning. She sounded, rightfully, intruded upon. Neither of us mentioned the fact that she was at Ventana. I told her my concerns. She couldn't recall either meeting or being hit on by anyone of Michael's description. Yes, she would be careful. She wouldn't be alone, she assured me. Cryptically. I spared her news of Cicero's death; she'd know that the moment she was home opening her mail.

Adrienne finally returned my call at twelve-thirty.

"Can I invite myself to that party you guys are going to tomorrow night?" I asked.

Adrienne's voice was sympathetic and suspicious. She exhaled before she began. "I can check. I'll be happy to see if we can bring you. You're sure you're up for this? It's not your kind of party."

"I promise to be pleasant."

"And wear a costume?"

I cringed. I was allergic to costume parties. "If required. Will you help me with it?"

"You're as helpless as Peter."

"I sense some gender discrimination."

"I don't know when I can reach Binky, so why don't you just count on it until you hear from me. I'll convince her somehow."

"Binky?"

"Don't start, Alan. I swear I'll be furious if you make me regret this. We'll probably leave here about eight-thirty. Call me tonight about your costume. At least try and think of something on your own. I will help you accessorize. Bye."

Accessorize? I thought; I am inviting myself to a party thrown by somebody named Binky that requires that I accessorize?

The party that I invited myself to was an annual affair that coincided with the Halloween Mall Crawl. The party was held in the offices of Binky's design firm, Purple Mountain Majesty, whose office suite overlooked the Halloween festivities and insanity on the mall in the manner that sky boxes protected the elite at football stadiums. Adrienne didn't know that Binky and I had met before. Binky had attended the open house that Dana Beal, the architect upstairs from Diane and me, threw to celebrate the opening of her business. Within moments of my introduction to Binky I had apparently insulted her with a benign inquiry about her "decorating business." She had corrected me, with some contempt, "Decorators are housewives with flair. I," she'd said, "am a designer."

There was a time when I bristled in a similar way when people called me a counselor, not a psychologist. Actually, I bristled, but I'm relatively certain that I was incapable of bristling with Binky's sparkling acidity.

Adrienne's tie to Binky was her husband, Thomas Usokowski, M.D., a urological colleague whom Adrienne viewed with rare respect. In deference to him, twice a year, Halloween and Bastille Day, Adrienne and Peter donned strange finery and acted as though Binky's concept of societal splendor were something more than kitsch.

Peter's off-center view of the world made him an instant hit at parties like those Binky threw. He was, in his sparse philosophical soup, quintessentially Boulder. People embraced him the way they embraced fire walking, high colonics, and sadistic bodywork—with public acceptance and private skepticism. In Boulder, being of narrow mind was a much worse sin than appearing stupid. Those days I often felt like the most endangered of local fauna: someone capable of both.

For pragmatic reasons I decided to be a pirate captain at Binky's soiree. A pirate so that I could carry a looking glass; a captain so I could wear a big coat to ward off the cold if I succeeded in my surveillance and wandered outside. My memory of old pirate movies was that the plebes were never permitted outerwear. I had an eye patch that an ophthalmologist had given me while my eye recovered from some strange fungal process that I had diagnosed as leprosy. A costume store in Denver agreed to hold a pirate's hat until six that evening, and I planned to wear an old black cape that Merideth had left behind because she'd acquired it before she began her conversion to natural fibers. Except for a few accessories, I was set. Adrienne would be impressed.

The trip to Denver withdrew two and a half hours

from my day. I had left a message with Lauren to call my answering service to page me when she was free, but my pager stayed silent all afternoon.

Two guys from a glass company in Louisville, the community neighboring Boulder to the east, met me at the house at four-thirty and efficiently replaced the large pane in the living room. They were straightforward blue-collar types, people I didn't even suspect of having set aside their master's degrees in cellular biology to become salt-of-the-earth glaziers. Peter came over while they were finishing up, and since it was their last call of the day, they joined us for a beer. Peter, his long hair, his excitement at scoring some esoteric African woods, and the fact that I was getting used to my pirate hat, all conspired to leave the craftsmen acting suspiciously like tourists. My story about the meteorite pool ball was met with stone-faced nods. They wanted to leave the impression that replacing picture windows destroyed by billiard balls was nothing new to them. I had no doubt, when they left, that their friends in one of the Main Street saloons in Louisville would soon be hearing about the strange service call they'd made in Boulder.

I decided to be as charitable as I could about Binky.

Adrienne had used up what was left of her goodwill with Binky to get me an invitation to the party. I tried to be suitably grateful. My friend touched up my costume with a scarf of hers and an old white shirt of Peter's, and rummaged through my closet for a replacement after rejecting my choice of trousers. She said she would do my eyes and makeup tomorrow. Great.

The winds were doing guerrilla strikes into town. Still air would dissipate in the blink of an eye, and a frosty gale would knife out of one of Boulder's many canyons. By the time the blows reached east Boulder they had coalesced into a rhythmic pulse that never quieted. Merideth's cape was my only salvation as I crossed the brown grass and gravel back to my house.

Walking into the house was when I missed Cicero most.

Since Merideth left me, Cicero had become the one who listened best. Actually, the truth was that even before Merideth's departure Cicero was probably the one who listened best. Cicero, bless her heart, rarely had anything more on her mind than the nearest morsel or the most compelling current noise. She was almost perfect therapist material.

The pool ball puzzle had simmered through the day's chaos without ever reducing to a palatable consistency. I reassured myself that I had covered my bases with Merideth. Lauren, as usual, was being difficult.

Despite the fact that even in my worst moments I didn't delude myself into believing that Cicero had understood what I said, the very presence of otological organs other than my own sanctioned talking out loud in an otherwise empty house. Some people couldn't read without moving their lips; my failure to solve the riddle spawned fears that I had evolved into someone who couldn't think without moving mine.

The ways that I would miss my dog were barely starting to accumulate.

Forty

The city of Boulder recognized the Mall Crawl with the same reluctance that parents recognize adolescence. It was never welcomed, but at some point its presence was acknowledged with resignation.

On some Halloween shortly after the mall was completed in the late seventies, the open-air carnival atmosphere attracted, as inexorably as white light draws miller moths, costumed exhibitionists eager to display their outrageousness of dress and/or behavior to each other or to the endless parade of Boulderites and visitors who loved to examine evidence of the town's warped superego. Initially the gathering of the watched and the watchers was a prelude to serious partying in other venues. By the early eighties, however, the Mall Crawl, as the four-block-long Halloween party became known, was the end in itself. The city was forced to close streets, put dozens of police on overtime, and then stand back helplessly as thirty to forty thousand bizarrely costumed citizens of many planets paraded up and down the mall. And drank. And did drugs.

There were always fights. There were always overdoses. There was always vandalism. But considering the incredible number of people operating under the joint and several disinhibitors of alcohol, chemicals, and disguise, most everyone in Boulder agreed, on each of the mornings after, that it could have been worse.

Merideth and I went once. The nicest thing I could say about the experience was that it was memorable. One group of people were convincingly dressed as contraceptives — a foil punch-out of a month's cycle of birth control pills, a condom (in the "on" position), a diaphragm, a Copper-7 IUD, and a nun. Others wore more pedestrian attire: clowns, political figures, film characters, or the sputum of the year's commercial messages. The sheer numbers rendered walking improbable and quiet conversation unheard of. Early in the evening people were playful and a little drunk; later they were meaner and a lot drunk.

My general tendency was to avoid crowds whenever possible. I left baseball games in the eighth inning, football games at the two-minute warning, and always viewed encores at concerts from the back of the arena. The Mall Crawl was not my idea of fun.

I had invited myself to Binky's party to achieve a vantage point from which to spy on Lauren Crowder. More specifically, on her date. I wanted that date not to be Michael McClelland Morton. There was an image floating in my mind of Venetian masked balls and sophisticated people waltzing in anonymity. I saw my task as simple: to charm the mask off Lauren's paramour.

Once I accomplished plan A, I would wing it and somehow convince the deputy district attorney of the danger she was in.

Adrienne saw something sinister in my choice of a pirate's costume, considering her husband was dressing as Peter Pan. "No hooks, no wooden leg, no confusion," I insisted.

She was quite convincing as an elfin Marie Antoinette. For all I knew, Marie could've actually been only five feet tall, but I doubted it. Adrienne wore a long, or at least floor-length, flowing gown that I had no trouble accepting as eighteenth century, heavy makeup, and an ingenious miniature guillotine for a hat. She carried a small white bakery box on a string.

The makeup she applied to my face had transformed me. Thick eyeliner, powder and rouge, lipstick — I became the pirate queen. She suggested I carry the stem of a long-stem rose between my teeth, not so much as an accessory, I suspected, but rather to force me to keep my mouth shut around our hostess. I declined.

Adrienne was suspicious when I insisted on taking two cars downtown but began to see some advantages looming when I led their Land Cruiser into the small lot behind my office building. "If I knew you had reserved parking, Alan, I would have gotten you invited long before this."

Walking, we crossed Ninth at Walnut and joined an unlikely procession down Pearl toward the mall. Our progress was retarded by the misfortune of strolling behind two people dressed as Siamese twins joined at the cranium. It was going to be a long night for the twins.

Two blocks away the sidewalks barely permitted ambulation; by the time we were opposite the *Daily*'s brick wall of a facade, the walk had become a creep. Entering the mall at the west end was a ludicrous proposition. The mass of browsing humanity looked impenetrable. Peter suggested an alley approach to the problem and led us down the narrow service drive behind the shops on the southern side of Pearl.

We crossed back to the mall through the bank plaza in the twelve hundred block and spent ten minutes weaving through the crowds to the door to Purple Mountain Majesty.

An immense, bare-chested, black-hooded man with a mace asked for our tickets as soon as we opened the door. When it closed behind us, I began to recognize, in the ensuing quiet, the extent of the cacophony we were privileged to leave behind.

The spartan simplicity of Binky's design firm had cost a small fortune to achieve; the budget, no doubt, had been more Athens than Sparta. In its precostumed state, black tile work areas gave way to dark gray carpets. Black halogen lamps lit every horizontal surface. The walls were stark white, although each doorway was outlined in a color borrowed from a child's rainbow of tempera.

For this party, the black-and-white space had become a canvas for an Elizabethan fantasy. Pillars reached incongruously through absent panels in the suspended ceiling. Murals hand-painted for the occasion covered large expanses of wall. The Italian lamps were on the floor, their stark light washing up the muraled walls. The drafting tables were set to horizontal, covered with rich cloths and piled high with food. The broad windows overlooking the mall were draped with red velvet. Jesters or fools, the toes of their shoes curling up—Binky was apparently not averse to blending centuries—circulated with champagne glasses or took drink orders and disappeared into back rooms to have them filled. Thirty-five-inch television monitors sat high on racks in the far corners of the room, their screens filled with images of the fermenting madness taking place in the public arena below. I couldn't determine where the cameras were hidden.

At the top of the stairs Adrienne had been

whisked away with echoes of "Ooooh, I love your costume!" in her wake. Peter Pan and I moved cautiously to a corner overlooking the mall.

"Is it like this every year?" I asked.

"This opulent every year, yes. But always different. Last year this place was a lunar surface, the year before a street in Montmartre." Peter said this with an attempt at evenness; the artist in him had trouble with so much being invested in something so transient. If conversation dragged, we could always replay the one we had about Christo. "I suspect we won't see Marie again until long after the Revolution," he added.

"I guess I owe Adrienne one," I said. "I assumed this was a typical Boulder party, whatever that is. I can only guess that getting an invitation here is like being invited to dine with the queen." I stepped out of the seclusion of the corner to pluck a couple of glasses of champagne off a tray borne by a passing wench and retreated quickly. "This patch is a pain. I'd forgotten how irritating it is to have it on."

"You're right," Peter said. I looked at him with non sequitur in my eye. "You do owe Marie one for getting you in here." He smiled at me and doffed his green felt cap. "Will you excuse me, sir?" Peter Pan took off in search of Never-Never Land.

So that we privileged few could observe the festivities below, settees were placed like bleachers before the velvet-draped windows overlooking the mall, a second row angling off closer to the walls on raised platforms. I took a seat in the corner, set my champagne glass on the floor, and raised the monocle to my unpatched eye.

My efforts to find Lauren were going to be futile. The angle from the second-floor perch obscured most faces in the crowd below unless I pointed the glass west toward Broadway, where the pedestrian lights at the corner flashed their rhythmic signals to the apparent attention of no one. Waves of pedestrians pulsed from east and west curbs in response to some random tides generated farther down the mall. The sides met with resistance in the middle of Broadway and then were slowly absorbed into the masses on the opposite curb. Few cars made their way through the morass.

Horns honked. Aliens yelled. Ancient Egyptians swayed.

And there were a thousand clowns. I thought of Jason Robards and wondered how many Eskimos. I decided that if luck was on my side, Lauren would be an arctic beauty. But my eyes stayed peeled for Bozo and Chuckles.

A psychologist's responsibility to break confidentiality, the "duty to warn," was activated when "a moment's reflection" permitted the psychologist to identify the potential victim of an overt threat. My reflections, now hours longer than an instant, left me in a quandary, which I continued to review while I left the monocle fixed on the masses at Broadway and Pearl.

Michael McClelland Morton had not made a verbal threat, nor had he verbally identified a victim. Yet I was certain that the threat and the identity of the victim were clear. My responsibility, legally, was to make an "appropriate intervention"—warn the victim, tell the police, involuntarily hospitalize the patient/murderer-to-be. I had attempted to warn the victim. My current plan was to notify the police as soon as I had hard evidence linking Michael with Lauren, something I hoped to achieve during this bizarre parade. The third option seemed unfeasible; I could only put Michael McClelland Morton in the hospital with the assistance of the police. And in the unlikely event they cooperated, I was relatively certain he would be back out as soon as the seventy-two-hour involuntary hold period was up.

The four ball had crashed through my window after Michael's therapy had terminated. That fact increased my degrees of freedom by one. I could tell anybody about that. What I had trouble doing, however, was communicating the significance of that event without breaching the confidence of the previous therapy. And even then I wasn't at all sure anyone would believe me. Specifically, I wasn't sure either Lauren or Purdy was predisposed to believe me.

While I pondered all this, a lithe young woman in a flesh-colored body stocking inadequately covered with bright feathers sat down next to me on the settee. "Hi," she said, smiling, "can I have a look?"

My response was a hesitant, "Sure." As she peered through my looking glass and I looked at her, my ambivalence waned, however, and I wondered, among more prurient thoughts, how she was going to get the glitter out of her long blond hair. She was stunning.

"Looking for a merchant ship to plunder?" She raised her sparkling eyebrows when she talked and held the tip of her tongue between her teeth when she finished. She took the long glass down from her eye, collapsed its telescoping elements once, and slowly opened it back up to its full length before handing it back to me.

"Did you see any out there?" I asked. That's as smooth as I get.

"No ships. Many drunken sailors. My name is Marla."

At this point I was quite ambivalent. It was not often that I was the object of such unabashed flirtation. It was, fortunately, even rarer that I followed murderers around. "I'm Alan," I said, holding out my hand, which she shook and then immediately grasped in both of hers. There was no way to keep my hand in hers and not turn toward her on the fabric-covered bench. She knew that.

Marla wore a costume that demanded perusal; the shadows and bulges on the sheer stocking were more enticing than covered trays at a banquet after a fast. But the situation was one where I had been socialized not to stare. One of my girlfriends in college, noting my examination of her breasts on our first date, had said, "They don't talk, why don't you look up here." So I tried to look at the part of Marla that talked, not the part of her that was shouting.

"Would you dance with me?" she asked, the tongue in the teeth again.

Not trusting my own tongue to behave, I merely nodded, and we walked to the back of the room where a small wooden dance floor had been set up between the TV monitors. Peter Pan saw the plumed Godiva leading me to the dance floor, and he mouthed some lewd affirmation.

Marla trailed an aura of flora and spice. She turned as we reached the other dancers and said, "Who does your makeup, Captain?" The music was something by Phil Collins that I didn't recognize. A few of the couples were succeeding in dancing to its moderate rhythm, although most had collapsed into ignoring the beat and were slow-dancing to some other tune. I took Marla's hand to join the few, she moved mine around to a spot quite low on her back and moved in close to me to join the many.

When I looked up Marie Antoinette was laughing, her arm around Peter Pan.

"Marie Antoinette," I said in reply to the earlier question.

She lifted her head off my shoulder and looked around, seeing Adrienne's interpretation of French

323

royalty. "She's your—"

"Next-door neighbor," I said.

Lauren's date had little of my attention for the next few minutes. My body was doing what my eyes could not, mapping as much of Marla's firm form as it could. She smelled heavenly, felt heavenly, and didn't complain about my dancing.

At that moment Lauren, her face in greasepaint but her cascade of black hair uncovered, moved slowly into the upper left corner of one of the TV monitors. Her right hand trailed behind her, fingertips curled into those of a tall man in a white sweat suit, a computer keyboard attached to his chest on some type of frame, his head enclosed in what looked like a real twelve-inch bronze glass monitor. Great costume.

Marla noticed before I did that I had stopped dancing. She said, "Alan . . . Captain . . . what's up?"

"I need to follow that clown," I said, more to myself than to her. My presence of mind was not completely gone, however. I manufactured a smile and said, "I'll see you a little later," to Marla.

I lost a minute retrieving my cape and another going back to the monitor to identify the last known location of Lauren and Byte-Man on the mall.

A plea in Adrienne's eyes said, "Oy." Ignoring it, I turned to rush down the stairs and used both handrails to reach the door in three bounds.

Then I was gone.

Forty-one

I walked from the banquet at the castle into a marketplace of wide-eyed fools. The bizarreness throbbed.

The air was cold and dry, the night sky partially obscured by clouds, the stars rendered invisible by the umbrella of incandescence over the mall. It took me five minutes just to get to the place on the mall where the camera had recorded Lauren's passing. Following the path she was headed on in the tape was as futile as trying to catch the horse in front of me on a carousel. I could bare my teeth and gallop, but my progress was to be determined by other factors.

Yielding to a hope that Lauren and her companion might have stayed in the vicinity, I jumped onto a planter box that had just been vacated by a young man dressed in a Neanderthal costume that permitted him to display the fruits of many hard hours in the gym or a few expensive ones in the drugstore. The caveman had leaped from the planter to a light standard and was doing chin-ups to the shouted count of the adoring masses. The light standard swayed, and a squadron of police moved in to discourage anyone else from joining the acrobatics. I stepped back and balanced myself on a piece of jutting flagstone a couple of feet up the wall of the adjacent bank. I scanned the crowd for a bobbing computer monitor.

"Down. *Now! You!*"

"Me?" I asked the red-faced cop.

"Down! Get the fuck down!" I jumped into the dirt of the big planter and threaded through a few people before I stepped down in front of the cop. He was young, angry, and eager to be obeyed. I was chastised, costumed, and willing to be obsequious.

"This way," he ordered, gripping me firmly above the elbow.

I complied, trailing in the wake he made as he moved around the corner to Thirteenth where three squad cars were parked. The reinforcements were holding nightsticks.

"ID, please." He was breathing heavily, his polite words an obvious concession to decorum that he would have just as soon dispensed with. I pulled out my driver's license and handed it to him.

"This is enough of a zoo without citizens"—he turned the word into a profanity—"like you scaling buildings and busting their heads open."

"I'm sorry, Officer. I got separated from someone, and I was trying to get up high enough to see over the crowd to find them." He seemed mollified by the fact that I wasn't going to give him a hard time. "I promise"—I raised my hands—"no more climbing."

Before he responded, a quiet voice intruded. "Why, it's Doctor Deadly. Can't seem to stay away from us, can you? What is it? Love? Or maybe a new corpse for us?" Purdy was wearing a heavy wool overcoat with tiny lapels. It was such a nice piece of clothing that he looked out of uniform. For a second it crossed my mind that he was in costume, too. "I'll take care of this one, Frank, thanks," he said to the young patrolman.

"Hello, Detective." Purdy's hands were buried in the deep pockets of his coat. He smiled and nodded in response to my greeting. "Can I talk to you for a minute?" I asked.

Purdy buried his lower lip in his mustache and just

continued nodding. Closing his eyes, he gestured with his bowling ball of a head to follow him. We got into the backseat of one of the squad cars.

"I think Deputy District Attorney Crowder is in danger." As I spoke, I saw my reflection in the rearview mirror of the car. The fact that I was in costume had temporarily escaped my consciousness. "Jesus," I said.

"What?"

"Nothing."

"Nothing what? Nothing about Crowder?"

"No. Jesus nothing. The part about Lauren is true. I think she's in danger."

"Go on," he said. Then he smiled. "Given the life expectancy of people you know, I have to take this seriously. Go on."

"Somebody threw a pool ball, a billiard ball, through the living room window of my house Wednesday night. A four ball. I think it was a message telling me that Lauren is in danger."

"Makes perfect sense to me," he said. "That's how I read it. Every time a pool ball goes into a living room in this town you just automatically write off a deputy DA."

I ignored the sarcasm and felt pretty smug about doing so. "Lauren Crowder plays tournament-quality pool, pocket billiards, whatever. She has a big carved table in the living room of her house. Somebody was telling me that they know that. And I think they were telling me that they can get to her. Like they have gotten to others I know."

"Others? Plural." Purdy was quick.

"Well, one other, at least." I didn't want to explain to Purdy about the turtle at this late date.

"So you know who this pool ball hurler is?"

I sighed. "This is slippery ground, Detective." I waited for a sign that the burly man next to me acknowledged my dilemma. What I got was a slow perusal of my makeup. "What if a psychologist, like myself, had an idea who had done something like throw this billiard ball, but knew it only because of things that he had learned in psychotherapy. That would be confidential. Right? And there are only limited rationales for breaking that confidentiality, one of which is the 'duty to warn.' You're familiar with the 'duty to warn,' aren't you, Detective?" Purdy's head was in an almost continual bob. "Well, just suppose this psychologist might be willing to divulge some confidential information, but only if he had some assurance that somebody would take him seriously about the threat he perceived somebody like Deputy District Attorney Crowder to be in. I mean, he wouldn't feel comfortable divulging the information if nobody was going to take it seriously, would he?"

" 'Course not," said Purdy.

"So suppose this psychologist knew that the same guy he suspects of doing something like throwing this pool ball through his window also did something like what happened to my dog, you know, the neck shaving? Suppose the psychologist divulged that, would a police officer, like yourself, take that association seriously?"

"This cop supposes that a cop like myself would say that ain't enough." Purdy was guessing that I had an ample inventory of information with which to barter; he had little to gain by being agreeable to my first offer.

"Okay. Just suppose that this psychologist knew, I mean *knew*, that the guy who did something like throw the pool ball and something else like barber my dog also committed a certain violent felony that has perplexed the local authorities. What if the psychologist divulged something like that—would a cop, like yourself, take that seriously enough to show some concern about Deputy District Attorney Crowder?"

"How violent a felony?"

"As violent as they come." Nobody had been murdered in Boulder since Gretchen.

Purdy had the information he wanted. "A cop like myself would be intrigued. First, though, he would want to remind this psychologist, like yourself, that if he is aware of a threat to an individual, one of his responsibilities is to inform the intended victim."

"Let's just say that in this circumstance the intended victim told the psychologist to fuck off."

Purdy was silent for a full minute. "Lauren Crowder plays pool? Damn." He spent a moment digesting the image. "And you know who threw the pool ball?"

I nodded.

"And where do you think this person who threw the pool ball is?"

"When your colleague accosted me, I was trying to spot Lauren and her date. My concern is that Lauren is enjoying an evening with the pool ball thrower even as we speak."

"She's here? Right now?"

"Yes."

"With him?"

"I don't know. The guy she's with has a mask on."

"Maybe we can find her, have a chat?"

"Maybe, Detective."

"If this is jealousy talkin', if you're shittin' me about any of this, Doctor Deadly, I'll cut out your heart and feed it to my dog." He started to lift his big frame out of the car and stopped as I was trying to unwrap myself from Merideth's cape, which in the closed car had released its aroma of old Opium perfume. "I wonder, you know, if the psychologist, the imaginary one, could have guessed what kind of car this guy might drive?"

"Those sorts of things don't come up in therapy very often. He probably never even heard about the multi-valve red Honda Prelude a guy like this might drive.

So I can't help you."

I told Purdy where I had seen them heading and described their costumes. He pulled a radio from under the folds of his coat and said something into it about a tall guy with a computer monitor for a head. "Let's go for a walk," he said to me. I gazed at the quasi-human glacier impeding us. Yeah, right.

Purdy's receiver crackled and squawked a few minutes later. We had progressed about twelve feet. He put the black Motorola under his coat and said, "Follow me."

We moved through the crowds, hugging storefronts, crossed Broadway, and stopped outside the bookstore. "They were here when I got that call."

I backed up to the bookstore wall, put my right foot on the ledge of the display window, and pushed myself up, keeping my balance with a hand on Purdy's shoulder. "There they are," I said, and jumped down. "They're heading off the mall, at the other end."

The illusion of being able to cover one hundred feet of paving brick in less than five minutes died hard. When we arrived, panting and pissed, at the end of the mall, Lauren and her date were not to be found.

"If we had a uniform with us, we would have made it. They act like icebreakers during shit like this," Purdy said.

I didn't offer my impression that people were treating his pleas of, "Stand back, police," as Halloween guerrilla theater. It wasn't his fault; he was, after all, being tailed by a pirate in drag.

What I did say was, "I appreciate you taking this seriously, Detective."

He said, "Don't. Look, I got a job to do. You're a citizen with information to help me do my job. That's all. I suggest you think about what you legally feel obligated to tell the police about all this. Understand? Now get out of my face. Have fun. Don't drink and drive."

"Are you going to talk to Lauren?" My face was as stony as I could make it beneath the powder and the rouge.

"I'll think on it." The tone he employed informed me that I had pressed him as much as I would be permitted before he became less accommodating.

"You've done your bit, Gregory." Purdy glared at me and spoke as if he were talking to a Boy Scout who had somehow met the criteria for a merit badge while leaving any number of little old ladies stranded on curbs. "You told her something and you told me something. You can go home and rest gently at having protected your cherished professional ethics and simultaneously covered your ass from lawsuits. Don't let your dreams be disturbed by the slime you could clean off the streets."

"Cleaning the streets isn't my job. Treating people with problems is." It sounded lame to me. I was rather sure it would sound lame to him.

"The job, *my* fucking job, is cleaning the goddamn streets. When people like you fail to do your fucking job, my fucking job is just a little fucking harder."

"I'm not perfect at what I do, Detective."

"I've noticed. The coroner's noticed. Good night. *Doctor* Deadly."

Binky's party had become even more crowded in my absence. Despite myself, part of me wanted Marla to be waiting near the top of the stairs, anxious for my return. I spotted her, instead, on the dance floor. Her fluid hips were thrusting in counterpoint to those of a tall man dressed as a wizard.

A regal voice from behind me said, "Welcome back,

Captain Hook."

"Hi, Ren."

"Marie. Miss Antoinette," she corrected me, heavily caked eyes closing for a second or so.

"Marie."

"Your arrest was recorded on video. So far it's been the high point of the party. You planning an encore?"

"I wasn't arrested."

"Whatever."

I was almost too distracted to notice how miffed she was. Almost.

"What's up, Ren?"

"You are here"—Ms. Antoinette spread her regal arms to display her kingdom—"at my invitation, under my sponsorship, if you will. Binky's noticed your erratic behavior and is subtly trying to convince herself and anyone who asks that your stunt was scripted. Part of the 'ambiance.' "

My lips turned up just a little bit. "You're thrilled, aren't you? You've found a relatively insulated way of annoying her. You can thank me later."

"For the record, I'm livid," said Adrienne, regally.

"For the record, I'm chastised and on my way to the Bastille."

"So," she said, "I'm sorry about the bird of paradise." She gestured toward undulating Marla.

I shrugged wistfully and raised an eyebrow.

"She's not what you need, Alan. You're suffering from malnutrition and she's a Big Mac. But, I guess, even junk food can be nutritious for starving people, and let's face it, you're in a famine." She paused, eyeing Peter, his head bent in serious discussion with a woman about four feet six inches tall dressed as a vegetable. Adrienne gestured toward him with her cake box. "He's got this thing about diminutive women." Adrienne never said "short." "You gonna tell me what that was all about down there on the mall? The bounding exit, the scaling buildings, the cops?"

"I thought I saw Lauren. That's all."

"That's all? All right, all right. You'll tell me when you're ready."

"I'm gonna go," I said. "You know where Binky is? I want to thank her."

"Don't do me any favors. The stairs are behind you. Slink. And please, stay off camera." She kissed me on the cheek and tiptoed over toward her husband.

Forty-two

Either the forced march up the mall behind Purdy or the spray of innuendo he departed behind left me coated with a thin film of sweat. Merideth's cape was an inadequate wrap in both size and design, and I arrived at my office chilled after leaving the party.

Purdy's words had stung.

Mostly because he was right. I was trying to walk a probably nonexistent line between my ethical responsibility to maintain confidentiality and my moral responsibility to interfere with an upcoming homicide. Purdy didn't feel good about it. I didn't feel good about it. And I could guess that Michael McClelland Morton wouldn't feel too great about it, either. Thinking about my life without the context of Karen Hart's death did not come easy to me then, but I tried to imagine how I would have handled the situation with Michael if I hadn't been beat up by Karen's death and what had happened after it. In truth, I would probably have clung more rigidly to the ethical guidelines. And the ethical guidelines told me I could only exercise the duty to warn if . . .

The clothes I had left in the Subaru weren't quite warm enough for the last hours of the last day of October. But they were all I had. In two minutes I transformed myself from pirate queen to inconspicuous pedestrian. Brown corduroys, blue-and-maroon sweater, and my old Nikes. The makeup came off reluctantly. I wished I had paid more attention to the hundreds of opportunities I had missed to observe the intricacies of makeup removal during Merideth's nightly ritual. By the time I finished scrubbing, my face was red and blotchy and my eyes looked mildly diseased.

The decision to swing by Lauren's house on my way home, and then, if necessary, to head up to Michael's house on Lee Hill, was the result not so much of deliberation as of wishful thinking. There remained a slight possibility that I would see a car I didn't recognize in front of her house and that I could convince myself that Lauren's vulnerability to assault by Michael wasn't an imminent problem.

The Subaru started hard, making sputtering and missing noises to remind me that it wasn't winterized. I crossed Canyon Boulevard at Ninth and passed over Boulder Creek. Three more turns through the dark old neighborhood of well-spaced houses, and I was on Lauren's street. Her house sat at the crest of a blister of a hill. The house was unlit, but the front yard was illuminated by the lane's only streetlight. The Rockies loomed immense and gray to the west. She usually parked the Peugeot in a gravel space on the south side of the house. Three-foot-high berms capped by dense euonymous partially screened the spot from view. But from the angle where I sat in the Subaru, I could see that the space was filled.

With a bright red Honda.

My ego defenses were active enough and irrational enough that I let denial fuel the thought that maybe it wasn't Michael's car. Hondas all look almost the same from the rear, right? Wrong.

It was Michael's multivalve Honda Prelude. Illinois plates.

Disdaining further subterfuge, I walked boldly to the

front door and rang the bell. No answer. I knocked, first with my knuckles and then with my fists. No answer.

Where was Lauren's car?

I walked around the side of the house and then around back. I heard a car on the street, and then the noise faded. Lauren's house was dark. The doors were locked. The rooms I could peer into were in meticulous order. I didn't see any bodies sprawled in unnatural positions on the floor. Through the kitchen door I could see a note on yellow lined legal paper taped to a plastic spray bottle on the kitchen table. A pale green water pitcher sat next to the spray bottle.

Breaking the kitchen window with a rock was an option, inelegant, but an option. Instead I chose to go back to the Subaru and rummaged around to find another of my chronically underpowered flashlights in the glove compartment. Trying to appear as if I belonged, I didn't look around to see if any of the neighbors were watching. The angle from the kitchen door made the light from the flashlight reflect off the note as though it were a mirror. To change angles, I climbed behind some overgrown lilacs and tried the window over the sink. Bingo.

Somebody. Do you mind something something plants. Big question mark. Thanks for getting the something. We'll be back Monday something. Seven digits, preceded by a one, the first number was a nine. A single scripted *L* at the bottom of the page.

She went to Aspen. She took the Peugeot. And she took Michael with her.

As I solved the equation for X, I stepped backward onto the lilac and snapped a fair-size branch. The loud crack startled me into rotating rapidly and breaking off another one.

I ran back around the house, jumped into the wagon, cranked a U-turn, and weaved back toward Arapahoe. I cut off on Ninth and accelerated south to Baseline, feinted a stop, and hooked left on Baseline to Broadway. Green light. On South Broadway I stopped at a gas station below the mesa edifice where Michael Morton worked and filled the tank. I bought an obscenely large cup of steaming brown liquid purportedly brewed from ground coffee beans, and a big bag of Chee-tos and screeched off south on 93 toward Golden.

The Subaru was doing seventy on the two-lane road as I sped past the Rocky Flats Nuclear Weapons Facility. The cutoff to Coal Creek Canyon often shielded state patrol cars, so I slowed to sixty. A few miles farther on, in Golden, the streets seemed to have a cop or sheriff's car on every corner; I assumed they were Halloween precautions. I picked up I-70 south of town and set the cruise control at seventy-two as I climbed into Mt. Vernon Canyon. The Subaru humored me for a few hundred yards and then begged to be downshifted.

Approaching Idaho Springs, I was struck by the possibility that Independence Pass would be closed for the season. Would my three-and-a-half-hour drive become even longer? The fall on the Front Range had been mild, but that didn't mean one good dump of snow hadn't closed the high pass into Aspen. I chose not to worry about it, remembering that there would be a sign posting the status of the pass on I-70 just before Copper Mountain.

The snow gods blessed me; the pass remained open. Given Lauren's vision problems and her vertigo, I guessed that she would have Michael drive and that she would insist he avoid the nauseating curves of Independence Pass and take the long way around, despite the possibility of construction delays in Glenwood Canyon. I was at least an hour behind them; I figured to make some of that up by taking the shorter route.

I continued to rush as though hurrying would make a difference. During the drive I had ample time to question my rationale for making this trip in the middle of the night.

Between yawns I could confuse myself with the possibility that I had misread Michael's recent message. Then I would open the window, wake up with a blast of cold thin mountain air, and reassure myself that warning Lauren was the only prudent thing to do.

I thought about the past two years. Merideth leaving. Karen Hart dying. Anne's accident. Gretchen's murder. Cicero. Lawyers. Lawsuits. And Michael.

I pondered Michael's relationships with all the other players, and the connection struck me as I rifled past the vile scars left by the purveyors of molybdenum on the mountain faces near Climax. My foot eased off the accelerator, the fatigue deserted my eyes and chest, and certainty erased doubt.

Of course he was going to hurt her. There was no doubt that Lauren was Michael's next victim. And there was no doubt why. When I realized who had been the target all along, it was clear that everybody else, including me, had just happened onto the scene. We were merely the hammers used to pound the nail.

I should, of course, have seen it all sooner. The pieces were there. Or at least the proper pieces were missing. Any of the questions about Michael that had perplexed me, if answered, would have solved the puzzle.

And the whole time I played right into his hand.

A recent storm's residue of snow dusted the plains around Leadville and carpeted the steppes at the base of the Collegiate Peaks. Meager moonlight flared off the still waters at Twin Lakes, and I considered simply stopping at a phone and calling the Aspen police or Pitkin County sheriff or whoever. I played the imaginary dialogue in my head, fantasized briefly that I wouldn't be mistaken for a crank, hallucinated that I actually convinced some uniformed knight to drive out to Jake's house to save Lauren, and then was slapped back to reality by the stark truth of Lauren's certain explanation to the officer that I was a jealous fool, and thanks, she wasn't in any danger.

I managed to pass an old Thunderbird before the switchbacks at the entrance to Independence Pass and didn't see another car on my side of the road until I was winding into Aspen.

Only two wrong turns impeded my arrival at Lauren's timeshare. To be safe, I parked just past it on the quiet street despite my assumption that these vacation homes would be empty during Aspen's lull in seasons. The autumn leaf spectacular was rapidly becoming mulch, and Aspen Mountain and Snowmass were at least three or four storms away from their traditional Thanksgiving opening.

I marched to the house resolutely. Instead of knocking I checked the garage window for Lauren's Peugeot. It was there.

I walked to both sides of the house. All the windows were dark. I cut through a neighbor's property to the path along the Roaring Fork that fronted the house. Dim lights illuminated the ceiling of the living room on the top floor. No other signs of occupancy were apparent.

My options were too many. Climb onto the deck outside Lauren's bedroom, hope she was sleeping alone, and try to convince her that the guy she was spending the weekend with had other, violent, things on his mind. Or. Climb onto the deck outside the bedroom where I had slept a few months before, wake Michael, if he was sleeping alone, and try to convince him not to hurt Lauren. Or. Pound on the front door, wake everybody up, and . . .

It was almost three o'clock in the morning. I was exhausted.

On the interminable trip over the mountain pass into town, I had been unable to solve a simple dilemma. I could almost convince myself of my right to waive Michael's privilege because I feared Lauren was in "imminent danger," but I was left with the discomfiting reality that there was very little information in Michael's clinical record that would convince Lauren, or anyone else, that she was in jeopardy. Sure, Michael had confessed to some crimes, including murder. Actually he had said, "You figured out that I killed her," never identifying Gretchen as his victim. Any skeptical audience would point out to me that I was grasping at straws in my accusation of Michael. Anyway, he would vociferously deny saying those things to me, and Lauren was certainly stubborn enough to believe him rather than me.

I was willing, though not eager, to be humiliated in order to convince Lauren of the peril she was in. I wasn't, however, willing to humiliate myself and fail to convince her. I needed a plan.

I took off my Nikes and climbed in my stockinged feet onto the deck outside her bedroom window. After finding a vantage from which I could see her bed, apparently with only one body in it, I waited patiently until the body heaved in a sigh and rolled over.

It appeared that I had some time. I considered curling up like a watchdog and sleeping on her deck, but acute hypothermia seemed to be the most likely outcome of that. I thought of breaking into her house and skulking about as an unseen guardian. If either Lauren or Michael discovered me there, though, I'd certainly spend the rest of the night in the local pokie.

I decided to get some sleep and do my confronting the next day.

Forty-three

The clerk at the Pitkin Inn was unenthused about my middle-of-the-night check-in. I pleaded for a room, exaggerated by telling him I was a regular customer (Merideth and I had stayed there once before while I attended a seminar in town), lied about my car breaking down on the pass, and finally bribed him with a forty-dollar tip.

The room was frilly and floral, but the bed was firm and the sheets soft. I checked my reasoning one last time for fatal errors, cleared my head, and slept with Laura Ashley.

I woke at seven, feeling surprisingly refreshed, and had a big breakfast in the inn's little dining room, which I had to myself. The round four-top where I sat with only the Sunday *Denver Post* for company edged into a bay window that sparkled with morning light. The night clerk stopped by while I finished a third cup of coffee and apologized for his mood the night before. I told him it was understandable and thanked him for his consideration in giving me a room. We each allowed the other the privilege of recouping some dignity. He didn't, however, return the tip.

A plan had surfaced during the night. Broad outlines evolved through gradual metamorphoses into workable details as I lingered after breakfast.

Near nine I signed the breakfast tab and hurried to the drugstore on Main Street, hands in my pockets for warmth. I bought a toothbrush, toothpaste, razor, and shampoo and hustled back to the inn to put them to use. My room was cozy and bright when I returned, the bed crisply made, a fresh, single pink rose in the vase by the window. I showered long, permitting the final details of my plan to reassure me that the proposal was an adequate response to my quandary.

A troubling image threatened to attack my growing contentment, however, as dramatic visions of what Lauren and Michael might be doing in that grand house on the Roaring Fork skipped across my imagination. I had two fears—that they were engaged in some passionate replica of my first morning in Mexico with Lauren, or that Michael had already, or was about to, hurt her. My gut feeling said that with a weekend in paradise ahead of them, the former was more likely than the latter.

To be reassured, I called Jake's house. Lauren answered. I hung up.

I tried not to think about how much was riding on my timing being right.

It was near ten when I started making my calls, long-distance card in hand. Merideth had taught me, back in her real estate days, never to discard a phone number, and it was one of a thousand lessons I still thanked her for. The telephone directory in my Day-Timer provided the numbers I needed, and the motivation that came from being cornered provided the chutzpah.

Valerie Goodwin sounded pleased to hear from me. Her cooperation was probably contaminated by voids on her social calendar. Anyway, I sketched the outline of my plan and received her permission to proceed; she agreed to grant me the right to discuss Karen's treatment with Lauren and Michael and promised to put the release in writing and get a copy to me in the mail. Michael's name meant nothing to her.

Phil Hubbard was more reluctant to comply because I was more restricted in what I could tell him. I told him that giving me the permission I wanted might make sense of some of the things that were so confusing to him. He was suspicious of the need to include the man I called Michael McClelland in the release of information I was asking him to sign on behalf of his deceased wife. There was no way he could know of his employee's pseudonym. He asked me directly if his cooperation would help him solve his obsession. The answer, I said, was yes, I thought so. The reality was maybe. With obvious ambivalence he granted me permission to talk to Lauren and Michael about Anne Hubbard, took my dictation of release language over the phone, and promised to sign it and put it in the mail.

My call to Cleveland went unanswered at ten. At eleven a woman said that her mother-in-law would be back after church. I said I would call back.

The chill had tempered by the time I walked across Main Street into town. Autumn warmth in the Rockies is deceptive. Warmth that seems forever when one is standing immobile evaporates with the first movement of a muscle or the first wisp of a breeze. My first stop was a ski shop selling last season's rejects at deep discount. I bought a sleek parka filled with goose down, and a pair of gloves. The first bike shop I went to was in the process of changing over from summer sports to winter sports. Their rental bikes from the previous summer were for sale, not rent. I moved on until I found one that would rent me a solid bike for the rest of the day. I paid a few extra dollars for damage insurance and another buck to rent a lock.

I thought seriously about buying a gun. Then I thought seriously about the fact that I was terrified of them, didn't know how to use one, didn't think I could actually pull the trigger of one that was pointed at somebody, and that if this scenario played out so that one was necessary, I had blown it.

I locked the red Trek mountain bike outside the inn and tried Gretchen's mom one more time. She cried when I mentioned her daughter's name but recovered her composure quickly.

She apologized. I said, Don't. I told her what I wanted and told her I thought it might provide some clues to help solve her daughter's murder. She asked if the police were involved. I told her no, but that nice deputy district attorney, Ms. Crowder, and another man, a Mr. McClelland, would be there. If Ms. Crowder was part of it, sure, I could have permission to talk about Gretchen's therapy, she told me. I thanked her, telling her I would also need the permission in writing and dictated language to her over the phone. She took Michael McClelland's name in stride. Thank you, Doctor, she said.

My ducks were all in a row.

I retrieved the bike and rode down the hill next to the Hotel Jerome. I caught the bike path just past the post office and played with the gearing as the strobe lights of aspen-tree-interrupted sunshine played off my body. The Trek was a solid bike, but I missed the feel and spring of the Deore-equipped Bridgestones Jake kept in his garage.

The wooden bridge traversing the Roaring Fork was lit by unfiltered light, the cold water below rushing and bouncing over the rounded rocks. I remembered times with Lauren and times with Merideth. Better times. I pulled my L.A. Dodgers cap low over my face and pedaled down the trail.

It was almost two o'clock when I rode past Jake's house. The correlation between time of day and Lauren's holiday siesta schedule should be a perfect 1.0, I reminded myself, and allowed the house only a brief glance as I sped by. Michael was standing on the living room deck, hands on the railing, looking as if he owned the place. He wore a blue long-sleeve polo shirt and black jeans. He didn't react to my passing by.

Two houses farther down the trail I pushed the bike, and myself, through an initial test, riding through brush and rocks up the steep hill to the road above the house. The versatility of the mountain bike was a joy; it seemed

344

capable of going anywhere. The street I had parked on the night before was empty, the expensive homes in pre-winter hibernation.

Counting on Michael staying on the other side of the house, I walked into the garage, raised the hood on the Peugeot, removed the distributor cap, which I hid behind some firewood, and remounted the bike for a hair-raising downhill journey back to the trail by the river.

Another bike drifted down the trail from town. The rider stopped well short of the house and sat on a big rock overlooking the river. He or she was far enough out of the way that I didn't have to be concerned.

Michael had pulled a chair up to the railing and was sitting in the afternoon sun.

Since the other rider had stopped upstream from the house, I parked my bike about fifty yards downstream and pretended to be reading a paperback that I had removed from the Pitkin Inn's convenience library.

Lauren arrived, right on cue, a little after three. She wore her yellow sweats, her black hair was down and blown slightly by the breeze. Each hand grabbed the bicep of the opposing arm. She spoke something to Michael from a few feet away. He turned, bounced up from the chair, and walked over to her. He put his arms around her, but she left hers where they were. Was she cold, reticent, or both? I hated watching this. She said something that caused him to free her and preceded him back into the house.

Now what?

The Trek lurched over rocks as I headed back up the hill to the road, feeling a little more comfortable with the bike with each ascent. I coasted down toward the front of the house. An Aspen Police Department Saab patrol car moved quietly by. I waved. The officer nodded and continued to patrol.

Lauren and Michael were both awake. Now was as good a time as any to have the talk I had been rehearsing. I preferred, I decided, to do this in the daylight.

When I was twenty feet from the driveway, the garage door opened, the mechanical clanging of steel rollers in steel tracks startling me. My plan didn't include responses to a lot of contingencies. Caught off guard, I ventured past the house, following the street around a bend a hundred yards ahead. When I looked back I saw Lauren and Michael getting settled on the mountain bikes from the garage. I waited for them to mount and take off and then followed them down the road. I knew the way. Between the houses I could see another rider on the trail, off his bike, looking up at me as I went by.

I quickly decided that, for what I had in mind, the trail was almost as good a venue as Jake's house.

Instead of following Lauren and Michael, I turned back down the hill between the houses. I would ride up the trail and meet them where the road merged close to the trail a quarter mile downstream. The guy on the bike below mounted and took off upstream as I headed down the hill. Not bothering to pause at the bottom, I angled off and caught some air before the fat tires thudded on the trail. I needed to buy myself one of these, I said to myself, patting the bike's frame as though it were a steed to be reassured and praised.

Michael led Lauren as they joined the trail just where I had predicted. He hotdogged off the pavement, climbing little hills into the forest, splashing down into the shallow banks of the river; Lauren kept a steady, slow pace on the trail. I stayed well back.

They rode for almost a half hour, moving from paved trail to packed trail and up to the steep sections where the trail clung to hillsides way above the river. Finally they stopped.

I didn't. I rode right up to where the two of them sat holding hands on a rock, took off my cap while still straddling the bike, and said, "Hello."

Michael shook his head just a little and said, "Hello." He had been waiting for this moment for fifteen years.

Lauren just glared.

Forty-four

"What're you doing here?" Lauren was angry. She was also, it appeared, appalled.

"Just enjoying a weekend in the mountains. I have fond memories of this place." I was aware of no one who could precipitate contentiousness in me as quickly as these two people.

"Please." She turned the word into two long syllables.

Michael stood and moved forward a step, letting go of Lauren's hand. "This might have something to do with me," he said.

"You know him?" Lauren spat the question at Michael, suddenly recognizing she was operating with a handicap, obviously perplexed that she didn't know the nature of her disadvantage.

"You could say that."

"Alan, what the hell is this all about? If you're entertaining any illusions that your display of possessiveness is somehow attractive or endearing, you're sadly mistaken. I find your jealousy and intrusiveness to be childish."

"This has to do with a lot of things, Lauren. Possessiveness is one of them. But not my possessiveness of you. It has to do with this man's"—I pointed at Michael—"possessiveness."

"You don't know shit, Alan. How he treats me is between him and me."

"I'm not here about his treatment of you. Thus far, anyway. I'm here because of what he's done in the past with other women and what he might be planning with you in the very near future. This may be hard for you to believe, Lauren, but you are, to him, only an extra on this set, not the star."

"How dare you?" She started to rise from the rock.

All the light in the Roaring Fork valley was subdued, the sun having moved behind the steep peaks to the west. The air continued a rapid transformation from crisp to cold. Neither Lauren nor Michael was dressed for an All Saints' evening on the trail. I was. She wore skintight black stretch pants that disappeared into the top of bulky red socks and a long, thick cable-knit turtleneck. Michael wore the clothes he had been wearing on the deck and a jean jacket.

"For a moment, Lauren"—I raised my voice—"please shut up. For once, just listen. Please."

She reclaimed her spot on the rock and heeded my suggestion. She was quiet and attentive. I was taken aback.

My plan depended on Michael accepting his role in this production. I didn't acknowledge him further as I recited the prologue.

"Lauren, you've asked me, a number of times, to discuss a case I've had in treatment. I've been forced, because of lack of permission, not to discuss that case with you. The case involves someone you know as 'M.' " I looked at Michael. His face was impassive; he displayed no anxiety or alarm.

"I still can't tell you about that case. But there are some others that I can tell you about that you might find enlightening. Do you mind?"

"Really, Alan, this isn't the time—"

"But it is," I interrupted, "trust me. By the way, I've requested and have received permission to discuss these matters not only with you, but with your companion as well. Shall we?"

Neither responded. Not responding, for Lauren, required significant effort. I lifted my right leg off the bike, dismounted, and leaned the chunky bicycle against a bare aspen tree across the trail. There was a rock slightly downhill from where Lauren sat. I perched on it, feet resting solidly on its sloping face. Michael stood pat, between Lauren and me, slightly to my right.

"Where to start? How about with a woman named Anne Hubbard? Remember her? She was a city councilwoman who died in a single car crash last Memorial Day weekend." Lauren indicated she was with me. I had her attention. "Well, she was a patient of mine. Her husband, Phil Hubbard, has given me permission to discuss her case with you both." I waited for objections and continued, "Anne was a very talented politician with a wreck of a marriage. Maybe not a wreck, but a passionless relationship devoid of intimacy. She wanted to blame her husband for all of that — coming to see me was a way of recognizing she contributed to the blight. Anyway, last spring she had an affair. Her husband" — I exaggerated — "knows all about it." Michael's face twitched. I assumed the twitch was at his fear that Phil Hubbard knew that Michael had been sleeping with his wife. Michael didn't know that Phil didn't know. "As a matter of fact, she was driving down from her lover's house when she died. A little drunk. A little pregnant."

Michael exhaled. I'd hit a nerve; he hadn't known about the pregnancy. His face was screened from Lauren's view. Lauren looked sharply at me and guessed, "That postmortem you wanted a while back. It was hers?"

"It was," I affirmed. "By the way, Anne was killed on Lee Hill Road near North Broadway. Where do you live?" I turned my attention toward Michael and pointedly examined his face.

He stayed silent. Lauren leaned forward to look at his stony countenance. "I don't need to conspire in this charade with you," he said finally.

Lauren interjected, "He lives on Lee Hill. So what?"

I shrugged. "And where do you work?" I asked Michael. The whisper returned: "At NCAR." N-car.

349

"So does Phil Hubbard," I said. "Interesting. What lab do you work in?"

Lauren was leaning forward, trying to see Michael's face in the dying light.

He whispered again, "Severe Storms. Phil Hubbard is my supervisor."

"Mmmm," I muttered. I conjured an image of Lauren completing a prosecution. This time she was my jury.

"So. Anne had an affair with somebody who lived up Lee Hill. And your friend here, Lauren, happens to meet that criterion. And he works for her husband to boot. Mmmph."

"Alan, this is tedious, what're you getting at? So he had an affair with a married woman?"

"Not just a married woman. His boss's wife."

"Okay. His boss's wife."

I held my hands out, begging her patience. "I'm trying to establish a pattern here," I said, images of famous movie lawyers providing my role models. "Next? How about Gretchen Kravner? She was murdered in September. She was one of my patients as well. You have her chart, Lauren, but your friend here may need some details to get oriented. He probably doesn't know that she told her psychologist — me — that she'd learned from a friend of hers at a travel agency of the destination and dates of a trip to Mexico that he was planning a couple of months ago. He also probably doesn't know" — I was guessing now — "that her psychologist knows that she told an acquaintance or two about that knowledge as well. You remember, Lauren, of course, that one of the people she knew was 'M,' that person I can't talk about, someone she met in my waiting room." I paused and looked at Michael. "Are you with me?" His face remained impassive.

"Good," I said. "Anyway. This next part is not gonna be news to either of you. You must remember the last time the three of us were together." I said this in the voice of familiarity usually reserved for reintroduction of people who don't recall that they've met before. Lauren raised one corner of her closed mouth and arched her eyebrows. I nodded to her. "Yes, that's right. Lover's Beach. Cabo San Lucas," I continued. "Remember?" Lauren stood up and walked next to Michael, as though to look at him for the first time.

"Was that you, Michael? In Mexico?"

"Just a coincidence. Serendipity," he muttered.

"Why haven't you told me you saw me there?"

"I'd forgotten. It's been unimportant."

I was counting on Lauren remembering her assumption that the person on the beach had been a patient of mine. I couldn't reveal that now.

Lauren sat back down. She raised her knees up near her shoulders and crossed her arms over them.

The next words were directed at Michael: "I've been wondering whether you knew Gretchen Kravner. Maybe you were one of the friends she told about my trip — well, our trip." Michael was between a rock and a hard place, literally and figuratively. He couldn't tell me I had no right to question him like this without acknowledging that he was my patient. And the fact that he was my patient was something he couldn't afford to have Lauren know, since she was looking for a male patient of mine with a first initial 'M.' And he couldn't answer the question truthfully for the same reason. So he stonewalled.

"This is getting boring. Lauren, let's go."

"Answer him," she said, suddenly the prosecutor again, certainly not bored.

He continued to stand, silent, his hands now fists. A scratching sound interrupted the quiet somewhere behind me on the trail; the flutter of falling pebbles started loudly and then quelled. Michael's eyes left me for an instant before returning to lock on.

"Michael, answer him," Lauren admonished. I had little doubt that she'd finally begun to wonder about his first initial.

"No need for any hostility, Lauren. Permit me to continue." I was enjoying feeling some leverage over her. Over both of them.

"Karen Hart," I said.

Michael's fists straightened. His shoulders slackened. His eyes blazed.

"Another one of my patients. You must've read about her in the papers. Killed herself almost a year ago. Since then I've been accused of having been sexually involved with her during her treatment. It's been in the papers," I repeated, my voice even.

Lauren's face belied her befuddlement at the mention of Karen Hart.

"Karen's is a particularly tragic story. Her friend, her appointed personal representative, has approved my revealing some of the details of that tragedy to the two of you. I saw Karen in treatment for quite a while. I knew her well. She dredged up horrors of her childhood in my presence. We shared that. She felt rage that she couldn't have previously imagined. At first that rage was misdirected. I got more than my share. Her friends got more than theirs. Unsuspecting strangers were occasionally mowed down by its intensity. Then the light of her rage became focused, like a laser. At first she aimed it at herself, for being a child once, then at her father, for failing to protect her. Finally, she targeted her stepbrother. Who had raped her repeatedly for almost three years of her fractured childhood."

Lauren's eyes were locked on mine. I broke mine free to assess Michael. His demeanor had flattened; he looked anesthetized.

"She killed herself last year after he tracked her down and raped her again. She hadn't seen or heard from him in six years, and Thanksgiving weekend a year ago, he arrived on her doorstep and stole her reclaimed soul.

"There's something about Karen that I've told no one, not even the police. Before she went home and drank the whiskey and took the pills, she wrote me a note and dropped it by my office. She didn't even struggle, she wrote, during the rape." I permitted this image to filter back to Michael.

"This stepbrother, by the way, committed the first of these assaults in England. You ever live there, Michael?" This man who said "in hospital" not "in the hospital"; this man who said "nicked," not "stolen" or "ripped off."

He was a statue.

"Whatever. Take a moment and see if you can recall some months you spent in London as an adolescent. This stepbrother was about six years older than her. She'd be twenty-four now, had she lived. How old are you, Michael?"

Lauren was leaning back, as though the rock on which she was perched had a corner in which she could cower.

"What would you guess the stepbrother's name was, Lauren?"

She mouthed the word. I said it out loud, "Michael."

"Did you know Karen Hart, Michael? Know anything about her stepbrother? Know Sheldon Hart? Ever pimped him over quiche at Le Français?

"Have you ever committed sexual assault on a child? Or rape?"

It was hard to tell what happened next. I think Lauren fell sideways off the rock. The squeal she made ruptured Michael's catatonia. At first I thought he jumped to help her back up. When he raised her off the ground, though, one of her arms was bent behind her back. The forearm of Michael's right arm was crossed over her throat.

I stood up and took one step before I saw from the anguish on Lauren's face that Michael had tightened his grip on her arm and her throat. "It's over, Michael. Let her go," I said, part of me actually expecting him, despite everything, to be reasonable. He didn't move. Lauren's eyes were terrified, her gaze uneven. "Everything's been predicated on your being able to move over this terrain undiscovered. It's over. Your stepfather is going to know it all. Let her go. Don't make things worse for yourself. I'll help you get a lawyer."

"I can't. Leave us alone. Go," he said, the whisper replaced by a calm, modulated voice.

"I can't do that," I said.

I should have bought the gun.

I lived in a world where words were magic, where suicides were postponed by the right phrase, where wounds were cauterized by understanding and well-spoken compassion, a world where lives were corrected by language and feeling and thought. Once again I had misunderstood Michael. The reason I didn't know him well was because he didn't inhabit the same world I did.

Three feet behind Michael was a cliff upholstered with big rocks. It led, after fifty or sixty vertical feet, to the river flowing, angry and loud, through the narrow framed by the cliff. I processed rapidly whether suicide, homicide, or both were likely to be Michael's next move. I tried to work out scenarios where he was more concerned with revenge or more concerned with escape.

Ray Farley had said once or ten times, during supervision, that in the course of psychotherapy a safe maxim for a therapist was "not to bother the transference unless it was bothering you." Michael's transference *was* bothering me. So I interpreted the whole thing to him.

"Look at her, Michael. She's not your sister. Look at me. I'm not your father. It's as if" — I emphasized the words *as if* and then, for good measure, repeated them — "as if it were all the same as it was back then. He wronged you, Michael, he sucked you in and deserted you. You tried to get back at him through Karen. You're still trying. Look at that woman, Michael. She's not Karen. I'm not Sheldon Hart. You're not that little boy. You have other choices now. You're not hurting him anymore, Michael. You're only hurting yourself." It felt odd to be having this conversation outside of my office.

His eyes lacked any expression, and I couldn't tell if I was being heard. The prospect of his entering a dissociative state concerned me.

"I need to go," he said calmly.

"Fine. Let go of Lauren, get on your bicycle, and go. We won't follow you." He pulled Lauren backward a step, his back foot resting on the loose dirt at the edge of the cliff. "Michael, behind you, please be careful," I said calmly so as not to alarm him.

"Thank you," he said, and edged Lauren toward the trail and their parked bikes.

The mood created by our calm voices and civility was shattered by a shout from behind me. "Everybody stay where you are. Police." Silence for a few moments. I didn't turn, being much more concerned with Michael than with Aspen's cops. Footsteps on the trail.

"Hello, Doctor. Ms. Crowder," said Detective Sam Purdy.

"You. Let go of her, raise your hands, and step back. Slowly." Purdy was beside me now, his gun in his hand.

"I can't do that," said Michael. He edged back toward the cliff, keeping Lauren in front of him as a shield. "Throw your gun down now, Officer. Over here, by me. Or she and I will jump." He spoke with ingrained middle-class deference to a law enforcement officer. A moment passed. "We'll do it," he declared.

"He will," I said to Purdy. "Your timing sucks."

Purdy now gripped the gun in both his hands. His feet, in heavy black shoes with rubber soles, were slightly more than shoulder-width apart. He wore the overcoat I had seen on him the night before. I wondered how he'd known where we were. "My timing sucks? What kind of game you been playing up here? How many choices did I have left, assbite?"

"I told you she was in danger."

"Fuck you," he said. I had enough composure to read the profanity as an expression of his circumstances and not as an epithet for me. Well, not totally, anyway.

"He'll kill her," I said, as much to regain some alliance with Michael as to provide some reality base for Purdy.

Forty-five

Purdy straightened his stance, took his right hand off the grip of the revolver, and grabbed it by the barrel. With his left hand he opened the cylinder and emptied the shells on the dirt. He kicked them away with his right foot, scattering them into the sparse brush and fallen leaves.

"That's your only gun?" Michael asked. Purdy pressed his thin lips together tighter, seemed to fight an impulsive sarcastic retort, and said simply, "Yes."

"Now throw the gun over this way." Purdy snapped the gun shut and tossed it a few feet in front of Michael.

"Together, both of you sit on that ledge facing the river. Hands behind your heads so I can see them." I took one last look at Lauren before I obeyed. Her face pleaded for help.

I moved with Purdy toward the ledge, planning which way I would roll if I heard Michael moving toward us. So little light remained that our shadows were more imagined than real. White needles of phosphorescent light were the only visible evidence of the raging water below.

Shuffled footsteps moved away, across the trail. "Down," he said quietly, to Lauren. "No, just bend." As I rotated my neck I heard, "Don't turn." Michael's voice was calm and methodical, the voice of somebody who had flown before inside the hurricane. Or of somebody who had Halothane for breakfast.

A crash and thud intervened. Twenty seconds later, another. The sound of a bike falling over, and then a final crash and thud.

"She and I are going to walk down the trail a little ways. Then I'm going to release her. No, wait. You. Policeman. Take off your coat and give it to me." The big cop was unfortunate enough to be closer in size to Michael than I was. He was also unfortunate enough to have the radio unit he carried under the bulky coat revealed. Michael said, "You should've told me you had that. Throw it over here." Purdy obeyed. "Damn," Michael said, considering what the radio might mean. Twenty seconds later I saw a black object head out over the river and heard it crash on the rocks below. The sounds of Michael wriggling into the coat completed the aria.

"We're going to walk to the first bend in the trail. I'll release her there. Stay where you are until she gets back or I'll kill her. Okay?"

He seemed to want an answer. "Okay," I said.

Purdy and I turned our heads simultaneously to watch him back down the hill, Lauren still bound by his left arm around her throat. His right arm guided one of the mountain bikes beside him. One of the Bridgestones.

Muted sounds drifted up from the bend, and we saw Lauren's dark silhouette move from vertical to prone. Michael jumped on the bike and took off down the mountain.

We jumped up and raced down the trail to Lauren. Purdy stood back as I lifted her from the ground. She was weeping. I released one arm, then the other, slithered out of my new parka, and wrapped it over her shoulders. Her head pressed against my chest, and I rocked her slowly until the whimpering slowed. "Are you okay?" I finally asked.

Her head nodded a silent assent.

"Let's get off this mountain, gang," Purdy said.

"You up to it, Lauren?"

"Yes."

Purdy moved back up the trail and fell to his hands and knees. He found his revolver easily in the darkness. After a few futile minutes he gave up trying to locate any of the bullets.

"Do you have any more?" I asked him.

"Whattya think I am, Dirty Harry? Shit."

His white shirt looked disembodied as it floated across the darkness to the other side of the trail. The shirt bent and extended its arms. "He crushed the front wheels of the bikes. We'll have to walk."

He blew past us at some military pace. "I'll go first."

Lauren walked on her own, holding on to my left arm as we descended. "You can't see well, can you?" I said in a voice too quiet to reach Purdy. Lauren shook her head.

"Was that a 'no'?"

"Yes. It was a 'no.' "

"How bad?"

"It seems worse in the dark. But I can make it."

"Hold on. We'll get down."

"Don't worry. I'll hold on."

The exercise helped retard the growing cold. Lauren stumbled at times, resorting to prancing in a fashion that, in more amusing circumstances, would have been reminiscent of Clydesdales. Purdy turned to check on our progress, or lack thereof, every twenty or thirty seconds. Twice he hissed, "Stop," so he could convince himself that Michael wasn't waiting in ambush.

The risk of Michael waiting for us seemed slim to me. He'd had an opportunity to kill us much more easily at the top of the hill. He'd chosen not to. Purdy was being overly suspicious. Okay, paranoid. When I thought more on it, though, I decided paranoia wasn't a bad character trait in a point man.

As we entered the segment of the trail where expensive homes clung to the hill above the river, Lauren said, "Do you have any idea what it's like to be constantly apologizing to somebody? God. I'm sorry I didn't listen to you about this. I am so sorry." She hesitated, then continued, "But, Alan, I checked for the four ball. I did, really. It wasn't missing. I thought, I thought you were—"

"Being a jerk?" I said. "I blew it up there, Lauren. I almost got you killed. I misread him for the tenth time. I'm sorry, too."

The rhythm of our march propelled us another quarter mile until I yelled to Purdy, "Take the fork to the left, Detective. I don't think she can manage the steep trail to the house." Purdy obeyed silently, and in a few yards we were on the paved road that would lead us to Lauren's house. We walked for another minute before a blue Saab patrol car drifted into view. Purdy ran out, flagged it down, held out his badge, and barked staccato cop talk with the driver. The Aspen policeman grabbed the radio, spoke for almost a minute, turned back to Purdy, asked a question, and spoke for another minute. Purdy told us to get in the backseat of the squad car.

The Boulder detective jumped in the front seat and said, "This is Officer"—he leaned forward to read the name tag once again—"Rodriguez. Tell him which house." Lauren said the address. Officer Rodriguez repeated it into the radio, and we, as they say, rolled.

"Stay in the car," Purdy said less than a minute later as we arrived. He exited immediately and began to walk toward the house, which was dark. He was carrying a rifle that Rodriguez had allowed him. Another squad car joined us and then, silently, one more. A total of three more officers, two men and a woman. They huddled for a moment and moved toward the house. Rodriguez yelled for Purdy to wait. Purdy, of course, didn't.

"Got the key?" I asked Lauren.

"No. Mike carried them. I didn't have any pockets. He probably took the car. I should tell them what kind it is."

"I disabled your car. He doesn't have it."

"You what?" Her voice was full with fatigue. "Never mind."

It took the cops fifteen or so minutes to secure the place. The female officer came out to get us. Lauren was asleep on my shoulder.

I roused her and led her inside. One of the officers drew me away from her as soon as we walked in the door. Another escorted her to the living room.

"Let me make coffee, first, please. She's freezing." Actually, coffee third. First was peeing, second was turning up the thermostat.

At the dining room table, I gave my version of what happened. Lauren was interrogated in the living room. Purdy flitted back and forth, offering suggestions and clarifications. Mostly he got exasperated at the details I refused to divulge about my ex-patient.

A trim, tanned man in good wool trousers and a Mister Rogers cardigan arrived about a half hour into the interview, and after he consulted with everybody who was wearing a gun, Lauren and I got to start all over, one at a time, answering his questions. Everybody except Purdy demurred to him. Purdy interrupted the interrogation whenever he decided I was being treated with too much deference.

During Lauren's turn with the boss, a locksmith arrived to change the locks. It was almost ten when we finished our interrogations. Lauren looked like an ice sculpture too long in the sun. Her features sagged and had lost their definition. Even Purdy looked tired.

"How did you know where we were?" I asked him.

"I followed you. I'll tell you tomorrow. We'll have lots of time for show-and-tell when we drive down to Boulder in the morning for another day of tell-me-what-you-know. So get some rest."

"Where is he? Do they know?"

"He can't have gotten far. He took most of his things from the house, and the bike he was on is gone. They're pretty sure he's in the valley. The roads out were sealed before he could have gotten that far, even if he stole a car. They'll get him soon." He shook his big head and thought for a minute. "But Ted Bundy got out of this valley bein' chased by a battalion, and I don't think he was any smarter than our guy is. So who knows? We'll protect the two of you until he's found. Don't worry."

"Thanks, Detective." I wasn't worried.

"Yeah. Whatever." He almost said "Thank you" in return. I was sure of it.

"I'm gonna stay here with her tonight," I said. "If you need a place to stay, you can have my room at the Pitkin Inn. It's paid for." I held out the key.

"Thanks. It'll probably be more comfortable than the living room sofa one of the local guys"—he waved at the uniforms—"gave me last night."

Lauren refused my offer to fix her something to eat. She wanted to go to bed. The guy in charge told us that there would be an officer outside the house all night and, after confirming with the uniforms that the bedrooms were secure, said to get some rest.

She said good night to the crew and thanked them and let me help her down the stairs. She kissed me on the cheek at her bedroom door and asked if I would stay.

"Whether you want me to or not. I'll be right upstairs."

"Thanks, Alan."

"It's okay."

"Yeah. It is now. Good night."

The room I had stayed in a few months before was obviously the one that Michael had been using. I was relieved to see signs of his habitation. I wanted to believe that Lauren hadn't slept with him. I claimed an empty, identical suite on the other side of the landing on the level above Lauren's room and went back up the stairs to say good-bye to the gang in blue.

One of the officers handed me the new set of house

keys and the bill from the locksmith. I pocketed them as though they were mine.

Purdy asked his colleagues for a ride to the Pitkin Inn. The cops gave him shit about his uptown tastes, and everybody departed after a last look around.

"Somebody'll be outside all night. Me first," said Rodriguez.

I showered long and hard and replayed my mistakes, which took a while. I knew I wouldn't sleep until I let go of them. When I finished in the bathroom I heard the muted sounds of late night television coming through the floor below.

Well, I'm not the only one who can't fall asleep, I thought.

I toyed with the idea of offering Lauren some company, discarded it, and climbed into the double bed.

Forty-six

The sheets relinquished their chill reluctantly. For five minutes I stayed in one position to reduce my exposure to cold spots before finally yielding to my inability to sleep.

The big television upstairs was a tempting diversion. I assumed Jake had cable. But it meant getting out of bed into the cold house. My toes voted no.

In the void created by the absence of both sleep and distraction, and in my determined need for closure, I permitted the raw footage of my relationship with Michael to roll in my head.

The chronological review of events reached Gretchen Kravner's murder when I realized with a jolt of adrenaline that Michael wasn't finished.

The sweater itched my chest as I pulled it on without a shirt. My corduroys had assumed the temperature of the room and felt like sheets of ice as I slid them on. I shivered and left my feet bare.

The TV was too loud.

I knew that before I left the room.

As I descended to the lowest level of the house, the volume of the TV seemed even louder. Something was wrong. The oak on the stairs leading to the master suite silently absorbed my steps.

Maybe I should get the cop, I thought.

And maybe you are just being stupid, I replied.

The door to the bedroom had no lock, and it opened quietly into a small foyer. Doors led to a diagonally tiled bathroom and a closet that could store a small Cessna.

The TV blared. A rerun of *Cheers* before Coach died.

A mirrored wall reflected half the room. The room was painted in pastel shades of blue; it was sparsely furnished and huge. The part I could see was as big as my living room and contained no bed, just a sitting area with an upholstered chaise and two matching chairs.

I was terrified of finding Michael in the room. If he was there, I would delight in hurting him. I was also more than a little leery of Lauren's rage at my intruding on her without warning should Michael not be there. She, I feared, would delight in hurting me.

A silk ficus framed the corner of the foyer where it turned into the bedroom. I crept low and peeked in between the branches.

Lauren lay in bed naked, a silent scream locked in her throat by a mouthful of blue-and-white fabric securely tied around her face. Fear pressed her back into the lacquered headboard of the big bed.

Michael stood by the side of the mattress, dropping his shirt to the carpeted floor. One hand held a hunting knife, the other fumbled to unbuckle his belt. His face was impassive, not threatening. If not for the knife, he would have appeared to be a husband preparing for bed.

I waited until he lifted his left leg to raise it from his trousers, then ran and dove at him, screaming at Lauren to run.

She did.

Which freed Michael to turn the knife toward me. His balance was compromised by being tangled in his trousers, though, and the slash he made at me behind his back missed its mark. I rolled against the backs of his knees, and he fell over me onto his back. He tripped me with his left foot as I tried to raise myself against the bed and run. As I fell, I was able to tumble across the bed and put it between us. Unfortunately he was between me and the door.

He stood and faced me. His pants were gone. The swollen glans of his erection peeked from the top of his bright blue briefs.

The angle to the bedroom door might have permitted Cicero to outrace Michael to the exit, but I couldn't do it. And he knew it. The goddamn room was contemporary to the point of sterility. There wasn't a loose object within reach to use as a weapon or a shield. I leaned forward and pulled a sheet from the bed. I rolled it first around one fist, then the other, pulling it taut in front of me. Michael was edging around the bed. I jumped up on it, deciding to defend the high ground.

Lauren would get the policeman from outside. I needed to stay alive for a few minutes. Only a few minutes.

Michael plotted his assault. Muscles rippled in his arms and legs. Somehow his nakedness accented my disadvantage, not his.

He feinted left and right and studied my instinctive responses. Then he stepped up on the bed. The knife shot forward in a fake thrust at my gut. I fell for the feint and slashed down with the sheet. But Michael had pulled the blade back and was slashing it back up before I recovered my balance. I caught his wrist with the sheet as I desperately pulled it back up and heard the knife tear the flesh of my left shoulder. Michael stepped back to enjoy his handiwork.

I didn't look but could feel the flood of warm blood down my abdomen. The sweet, metallic smell seemed to fill the room. Lauren, where are you?

My arm still worked. The pain was manageable, deep but not sharp, like sound under water.

Michael tried the same move again. I caught the blade in the sheet this time and lurched upward with all my strength. The knife flew from his hand, thumped the ceiling above the bed, and came down impaled in the mattress. He rushed me.

My hands were twisted in the damn sheet, which had been a creative defense against the knife but was a disaster against a head butt. The wall behind the bed felt as if it were made of brick as I thudded against it. My right hand worked free of the sheet first; my left hand was growing increasingly reluctant to follow commands from my overstimulated and underoxygenated central nervous system.

As he shifted his weight to augment his leverage for pummeling me, I grabbed a handful of his hair, yanked him to my right, planted my left foot on his chest, and kicked him from the bed.

He rolled quickly to his knees. The knife was closer to me than to him. Unfortunately it was closer to my left hand than my right. I was losing a lot of blood. Soon this battle would be over by default.

Lauren???

He lunged for the blade. I let him.

Using the last of my strength, I timed a kick to where his head would be and landed a solid blow that resonated all the way up to my hip. He fell to the floor, stunned.

I tried to jump from the bed, but my legs collapsed under me. My head was twisted over my shoulder as I crawled toward the door. Whatever had been protecting me from the pain of my wound departed in a wisp. In agony I left a trail of red slime on the thick carpet, a parody of a snail in a three-point stance.

He laughed when he recovered and saw me. He pulled the knife from the mattress, crept across the bed, swung his legs onto the floor, and raised the blade.

That's when Lauren shot the Tizio.

If she had been aiming at the Tizio, it would have been a great shot. The Italian floor lamp was a skeleton

366

of long thin black arms. A tough target at twenty feet.

Michael and I both assumed that he was the actual target. Which meant that Lauren had missed by a good two feet. The fact that she was holding a revolver meant that something bad had probably happened to the policeman guarding our perimeter. I was about to ask Lauren where he was when the room exploded.

She had fired again. I jumped as much as I could, which wasn't much. My adrenals kicked out their reserve supply of hormone.

The gun was so loud. Was this what gunpowder smelled like? Four million caps?

The sliding glass door to the deck disintegrated. The cold air felt good. I appreciate the ventilation, honey, but a little more to the left next time, please.

Michael and I were frozen in our places. We both looked at Lauren. Her legs were bare, her feet adorned with knee-high boots covered with synthetic animal fur. A vaguely Native American design was stitched up the sides. A man's Gore-Tex pullover reached to the tops of her thighs.

"Don't," she said as Michael emerged from his catatonia. "Drop the knife," she instructed, "to the side." I was in front and, although it seemed incongruous to the circumstances, was grateful for the clarification.

Michael didn't drop the knife. He took a step toward her with his left foot. She fired again. He cringed and paused. He and I wondered where the bullet went.

Missing a two-hundred-pound man three times from eight feet seemed like an impossibility, even for an amateur. My brain was fortified with barely enough oxygen to permit me to wonder if Lauren could even see him. And if she could, how many of him was she seeing? This wasn't good.

My good hand was only eighteen inches from Michael's left foot. The knife in his hand was only four feet from my neck.

Lauren turned ninety degrees and looked back toward Michael from over her left shoulder. Her right arm extended across her body, holding the gun.

I swear I'll kill you. Drop it. *Now!* She screamed the last word. She was begging to be freed from an impulse to simply murder him.

He didn't hesitate. He lunged over me, lurching directly for Lauren with the knife. I managed to hook his foot as he flew by. I barely deflected him; he still had plenty of momentum to reach her.

She fired again. The bullet suspended Michael in the air above me for a moment, like Michael Jordan defeating gravity at the top of his jump shot. I saw a small circle of skin on his chest implode into a dark hole and watched a fine mist of blood settle gently into the air above him like a webbed parachute of fine silk thread.

His body fell heavily, the knife gripped tightly in his hand.

For a few seconds we were all stationary.

Michael broke the mood with a hissing scream.

Lauren was still, the gun pointed horizontally toward where Michael had been standing moments before. A shudder and groan shook him as his upper torso stayed glued to the carpet, his arms and legs convulsing once more, the point of the knife finally being buried in the carpet inches from Lauren's furry paw, the bare toes of his left foot buried in the sticky wound of my shoulder.

When I woke up the familiar gang was all back, together with some new faces. Ambulance attendants had an IV rushing clear fluid into my arm and a pack of bandages heavy on my chest. Lauren was in her warm-ups, talking to Purdy and the guy in charge from Aspen. One of her hands ran arrhythmically through her hair.

My attempt to say hello came out in a rasp.

She turned from the policemen and knelt next to the

narrow stretcher and brushed me with a kiss.

"How did you know?"

"You hadn't slept with him yet." The hopeful words were mangled by my tongue sticking to all the dry spots in my mouth.

"No. I hadn't."

"That's how I knew," I said.

Forty-seven

Purdy's face, not Lauren's, greeted me at Aspen Valley Hospital the next morning.

The pain in my shoulder and chest convinced me of two things: that the knife was still in there somewhere, and that somebody else was getting my morphine.

The Boulder detective had an endless variety of ways to ask the same questions and blatantly took advantage of my insufficient analgesia to attempt to pry from me some confidential information about Michael. His repetitive bludgeoning was almost successful; at one point I resorted to using the nurse call button to deflect him. When he finally accepted that I would reveal no more from any of the psychological records, he pushed me for how I knew that Michael might have gone back to rape Lauren.

"My guess is that he didn't want to have to rape her. He was willing to, certainly, but mostly he needed me to know that he'd slept with her. When she refused, it became rape. The other women, the traffic accident, the suicide, and Gretchen—they all died shortly after having intercourse with him. I thought about it and decided he would feel pressure to keep the circle unbroken." I paused and tried to shift my weight so that my shoulder stopped radiating pain. The effort was unsuccessful. "Lauren had told me that Gretchen's murderer had entered the house through a window that you guys—you detectives—thought he had left open at an earlier time. I just guessed that Michael might try the same thing here—use the time he had alone in the house to pack up like he was going and leave a window unlatched so that he could return.

"No rocket scientist deductions, Detective. I'm just somebody who believes that the only way to have a chance at predicting future behavior is by paying attention to past behavior. I got lucky once when I found him. I got lucky twice that Lauren was resourceful." He stared at me for a moment, processing the possibility that I wasn't telling him all I knew.

To distract him I said, "Yesterday, you promised you'd tell me how you ended up on that trail with us."

He smiled, which made his immense head seem even bigger. His voice was patient and patronizing. "You gave me enough information on Saturday night, at the Mall Crawl, that I thought you thought you knew something. Being a little protective of a certain deputy district attorney, and looking for any decent excuse to depart from the lunacy on the mall, I decided to check her house for that red Honda. As you well know, it was parked outside. I called the plates in for a check, which took a while—since they were out of state—and was sitting there waiting for a reply when you show up looking for all the world like a burglar.

"You prowl around enough to convince yourself that something warrants you jumping into your Subaru and acting like it's a goddamn Corvette. So I follow you, figuring that you're heading for lover boy's house. While you're getting gas and munchies on South Broadway, my vehicle check comes in with this guy's name and two priors. One for disturbing the peace, the other for assault. Charges dropped. Anyway, I decide that this Michael Morton could be 'Mickey' could be 'M,' so I get serious in my following.

At first, I convince myself that you're going maybe to Eldorado Springs, then I'm sure you're going no farther than Coal Creek Canyon, then I'm willing to accept that we're going maybe all the way to Golden, on and on, until we stop in fucking Aspen. When I finally tuck you into bed I got like two drops of gas left. I check in with the local boys, who give me a place to sleep and a radio and tell me to call if I need any help. The next day I borrow a bike and watch you doing a motocross up and down that hillside. Finally I follow the parade up the damn trail and spend twenty minutes trying to hear your prosecution over the white noise of the damn river. When you manage to fuck things up, I rush in and play the Lone Ranger. You know the rest."

"One question and one favor," I said.

"I make no promises," he replied.

My hair was greasy and plastered to one side, my mouth felt as if a bird with bad hygiene had used it for a nest overnight, and the pain in my upper body erupted anew with every minute movement. I wasn't up to sparring with Purdy. At some level I felt that he was trying to convince me that the only reason I wasn't in his custody was that I was the one who'd figured out that Michael was going to stay around for another chance at Lauren.

From Purdy's questions, I had surmised that Rodriguez was the cop Michael had assaulted outside the house and that his condition was very poor. Michael, too, was alive, but barely. Both had been transported to Denver hospitals by air ambulance after being stabilized in the hospital where I lay.

"You going to search his house?" I asked finally.

"That's your question? That's easy. Sure, we're gonna search it."

"I want you to look for something for me."

He looked at me unevenly. Purdy liked me at some

level. But the level wasn't anywhere close to the surface. What was close to the surface was his suspicion that I was mixed up in this mess in some quasi-criminal way.

"Unofficially? I can't do that." He said it with a voice that said he could do it, but the price would have to be right.

"It doesn't have to be unofficial," I told him. He looked disappointed. "But I want you to arrange it so I can have access if you find what I want." He looked as if he had been counting cards and lost his place.

"I can't promise you that."

"Then I don't tell you what to look for. Good-bye, Detective."

"We'll find whatever it is you want without your help. I don't need to make any arrangements with you."

"You may or may not find it without my help. What you need my help to do is to understand the importance of what you find. It's all gonna be shrink talk." I didn't have the energy to argue with him anymore. "I'm tired. Please go."

The big man pulled himself up from the empty bed where he was sitting. He turned and walked to the door. At the last moment he relinquished his poker face, stepped out of his bluff, and said, "I owe you one. Whattya want?"

"What you need to look for are some diaries written by his stepsister. I think he went back to her house after she killed herself. The diaries were incriminating, so he took them. I don't know what they look like."

"And you'll interpret them for me?"

"You know me better than that, Detective. I'll draw you a picture. You'll have to connect the dots."

Purdy laughed. I laughed with him and felt like I had been split open with a cleaver.

"You got any other tips for the real cops?"

"Sure. Since you asked. Compare the semen samples from all the dead women." He wrote something down. "Where's Lauren?" I asked him.

"You said one question."

"Don't be a jerk."

"I saw her for breakfast this morning. She's already headed back to Boulder. Had to fly to Denver; somebody's gonna pick her up. By the way, where the fuck did you put her distributor cap?" Without waiting for an answer, he walked out the door and closed it gently.

Ten seconds later he stuck his head back in. "What you did last night was balls-on. Stupid, but balls-on. I won't forget it."

I agreed with him.

Forty-eight

Diane and Raoul drove up to Aspen to ferry me
and the Subaru home. Two days in the hospital felt
like five years.

Lauren didn't call.

Raoul took my car, and Diane drove me down in
the Saab. She had most of the story out of me before
we hit Leadville.

"How did you finally put it together?" she asked,
hands at ten and two, eyes hard ahead, pushing the
9000 like a sports car.

"Transference." I rubbed my eyes with the fingers of
my good hand, discovering that left hands were intended by nature to rub left eyes — eye rubbing becoming another in a growing list of activities that did not
cross the midline with grace. "At the end I understood
the transference. Once I saw the connection between
Michael and Sheldon Hart, the pieces fell together."

Talking seemed to upset the fragile comfort I had
attained in positioning my sore body in the car. Timo-
rously, I resettled myself and bore on. "I was familiar
with the pattern, Diane; he'd described it to me ten
times. I just didn't see it coming. So, as you'd expect,
he started making me live it. But I didn't put it all together until I knew that Karen's father was Michael's
stepfather.

"Once I knew that, it made perfect sense that he

375

had been involved with Karen's death.

"Michael's natural father had deserted Michael and his mother when Michael was five or so. His mom re-married Sheldon Hart, who inherited all the wrath and suspicion Michael had developed for his father in the intervening years. Hart became the object of all this kid's ambivalence. He was savior and he was Satan to Michael. When Michael saw his stepfather as Satan, he molested his little stepsister, Karen, who idolized her relatively neglectful father. This, of course, was an effort to hurt his stepfather. But it was Michael's secret. Karen wouldn't tell—she was terrified of being blamed and rejected by her father. Michael needed to find some way of letting his stepfather know he was getting even. So he left clues, I guess, that Sheldon Hart ignored. Like most parents in incestuous families, he didn't want to know.

"It was almost perfect for Michael. He got to shit in his stepfather's home and never be blamed.

"When Michael took the job at NCAR in Boulder and showed up out of the blue to visit his stepsister, she told him, I'm guessing now, that she was going to tell her father everything. So he raped her again in some pathetic rage. Or maybe he had planned to rape her all along. I don't know. Then Karen killed herself. Michael was let off the hook—relieved. Sort of. He'd been robbed, though, of his way of dispelling his anger at Sheldon Hart.

"But the rage wasn't gone, of course. So he made the transition from Sheldon Hart to a stand-in for Sheldon Hart—Phil Hubbard, his boss, the perfect object for his transference. Perfect because he was a distant, powerful male, like Sheldon Hart. Perfect, too, because in Phil's wife, Anne, there was a surrogate for Karen Hart. Michael started an affair with Anne, but after a while she decided to tell her husband. Michael told me that himself. And then she died in a car wreck. Once again he was relieved, his safety protected. And the pattern had crystallized. When the women he used in his bizarre acting out died—he felt better.

"I was not a perfect transference object, like Phil Hubbard. I was made eligible, in a way, by the energy lost in Michael's explosive transition from sick to psychotic. I was chosen, I think, because I was a common denominator, somebody both his stepsister and Anne Hubbard had positive relationships with. So I became the next transference object, the next man to play his father's role in this sad production. He met Gretchen, who thought I walked on water, and that alone qualified her to be the next victim. So Michael cast her in Karen's role and proceeded to find a way into her pants. The man, I guess, could be pretty charming. She knew I would have concerns about two of my patients dating, probably felt guilty about keeping it from me, and told him she was going to tell me she was dating one of my patients. Michael couldn't afford to have me know. He killed Gretchen to protect his secret. Momentum had carried him from precipitated death to circumstantial death to murder.

"I think Michael got scared here and there and backed off. He tried to temper his acting out. He did the bit with Cicero and with the turtle in your car, hoping, I think, that I was smart enough to stop him. I wasn't. And then I kicked him out of treatment. He, of course, couldn't take the rejection.

"He went after Lauren, whom he knew I'd been seeing. He'd seen us together in Mexico; had probably seen her picture in the paper. He somehow managed to meet her, asked her out, and left a trail of pool balls even I couldn't misread. The rest is in the tabloids."

Diane downshifted and blew past a Dodge Aries in

about three nanoseconds. I winced and checked my watch to see whether enough time had passed so I could swallow more Tylenol fours. The doctor had said two pills every four hours. From moment one, however, he and I had disagreed on the extent of my agony, and now that I was free of his control I was intent on dosing myself a little more liberally.

"Why didn't he take the guns?" Diane asked.

"You mean from his house? Why didn't he bring one?"

"No. Why didn't he take the detective's gun on the trail? And why didn't he take the cop's gun after he bludgeoned him outside the house?"

"I've wondered about that, too. I think he wanted it to be over. It's why he left me such a well-marked trail. I think he needed to be the final victim in all this. It had to come down to him and me. That's the ultimate reenactment in the transference."

We were on a straightaway. She turned her serene face toward me and said, "You're lucky you're talking to another shrink. I'm not sure anybody else would let you get away with saying something like that. But," she continued, "I think you're right."

During the rest of the week, Peter and Adrienne took turns nursing me back to some semblance of health.

Diane visited frequently and always let me know that Lauren called her daily to ask how I was recovering. I would say, "And is she okay?" and Diane would say, "Yeah, okay," neither relishing nor abusing her role as intermediary. I would worry out loud about my remaining patients, and Diane, who was covering, would assure me that all was well, or at least under control.

I left messages on Lauren's machine that were never returned.

Purdy found the diaries that I suspected Michael had taken from his stepsister's apartment. They detailed her memories of his prolonged abuse of her. A final entry described the last rape as though she had been only a disinterested witness. I ached for her all over again.

Jon Younger used the diaries in Michael's possession as leverage to get Sheldon Hart to drop his lawsuit and to relinquish *Domain of the Heart* to Valerie Goodwin. My big lawyer tried to reassure me that the hearing scheduled before the state grievance committee would be pro forma. I wasn't convinced.

The *Daily* published as many details of the attack in Aspen as they could. Front-page photographs for two days. A follow-up by Joseph Abiado, a few days later, on the dropping of the lawsuit against me, was on the bottom of page five opposite an ad for a new kind of environmentally sensitive disposable diaper. Diane suggested I take advantage of my celebrity and offer an interview to get my side of the story on page one. I was thinking about how to manage it.

Both Merideth and my mother called and offered to visit. I turned them down for similar reasons.

I called Valerie Goodwin, Gretchen Kravner's mother, and Phil Hubbard and told them what I could without crossing the boundaries of privilege. They expressed gratitude, and that felt good.

Winter's first big snow had blasted Boulder and my arm was out of its sling when I answered the door the morning of the Saturday after the Aspen shoot-out.

379

Lauren stood examining the doorstop as if she were an appraiser and it was made of gold. She wore mittens, hat, and muffler and said, "Can I come in?" without looking at me. She leaned inside and set a long white box in the corner, kicked her nylon boots on the door frame in a futile attempt to loosen some of the wet snow, stepped into the house, and let me take her coat. She faced the oak coat tree while she removed the remaining winter wool.

"It's odd without Cicero here," she began.

"Yes," I replied. I reached up with my right hand and slid my fingers over the cold skin on the back of her neck. I cleared a small spot and kissed her there, then buried my face in her hair and reached around and hugged her across her abdomen.

She turned, keeping her head down. "I'm sorry," she said, "for not calling."

"Accepted," I said, biting my tongue.

"I haven't known whether to be grateful to you for saving my life or furious at you for risking it."

"You don't have to choose, you know. You can be both."

"That's what Dr. Washburn said," Lauren offered, her voice tentative.

"You're seeing Rebecca for therapy?"

She nodded, then looked up, caught my eyes, and turned her head slightly away. "She says I have intimacy issues. Things I do to keep men from getting too close. There are a lot of things I've never told anybody about my father. She says I haven't come to terms with my MS, either." She turned back to me, meticulously gauging my reaction. I was wearing my best therapy face. "I've also had trouble shaking the images of that last day. Of shooting him. Part of me is guilty. Part of me still wishes he had died. I suppose all of that will take time to work out."

I nodded concurrence. "You saved my life, lady."

"And you mine. I guess we're even."

"Rebecca's real good, Lauren. I'm glad for you." I think I passed a test by not saying, "I told you so." She put both her arms around my neck and squeezed me tight. My shoulder screeched in protest.

"The box, it's for you," she whispered. "It's a cue stick."

I hugged her just a little tighter, said, "Thank you," and told her I was leaving the next day to see Merideth.

Her hold on me slackened for half a breath. "To get back together?" she asked, her lips brushing my ear.

"To say good-bye," I said.

She, too, passed a test by not saying, "I told you so."

Acknowledgments

Patricia Nelson Limerick, Jeffrey Limerick, and David Stanford helped opened doors to which I had no keys. My sincere thanks to each of them.

I am also grateful to ex-Deputy District Attorney Mary Malatesta, Division Chief Hal Nees of the Boulder Police Department, Stanley Galansky, M.D., and Marc Vick, who instructed me about their respective professions and avocations. And to Kathy Mahoney, who assisted in many small ways.

I am fortunate to have kind friends who encouraged me and offered valuable suggestions along the way. Their varied perspectives taught me essential lessons about the diversity of readers; their generosity and caring taught me volumes about friendship. To them, and to my supportive family, I am deeply indebted.

Part of the bounty of this project has been the opportunity to work with Al Silverman and Jean Naggar, two wise, gracious people it would be a pleasure to know in any circumstance. In this one, it's been a privilege.

And especially, Rose: Thanks are not enough, for without your quiet faith this never would have gone beyond a dream.